A YOUNG GIRL'S WOOING

E. P. ROE

A Young Girl's Wooing

E. P. Roe

PO Box 2211
Fairfield, IA 52556
www.1stworldlibrary.com
First Edition

LCCN: 2009923374

Softcover ISBN: 978-1-4218-8823-1
Hardcover ISBN: 978-1-4218-8922-1
eBook ISBN: 978-1-4218-8724-1

1st World Library Literary Society

Giving Back to the World

"If you want to work on the core problem, it's early school literacy."

- James Barksdale, former CEO of Netscape

"No skill is more crucial to the future of a child, or to a democratic and prosperous society, than literacy."

- Los Angeles Times

"Literacy... means far more than learning how to read and write... The aim is to transmit... knowledge and promote social participation."

- UNESCO

"Literacy is not a luxury, it is a right and a responsibility. If our world is to meet the challenges of the twenty-first century we must harness the energy and creativity of all our citizens."

- President Bill Clinton

"Parents should be encouraged to read to their children, and teachers should be equipped with all available techniques for teaching literacy, so the varying needs and capacities of individual kids can be taken into account."

- Hugh Mackay

CONTENTS

I. A CRESCENT OF A GIRL 9

II. GRAYDON MUIR 17

III. THE PARTING 27

IV. EFFORT 36

V. ACHIEVEMENT 47

VI. THE SECRET OF BEAUTY 56

VII. NOT A MIRACLE 65

VIII. RIVAL GIRLS 74

IX. THE MEETING 92

X. OLD TIES BROKEN 102

XI. "I FEAR I SHALL FAIL" 112

XII. THE PROMPTINGS OF MISS WILDMERE'S HEART 120

XIII. "YOU WILL BE DISAPPOINTED" 137

XIV. MISS WILDMERE'S STRATEGY 146

XV. PERPLEXED AND BEGUILED 155

XVI. DECLARATION OF INDEPENDENCE 172

XVII. NOT STRONG IN VAIN 180

XVIII. MAKE YOUR TERMS 191

XIX. AN OBJECT FOR SYMPATHY 203

XX "VEILED WOOING" 210

XXI. SUGGESTIVE TONES 225

XXII. DISHEARTENING CONFIDENCES 233

XXIII. THE FILIAL MARTYR 240

XXIV. "I'LL SEE HOW YOU BEHAVE" 247

XXV. GOSSAMER THREADS 260

XXVI. MRS. MUIR'S ACCOUNT 266

XXVII. MADGE'S STORY 276

XXVIII. DISPASSIONATE LOVERS 289

XXIX. THE ENEMIES' PLANS 301

XXX. THE STRONG MAN UNMANNED 312

XXXI. CHECKMATE 326

XXXII. MADGE IS MATTER-OF-FACT 334

XXXIII. THE END OF DIPLOMACY 347

XXXIV. BROKEN LIGHTS AND SHADOWS 356

XXXV. A NEW EXPERIMENT 365

XXXVI. MADGE ALDEN'S RIDE 370

XXXVII. "YOU ARE VERY BLIND" 381

XXXVIII. "CERTAINLY I REFUSE YOU" 392

XXXIX. "MY TRUE FRIEND" 400

XL. THE END OF THE WOOING 411

CHAPTER I

A CRESCENT OF A GIRL

When Madge Alden was seventeen years of age an event occurred which promised to be the misfortune of her life. At first she was almost overwhelmed and knew not what to do. She was but a young and inexperienced girl, and for a year or more had been regarded as an invalid.

Madge Alden was an orphan. Four years prior to the opening of our story she had lost her mother, her surviving parent, and since had resided with her elder sister Mary, who was several years her senior, and had married Henry Muir, a merchant of New York City. This gentleman had cordially united with his wife in offering Madge a home, and his manner toward the young girl, as far as his absorbed and busy life permitted, had been almost paternal. He was a quiet, reticent man, who had apparently concentrated every faculty of soul and body on the problem of commercial success. Trained to business from boyhood, he had allowed it to become his life, and he took it very seriously. It was to him an absorbing game—his vocation, and not a means to some ulterior end. He had already accumulated enough to maintain his family in affluence, but he no more thought of retiring from trade than would a veteran whist-player wish to throw up a handful of winning cards. The events of the world, the fluctuations in prices, over which he had no control, brought to his endeavor the elements of chance, and it was his mission to pit against these uncertainties untiring industry and such skill and foresight as he possessed.

His domestic life was favorable to his ruling passion. Mary Alden, at the time of her marriage, was a quiet girl, whose early life had been shadowed by sorrow. She had seen her father pass away in his prime, and her mother become in consequence a sad and failing woman. The young girl rallied from these early years of depression into cheerfulness, and thoroughly enjoyed what some might regard as a monotonous life; but she never developed any taste for the diversions of society. Thus it may be surmised that Mr. Muir encountered no distractions after business hours. He ever found a good dinner awaiting him, and his wife held herself in readiness to do what he wished during the evening, so far as the claims of the children permitted. Therefore there were few more contented men in the city than he, and the name of Henry Muir had become a synonym among his acquaintances for methodical business habits.

In character and antecedents his younger brother, Graydon Muir, who was also an inmate of his family, presented many marked contrasts to the elder man. He had received a liberal education, and had graduated at a city college. He had developed into one of the best products of metropolitan life, and his defects were chiefly due to the circumstances of his lot. During his academic course he had been known as an athletic rather than a bookish man, and had left his Alma Mater with an Apollo-like physique. At the same time he had developed fine literary tastes, and was well informed, even if he had not gone very deeply into the classics and the sciences that were remote from the business career which he had chosen. After a brief interval of foreign travel he had entered his brother's office, and was schooling his buoyant, pleasure-loving temperament to the routine of trade. When business hours were over, however, Graydon gave himself up to the gratification of his social tastes. His vitality and flow of spirits were so immense that wherever he went he always caused a breezy ripple of excitement. Even veteran society girls found something exhilarating in the mirthful flash of his blue eyes, and to be whirled through a waltz on his strong arm was a pleasure not declined by reigning belles. Many looks that to other men might have been the arrows of Cupid were directed toward him, but they glanced harmlessly from his polished armor. Society was to him what business was to his brother,—an arena in which he easily manifested his power. At the same time he was a manly fellow, and had no taste for corner flirtations or the excitement of drawing perilously near to a committal with those who would have responded to marked attentions. The atmosphere he loved was that of general and social gayety. The girls that he singled out for his especial regard were noted for their vivacity and intelligence, as well as their beauty. Meanwhile he had won a reputation for his good-natured attentions to "wall-flowers." Such kindly efforts were rarely made at the promptings of conscience. The truth was, he enjoyed life so fully himself that he disliked to see any one having a dismal time. It gave him genuine pleasure to come to a plain-featured, neglected damsel, and set all her blood tingling by a brief whirl in a dance or a breezy chat that did her good, body and soul, so devoid of satire or patronage was the attention. His superb health and tireless strength, his perfect familiarity with the usages of society, and his graceful decision of action made everything he did appear as easy and natural as the beat of a bird's wing upon the air, and in his large circle it was felt that no entertainment was complete without his presence.

Graydon was still attending college when Madge Alden first became associated with him in her home-life. She was then but thirteen, and was small and slight for her age. The first evening when she came down to dinner, shrinking in the shadow of her sister, lingered ever in her memory. Even now it gave her pain to recall her embarrassment when she was compelled to take her seat in the full blaze of the light and meet the eyes of the one to whom she felt that she must appear so very plain and unattractive. Clad in the deepest mourning, pallid from grief and watching at her mother's bedside, coming from a life of seclusion and sorrow, sensitive in the extreme, she had barely reached that age when awkwardness is in the ascendant, and the quiet city home seemed the centre of a new and strange world. One other thing she remembered in that initial chapter of her life,—the kindly glances that Graydon Muir bent on the pale crescent of a girl who sat opposite to him. Even as a child she knew that the handsome young fellow was not secretly laughing at or criticising her, and before dinner was over she had ventured upon a shy, grateful glance, in reward for his good-humored efforts to break the ice.

There had, in truth, been no ice to break. The child was merely like a plant that had grown in the shade, and to her the strong, healthful youth was sunshine. His smile warmed and vivified her chilled nature, his hearty words and manner were bracing to her over-sensitive and timid soul, and his unaffected, unforced kindness was so constant that she gradually came to regard it as one of the best certainties of her life. She soon learned, however, that behind his sunny good-nature was a fiery and impatient spirit, ready to manifest itself if he was chafed beyond a certain point, and so a slight element of fear was mingled with her childlike affection.

He had sufficient tact to understand Madge's diffidence, and he knew that their family life would soon banish it. He welcomed this pale slip of a girl to their home circle because it gave him pleasure to pet and rally such a wraith into something like genuine existence. He also hoped that eventually she would become a source of amusement to him. Nor was he disappointed. Madge's mind was not colorless, if her face was, and she gradually began to respond to his mirthfulness, and to take an interest, intelligent for a child, in what occupied his thoughts. Kindness creates an atmosphere in which the most sensitive and diffident natures develop and reveal themselves, and Madge Alden, who might easily have been chilled into a reticent and dispirited girl, eventually manifested an unusual versatility of fancy and thought, acquiring also no slight power of expression.

Thus Graydon obtained his reward. His brother was a grave and silent man, to whom few themes could be broached except those of business and the events and politics of the day in their relation to trade. His sister-in-law was absorbed in household and family cares, but Madge's great black eyes responded with quick appreciation to all that he said, and their merry nonsense often provoked a smile upon even the face of Mr. Muir. The good-natured sympathy of the young man therefore passed gradually into a genuine fraternal regard, and he rarely came home of an evening without bringing flowers, bonbons, or some other evidence that he had remembered her. Unconsciously to herself, he became more to her than her sister, who was indulgent in the extreme, but not very demonstrative. Her shyness disappeared, and his caresses seemed as natural as those of an elder brother, in which light she regarded him.

Thus time passed on, and the girl rapidly approached the stature of womanhood. Apparently she grew too fast for her slight reserve of physical strength. She nominally attended a fashionable school, but was often absent from ill health, and for this reason her sister permitted her to follow her own moods. Indolence and inanition accounted largely for her lack of strength. Exercise brought weariness, and she would not take it. Nothing pleased her more than to curl up on a lounge with a book; and her sister, seeing that she was reading most of the time, felt that she was getting an education. To the busy lady a book was a book, a kind of general fertilizer of the mind, and as Madge usually took cold when she went out, and was assuredly acquiring from the multitude of volumes she devoured all the knowledge a woman needed, she was safer in the evenly heated city house. The sisters had independent fortunes of their own, and the great point in Mrs. Muir's mind was that they should live and enjoy them. If Madge was only sufficiently coddled now while she was growing, she would get strong eventually; and so the good lady, who had as much knowledge of hygiene as of Sanscrit, tempted the invalid with delicacies, permitted her to eat the confectionery that Graydon brought so often, and generally indulged a nature that needed wise and firm development.

Thus Madge lived on, growing more pale and languid with each succeeding year. The absence in the mountains and at the seashore which Mr. Muir permitted to his family every summer brought changes for the better, even though the young girl spent most of the time in a hammock or reclining in the stern of a sail-boat. She could not escape the invigoration caused by the mere breathing of pure air, but during the winters in town she lost all and more than she had gained, and sunk back into her old apathetic life.

This life, however, contained two elements which gave some color and zest to her existence. All through the day she would look forward to Graydon's return from business, and when she heard his latch-key the faintest possible color would steal into her cheeks. Up-stairs, two steps at a time, he would come, kiss her, waltz her about the room with a strength which scarcely permitted her feet to touch the floor, then toss her back on the lounge, where she would lie, laughing, breathless, and happy. With a man's ignorant tolerance he accepted her character as an invalid, and felt that the least he could do was to brighten a life which seemed so dismal to him. When he came down dressed for dinner or some evening engagement, she looked at him with a frank, admiring pride that amused him immensely. When he returned earlier than usual he often found her still upon the lounge with her inevitable book, usually a novel, and then he would take her upon his lap and call her his "dear little spook, the household ghost that would soon cease to cast a shadow;" and she, with a languid curiosity, would easily beguile from him a portrayal of the scenes through which he had just passed. She cared little for them, but from his stores of vitality and strength he imparted life to her, and without understanding why, she simply knew she was happy.

Apart from her fondness for the unreal scenes presented by the miscellaneous books she read—scenes all the more unreal because she had no experience by which to correct them—she had one other taste which promised well for the future—a sincere love of music. She was taking lessons, but it was from a superficial teacher, who was content to give her pretty and showy pieces; and she brought even to this favorite study the desultory habits which characterized all her efforts to obtain an education. When she sat down to her piano, however, nature was her strong ally. Her ear was fine and correct, and her sensitive, fanciful spirit gave delicacy and originality to her touch. It scarcely seems possible for one to become a sympathetic musician without a large degree of imagination and a nature easily moved by thought and feeling. The young girl's thoughts and feelings were as yet very vague, not concentrated on definite objects, and yet so good a connoisseur as Graydon often acknowledged her power, and would listen with pleased attention to her girlish rendering of music made familiar to him by the great performers of the day. He enjoyed it all the more because it was her own interpretation, often incorrect, but never commonplace or slovenly; and when her fingers wandered among the keys in obedience to her own impulses he was even more charmed, although the melody was usually without much meaning. She was also endowed with the rudiments of a fine voice, and would often strike notes of surpassing sweetness and power; but her tones would soon quaver and break, and she complained that it tired her to sing. That ended the matter, for anything that wearied her was not to be thought of.

Thus she had drifted on with time, unconscious of herself, unconscious of the influences that would bring to pass the decisive events in the future. She was like multitudes of others who are controlled by circumstances of their lot until the time comes when a deep personal experience applies the touchstone to character.

CHAPTER II

GRAYDON MUIR

Madge Alden was almost seventeen, and yet she was in many respects a child. Scenes portrayed in books had passed before her mind like pictures, having no definite significance. Mr. Muir was to her like some of the forces in nature—quiet, unobtrusive, omnipotent—and she accepted him without thought. Her sister was one whom she could love easily as a matter of course. She was an indulgent household providence, who cared for the young girl as she did for her own little children. If anything was amiss in Madge's wardrobe the elder sister made it right at once; if Madge had a real or imaginary ailment, Mary was always ready to prescribe a soothing remedy; and if there was a cloud in the sky or the wind blew chill she said, "Madge, do be prudent; you know how easily you take cold." Thus was provided the hot-house atmosphere in which the tender exotic existed. It could not be said that she had thrived or bloomed.

Graydon Muir was the one positive element with which she had come in contact, and thus far she had always accepted him in the spirit of a child. He had begun petting her and treating her like a sister when she was a child. His manner toward her had grown into a habit, which had its source in his kindly disposition. To him she was but a weak, sickly little girl, with a dismal present and a more dreary outlook. Sometimes he mentally compared her with the brilliant girls he met in society, and especially with one but a little older than Madge, who appeared a natural queen in the drawing-room. His life abounded in activity, interests, and pleasures, and if it was his impulse to throw a little zest into the experiences of those in society who had no claims upon him, he was still more disposed to cheer and amuse the invalid in his own home. Moreover, he had become sincerely fond of her. Madge was neither querulous nor stupid. Although not conceited, he had the natural vanity of a handsome and successful man, and while the evident fact that he was such a hero in her eyes amused him, it also predisposed him to kindly and sympathetic feeling toward her. He saw that she gave him not only a sisterly allegiance, but also a richer and fuller tribute, and that in her meagre and shadowed life he was the brightest element. She tried to do more for him than for any one else, while she made him feel that as an invalid she could not do very much, and that he should not expect it. She would often play for him an hour at a time, and again she would be so languid that no coaxing could lure her from the sofa. Occasionally she would even read aloud a few pages with her musical and sympathetic voice, but would soon throw down the book with an air of exhaustion, and plead that he would read to her. In her weakness there was nothing repulsive, and without calculation she made many artless appeals to his strength. He generously responded, saying to himself, "Poor little thing! she has a hard time of it. With her great black eyes she might be a beauty if she only had health and was like other girls; but as it is, she is so light and pale and limp that I sometimes feel as if I were petting a wraith."

Of late she had begun to go out with him a little, he choosing small and quiet companies among people well known to the

Muirs, and occasionally her sister also went. Her role of invalid was carefully maintained and recognized. Graydon had always prided himself on his loyalty as an escort; and as long as he was devoted, the neglect of other young men was welcomed rather than regretted; for, except toward him, all her old shyness still existed. With the consciousness that he was caring for her she was well content with some half-secluded nook of observation, from which she looked out upon scenes that were like an animated story. She wove fanciful imaginings around those who attracted her attention, and on her return laughingly discussed the people who had passed, like players, before her eyes. Graydon encouraged her to do this, for her ignorance of society made her remarks original and amusing. He knew the conventional status of every one they met as accurately as his brother recognized the commercial value of the securities that passed under his eye, and Madge's estimates often seemed absurd to the last degree.

Whenever she went out with Graydon his course was eminently satisfactory; she never felt herself neglected, while at the same time she saw that his attentions were welcomed everywhere. She never lost her serene sense of proprietorship, and only grew more fond of him as she noted how readily he left the side of beautiful and gifted women to look after her. He had often laughingly asserted that he went into society only for amusement, and his course under her own observation confirmed his words.

Early in the winter during which our story opens, she had caught a succession of colds, and one proved so severe and obstinate that her friends were alarmed, fearing that she was going into a decline. She slowly rallied, however, but was more frail than ever. Before the gay season closed, just preceding Lent, Madge received an invitation to a very large party. Graydon urged her to go, remarking that she had not yet seen society. "Don't be afraid, I'll take care of you, little ghost," he said, and with this assurance she accompanied him, contrary to her sister's advice. It was indeed a brilliant occasion. The wide rooms of a Madison Avenue palace were thronged, and she had never even imagined such toilets as caught her eye on every side. There were so many present that she could easily maintain her position of quiet spectator, and her eyes dilated with pleasure as she saw that Graydon was as much a leader as at other places where comparatively few were present.

At last her attention was attracted by one who was evidently a late comer, and whose presence appeared to fill the apartment. All the others paled before her, as do the stars when the moon rises among them. She was evidently young, and yet she did not suggest youth. One would almost imagine that she had never had a childhood or a girlhood, but was rather a direct creation of metropolitan society. Her exquisitely turned shoulders and arms were bare, and the diamonds about her neck were a circlet of fire. The complexion of her fair oval face was singularly pure, and the color came and went so easily as to prove that it owed nothing to art. The expression of her gray eyes was rather cold and haughty when at rest, and gave an impression of pride and the consciousness of power. The trait which to the observant Madge seemed most marked at first, however, was her perfect ease. Her slightest movement was grace itself. Her entire self-possession was indicated by the manner in which she greeted the men who sought her attention, and many there were. She could be perfectly polite, yet as repellent as ice, or she could smile with a fascination that even Madge felt would be hard to resist. This girl, who was such an immense contrast to herself, wholly fixed her attention as she stood for a few moments, like a queen, surrounded by her courtiers.

Graydon had gone for a glass of water, and meeting a friend had been detained for a brief space. Madge saw him coming, saw his eye light up with admiration as he caught sight of the beautiful stranger, but he came directly to her, and asked, genially, if there was anything else she would like.

"Yes. Who is that girl yonder?"

"Miss Wildmere. Isn't she lovely? She promised me, last week, her first dance for this evening. Will you excuse me for a little while?"

"Certainly;" and yet she was conscious of a sudden and odd little protest at heart.

He approached the beauty. Miss Wildmere's face flushed with pleasure and softened into a welcoming smile, such as she had not yet bestowed upon any who had sought her favor. Then, in swift alternation, she bent upon Madge a brief, cold glance of scrutiny. So brief was it, and so complacent was the expression of the belle as she turned away, that the pallid, sensitive girl was told, as by words, "You are nothing."

That glance was like a sharp, deep wound, and pierced where she was most vulnerable. It said to her, "You are not capable of being anything to Graydon Muir. I am not in the least afraid of you."

What was she to him? What did she wish to be? To these questions Madge had but one answer. Any and every girl, in her belief, would be only too glad to win him. He had said that Miss Wildmere was lovely; his eyes had expressed an admiration which he had never bestowed upon her; he had led the beauty away with a glad content in his face, and the crowded room was made empty by their absence.

She was no longer conscious of weakness, but, obeying her impulse, sprang up and followed them to the ballroom. Concealed by a little group she stood, unwearied, and watched them as they glided hither and thither with a grace that attracted many eyes. The music appeared to control and animate them, and their motion was harmony itself. Graydon evidently thought only of his fair partner; but her swift glances were everywhere, gathering the rich revenue of admiration which was freely offered. For a second she encountered Madge's large black eyes, full of trouble, and a satirical smile proved that she enjoyed the poor girl's solicitude. To deepen it she looked up at Graydon and said something that caused his face to flush with pleasure. His response was more decisive, for the swift color came into her face, and her eyes drooped. The by-play was momentary, and would not have been seen by a less vigilant observer than Madge; but to her it gave the undoubted impression that they were lovers. When Miss Wildmere looked again to see the result of her unkindly strategy, Madge was gone.

In reaction she had grown almost faint, and reached her former retreat with difficulty. But all her latent womanhood speedily rallied to meet this strange and but half-comprehended emergency. The impulse now uppermost was to retain her self-control and reach the seclusion of her own room. How she was to endure the long hours she scarcely knew. She did not dare to think. Indeed, the effort was scarcely possible, for her mind was at first in tumult, with only one thing clear, a poignant sense of loss and trouble.

Graydon was a long time away, longer than he had ever been before when acting as her escort. While she felt this neglect, and interpreted it naturally, she was not sorry. She dreaded meeting him again. In one brief hour her old ease and freedom with him had gone. She wondered at the change in herself, yet knew that it was as definite and decided as if she had become another person. When be had brought her the glass of water she could look into his face with the frank directness of a child. Why could she not do so now? Why did she almost tremble at the thought of his glance, his touch, his presence? She knew that he would come back with his old genial, kindly manner—that he would be the same. But a change had occurred in her which made the fabled transmutations of magic wands seem superficial indeed. Would he note this change? Could he guess the cause? Oh, what *was* the cause? Even her pale face grew crimson, for there are truths that come to the consciousness like the lightning from heaven. She did not need to think, to weigh and reason. A woman's heart is often above and beyond her reason, and hers had been awakened at last by the all-powerful touch of love.

The time passed, and still Graydon did not come. He was not absent very long, and yet it began to seem terribly long to her. She had overrated her powers, and found that even pride could not sustain her. She had no reserve of strength to draw upon. The heat of the room grew oppressive, and she was unaccustomed to throngs, confusion, and noise. The consciousness of her weakness was forced upon her most painfully at last by the appearance of Miss Wildmere on Graydon's arm. The belle was smiling, radiant, her step elastic, her eyes shining with excitement and pleasure. Her practiced scrutiny had assured her that she was the queen of the hour; the handsomest and most courtly man present was so devoted as to suggest that he might easily become a lover; she had seen many glances of envy, and one, in the case of poor Madge, of positive pain. What more could her heart desire? Graydon conducted her to her chaperon, near whom half a dozen gentlemen were waiting for a chance to be his successor; and, having obtained her promise for another dance later in the evening, he turned deprecatingly to Madge. His apologies ceased before they were half spoken. She looked so white and ill that he was alarmed, and asked permission to get her a glass of wine.

"No, Graydon," she said, then hesitated, for she felt the color coming into her face, while a strange blur confused every object in the room. "I'm very, very sorry," she added, hastily, after a moment. "I ought not to have come. I'm not equal to this. It wouldn't take you very long to drive home with me, and then you could return. Please, Graydon."

Her tone was so urgent, and she appeared so weak, that he complied at once, saying, with much compunction, "I should not have left you alone so long, but supposed you were amusing yourself by looking at the people."

She did not trust herself to reply. Her one thought was to reach the refuge of her own apartment, and to this end she concentrated her failing energies. The climb to the ladies' dressing-room was a desperate effort; but when she was once outside the house the cold, pure air revived her slightly.

"You can excuse me to our hostess—she will not care," she faltered, and it seemed to her then that nobody would care. Miss Wildmere's glance had conveyed the estimate of society. If she could believe herself first in Graydon's thoughts she would not be cast down, but now the truth was overwhelming.

She leaned away from him in the corner of the carriage, but he put his strong arm round her and drew her to his breast. She tried to resist, but was powerless. Then came the torturing thought, "If I repel him—if I act differently—he will guess the reason," and she was passive; but he felt her slight form tremble.

"My poor little ghost, you are ill in very truth! I'm indeed sorry that I left you so long."

"Believe me, Graydon, I am ill. Please let that excuse me and explain. Oh, that I—I were strong, like Miss Wildmere!"

"Isn't she a beauty?" exclaimed the unconscious Graydon. "The man who wins her might well be proud, for he would have competitors by the score."

"Your chances seem excellent," said Madge, in a low tone.

He laughed complacently, but added: "You don't know these society belles. They can show a great deal of favor to more than one fellow, yet never permit themselves to be pinned by a definite promise. They are harder to catch and hold than a wild Bedouin; but such a girl as Miss Wildmere is worth the effort. Yes, Madge, I do wish you were like her. It would be grand sport to champion you in society and see you run amuck among the fellows. It's a thousand pities that you are such an invalid. I've thought more than once that you were designed to be a beauty. With your eyes and Stella Wildmere's health you would be quite as effective after your style as she is in hers. Never mind, little sister, I shall stand by you, and as long as I live you shall always have a luxurious sofa, with all the novels of the northern hemisphere at your command. Who knows? You may grow strong one of these days. When you do I'll pick out the nice fellows for you."

At every kindly word her heart grew heavier, and when the carriage stopped at their door she could hardly mount the steps. In the hall she faltered and caught the hat-rack for support. He lifted her in his arms and bore her easily to her room, her sister following in much solicitude. "It's nothing," said Madge; "the company was too large and exciting for me. There was no need of Graydon's carrying me upstairs, but he would do it."

"You poor dear!" began her sister, broodingly. "I feared it would be so. Graydon is made of iron, and will never realize how delicate you are."

"He's very kind, and more considerate than I deserve. As he says," she added, bitterly, "I'm nothing but a ghost, and had better vanish."

"Nonsense, Madge," said the young man, with brusque kindness. "You know I want you to haunt me always. Good-by now, little sister. I shall be *de trop* if I stay any longer. You'll be better in the morning, and to-morrow evening I'll remain home and entertain you."

CHAPTER III

THE PARTING

At last Madge was alone. Her sister had suggested everything she could think of, meanwhile bewailing the young girl's extreme imprudence. Madge entreated for quiet and rest, and at last was left alone. Hour after hour she lay with wide, fixed gaze. Her mind and imagination did not partake of her physical weakness, and now they were abnormally active. As the bewilderment from the shock of her abrupt awakening passed, the truth hourly grew clearer. From the time she had first come under her sister's roof Graydon Muir had begun to make himself essential to her. His uniform kindness had created trust, freedom, and a content akin to happiness. Now all was swept away. She understood that his love was an affection resulting from pity and the strong, genial forces of his nature. The girl who could kindle his spirit and inspire the best and most enthusiastic efforts of his manhood must be like Miss Wildmere—strong, beautiful, capable of keeping step with him under society's critical eyes, and not a mere shadow of a woman like herself. Her morbidly acute fancy recalled the ballroom. She saw him again after his return, encircling the fair girl with his arm, and looking down into her eyes with a meaning unmistakable. Oh, why had she gone to that fatal party! The past, in contrast to the present and the promise of the future, seemed happiness itself.

What could she do? What should she do? The more she thought of it the more unendurable her position appeared. In her vivid self-consciousness the old relations could not continue. Heretofore his caresses had been a matter of course, of habit. They could be so no longer. She shrank from them with inexpressible fear, knowing they would bring what little blood she possessed to her face and very brow in tell-tale floods. The one event from which her sensitive womanhood drew back in deepest dread was his knowledge of her love. To prevent this she would rather die, and she felt so weak and despairing that she thought and almost hoped she would die. If she could only go away, where she would not see him, and hide her wound! But how could she, chained near his daily presence by weakness and helplessness?

Thus through the long night her despairing thoughts went to and fro, and found no rest. Miss Wildmere's cold glance met her everywhere with the assurance that such a creature as she could never be anything to him, and, alas! his own words confirmed the verdict. Love that gives all demands all, and such pitiful affection as he now gave was only a mockery. The morning found her too weak to leave her room, and for the few following days she made illness her excuse for remaining in seclusion. As Graydon looked ruefully at her vacant chair the fourth evening after the company, Mrs. Muir remarked, reproachfully, "I hope you now realize how delicate Madge is. You never should have coaxed her to go to that party."

He was filled with compunction, and brought her flowers, boxes of candy, books, and everything which he imagined would amuse her. At the same time he was growing a little impatient and provoked. He knew that he had taken her from the kindest motives. Now that she gave up utterly to her invalidism, he was inclined to question its necessity. He found that he missed her more than he would have imagined, and his brief hours at home were dreary by reason of her seclusion.

"Why don't you call in a first-class physician and put Madge under a thorough course of treatment?" he asked, irritably. "She has no disease now that I know anything about, and I don't believe it's necessary that she should remain so weak and lackadaisical."

"We did have our doctor call often, and he said she would outgrow her troubles if she would take plenty of fresh of fresh air and exercise. And now she positively refuses to see a physician."

"I wouldn't humor a sick girl's fancies. She needs tonics and a general building up. With your permission I'll stop on my way downtown to-morrow and tell Dr. Anderson to call."

Mrs. Muir repeated the conversation to her sister, with the literalness of which only unimaginative women are capable. Madge turned her face to the wall, and said, coldly and decisively, "I refuse to see a physician. I am no longer a child, and my wishes must be respected." After a moment she added, apologetically: "A doctor could do me no good. I shall soon be stronger. You understand me better than Dr. Anderson can. You are the best and kindest nurse that ever breathed, and I've had enough of doctors. I'll take anything you give me."

These politic words appealed to Mrs. Muir's weak point. Nothing pleased her better than to believe that she could act the part of physician in the family, and prescribing for Madge was a source of unflagging interest. When she informed Graydon of their decision in the morning, he muttered something not very complimentary to either of the ladies; but his good-nature prevailed, and instead of the doctor he ordered a superb bouquet of Jacqueminot roses.

Meanwhile events were taking place of which Madge had no knowledge, but which would favor the plan slowly maturing in her mind. Mr. Muir's business affairs had been taking a turn which made it probable that he would soon have to send his brother abroad. As long as there was uncertainty the reticent man said nothing, but at last he received advices which brought him to a prompt decision, and Graydon was told that he must go at once. The young fellow submitted with fairly good grace. A brief foreign residence had its attractions, but it interfered with his incipient suit to Miss Wildmere. He felt that he had not gone far enough for a definite proposal, but he showed, during the brief call that his time permitted, an interest which the young lady well understood. Since he was to be absent for an indefinite period, and would have no chance to observe her other little affairs, she permitted herself to be gracious and regretful up to the point of inspiring much hope for the future. With a nicety of tact—the result of experience—she confirmed his view that they had made favorable impressions on each other, and that for the present they must be content with this.

He had but a day in which to make his preparations in order to catch a fast steamer that sailed at daylight the following morning. Madge's first sensation when she learned of his near departure was one of immense relief. The possibility which she had so dreaded could not now be realized, and her plan could be carried out with far less embarrassment. But as time passed, and she knew that their separation was so near, her heart relented toward him with inexpressible tenderness. The roses that perfumed the room were a type of his unstinted kindness and consideration. She was just enough to acknowledge that these were even more than she could naturally expect from him—that the majority of young men would have treated her with a half contemptuous pity which she was now beginning to admit would be partially deserved. On the occasions when she had gone out with him she had learned how unattractive in society her pale face and shy ways were. Such attentions as she had received had been to her sensitive spirit like charity. Graydon had been animated by unaffected good-will and an affection that was, after its kind, genuine. While she felt that it would be no longer possible to receive these mild manifestations of regard while giving something so different, she still knew, with a half despairing sinking of heart, how blank and desolate her life would be without them. She must meet him once more, and word was sent that she would receive his good-by after dinner. Having safely passed this one interview, she hoped that she might be able to control the future, and either cease to be, or bring about changes upon which she had resolved.

Only a soft, dim light shone in her room when he came to say farewell.

"Why, Madge," he exclaimed, "you are better! You actually have color. Perhaps it is fever, though," he added, dubiously. "At any rate, it's very becoming."

"I think it must be the reflection from your roses there, you extravagant fellow," she replied, laughing.

"That's famous, Madge. If you will laugh again like that I'll send you a present from Paris. Dear Madge, do get well. Don't let us have anything dismal in our parting. It's only for a little while, you know. When I come back it will be summer, and I'll take you to the seashore or mountains or somewhere, and help you get well."

"You are very kind, Graydon. You have been a true brother to me from the time you tried to cheer and encourage the pale, frightened little girl that sat opposite you at the dinner-table. Don't you remember?"

"Of course I do. It seemed so droll to me that you were afraid when there was nothing to be afraid of."

"My fear was natural. Little as I know of the world, I know that—at least for one like me. It may seem weak and silly to you, but, brought up as I had been, I was morbidly sensitive. You might have meant to be kind and sympathetic and all that, and yet have hurt me cruelly. I have been out with you enough to know how I am regarded. I don't complain. I suppose it is the way of the world, but it has not been your way. You have brought sunshine from the first, not from a sense of duty, not out of sheer humiliating pity, but because it was the impulse of your strength to help and cheer one who was so weak, and if—if—anything—Well, I want you to know before you go away that I appreciate it all and shall never forget it."

"Oh, come, Madge, don't talk so dismally. What do you mean by 'if—if—anything'? You are going to get strong and well, and we will open the campaign together next fall."

She shook her head, but asked, lightly, "How will Miss Wildmere endure your absence?"

"Easier than you, I imagine. She knows how to console herself. Still, as my little sister, I will tell you in confidence that she was very kind in our parting interview. How much her kindness meant only she herself knows, and I've been in society long enough to know that it may mean very little."

"Are you so wholly bent upon winning her, Graydon?"

"Oh, you little Mother Eve! You are surely going to get well. There is no sign of longevity in a woman so certain as curiosity. I've not yet reached the point of breaking my heart about her, whatever she does. Wouldn't you like so beautiful a creature for your sister?"

"The contrast would be too great. I should indeed seem a ghost beside her. Still, if she would make you happy—" But she could go no further.

"Well, well, that's a very uncertain problem of the future. Don't say anything about it at home. My brother don't like her father. They do not get on well in business. Let us talk about yourself. What are you going to do while I am gone?"

"What can such a shadow as I do? Tell me rather what you are going to do, and where you'll be. You are real, and what you do amounts to something."

"There's one thing I'm going to do, and that is, write you some jolly letters that will make you laugh in spite of yourself. They will be part of the tonic treatment that I want you to promise me to begin at once."

"I have already entered upon it, Graydon," she said, quietly, "and I don't think any one will value your letters more than I, only I may not get strong enough to write very much in reply. I've never had occasion to write many letters, you know. Tell me where you will be and what you are going to do," and she leaned back upon her lounge and closed her eyes.

While he complied, he thought, "She has grown pale and thin even to ghastliness, yet I was sure she had color when I first came in. Poor little thing! perhaps her fears are well founded, and I may never see her again;" and the good-hearted fellow was full of tender and remorseful regret. He was quite as fond of her as if she had been his own sister, perhaps even more so, for his affection was not merely the result of a natural tie, but of something congenial to his nature in the girl herself, and it cut him to the heart to see her so white and frail. He stopped a moment, and she opened her eyes and looked at him inquiringly.

"Oh, Madge," he broke out, "I'm so sorry I took you to that confounded party. You seemed getting on hopefully until that blasted evening. You must get well enough to haunt me after your old fashion. You don't know what a dear little sister you have become, and I didn't know it myself until you were secluded by illness, and all through my fault. You have barricaded yourself long enough with that stand and its vase of roses. I'm not going to say good-by at this distance." He removed the stand, and seating himself by her side, he drew her head down upon his shoulder and kissed her again and again. "There now," he continued, "you look perfectly lovely. Kisses are a part of the tonic treatment you need, and I wish I were going to be here to give them. Why, you queer little woman! I did not know you had so much blood in your body."

"It's—it's because I'm not strong," she said, struggling for release. Suddenly she became still, her face took on almost the hue of death, and he saw that she was unconscious.

In terrible alarm he laid her hastily on the lounge, and rushed for Mrs. Muir.

"She has merely fainted," said that experienced woman, after a moment's examination. "You never will learn, Graydon, that Madge is not as strong as yourself. Call one of the maids, and leave her to me."

That was the last time he saw Madge Alden for more than two years. She soon rallied, but agreed with her sister that it would be best not to see him again. She sent him one of his own roses, with the simple message, "Good-by."

Late at night he went down to the steamer, depressed and anxious, carrying with him the vivid memory of Madge lying white and death-like where he had laid her apparently lifeless form.

"I shall never see her again," he muttered. "Such weakness must be mortal."

CHAPTER IV

EFFORT

The deep experience, the touchstone of character, of latent power, if such existed, had come to Madge Alden. For days she had drifted helplessly on the rising tide of an apparently hopeless love. With every hour she comprehended more fully what Graydon Muir had become to her and all that he might have been. It seemed that she had been carried forward by a strong, quiet current, only to be wrecked at last. A sense of utter helplessness overwhelmed her. She could not ignore her love; it had become interwoven with every interest and fibre of her life. At first she contemplated it in wonder, in deeply troubled and alarmed perplexity. It was a momentous truth, that had suddenly been made known as some irretrievable misfortune might have been revealed. She had read of love as children hear of mental anxieties and conflicts of which they have no comprehension. As she grew older it had been like poetry, music, romance—something that kindled her imagination into vague, pleasant dreams. It had been as remote from the present and her own experience as lives of adventure in strange and foreign lands. She had awakened at last to find that it was like her vital breath. By some law of her nature she had given, not merely her thoughts and affection, but her very self to another. To her dismay it made no difference that he had not sought the gift and was not even aware of it. Circumstances over which she had no control had brought her into close companionship with Graydon Muir. She had seen him almost daily for years; she knew him with the intimacy of a sister, yet without the safeguard of a natural tie; and from his genial kindness she had drawn almost all the life she had ever possessed. With an unconsciousness akin to that of a plant which takes root and thrives upon finding a soil adapted to it, her love had been developed by his strong, sunny nature. She soon recognized that it was a love such as she had never known, unlike that for her mother or sister or any one else, and it seemed to her that it could pass away only with herself. It was not a vague sentiment, an indefinite longing; it was the concentrated and imperious demand of her whole being, which, denied, left little indeed, even were the whole world hers. Yet such were the cruel conditions of her lot that she could not speak of it even to one whose head had been pillowed on the same mother's breast, and the thought that it might be discovered by its object made her turn cold with dread. It was a holy thing—the spontaneous product of an unperverted heart—and yet she must hide it as if it were a crime.

Above all the trouble and turmoil of her thoughts, clear and definite amid the chaos brought into her old quiet, languid life, was the impulse—the necessity—to conceal that which had become the mainspring of her existence. She had not the experience of one versed in the ways of the world. How could others—how could he—be kept in ignorance of that of which she was so painfully and vividly conscious? Therefore, overwhelmed with dread and a sense of helplessness, she yielded to her first impulse to hide, in order that what seemed inseparable from herself might be concealed.

But she knew that this seclusion could not last—that she must meet this first and great emergency of her life in some other way. From the strong wish to obtain safety in separation, a plan to bring it about gradually took form in her mind. She must escape, either to live or to die, before her secret became known; and in casting about for the means, she at last thought of a family who had been the kindest of neighbors in the village where her mother had died. Mr. Wayland and his wife had been the truest and most sympathetic of friends to the widow and her orphan children, and Madge felt that she could be at home with them. Mrs. Wayland's prolonged ill-health had induced her husband to try, in her behalf, the remedy of an entire change of air and climate. Therefore they had removed, some years before, to Santa Barbara, on the Pacific coast. The signal success of the experiment now kindled a glimmer of hope in poor Madge. That remote city certainly secured the first requisites—separation and distance—and the fact that her friend found health and vigor in the semi-tropical resort promised a little for her frail young life. She had few fears that her old friends would not welcome her, and she was in a position to entail no burdens, even though she should remain an invalid.

The practical question was, How should she get there? But the more she thought upon the plan the more attractive it grew. The situation seemed so desperate that she was ready for a desperate remedy. To remain weak, helpless, and in perpetual dread was impossible.

Her mind also was clear and strong enough for self-arraignment, and in bitterness she partially condemned herself that she had lost her chance for happiness. Her conscience had often troubled her that she had given up so weakly to the habit of invalidism, but she had never had sufficient motive for the vigorous and sustained effort essential to overcome it. Indeed, her frailty had seemed a claim upon Graydon, and made it more natural for him to pet her. Now that she was thinking deeply, she was compelled to admit that her ill health was to some extent her fault as well as her misfortune. Circumstances, natural indolence, and her sister's extreme indulgence had brought about a condition of life that propagated itself. One languid day was the parent of another, it was so much easier to dawdle than to act. Thus she had lost her opportunity. If he had won health, even Graydon said it would have brought her beauty. She might have secured his admiration, respect, and even love, instead of his pity. What could be more absurd than to imagine that he could give aught else to one like herself? "Oh, what a blind fool I have been!" she moaned—"blind to the wants of my own heart, blind to the truth that a man needs a strong, genial companion, and not a dependent shadow."

Graydon's sudden departure took from her project many obstacles and embarrassments. She was not afraid of her sister or her remonstrances, and felt that she could convince Mr. Muir that the change gave the best promise for the future. Graydon's objections would have been hard to meet. He might have been led to guess her motive or insist on being her escort. Now it was merely a question of gaining sufficient strength for the journey and of being resolute.

Mrs. Muir's opposition was not so great as Madge had feared, and Mr. Muir even approved of the plan. The shrewd merchant's judgment was usually correct on all practical matters, and he believed that Madge's best chance was in a radical change. He saw that his wife's indulgence tended to confirm her sister's lack of energy, and that it would be best for Madge to spend the next few years with one who had regained her health by wise endeavor. Mrs. Muir soon saw everything as her husband viewed it, and the young girl prepared for a new world and a new life.

It was indeed a wise decision. There could be no more aimless drifting and brooding. A telegram to Mr. Wayland brought immediate acquiescence in the project, which was arranged more in detail by letters. Madge strove in every possible way to fit herself for the journey, and was surprised at her success. Better than all tonics was the diversion of her thoughts, the prospect of change, the necessity for action. In her thoughtful prudence she even satisfied Mrs. Muir's solicitude, for the young girl realized more fully every day how much depended upon her plan. It seemed to her that there could be no greater misfortune than to become so ill again that in helplessness she must await Graydon's return. Therefore, every faculty of mind, every power of body, was exerted to accomplish her purpose; and, while her farewell to her sister and Mr. Muir was tender and full of gratitude, the consciousness of escape was uppermost in her mind. An elderly friend of Mr. Muir would be her escort to San Francisco, and in that city Mr. Wayland was to meet her.

She arrived safely at her far-distant home, greatly worn and exhausted indeed, but calm in mind from a sense of security. Mrs. Wayland greeted her with her old-time cordiality, and gave herself heartily to the task of rallying the frail girl into health.

During the days of absolute rest which followed the journey, Madge's thoughts were busy. The width of the continent would separate her from the past and those associated with it. Both the breadth of the continent and the ocean were between her and him from whom she had fled; yet he was ever present to her imagination. In this respect the intervening miles counted for nothing. She had not hoped that they would. She could conceive of no plan of life that left him out, yet she felt that she must have some object to look forward to, some motive for action. The spirit she had recently shown in taking so decisive a step proved her to possess a latent force of character of which she herself had not been conscious. She would not sit down to dream and brood away the future. She could never hope for Graydon

Muir's love. He would soon return to New York, and the idea that Miss Wildmere or any other girl would remain cold to his suit was preposterous. Yet if she lived she must meet Graydon again, and she now felt that she would live. The decision she had manifested at the crisis of her life was kindling her nature. She was conscious of a growing inclination to prove to Graydon that she was neither "weak nor lackadaisical." The reproach of these, his words, haunted her and rankled in her memory. If she could only make him respect her—if she could only win such a look of admiration as she had seen upon his face when he first recognized Miss Wildmere at the party, it would be a triumph indeed.

Thus a new plan, a new hope, was developed, and became the inspiration of effort. She listened unweariedly as Mrs. Wayland related how she had turned the tide of her ebbing vitality. Thus Madge gained the benefit of another's experience. Little by little she sought to increase her slender resources of strength. The superb climate enabled her to live almost in the open air, and each day she exulted over an increase of vigor. Almost everything favored her in her new home. When she was well enough to go out much the strangers had gone, and everything in the town was restful, yet not enervating. The Waylands, while on the best terms with other permanent residents, were not society people. Mrs. Wayland had become satisfied with that phase of life in her youth. Her husband was a reader, a student, and something of a naturalist. The domestic habits which had been formed while Mrs. Wayland was an invalid still clung to them. While never ceasing to be kind neighbors, they were more than content with books, nature, and each other. Madge therefore had access to a very fine library, and the companionship of intellectual people who had known from contact the present world, and in whose cultivated minds dwelt the experiences of the past. Her friends were in the habit of discussing what they read, and the basis of much of their enjoyment—as of all true companionship—was harmonious disagreement. Thus the young girl was insensibly taught to think for herself and to form her own opinions. They also proved admirable guides in directing her reading. She felt that she had read enough for mere amusement, and now determined to become familiar with the great master-minds, so far as she was capable of following them, and to inform herself on those subjects which Mr. Wayland declared essential to an education.

If circumstances within doors were conducive to mental growth, those without were even more favorable to physical development. The salt air and softly tempered sunshine were perpetual tonics. The place was full of exquisite flowers. She felt that she had never seen roses until she came to Santa Barbara. To a wounded, sensitive spirit there is even a healing influence in the brightness and perfume of flowers. They smiled so sweetly at her that she could not help smiling back. The sunny days passed, one so like another that they begot serenity. The even climate, with its sunny skies, tended to inspirit as well as to invigorate. Almost every day she spent hours in driving and sailing, and as the season advanced she began to take ocean baths, which on that genial coast are suitable almost all the year round. Going thus to nature for healing, she did not appeal in vain. Strength and grace were bestowed imperceptibly, yet surely, as spring clothes the leafless tree.

A love such as had grown unbidden and unconsciously in Madge's heart could not be content with the meagre reward of a little admiration. Such an affection was softening and ennobling in its character, and the mere desire to compel Graydon to glance at her as she had seen him look at Miss Wildmere grew into the higher ambition to become such a woman as would approach in some degree his ideal. She knew his tastes, and as she thought over the past she believed she could gauge his character as could no other. She soon recognized that he was not an exceptional man, that she was not worshipping a hero. He himself would be the last one to claim pre-eminence among his fellows. But his genial, open nature, his physical strength, and his generous, kindly impulses made him an eminently lovable man, and—well, she loved him, and believed she ever should. Frail and defective in almost every respect herself, she would have thought it absurd to cherish some lofty and impossible ideal. He was hearty, wholesome, honest, and she soon began to see that it would be a better and a nobler thing—a nearer approach to happiness—to become a woman whom he could trust and respect than merely to win a little admiration as a tribute to ephemeral beauty.

She would attain beauty if she could, but it should be the appendage, the ornament of mind and character. She, who had seemed to him weakness itself, would aim to suggest eventually that noblest phase of strength—woman's patience and fortitude.

It must not be supposed that Madge reached these conclusions in days, weeks, or even months. Her final purposes were the result of slow, half-conscious growth. Right, brave action produced right feeling, and there are few better moral tonics than developing health. With richer, better blood came truer, higher, and more unselfish thoughts. She found that she could not only live, but that vigorous, well-directed life is in itself enjoyment. It was a pleasure to breathe the pure, balmy air, even when reclining in a carriage or a sail-boat, and as she gained strength sufficient for exercise, she soon became aware of the rich physical rewards that wait upon it. Slowly at first, but with an increasing impetus, she advanced toward health, the condition of all genuine life. She at last exchanged her carriage for a saddle-horse.

Mr. Wayland had one taste in which his wife did not share—a love for horseback exercise, which, indeed, was one of the chief characteristics of the community. Madge knew that Graydon was extremely fond of a good horse, and that he rode superbly. To become his equal therefore in this respect was one of the chief dreams of her ambition. It was with almost a sense of terror that she mounted at first, but Mr. Wayland was considerate. Her horse was only permitted to walk, and she was taken off as soon as she was weary. Confidence increased rapidly, and eventually she became fearless and almost tireless. The beach was like a smooth, hard road-bed, and before the summer was over she thought little of a gallop of ten miles, with the breath of the Pacific fanning her cheek. When Mr. Wayland drove with his wife up through Mission and Hot Springs canons, or eight miles away to the exquisitely beautiful Bartlett Canon and the fine adjacent ranches, she accompanied them on horseback. As she flashed along past date-palms, and through lemon and orange groves, she began to appear semi-tropical herself. She also became Mr. Wayland's companion on his botanizing expeditions, and her steps among the rocks of the foothills and on the slopes of the mountains grew surer, lighter, and more unwearied. Color stole into her face, and a soft fire into her dark eyes when animated. Mrs. Wayland looked on with increasing delight, and thought, "She is growing very beautiful. I wonder if she knows it?"

Indeed she knew it well. What young girl does not? But Madge had a motive for knowledge of which Mrs. Wayland did not dream. In the main the girl was her own physician, and observed her symptoms closely. She knew well what beauty was. Her vivid fancy would at any time recall Miss Wildmere as a living presence; therefore her standard was exceedingly high, and she watched her approach to it as to a distant and eagerly sought goal. Other eyes gave assurance that her own were not deceiving her. The invalid on whom at first but brief and commiserating glances had been bestowed was beginning to be followed by admiring observation. Society recognized her claims, and she was gaining even more attention than she desired. As her strength increased she accepted invitations, and permitted the circle of her acquaintance to widen. It was part of her plan to become as much at home in the social world as Graydon himself. Nor was she long in overcoming a diffidence that had been almost painful. In one sense these people were to her simply a means to an end. She cared so little for them that she was not afraid, and had merely to acquire the ease which results from usage. Diffidence soon passed into a shy grace that was indefinable and yet became a recognized trait. The least approach to loudness and aggressiveness in manner was not only impossible to her, but she also possessed the refinement and tact of which only extremely sensitive natures are capable. A vain, selfish woman is so preoccupied with herself that she does not see or care what others are, or are thinking of, unless the facts are obtruded upon her; another, with the kindest intentions, may not be able to see, and so blunders lamentably; but Madge was so finely organized that each one who approached her made a definite impression, and without conscious effort she responded—not with a conventional and stereotyped politeness, but with an appreciative courtesy which, as she gained confidence and readiness of expression, gave an unfailing charm to her society. With few preconceived and arbitrary notions of her own she accepted people as they were, and made the most of them. Of course there were some in whom even the broadest charity could find little to approve; but it was her purpose to study and understand them and lose forever the unsophisticated ignorance at which Graydon had used to laugh.

Santa Barbara was a winter resort, and she had the advantage of meeting many types. In Mrs. Wayland she had a useful mentor. This lady in her younger days had been familiar with the best phases of metropolitan society, and she counteracted in Madge all tendencies toward provincialism. Thus it gradually became recognized that the "shy, sickly little girl," as she had been characterized at first, was growing into a very attractive young woman. Indeed, after an absence of only a year her own sister would scarcely have recognized her.

CHAPTER V

ACHIEVEMENT

Mrs. Muir of course heard often from her sister, and was satisfied with the general assurance that she was better and steadily improving. Madge, however, was rather indefinite in her information. As time passed, the idea of giving her friends in the East a surprise took possession of her fancy. She instinctively felt that she needed every incentive to pursue the course she had resolved upon, since she often suffered from fits of depression hard to combat. The hope of appearing like a new being to her relatives was another innocent motive for her long-prolonged effort. Circumstances had never developed epistolary tastes in the sisters, and they were content with brief missives containing general assurances that all was well. Mrs. Muir was one of those ladies who become engrossed with the actual and the present. Had Madge been in her old room she would have been looked after with daily solicitude; being absent, she was loved none the less, but was simply crowded from thought and memory by swarms of little cares. She was doing well, and her sister was satisfied. "'It's a wonderful climate,' Madge writes," she would say, "so even and dry. Madge doesn't take cold as she did here, and can go out nearly every day. Perhaps we ought to become reconciled to the fact that she will have to live there always, since here, with our sudden changes, she could scarcely live at all."

With the kindliest intentions Graydon had sought to initiate a vigorous correspondence. He had learned with immense relief of Madge's improvement through change of residence, and he felt that a series of jolly letters might bring aid and hopefulness. Her responses were not very encouraging, however, and business cares, with the novelty of foreign life, gradually absorbed his thoughts and time until correspondence languished and died.

"It's the old story," he thought, with a shade of irritation. "Letters cost effort, and she is not equal to effort, or thinks she is not."

If he could have seen Madge at that moment riding like the wind on a spirited horse he would have been more astonished than by any of the wonders of the old world.

To Madge his letters were a source of mingled pain and pleasure, but the former predominated. In every line they breathed an affection which could never satisfy. Coldness or indifference could not have so assured her that her love was hopeless; and when she sat down to reply, the language of her heart was so unlike that which she must write as to make her feel almost guilty of deliberate deception. Correspondence made him too vividly present, and she was learning that she had the power, not of forgetting him, but of so occupying her mind with tasks for his sake as to attain serenity. The days were made short by efforts of which he deemed her incapable, and weariness brought rest at night. But when she sat down with her pen, confronting him and not what she sought to do for him, her heart sank. He was too near and dear, yet too remote, even for hope.

This emotion is, however, the most hardy of plants, and

although she had often assured herself that she had never entertained it or had any reason to do so, almost before she was aware she found it growing in her heart. Business still kept Graydon abroad, although a year had passed. There were no indications that he was pressing his suit with Miss Wildmere, and our heroine's mirror and the eyes of others began to tell her that the confident belle would not now bestow a glance so cold and indifferent as to mean, "You can be nothing to him or to any one." Moreover, Miss Wildmere's coveted beauty might prove an ally. One so attractive would be sought, perhaps won, before Graydon returned, and absence might have taught him that his regard had been little more than admiration. Naturally Madge would not be inclined to think well of one who had brought so cruel an experience into her life; but, prejudice apart, the society girl had given evidence of a type of womanhood not very high. Even Graydon, in his allusions, had suggested a character repulsive to Madge. A woman "as hard to capture and hold as a 'Bedouin'" was not at all her ideal. The words presented to her one who was either calculating or capricious, either heartless or fickle.

"Truly," she thought, "if there was ever a man who merited whole-hearted, lifelong constancy, it is Graydon Muir; and if he even imagines Miss Wildmere incapable of this, why should he think further of her? Perhaps while beyond the spell of her beauty he has formed a truer estimate of her character, and has abandoned all thought of her as a mocking dream. Perhaps—"

Of what possibilities will not a young girl dream at the dictation of her heart? And as she saw the sharp lines of her profile softening into loveliness, the color fluctuating in her cheeks even at her thoughts, her thin, feeble arms growing white and firm, and the rounded grace of womanhood appearing in all her form, she began to hope that she could endure comparison with Miss Wildmere, even on her lower plane of material beauty. But Madge had too much mind to be content with Miss Wildmere's standard. She coveted outward attractiveness chiefly that the casket might secure attention to its gems. The days of languid, desultory reading and study were over, and she determined to know at least a few things well.

It was to music, however, that she gave her chief attention, since she believed that for this art she had some positive talent A German in the pursuit of health had drifted to the remote southern city. He was past middle age, but had retained through numberless disappointments and discouragements the one enthusiasm of his life; and in Madge he found a pupil after his own heart. While his voice had lost much of its freshness and power, his taste was pure and refined. He kindled in the young girl's mind something of his own love and reverence for music on its own account. To Madge, however, it would always remain a method of expression rather than a science or an art, and the old professor at last learned to recognize her limitations. She would be excellent in only those phases of music which were in accord with her own feeling and thought. She would not, perhaps could not, study it as he had done, for her woman's nature and the growing purpose of her life were ever in the ascendant; but under his guidance her taste grew purer and her knowledge and power increased rapidly. What she did she learned to do well. Even Herr Brachmann was often charmed by the delicate originality of her touch, which proved that her own thought and feeling were infused into the music before her.

But her voice delighted him most. With her increasing vigor was gained the ability to use her vocal organs in sustained effort. He guarded her carefully against over-exertion, and her advance was assured and safe. Note after note, true, sweet, and strong, was added to the compass of her voice, and this exercise reacted with increased benefit on her general health. One can scarcely become a vocalist without toning up the vital organs, and in learning to sing Madge provided an antidote against consumptive tendencies. Her gift of song at last began to attract attention. Strangers loitered near the Wayland Cottage during warm, quiet evenings, and in society she was importuned by those who had heard her before. She usually complied, for she was training herself to sing before an audience of one who was familiar with the best musical talent of the world. Not that she wished to invite comparisons with this kind of talent, but merely to sing with such simple sweetness and truth that Graydon would forget the trained professional in the unaffected charm of the natural girl.

The manner of those who listened stimulated her hope. At the first notes of her song all conversation ceased. Even the unappreciative were impressed by a certain pathos, an appealing minor tone, which touched the heart while pleasing the ear.

During the long summer that followed her first winter at Santa Barbara the little town sank into a semi-torpid state. Strangers disappeared. With many of the permanent residents to kill time was the main object of languid effort. To Madge the season brought varied opportunity. The old professor gave her much of his time. While others slept she read and studied. The heat, tempered by the vast Pacific, was never great, and the air had a vitality that proved a constant aid to her controlling motive. In the morning she rode or took some form of skilled exercise in which she knew Graydon to be proficient, and she rarely missed her ocean bath. Such health was she acquiring that it was becoming a joy in itself. As with all earnest, constant natures, however, her supreme motive grew stronger with time.

In August she received tidings from the East that caused much solicitude and depression. Graydon had returned for a brief visit, and had joined Mr. and Mrs. Muir at a seaside inn. "A Miss Wildmere is staying here also," her sister wrote, "and, somewhat to Mr. Muir's disapproval, Graydon seems not only well acquainted with her, but unusually friendly. Mr. Muir says that if she is like her father she is a 'speculator'; and from the attention she receives and the way she receives it one would think he was right. Graydon, however, seems to be her favorite, and if he could remain long enough it is not hard to see what might happen. But she is a great belle and a coquette too, I should imagine, and she has a large enough following to turn any girl's head. I don't wonder at it either, for she is the most lovely creature I ever saw, and yet she doesn't make a pleasant impression on me. The men are just wild about her. Mr. Muir looks askance at Graydon's devotion, and mutters 'speculator' when Miss Wildmere's name is mentioned. Graydon returns to Europe next week. He inquires often after you, and his questions make me feel that I don't know as much about you and what you are doing as I should. You write often, but somehow you seem remote in more senses than one. I suppose, however, you are reading as usual, and just floating along down stream with time. Well, no matter, dear. You write that you are better and stronger, and have no more of your old dreadful colds. You must spend next summer with us, even if you have to go back to Santa Barbara in the winter."

Neither the shortness of his visit nor the fascinations of Miss Wildmere prevented Graydon from writing Madge a cordial note full of regret that he should not see her. "You have indeed," he wrote, "vanished like a ghost, and become but a haunting memory. It is a year and a half since I have seen you, and I did not succeed in beguiling you into a correspondence. Like the good Indians, you have followed the setting sun into some region as vague and distant as the 'happy hunting-ground.' Mary says that you will come East next summer. The idea! Is there anything of you to come that is corporate and real? If I had the time I would go to you and see. I find Miss Wildmere just about where I left her, only more beautiful and fascinating, and besieged by a host. Absence makes my chance slight indeed, but I do not despair. She so evidently enjoys a defensive warfare, wherein it is the besiegers who capitulate, that she may maintain it until my exile abroad is over. This is to my mind a more rational interpretation of her freedom than that she is waiting for me; and thus I reveal to you that modesty is my most prominent trait. She may be married before I see her again; and should this prove to be the case I will show you what a model of heroic equanimity I can be."

Madge read this letter with a sigh of intense relief, and was not long in resolving that when he came again she would enter the lists with Miss Wildmere and do what her nature permitted before her chance of happiness passed irrevocably. Graydon's letter kindled her hope greatly. It seemed to her that she was to have a chance—that her patient effort might receive the highest reward after all. She thanked God for the hope. Her love was a sacred thing. It was the natural, uncalculating outgrowth of her womanhood, and was inciting her toward all womanly grace.

Madge did not believe her motive, her purpose, to be unwomanly. Should the opportunity offer, she did not intend to win Graydon by angling for him, by arts, blandishments, or one unmaidenly advance. She would try to be so admirable that he would admire her, so true that he would trust her, and so fascinating that he would woo her with a devotion that would leave no chance for "equanimity" were it possible for him to fail. If in her desperate weakness, in the chaos of her first self-knowledge, she could hide her secret, she smiled at the possibility of revealing it now that she had been schooled and trained into strength and self-control.

In her brief letter of reply to Graydon she wrote:

"That I still exist and shall continue to live is proved by my one trait which you regard as encouraging—curiosity. Please send me some books that will tell me about Europe, or, rather, will present Europe as nearly as possible in its real aspect. I may never travel, but am foolish enough to imagine that I can see the world from the standpoint of this sleepy old town."

"Poor little wraith!" said Graydon, as he read the words. "What a queer, shadowy world her fancy will create, even from the most realistic descriptions I can send her!" But he good-naturedly made up a large bundle of books, in which fiction predominated, for he believed that she would read nothing else.

The days gilded on, autumn merged into winter, and strangers came again. Madge was acquiring an experience of which at one time she had never dreamed. She found herself in Miss Wildmere's position. Every day she was put more and more on the defensive. Gentlemen eagerly sought her society, and her situation was often truly embarrassing, for she had as little desire that the besiegers should capitulate as she had intention of surrendering herself. In this respect Miss Wildmere's tactics were easier to carry out. *She* was not in the least annoyed by any number of abject and committed slaves, and she was approaching the period when she proposed to surrender with great discretion, but to whom was not a settled point.

Madge was beginning to make victims also, but she made them by being simply what she was, and those who suffered most had to admit to themselves that she was almost as elusive as a spirit of the air.

In the spring visitors to the health resort, returning to the East, brought to the Muirs rumors of Madge's beauty, fascination, and accomplishments. They were a little puzzled, but concluded that Madge had appeared well in a rendezvous of invalids, and were glad to believe that she was much better. Prudent Mrs. Muir wrote, however, "Do not think of returning till the last of May. Then we shall soon go to the mountains. This will be another change, and change in your case, you know, has proved so beneficial! We expect Graydon soon. He is tired of residence abroad, and has so arranged the business that a confidential clerk can take his place."

Madge smiled and sighed. The test of her patient endeavor was about to come.

CHAPTER VI

THE SECRET OF BEAUTY

Mr. and Mrs. Wayland had become so attached to Madge that they were the more ready to listen to her solicitation that they should accompany her East and visit their old haunts. "Very likely I shall return with you," said the young girl, "and make Santa Barbara my home."

This indeed was her plan should defeat await her. She had become attached to the seaside town, as we do to all places that witness the soul's deepest experiences and best achievements. She had learned there to hope for the highest of earth's gifts; she believed that she could live there a serene, quiet, unselfish life, her secret still unknown, should that be her fate.

The old German professor was almost heartbroken at her departure. "It vas alvays so," he said; "ven mine heart vas settled on someding, den I lose it;" but she reassured him by saying that there was no certainty that she would not return.

Mary Muir was so overwhelmed with astonishment that at first she scarcely returned Madge's warm embrace. She expected to find her sister much stronger and better; but this radiant, beautiful girl, half a head taller than herself—was she the shadowy creature who had gone away with what seemed a forlorn hope? She held Madge off and looked at her, she drew her to a mirror and looked at her again, then exclaimed, "This is a miracle! Why did you not tell me?"

"I wished to surprise you. I did write that I was better."

"This is not better; it is best Oh, Madge, you have grown so pretty you almost take away my breath—all travel-stained and weary, too, from your journey! What will not Henry say? I should scarcely have known you. Surely now you need not go back. You are the picture of health."

"We shall see," said Madge, quietly. "It may be best if I find that the East does not agree with me." She was fully determined to keep open her line of retreat.

Mr. Muir, in his quiet way, enjoyed the transformation as greatly as did his wife. He had foreseen changes for the better, but had not hoped for anything like this, he declared.

"I just want to be near when Graydon first sees you!" exclaimed voluble Mrs. Muir, at the dinner-table.

The remark was unexpected, and Madge, to her dismay, found the blood rushing to her face. Quick as thought she put her handkerchief to her mouth, and sought to escape notice under the ruse of a brief strangulation. "This is not going to answer at all," she thought. "I must acquire a better self-control." She at once began talking about Graydon in the most simple and natural manner possible, asking many questions. Mrs. Muir's intuition and powers of observation were not very great, and she was without the faintest suspicion of what was passing in Madge's mind. Keen-eyed, reticent Mr. Muir was not so unheeding, however. When Graydon's name was mentioned he happened to glance up from the dinner which usually absorbed his attention. In dealing with men he had acquired the habit of keen observation. During a business transaction his impassive face and quiet eyes gave no evidence of his searching scrutiny. He not only heard and weighed the words to which he listened, but ever sought to follow the mental processes behind them; and often men had been perplexed by the fact that the banker had apparently arrived at conclusions opposite to the tenor of their statements. When, therefore, he saw the color flying into Madge's face at the unexpected utterance of his brother's name, his attention was arrested and an impression made to which his mind would revert in the future. It might mean nothing; it might mean a great deal. Business and home life were everything to Mr. Muir, and Graydon's admiration of Miss Wildmere did not promise well for either.

The power that Mr. Muir had acquired mainly by practice Madge possessed by nature. As we have seen, she was quite free from that most unwomanly phase of stupidity which is often due to the heart rather than the head. Some women know what is told them if it is told plainly; others look into the eyes of those around them and see what is sought to be concealed. The selfish woman is self-blinded. She often has great powers of discernment, but will not take the trouble to use them, unless prompted by her own interests. Selfishness is too short-sighted, however, to secure lasting benefits. Usually, nothing is more fatal than the success of mere self-seeking. While Madge pressed unwaveringly toward the goal of her hopes, she did not do so in thoughtless or callous indifference toward those who had true claims upon her. With her sister she soon saw that all was well—that she was, as before, absorbed and content with the routine of her life. She was not so sure about her brother-in-law. During her absence lines of care had appeared in his face, and there was an abstracted and sometimes a troubled look in his eyes, as if he was pursued by questions that were importunate and even threatening. The indications of perturbation were slight indeed, but from his nature they would be so in any case. Thus the young girl also received an impression which awakened a faint solicitude. Mr. Muir, as her guardian and the manager of her property, had been a true friend and loyal to his trust. She entertained for him much respect and a strong, quiet affection. He did not dwell in her thoughts merely as one who was useful to her, but rather as one who had been true to her, and to whom she in her place and way would be true and sympathetic were there occasion.

Madge was wearied indeed by her long journey, but not exhausted. In sensations so different from those which had followed her journey to the West she recognized her immeasurable gain. Then she had entered Mrs. Wayland's cottage helpless, hopeless, a fugitive from her own weakness. By wise endeavor she had transformed that very weakness into her strength, and had returned to the scenes from which she had fled earnest and resolute—one who had made her choice for life and would abide by it. Womanly to her very finger-tips, she was acting with the aggressive decision of a man. Sensitive and timid beyond most women, she would not lose her happiness when it might be won in paths not only hedged about by all the proprieties of her lot, but also by a reserve and pride with which her own fine nature was pre-eminently endowed. That she loved Graydon Muir was a truth for life. If he could learn to love her from what she had sought to be, from what she simply was, he should have the chance. Her own deep experience had taught her much and given her the clew to many things. She had studied life, not only in books, but in its actual manifestations. Mrs. Wayland was a social mine in herself, and could recall from the past, volumes of dispassionate gossip, free from malice. In two years Madge had learned to know the world better than many who are in contact with it for long periods, but who see all through the distorted medium of their own prejudices or exceptional experiences. Although she was no longer unsophisticated she was neither cynical nor optimistic. Before her hope could be fulfilled she knew she must enter society, and she studied it thoughtfully—its whims and meannesses as well as its laws and refinements. If she ever reached Graydon's side she meant to stand there with a knowledge and confidence as assured as his own. She soon learned that it is common enough for women to seek to win men by every alluring and coquettish device. She would employ no devices whatever. She would merely reappear above his horizon among other luminaries, and shine with her own pure, unborrowed light. Then it must depend upon himself whether she ever became his own "bright particular star."

So much she felt she had a right to do, and no conventional hesitation as to her course stood in her way. Her love had become the governing impulse of her life, and its dictates were imperative until they trenched upon her sensitive, womanly pride. Then they were met as the rock meets the tide. She did not care what the world might think: it should never have occasion to think at all. Her secret was between herself and God. Graydon himself should never know it unless his name became hers.

How vividly her old haunts recalled him! There was the lounge on which he used to toss the "little wraith" after having carried her around in the semblance of a waltz. The sofa on which had taken place their strange parting still stood as of old in her room. There her head had sunk in unconsciousness upon his breast, the result of her vain, feeble struggle to escape from caresses so natural to him, but no longer to be received by her.

What way-marks in life mute, commonplace things become

in the light of memory! To her vivid fancy Graydon was again present in all the positions now made memorable by deep affection. The past unrolled itself again as it had so often done before. She saw the pallid, frightened child that scarcely dared to look deprecatingly at the handsome young collegian. She saw again the kind yet mirthful eyes that beamed encouragingly upon her. She remembered that in the unworthy past they had ever looked upon her with a large, gentle, affectionate tolerance, and she now took chiefly upon herself the blame for those years of weakness. Her present radiant health and beauty proved how unnecessary they had been, and her heart sometimes sunk at the thought of what they might cost her.

Mary had accompanied her to her room, and was asked, in a careless tone, what had become of Miss Wildmere.

"I was told incidentally the other day that she was as great a belle as ever. I had hoped that she would be out of Graydon's way before this time. I have heard, however, that great belles are often slower in marrying than the homeliest girls. If all is true that is said, this Miss Wildmere has made mischief enough; but I am not anxious that our Graydon should cut short her career—that is, if marriage would cut it short. I imagine she will always be a gay society woman. Well, Madge, I suppose you must make up your mind to be a belle yourself. Why don't you cut out this 'speculator,' as my husband calls her? If Graydon had my eyes it wouldn't be a difficult task."

"Graydon hasn't your eyes or mine either," was the brusque reply. "I propose to use my own. They may see some one that I have never met. One thing at least is certain—I don't intend to cut out Miss Wildmere or any one else. The man who wins me will have to do the seeking most emphatically; and I warn you beforehand, sister mine, that you must never let the idea of matchmaking enter your head. Since I have been away I have developed more will of my own than muscle. There is no necessity for me ever to marry, and if I do it will be because I wish to, not because any one else wants me to. Nothing would set me against a man more certainly than to see that he had allies who were manoeuvring in his behalf;" and she concluded with a kiss that robbed her words of a point too sharp, perhaps, for her sister's feelings. She knew Mrs. Muir's peculiarities well enough, however, to believe that such words were needed, and she had intended to speak them in some form at the earliest opportunity. Therefore she was glad that she could utter the warning so early and naturally in their new relations. Nor was it uncalled for, since the thought of bringing Madge and Graydon together had already entered Mrs. Muir's mind. A scheme of this character would grow in fascination every hour. Poor Madge was well aware that, with the best intentions, no one could more certainly blast her hopes than her sister, whose efforts would be unaccompanied by the nicest tact. Moreover, any such attempts might involve the disclosure of her secret.

"Well, you have changed in every respect," said Mary, looking at her wonderingly.

"For the better, I hope. My feeling in this respect, however, seems to me perfectly natural. I don't see how a self-respecting girl could endure anything except a straightforward, downright suit, with plenty of time to make up her own mind. I can do without the man who does not think me worthy of this, and could probably do without him any way. Because a man wants to marry a girl is only one reason for assent, and there may be a dozen reasons to the contrary."

"Why, Madge, how you talk! When you left us it seemed as if any one might pick you up and marry you and you would not have spirit enough to say yes or no. Have you had to refuse any one at Santa Barbara? Perhaps you didn't refuse. You have told me so little of what was going on!"

"That isn't fair to me, Mary. I explained to you that I wished to give you a pleasant surprise. To plan a pleasure for you was not unsisterly, was it? I haven't Miss Wildmere's ambition for miscellaneous conquests. Why should I write about men for whom I cared nothing and toward whom my manner should have made my spoken negative unnecessary?"

"Other girls would. Well, it seems that their suit was downright enough to satisfy you. Good gracious! How many were there?"

Madge laughed, yawned, and her sister saw that her dark eyes were full of the languor of sleep, which added to their beauty.

"Oh, not many," she drawled. "I'll gossip about them some time when not so tired. I'll indicate them by numerals. Why should I babble their names in connection with what they called so sacred? I wonder how many like sacred affairs had occurred before. If I tell you the story of the wooing of Number One, Two, Three, and so on, that will answer just as well, won't it?"

"No, indeed. I wish to know their names, family connection, and whether they were well off or not."

Madge again laughed, and began to disrobe, in order to indicate that their confidence must at least be adjourned for the present. Her sister came and felt her perfect arms and rounded, gleaming shoulders. "Why, Madge," she exclaimed, "your flesh is as white and smooth as ivory, and almost as firm to the touch! It's a wonderful transformation. I can scarcely believe, much less understand it. You have grown so beautiful that you almost turn even my head."

"There is nothing so wonderful about it, Mary. Almost any girl may win health, and therefore more or less beauty, if she has the sense and will to make the effort. You know what I was when I left home. I suggested doctors' bills more than anything else, and it was chiefly my fault;" and she sighed deeply. "When I went to work in a rational way to get strong, I succeeded. I believe this would be true with the great majority. Good-night, dear. When I am rested I'm going to help you in many ways, in return for all you did for that lazy, lackadaisical, limp little nonentity that you used to dose and coddle when you should have given her a good shaking."

"It's all a miracle," said Mrs. Muir to her husband, at the conclusion of lengthy remarks about Madge.

"As much a miracle as my fortune," was the quiet reply. "Madge has had sense enough to know what she wanted and how to get it."

CHAPTER VII

NOT A MIRACLE

Madge was simply fatigued from her long journey, and not oppressed with want of sleep, for in passing through uninteresting portions of the country she had given herself up to repose. The sense of weariness passed with the hours of night, and she was among the earliest stirring in the morning. Long before breakfast was ready she had her trunks partially unpacked, her mind meantime busy with plans for immediate action. At last her healthful appetite so asserted itself that she went down to the dining-room. Mr. and Mrs. Muir had not yet appeared, and she strolled into the parlor, opened her piano, and played a few runs. She found it sadly out of tune from long disuse. As this was not true of her voice, she began singing a favorite German song.

In a moment the house was full of melody. Clear, sweet, and powerful, her notes penetrated to the kitchen, where the maids were busy, and they stopped in spellbound wonder, with dish or utensil in hand. Mrs. Muir listened with her hair-brush suspended, while methodical Mr. Muir laid down his razor, and, going to the door, set it ajar. The song poured into the room like an harmonic flood. Before the first stanza was completed Mrs. Muir had on her dressing-gown and was stealing downstairs into the back parlor, and as Madge was beginning again she rushed upon her.

"Why, why," she exclaimed, "I thought Nilsson or Patti had got lost and taken refuge here! Can it be you? You are nothing but a surprise from beginning to end. When will the wonders cease? Are you sure that you are Madge?"

"Yes, and equally sure that I am hungry. When *will* you be ready for breakfast? I've been up these two hours."

"Well, well, well, what will Graydon say? He thinks you are still little better than a ghost."

"He will say that I have been very sensible, and he will find me very substantial and matter-of-fact. The question now uppermost is, When will breakfast be ready?" cried the young girl, laughing, in a childlike enjoyment of her sister's wonder, and a loving woman's anticipation of triumph over the man who had once called her "weak and lackadaisical."

She responded warmly to the embrace of Mrs. Muir, who added, "You have come back to us a princess. Why, even Henry, whom nothing moves out of the even tenor of his way, paused in his shaving, and with one side of his face all lathered opened the door to listen."

"You tell him," cried Madge, in merry vein, "that he has given me the greatest compliment I ever received. But compliments are not breakfast."

Mrs. Muir returned to complete her toilet, and her husband soon appeared.

"Madge," he said, greeting her kindly, "you have brought about great changes. How have you accomplished them all in so brief a time?"

"The time has not been so very brief," she replied. "I have been away over two years, remember. It's all very simple, Henry. I went to work to get well and to learn something, as you give your mind and time to business. In the Waylands, my old German professor, and especially in the magnificent climate I had splendid allies. And you know I had nothing else to do. One can do a great deal in two years with sufficient motive and steady effort toward a few points."

"What was your motive, Madge?"

A slow, deep color stole into her face, but she looked unflinchingly into his eyes as she asked, "Was not the hope of being what I am to-day, compared with what I was, sufficient motive?"

"Yes," he replied, thoughtfully, "it was; but it appears strange to me that more girls do not show your sense. Nine-tenths of the pallid creatures that I see continue half alive through their own fault."

"If they knew the pleasure of being thoroughly alive," said Madge, "they wouldn't dawdle another hour. I believe that I might have regained health long before if I had set about it."

"Well, Madge, as your guardian I wish to tell you that I am deeply gratified. You have done more for yourself than all the world could do for you. I am a plain man, you know, and not given to many words. There is only one thing that I detest more than a silly woman, and that is a heartless, speculating one. Both are sure to make trouble sooner or later. You certainly do not belong to the first type, and I don't believe you will ever make a bad use of the beauty you have won so honestly. Let me give you a bit of business experience, Madge. I have seen men falter and fail by the score downtown, and usually it was because women were playing the mischief with them—too often women of their own households, who had no more idea of the worth of a dollar, or how it is obtained, than a kitten. The one idea is to marry for money, and then to spend it in parade. I believe you will be like your sister Mary, who has given me a home, quiet, and peace." ("If I ever give a man anything I'll give him a great deal more than that," Madge thought.) "And now," concluded Mr. Muir, "speaking of money, I wish to go over your accounts with you soon, that you may know everything and understand everything. It's absurd for women to be helpless and dependent in this respect. You should know all about your property, and the time has come when you should learn what are regarded as safe investments, and what are not. My life is as uncertain as any other man's, and I intend that you sisters shall not be like two children, who must do blindly what some trustee tells you to do;" and Mr. Muir complacently led the way to the breakfast-room, feeling that as guardian he had done his duty both morally and financially.

It was his way to speak plainly and promptly all he desired to say, and then, according to his creed, if people had sense they would do what was wise; if they had not, the less said the better.

Mrs. Muir was voluble during the morning meal. Now that Madge had come again within the sphere of her domestic energy, she was fall of plans and projects.

"Of course," she said, "you have nothing to wear. The outlandish dresses that you had made at that jumping-off place in the West won't answer. As soon as the Waylands have made their call we must go out and begin ordering your summer outfit. Perhaps Mrs. Wayland will go with us."

"Patience, Mary. We are not ready to order outfits yet."

"Why not?"

"Because we do not want to buy what interested shopmen and milliners may choose to palm off on us. You live such a domestic life that you are scarcely better informed than I as to the latest modes. We will drive in the park, use our eyes on the avenue, and visit several fashionable establishments first. Then I wish to find a dressmaker who is not an idiotic slave of fashion, and who can modify the prevailing styles by taste and appreciation of the person for whom she works. The one whom I employ must make dresses for me and under my direction, and not dresses in the abstract, as if they were for the iron-framed form on which she exhibits her wares."

"Good!" cried Mr. Muir; "Madge's head is level. Let her have her own way, Mary, and she will come out all right."

"Well," said Mrs. Muir, "I suppose it will take a little time for me to get used to all these changes. Before she went away I used to do everything for her. I'm going to have my own way in one thing, however. You must not write to Graydon a word beyond the fact that Madge is here. You have both laughed at me and my wonder, and I'm going to have the compensation of seeing him transformed into exclamation points."

Madge now turned toward Mr. Muir, and he could detect not the slightest indication of embarrassment or overconsciousness, as she said, "Certainly, Henry, you must not spoil this little bit of prospective fun."

Madge did have her own way, and made her preparations with the quiet decision and thoughtfulness which now characterized her actions.

The Waylands were frequent guests at Mr. Muir's home for a time, and then departed to visit friends in the country.

Madge and her sister soon decided upon the Catskills as the place of their summer sojourn. The choice of this region, so accessible from the city, was pleasing to Mr. Muir.

"What are you reading?" he said, one evening, as he found Madge surrounded by books and pamphlets.

"Reading up on the Catskills and their vicinity. A place is far more interesting if you have associations with it, and I intend to be versed in all the stories and legends of the region. In this I have a little design upon you also. You look worn, Henry, and need rest and change. You are too much devoted to business. I'm going to 'frivol,' like the rest of the girls, in the evening—dance, and all that, you know, but I shall try to keep you among the hills, and inveigle you into long drives and walks by telling you exciting yarns that will take the place of the dissipations of business. You needn't think you will have to mope around the piazza, your body on a mountain and your mind in Wall Street. You are getting old and rich, and you must begin to take an interest in other things besides business."

"Now, that's thoughtful and kind of you," he said, and then he lapsed into a revery that the contraction of his brow showed to be not altogether agreeable.

At last he said, "Madge, I half believe you are right. I am and have been too devoted to business. It's all very well as long as you can drive it, but when it begins to drive you it is a hard task-master. The times are bad. Instead of making anything, one has to use all his faculties to keep from losing what he has made. It's getting to be a grind. I sometimes wish I was out of it, but suppose I shouldn't know what to do with myself."

"That's just it, Henry, you wouldn't. You must become interested in other things, and that's a process which requires time, and I'll help you."

"Oh, you," he said, laughing—"you will soon have all you can do to keep your beaux at bay."

"Beaux in this free and enlightened land have only certain rights which a girl is bound to respect. Should there be any, and they unreasonable, you'll see," she said, with a little decisive nod. Then she added, gravely: "I don't believe you would be content out of business, but I should think there was such a thing as trying to do so much business that it would become a burden, and, perhaps, a heavy one. You may think I'm a little goose, talking of what I know nothing about; but I've read a great deal, and, of late, books worth reading. I don't believe it is a good thing to change one's habits and pursuits suddenly; and what's more, Henry, I believe that when the times are better business will be as great a source of satisfaction to you as ever. As I suggested before, you must gradually become interested in other things which can take the place of business as you grow old."

"What a wise little woman we have become!" said Mr. Muir. "Here you are giving your guardian sound advice—you who, I imagined once, would take no more thought for the morrow than a lily of the field, and a very pale one at that. This is a greater change than any that Mary exclaims about."

"Perhaps you think me very presuming," answered Madge, coloring.

"No, I do not. I think you very sensible, and I think myself very fortunate in having such women in my household as you and Mary. I was blue when I came home to-night, but it inspirits a man to talk to such a girl. You have a power of good common-sense, Madge."

"Well, I have—I had—need of it."

"The majority would say you could afford to be silly. You have a snug fortune of your own, of which not a penny can be lost unless the bottom falls out of everything."

"I don't think any woman can afford to be silly. I know that's a sweeping word with you, and covers all feminine folly. What I meant is this: Money and every good thing in life was a mockery. I couldn't enjoy anything, and wasn't anything but a burden. I saw it all, and that I should have to throw nonsense overboard if I wished to be different. You will find that I have plenty left, however, before the summer's over. Now, let me read to you Irving's legend of poor old Rip. What if you have read it often? A little infusion of the champion sleeper's spirit is just what you need;" and with simple purity of tone and naturalness of accent she made the old story new to him.

"Madge," he said, as he kissed her good-night, "that is even better than your singing. I feel so freshened and heartened up that I'm another man, and in good trim for the fight to-morrow; for that is just what business has become—a regular defensive fight. You didn't think two years ago that you would send me down to Wall Street with a clearer head and better courage."

"No, indeed, I didn't dream of it, and I can scarcely believe it's true now. You used to seem to me like gravitation, that would always be the same to the end of time."

"Bah! A man is only a man, and he finds it out sooner or

later. There's Jack crying again, and Mary hasn't had a chance to come down. I'll take the child, for his teeth make him so nervous that he won't stay with the nurse."

"I'll try my hand at him to-morrow," said the young girl, and was absorbed in her reading again.

The days passed quickly, and Madge filled them full, as before at Santa Barbara. As the time approached for Graydon's return, she felt a quiet rising excitement akin to that which inspires a soldier when a campaign is about to open; but to her brother-in-law and sister she gave only the impression of decision of character and youthful, healthful buoyancy. She was good-cheer itself in the household, and helpful in every little domestic emergency. The servants and the children welcomed her like sunshine, and she made the evenings all too short by music and reading aloud. She blossomed out in her summer costumes like a flower, so becoming to her style had been her choice of fabrics and the taste with which they had been fashioned. June was passing. In a day or two more Graydon would arrive, and the fruition or failure of her patient endeavor begin.

CHAPTER VIII

RIVAL GIRLS

Instead of Graydon there came a letter saying that he would be detained abroad another week. The heat was oppressive, and the family physician said that little Jack should be taken to the country at once. Therefore they packed in haste, and started for a hotel in the Catskills at which rooms had been engaged. Graydon was to join them there as soon after his return as possible.

Madge looked wistfully at the mountains, as with shadowy grandeur they loomed in the distance. There is ever a solemnity about mountain scenery, and she felt it as she passed under the lofty brows of wooded heights. To her spirit it was grateful and appropriate, for, while she would lead among them apparently the existence of a young girl bent only on enjoyment, she believed she would leave them, either a happy woman, or else facing the tragedy of a thwarted life. Their deepest shadows might, even when her laugh was gayest, typify the despondency she would hide from all.

It was Saturday, and Mr. Muir accompanied his family. He and his wife looked worn and weary, for at this time circumstances were bringing an excess of care to both. Mrs.

Muir was a devoted mother, and little Jack had taxed her patience and strength to the utmost. A defensive warfare is ever the severest test of manhood, and Mr. Muir had found the past week a trying one. He had been lured into an enterprise that at the time had seemed certain of success, even to his conservative mind, but unforeseen elements had entered into the problem, and it now required all his nerve, all his resources, to meet the strain. Neither Madge nor his wife knew anything of this. Indeed, it was not his habit to speak of his affairs to any one, unless the exigencies of the case required explanation. In this emergency he was obliged to maintain among his associates an air of absolute confidence. Now that he was out of the arena he gave evidence of the strain.

Madge saw this, and resolved that her large reserve of vitality should be drawn upon. The tired mother should be relieved and the perplexed and wearied man beguiled into forgetfulness of the sources of anxiety. Jack would have indulged in a perpetual howl during the journey had not his attention been diverted by Madge's unexpected expedients, which often suspended an outcry with comical abruptness, while her remarks and questions made it impossible for Mr. Muir to toil on mentally in Wall Street. By reason of the heat the majority of the passengers dozed or fretted. She heroically kept up the spirits of her little band, oblivious of the admiring eyes that often turned toward her flushed, animated face.

There are few stronger tests than unflagging good-humor during a disagreeable journey with cross children. At last the ordeal came to an end, and in the late afternoon shadows they alighted at the wide piazza of the Under-Cliff House, and were shown to airy rooms, which proved that the guests were not kept in pigeon-holes for the sole benefit of the proprietor. Our heroine employed the best magic the world has known—thoughtful helpfulness. Mr. Muir was banished. "You would be as useful as a whale," she said to him, when he offered to aid his wife in unpacking and getting settled. "Go down to the piazza and smoke in peace. I shall be worth a dozen of you as soon as I take off my travelling-dress."

She verified her words, and before they were aware of it Mrs. Muir, who was prone to fall into hopeless confusion at such times, and the nurse were acting under her direction. The elder little boy and girl were coaxed, restrained, managed, and soon sent down to their father, redressed and serene. Jack was lulled to sleep in Madge's room. The trunks instead of disgorging chaos, were compelled to part with their contents in an orderly way. In little more than an hour the two rooms allotted to Mr. and Mrs. Muir, and the nurse with the children, took on a cosey, inhabitable aspect, and by supper-time the ladies, in evening costume and with unruffled brows, joined Mr. Muir.

"The idea of my ever permitting Madge to go back to Santa Barbara!" exclaimed Mrs. Muir. "This day alone has proved that I can never get on without her. Just go and look at your room, sir. One would think we had been settled here a week. You ought to pay Madge's bills, and give her a handsome surplus."

"If time is money," said Madge, "Henry will have to pay me well. He must stay and help me explore these mountains in every direction. But now let us eat, drink, and be merry, for to-morrow we shall go to church."

"I've half a mind to take you down to Wall Street with me next week," said Mr. Muir. "Perhaps you can straighten out things there."

"No, sir. I'm a woman's-rights girl, and one of her rights is to get things out of the way as soon as possible, so that people can have a good time. Thank heaven our affairs can be shut up in drawers and hung up in closets, and there we can leave them—in this case for a good supper first, and a long quiet rest on this piazza afterward. Don't you think you could find a drawer somewhere in which to tuck away your Wall Street matters, Henry? You won't need them till some time next week, for you must certainly spend two or three days with us."

Mr. Muir laughed. "I've heard of managing women before, but you beat them all. You have won, to-day, the right to manage for a while. I'll join you soon; then supper; and, as you suggest, I'll put the Wall Street matters somewhere and lock them up."

Thus their mountain sojourn began auspiciously. The supper was excellent, and they were in a mood to enjoy it; they found the piazza deliciously cool after the long hot day; and the faint initial pipings of autumn insects only emphasized the peace and quiet of the evening. The mountains brooded around them like great shadows, their outlines gemmed with stars, and the very genius of repose seemed to settle down upon the weary man and woman who were in the thick of their life's battle.

They were among the earliest arrivals at the house, and had a wide space to themselves. Indeed, they could have been scarcely more secluded at their own summer residence. For those seeking rest, an early flight to summer resorts brings a rich reward.

While her relatives dozed or merely revived sufficiently from time to time to make some desultory remark, Madge thought deeply. At first she had been disappointed at the postponement of Graydon's return, but she grew reconciled as she dwelt upon it. While hope was deferred, she enjoyed a longer lease of anticipation. When he did come she might soon learn that all hope was vain. Besides, the delay gave her time to familiarize herself with the region and its most beautiful walks and drives. The mountains, woods, and rocks should all be pressed into her service. They would not reveal her secret, and they might engender thoughts and words with which Miss Wildmere would be out of harmony.

"I've been thinking," Mr. Muir at last remarked.

"Nonsense! you've been asleep," Madge replied.

"No; I've thought profoundly."

"Not even a penny for any thoughts of yours since supper."

"They would be worth fortunes, life, health, happiness, to half the world."

"Then keep still till you have a patent, copyright, or something," said his wife.

"No. I rise simply to remark—also to retire—that a little oil keeps machinery from wearing out and going to pieces. Come now, old lady" (pulling his wife to her feet), "you are the better to-night, as I am, for the oil that Madge has slipped in here and there. I fear the machinery to-day would have run badly without it."

The group that gathered at the breakfast-table next morning bore early testimony to the tonic of the hills. Jack only was not so well, and Mrs. Muir remained with him, while Madge and Mr. Muir wended their way to a little chapel whose spire was the only summons to worship. A short, genial, middle-aged man met them at the door, with such hospitable cordiality as to suggest that he was receiving friends at his own home, and conducted them to seats. A venerable clergyman sat in the pulpit with a face full of quiet benignity. Every one who came appeared to receive an almost personal welcome; and Madge and Mr. Muir looked enviously at the self-appointed usher. It was as evident that he was not a professional sexton as that the little congregation could not afford such a luxury. No care clouded his brow. Evidently his future did not depend on fluctuations in the maelstrom of commerce, nor had he one hope so predominant over all others that his life was one of masked suspense, as was the case with poor Madge. He was rather like the rugged, sun-lighted mountains near, solid, stable, simple. No matter what happened, he would remain and appear much the same.

Such was the tenor of Madge's thoughts as she waited for the opening of service. Fanciful and imaginative to a great degree, she found a certain mental enjoyment in observing the impressions made upon her by strangers.

The service was brief and simple; the good old clergyman preached the gospel of hope, and his words calmed and strengthened the young girl's mind. She was made to feel that there is something more and better than present happiness—that there are remedies for earthly ills.

When she returned to the hotel she found that Mrs. Muir was worried about Jack, who was worse, and that a Dr. Sommers had been sent for. She could not help smiling when, a little later, the hospitable usher of the chapel came briskly in. She eventually learned that the doctor provoked smiles wherever he went, as a breeze raises ripples on the surface of a stream. He smiled himself when he met people, and every one took the contagion. He examined the baby, said the case would require a little watching until certain teeth came through, and then that there would be no further trouble. He spoke with the same confidence with which he would announce that July was near.

"You watch the case, then," said Mr. Muir, decisively. "I must be in town. If you can look after the child and save my wife from worry, my mind will be easy as regards this end of the line at least."

"All right, sir. We'll manage it. Healthy boy. No trouble."

"Have you lived long among the mountains, doctor?" Madge ventured to ask.

"I should think so. As long as I have lived. Was born and brought up among 'em."

"It must be dreary here in the winter," Mrs. Muir remarked.

"Not a bit of it. It's never dreary."

"How far among the hills does your practice extend?" Madge pursued.

"As far as I'll go, and I'm usually going."

"Perhaps you can give us, then, some advice as to drives and walks."

"Oh, lots, free gratis. I can tell Mr. Muir of a trout-stream or two, also."

"Doctor," said Madge, laughing, "I am very ill. I shall need much advice, and prescriptions of all the romantic walks and drives in the vicinity."

"And like most of the advice from doctors, it won't be taken.

A stroll on the piaza is about all that most ladies are equal to. You look, however, as if you should not fear a steep path or a rough road."

"You shall see," cried Madge.

"Yes, I will see," said the doctor, laughing, and bowing himself out. "I've seen a great many ladies who could dance miles, but were as afraid of a mountain as of a bear."

At the dinner-table Mrs. Muir said, laughingly, "In Dr. Sommers, Madge has found a kindred spirit—another oiler of machinery. If between him and Madge things don't go smoothly, the fates are indeed against us."

"When life does go smoothly, it is because of just such good, cheery common-sense," Mr. Muir remarked, sententiously. "I'm in the financial centre of this part of the world, and schemes involving millions and the welfare of States—indeed of whole sections of the country—are daily brought to my consideration, and I tell you again men are often in no condition to act wisely or well because the wear and tear of their life is greater after business hours than during them. Business maniac as Madge thinks me to be, little Jack is of more consequence than a transcontinental railway. I must face the music—the discord, rather—of Wall Street to-morrow. There is no use in protesting or coaxing; I must be there; but it's a great thing to be able to return with my nerves soothed, rested, and quieted. Heaven help the men who, after the strain of the day, must go home to be pricked half to death with pin-and-needle-like worries, if not worse."

"Please imagine Madge and myself making a profound courtesy for the implied compliment," said Mrs. Muir. "But can you not spend part of the week with us?"

"No. Graydon will soon be here, and there is much to be seen to. He writes that he has worked very hard to get things in shape so that he can leave them, and that he wishes to take a vacation. As far as possible I shall gratify him. He can be with you here, and come to town occasionally as I need him. It's all turning out very well, and I am better off than many in these troublous times."

The remainder of his stay passed quietly in absolute rest, and on the following morning he was evidently strengthened for the renewal of the struggle.

* * * * *

"Stella!"

Miss Wildmere remained absorbed in her novel.

"Stella!" repeated Mr. Wildmere, impatiently.

"What is it?" she asked, fretfully. "I'm in an exciting scene. Can't you wait awhile?"

"Oh, throw down your confounded novel! You should be giving your mind to real life and exciting scenes of your own. No, I can't wait and don't propose to, for I must go out."

The words were spoken in a small but elegant house, furnished in an ultra-fashionable style. Mr. Wildmere was a stout, florid man, who looked as if he might be burning his candle at both ends. His daughter was dressed to receive summer evening calls at her own home, for she was rarely without them. If the door-bell had rung she would have dismissed her exciting scene without hesitation, but it was only her father who asked her attention.

"Very well," she said, absently, turning down a leaf.

Her father observed her listless air and averted face for a moment with contracted brow, then quietly remarked, "Graydon Muir may return at any time now."

Her apathy disappeared at once, and a faint color stole into her face.

"Haven't you had enough of general attention and flirtation? I know that my wishes have little weight; you have refused not a few good offers and one on which I had set my heart; but let the past go. The immediate future may require careful and decisive action. I speak in view of your own interests, and to such considerations I know you will not be indifferent. If you were taking a natural and intelligent interest in my affairs you would have some comprehension of my difficulties and dangers. The next few months will decide whether I can keep up or not. In the meantime you have your opportunity. Graydon Muir will share in the fortunes of his brother, who has had the reputation of being very wealthy and eminently conservative. I have learned, however, that he has invested largely in one enterprise that now appears to be very dubious—how largely no one but himself knows. If this affair goes through all right you couldn't do better than develop Graydon Muir into an impatient suitor; and you had better keep him well in hand for a time, anyway. He is a good business man and far more to be depended upon than rich young fellows who have inherited wealth, with no ability except in spending it. If the Muirs pass through these times they will become one of the strongest and safest houses in the country. Remember that the *if* is to be considered. Mr. Arnault, too, is a member of a strong, wealthy house. I would advise you to make your choice between these two men speedily. You are not adapted to a life of poverty, and would not enjoy it. An alliance with either of these men might also aid in sustaining me."

Miss Wildmere listened attentively, but made no comment, and her father evidently did not require any, for he went out immediately. He understood his daughter sufficiently to believe that she needed no further advice. He was right. The exciting crisis in her novel was forgotten, and her fair face took on an expression that did not enhance its beauty. Calculation on the theme uppermost in her mind produced a revery in which an artist would not have cared to paint her. It was evident that the time had come when she must dispose of herself, and the question was, how to do it to the best advantage.

To Graydon she gave her preference. He was remarkably fine looking, and could easily be a leader in society if he so desired—"and certainly shall be," she thought, "if I take his name." As far as her heart spoke in the matter it declared for him, also. Other men had wooed and pleaded, but she had ever mentally compared them with Graydon, and they had appeared insignificant. She had felt sure for a long time that he would eventually be at her feet, and she had never decided to refuse him. Now she was ready to accept but for this ominous "if," which her father had emphasized. She could not think of marrying him should he become a poor man.

She neither liked nor disliked Mr. Arnault. He was a man of the world, reported wealthy, established in a large but not very conservative business. He had the name of being a little fast and speculative, but she was accustomed to that style of man. He was an open suitor who would take no rebuff, and had laughingly told her so. After his refusal, instead of going away in despondency or in a half-tragic mood, he had good-naturedly declared his intentions, and spent the remainder of the evening in such lively chat that she had been pleased and amused by his tactics. Since that time he had made himself useful, was always ready to be an escort with a liberal purse, and never annoyed her with sentiment. She understood him, and he was aware that she did. He took his chances for the future, and was always on hand to avail himself of any mood or emergency which he could turn to his advantage. In various unimportant ways he was of service to Mr. Wildmere, but hoped more from the broker's embarrassments than from the girl's heart.

"I might do worse," muttered the beauty—"I might do worse. If it were not for Graydon Muir, I'd decide the question at once."

The door-bell rang, and Graydon was announced. Even her experienced nerves had a glad tingle of excitement, she was so genuinely pleased to see him. And well she might be, for he was a man to light any woman's eyes with admiration. If something of his youth had passed, his face had gained a rich compensation in the strong lines of manhood, and his manner a courtly dignity from long contact with the best elements of life. One saw that he knew the world, but had not been spoiled by it. That he had not become cynical was proved by his greeting of Miss Wildmere. He was capable of hoping that her continued freedom, in spite of her remarkable beauty, might be explained on the ground of a latent regard for him, which had kept her ready for his suit after an absence so unexpectedly prolonged. Through a friend he had, from time to time, been informed about her; and there was no ring on her hand to forbid his ardent glances.

Never before had she appeared so alluringly attractive. He was a thorough American, and had not been fascinated by foreign types of beauty. In his fair countrywoman he believed that he saw his ideal. Her beauty was remarkable for a fullness, a perfection of outline, combined with a fairness and delicacy which suggested that she was not made of ordinary clay. Miss Wildmere prided herself upon giving the impression that she was remote from all that was common or homely in life. She cultivated the characteristic of daintiness. In her dress, gloves, jewelry, and complexion she would be immaculate at any cost. Graydon's fastidious taste could never find a flaw in her, as regarded externals, and she knew the immense advantage of pleasing his eye with a delicacy that even approached fragility in its exquisite fairness, while at the same time her elastic step in the dance or promenade proved that she had abundance of vitality.

Nothing could have been more auspicious than his coming to-night—the very first evening after his arrival. It assured her of the place she still held in his thoughts; it gave her the chance to renew, in the glad hours of his return, the impression she had made; and she saw in his admiring eyes how favorable that impression was. She exulted that he found her so well prepared. Her clinging summer costume revealed not a little of her beauty, and suggested more, while she permitted her eyes to give a welcome more cordial even than her words.

He talked easily and vivaciously, complimented her openly, yet with sincerity, and rallied her on the wonder of wonders that she was still Miss Wildmere.

"Not so great a marvel as that you return a bachelor. Why did you not marry a German princess or some reduced English countess?"

"I was not driven to that necessity, since there were American queens at home. I am delighted that you are still in town. What are your plans for the summer?"

"We have not fully decided as yet."

"Then go to the Catskills. Our ladies are there at the Under-Cliff House, and I am told that it is a charming place."

"I will speak to mamma of it. She must come to some decision soon. Papa says that he will be too busy to go out of town much."

"Why, then, the Catskills is just the place—accessible to the city, you know. That is the reason we have chosen it. I propose to take something of a vacation, but find that I must go back and forth a good deal, and so shall escape the bore of a long journey."

"You have given two good reasons for our going there. The place cannot be stupid, since we may see you occasionally, and papa could come oftener."

"Persuade Mrs. Wildmere into the plan by all means, and promise me your first waltz after your arrival;" and there was eagerness in his tone.

"Will you also promise me your first?"

"Yes, and last also, if you wish."

"Oh, no! I do not propose to be selfish; Miss Alden will have her claims."

"What, Sister Madge? She must have changed greatly if she will dance at all. She is an invalid, you know."

"I hear she has returned vastly improved in health—indeed, that she is quite a beauty."

"I hope so," he said, cordially, "but fear that rumor has exaggerated. My brother said she was better, and added but little more. Have you seen her?"

"No. I only heard, a short time since, that she had returned."

Madge had not gone into society, and had she met Miss Wildmere face to face she would not have been recognized, so greatly was she changed from the pallid, troubled girl over whom the beauty had enjoyed her petty triumph; but the report of Miss Alden's attractions had aroused in Miss Wildmere's mind apprehensions of a possible rival.

Graydon's manner was completely reassuring. Whatever Miss Alden might have become, she evidently had no place in his thoughts beyond that natural to their relations. No closer ties had been formed by correspondence during his long absence.

Further tete-a-tete was interrupted by the appearance of Mr. Arnault. The young men were courteous and even cordial to each other, but before half an hour had passed they recognized that they were rivals. Graydon's lips grew firm, and his eyes sparkled with the spirit of one who had not the faintest idea of yielding to another. Miss Wildmere was delighted. The game was in her own hands. She could play these two men off against each other, and take her choice. Mr. Arnault was made to feel that he was not *de trop*, and, as usual, he was nonchalant, serene, and evidently meant to stay. Therefore Graydon took his leave, and was permitted to carry away the impression that his departure was regretted.

"Mr. Arnault," said Miss Wildmere, quietly, "we have decided to spend some time at the Under-Cliff House in the Catskills. So you perceive that I shall be deprived of the pleasure of your calls for a while."

"Not at all. I shall take part of my summering there also. When do you go?"

"In a few days—sometime before the fourth. How fortunately it all happens!" she added, laughing. "When did you decide on the Catskills?"

"That's immaterial. When did you?"

"That also is immaterial. Perhaps you would like to ask mamma?"

"I'd rather ask papa—both, I should say," he replied, with a significant shrug.

"Do so by all means. Meanwhile I would suggest that a great many people go to the Catskills—thirty thousand, more or less, it is said."

"I had another question in mind. Is Graydon Muir going there in order to follow the crowd?"

"If he is going I suppose he will follow his inclinations."

"Or you?"

"Were that possible, I could not prevent it. Indeed, women rarely resent such things."

"No indeed. It is well you do not, for you would become the embodiment of resentment. How large is your train now, Stella?"

"You can dimmish it by one if you choose," she replied, smiling archly.

"I should be little missed, no doubt."

"I didn't say that."

"I'm more afraid of Muir than of all the train together."

"That's natural. The train has little chance collectively."

"Don't pretend to misunderstand me. There was unmistakable meaning in Muir's eyes."

"I should hope so. He means to help me have a good time. So do you, I trust."

"Certainly. You may judge of the future from the past," he added, significantly, as he rose to take his leave.

"Then the future promises well for me," she said, giving him her hand cordially; "for you have been one of the best of friends."

"And a good deal more. Good-night."

"Mamma," said Miss Wildmere, stopping at the nursery on her way to her room, "we must get ready to go to the Catskills at once."

"Why, Stella! This is the first I've heard of this plan. Your father has said that he doesn't see how we can go out of town at all this summer."

"Nonsense! I'll insure that papa agrees."

"I don't see how I can get ready soon. The baby is fretful, and I'm all worn out between broken rest and worry. Won't you take Effie for a little while?"

"Where's the nurse?"

"She's out. Of course she has to have some time to herself."

"You just spoil the servants. It's her business to take care of the child. What else is she paid for? Why can't one of the other maids take her?"

"Effie is too nervous to go to strangers to-night."

"Oh, well, give her to me, then."

The sensitive little organization knew at once that it was in the hands not only of a comparative stranger, but also of one whose touch revealed little sympathy, and its protest was so great that the tired mother took it again, while the beautiful daughter, the cynosure of all eyes in public, went to her room to finish the "exciting scene" at her leisure.

But the scene had grown unreal. Its hero was but a shadow, and a distorted one at that. The book fell from her hand; she again saw Graydon Muir coming forward to greet her with an easy grace which no prince in story could surpass, and with an expression in his dark blue eyes which no woman fails to understand. It assured her that neither in the old world nor in the new had he seen her equal.

"I wish it could be," she murmured; "I hope it can be; were it not for that 'if' it should be soon."

Thus, after her own fashion, another girl had designs upon Graydon.

CHAPTER IX

THE MEETING

Graydon had completed his final transactions abroad with more expedition than he had anticipated, and, having been favored by a quick passage, had arrived several days sooner than he was expected. Therefore he decided to accompany his brother to the Catskills on Saturday, spending the intervening time in business and such arrangements as would leave him free to remain in the country for a week or two. The second evening after his arrival again found him in Miss Wildmere's parlor, and before he left he was given to understand that Mrs. Wildmere had decided upon the Under-Cliff House also, and that they would depart on Saturday.

"Then you will be *compagnon de voyage*," said Graydon, with undisguised pleasure.

Somewhat to Mrs. Wildmere's surprise, her husband quietly acquiesced in his daughter's wishes, telegraphed for rooms, and desired his wife to be ready.

She was a quiet, meek little woman, whose life had somehow become entangled in a sphere which was not in harmony with her nature. Her beauty had faded early, and she had little force of character with which to maintain her influence over her husband. His life was amid the fierce excitements of Wall Street; hers, as far as she had a life, was a weary effort to keep up appearances and meet the expenses of a fashionable daughter, on an uncertain and greatly fluctuating income.

Mr. Wildmere informed her that his affairs would keep him in town until late in the following week, but that, as the house to which she was going was a quiet family hotel, she would have no trouble.

Mr. Muir had telegraphed the arrival of his brother, and the latter had written a few cordial but hasty lines to both his sister-in-law and Madge. Where he spent his evenings was unknown to Mr. Muir, but that gentleman had little trouble in guessing when he saw his brother greet the Wildmeres as if he understood their plans, and laughingly promise Mr. Wildmere that he would see the ladies and their belongings safely established in the Under-Cliff House. Graydon observed the slight cloud on his brother's face, but ignored it, feeling that his preference was an affair of his own. He believed that the long-wished-for opportunity to press his suit with vigor had come, and had no hesitation as to his purpose. He did not intend to act precipitately, however. He would first learn just how Mr. Arnault stood, and become reasonably assured by Miss Wildmere's manner toward himself that her preference was not a hope, but a reality.

The enterprise in which Mr. Muir had engaged, and which now so taxed his financial strength, was outside of his regular business, and Graydon knew nothing of it. The young man believed that his own means and exceptionally good prospects were sufficient to warrant the step he proposed to take. He assuredly had the right to please himself in his choice, and he felt that he would be fortunate indeed could he win one whom so many had sought in vain.

It never entered Mr. Muir's mind to interpose any authority or undue influence. He merely felt in regard to the matter a repugnance natural to one so alien in disposition to Mr. Wildmere and his daughter, and it was a source of bitter mortification to him that he now found himself in a position not unlike that of the broker, in what would appear, in the present aspect of affairs, to be an outside speculation. During the ride to the mountains he mentally compared Miss Wildmere's behavior with that of Madge a week before. Witnessing Graydon's evident infatuation, he would have been glad to recognize any manifestation of traits that promised well for his future; but the young lady was evidently altogether occupied with the attentions she received, her own beauty, and the furtive admiration of fellow-passengers. Poor Mrs. Wildmere and the nurse were left to manage the cross baby as best they could. Graydon once or twice tried to do something, but his strange face and voice only frightened the child.

To Madge it had seemed an age since the telegram announcing Graydon's arrival had thrilled every nerve with hope and fear. Then had come his hasty note, proving conclusively his affectionate indifference. She was simply Madge to him, as of old. He was the one man of all the world to her, and no calculating "if" would be the source of her restraint.

True to her old tactics, however, she had spent no time in idle dreaming. She had cultivated Dr. Sommers's acquaintance, and he had already accompanied her and her sister through a wild valley, on the occasion of a visit to one of his patients. Little Jack had improved under his care, and Mrs. Muir was growing serene, rested, and eager for Saturday. Madge shared her impatience, and yet dreaded the hour during which she felt that a glimpse of the future would be revealed. She had driven out daily with her sister, and familiarized herself with the topography of the region. Having formed the acquaintance of some pleasant and comparatively active people in the house, she had joined such walking expeditions as they would venture upon. In rowing the children upon a small lake she also disposed of some of her superabundant vitality and the nervous excitement which anticipation could not fail to produce. In the evening there was more or less dancing, and her hand was eagerly sought by such of the young men as could obtain the right to ask it. Mrs. Muir's remark that she would become a belle in spite of herself proved true; but while she affected no exclusive or distant airs, the most callow and forward youth felt at once the restraint of her fine reserve. Her sensitive nature enabled her, in a place of public resort, to know instinctively whom to keep at a distance, and who, like Dr. Sommers, not only invited but justified a frank and friendly manner.

As the time for the gentlemen to arrive approached, Mrs. Muir showed more restless interest than Madge. The one anticipated a bit of amusement over Graydon's surprise; the other looked forward to meeting her fate. Mrs. Muir was garrulous; Madge was comparatively silent, and maintained the semblance of interest in a book so naturally that her sister exclaimed, "I expect you will die with a book in your hand! I could no more read now than preach a sermon. Come, it's time to make your toilet. Let me help you, and I want you to get yourself up 'perfectly regardless.' You must outshine them all at the hop this evening."

"Nonsense, Mary! They won't be here for an hour and a half. I'm going to lie down;" and she went to her room. When her sister sought admittance half an hour later the door was locked and all was quiet. At last, in her impatience, she knocked and cried, "Wake up. They will be here soon."

"I'm not asleep, and it will not take me long to dress."

"Well, you are the coolest young woman I ever knew," Mrs. Muir called out, finding that admittance was denied her.

Madge had determined to spend the final hour of her long separation alone. Her nature had become too deep and strong to seek trivial diversion from the suspense that weighed upon her spirit. As she thought of the possibility of failure, and its results, her courage faltered a little, and a few tears would come. At last, with a glance heavenward which proved that there was nothing in her heart to keep her from looking thither for sanction, she left her room, serene and resolute. She had taken her woman's destiny into her own hand, to mold it in her own way, but in no arrogant and unbelieving spirit.

Mrs. Muir uttered a disappointed protest. "Oh, Madge, how plainly you are dressed!"

"I knew you wouldn't like it at first," was the quiet reply. By the time they had reached the parlor door opposite the office, near which they proposed to wait for the travellers, now momentarily expected, Mrs. Muir was compelled to acknowledge the correctness of Madge's taste. Her costume no more distracted attention from herself than would the infolding calyx of a rosebud. In its exquisite proportions her fine figure was outlined by close white drapery, which made her appear taller than she really was. A single half-open Jacqueminot rose, like the one she had sent to Graydon at their parting over two years since, was fastened on her bosom. Her dark eyes burned with a suppressed excitement. Her complexion, if not so white as that of Miss Wildmere, was pure, and had a richer hue of health. But she was pale now. Her red lips half destroyed their exquisite curves in firm compression. The moment had not quite come for action, when those lips must be true to herself, true to her purpose, even while they spoke words which might be misleading to others.

Mrs. Muir, with triumph, saw the glances of strong admiration turned toward her sister from every side. Madge saw them also, but only to read in them the verdict she hoped to obtain from the kind blue eyes for whose coming she waited.

Standing with Mrs. Muir, facing the long hall down which Graydon must advance, she knew she would see him before he could recognize her. How much of longing, of breathless interest, would be concentrated in those moments of waiting, she herself had never imagined till they were passing.

The stages began to arrive, with consequent bustle, and the hasty advance toward the office of men seeking to register their names early, in order to secure a choice of rooms. At last she saw Graydon's tall form and laughing face, and for a second something approaching to faintness caused her to close her eyes. When she opened them again they rested upon Miss Wildmere.

This young lady understood the art of making an impressive and almost triumphal entry on new scenes. Therefore she had been in no haste. Indeed, haste had no place among her attributes: it was ungraceful and usually not effective. When, therefore, the crowd had passed on, and there was a comparatively clear space in the hall, she advanced down it at Graydon's side as if her mind was wholly engrossed with their lively chat. Never for a second was she unconscious of the attention they attracted. Graydon was one at whom even men would turn and look as he passed, and she believed that there was none other who could keep step with him like herself. So thought the self-appointed committee of reception who always regard curiously the new-comers at a summer resort, and there were whispered notes of admiration as the two paused for a moment before the register and looked back. Then it was seen that a meek-looking little lady and a nurse and child were straggling after them, while Mr. Muir brought up the rear. Graydon had some light wraps thrown gracefully over his arm, but the merchant carried the less ornamental *impedimenta* of the party, for the earlier guests had already overladened the office-boys. He now handed the valise—a sort of tender upon the baby—to a porter, and rather grimly acknowledged Mrs. Wildmere's mingled thanks and feeble protestations.

"Please register for us," said Miss Wildmere, glancing carelessly yet observantly around. An intervening group had partially hidden Madge and her sister. It was also evident that Graydon was too much occupied with his fair companion to look far away. He complied, thinking, meantime, "Some day I may register for her again, and then my name will suffice for us both." The smile which followed the thought brought out the best lines of his handsome profile to poor Madge, who permitted no phase of expression on that face to escape her scrutiny. So true was the clairvoyance of her intense interest that she guessed the thought which was so agreeable to him, and she grew paler still.

Mr. Muir hastened to greet his wife, and then Graydon recognized her. He came at once and kissed her in his accustomed hearty way. Madge stood near, unnoted, unrecognized.

"Where's Madge? Isn't she well enough to come down?" he asked, his eyes following Miss Wildmere, who had entered the parlor, which she must cross to reach her room beyond. Mrs. Muir began to laugh immoderately, and Mr. Muir followed his brother's eyes with vexation. Graydon was on the *qui vive* instantly, and Madge drew a step nearer and began to smile. For once the punctilious and elegant Graydon forgot his courtesy, and looked at Madge in utter astonishment—an expression, however, which passed swiftly into admiration and delight.

"Madge!" he exclaimed, seizing both her hands. "I couldn't have believed it. I wouldn't believe it now but for your eyes;" and before she could prevent him he had placed a kiss upon her lips.

Miss Wildmere had seen the unknown beauty as she passed, had inventoried her with woman's instantaneous perception, had paused on the distant threshold and seen the greeting, then had vanished with a vindictive flash in her gray eyes.

Graydon's impetuous words and salute had produced smiles and envious glances, and the family party withdrew into a retired corner of the apartment, Madge's cheeks, meanwhile, vying, in spite of herself, with the rose on her breast. Graydon would not relinquish her hand, and, as Mrs. Muir had predicted, indulged in little more than exclamation points.

"There now, be rational," cried the young girl, laughing, her heart for the moment full of gladness and triumph. He was indeed bending upon her looks of admiration, delight, and affection.

"Why have I been kept in the dark about all this?" he at last asked, incoherently.

"For the same reason that we were. Madge meant to give us a surprise, and succeeded. I couldn't get over it, and they were always laughing at me, so I determined that I should have my laugh at you. Oh, wasn't it rich? To think of the elegant and travelled society man standing there staring with his eyes and mouth wide open!"

"I don't think it was quite so bad as that, but if it was there's good reason for it. Tell me, Madge, how this miracle was wrought!"

"There, that's just what I called it," cried Mrs. Muir, "and it's nothing less than one, in spite of all that Madge and Henry can say."

"When you are ready for supper I will show you one phase of the miracle," said Madge, laughing, with glad music in her voice. "Come, I'm not an escaped member of a menagerie, and there's no occasion for you to stare any longer."

"Yes, come along," added Mr. Muir; "I've had no roast beef to-day and a surfeit of sentiment."

The young fellow colored slightly, but said brusquely: "Men's tastes change with age. I suppose you did not find a little sentiment amiss once upon a time. Well, Madge, you are not a bit of a ghost now, yet I fear you are an illusion."

"Illusions will vanish when you come to help me at supper. We will wait for you on the piazza."

As she paced its wide extent, her illusions also vanished. Graydon had greeted, her as a brother, and a brother only. When the tumult at her heart subsided, this truth stood out most clearly. His kiss still tingled upon her lips. It must be the last, unless followed by a kiss of love. Their brotherly and sisterly relations must be shattered at once. No such relations existed for her, and only as she destroyed such regard on his part could a tenderer affection take its place.

With her as his sister he would be content; he might not readily think of her in another light, and meantime might drift swiftly into an engagement with Miss Wildmere.

CHAPTER X

OLD TIES BROKEN

"Madge," said Graydon, rejoining her on the piazza, and giving her his arm, while Mrs. Muir sat down to wait for her husband, "you wear a rose like the one you sent me when we parted so long ago. Oh, but my heart was heavy then! Did you make this choice to-night by chance?"

"You have a good memory."

"You have not answered me."

"I shall admit nothing that will increase your vanity."

"You will now of necessity make my pride overweening."

"How is that? I hope to have a better influence over you."

"As I look at you I regard my pride as most pardonable and natural. My old thoughts and hopes are realized beyond even imagination, although, looking at your eyes, in old times, I always had a high ideal of your capabilities. I should be a clod indeed if I were not proud of such a sister to champion in society."

Madge's hearty laugh was a little forced as she said, "You have a delightfully cool way of taking things for granted. I'm no longer a little sick girl, but, to vary Peggotty's exultant statement, a young lady 'growed.' You forgot yourself, sir, in your greeting; but that was pardonable in your paroxysm of surprise.

"What, Madge! Will you not permit me to be your brother?"

"What an absurd question!" she answered, still laughing. "You are not my brother. Can I permit water to run up hill? You were like a brother, though, when I was a sick child in the queer old times—kinder than most brothers, I think. But, Graydon, I am grown up. See, my head comes above your shoulder."

"Well, you are changed."

"For the better, in some respects, I hope you will find."

"I don't at all like the change you suggest in our relations, and am not sure I will submit to it. It seems absurd to me."

"It will not seem so when you come to think of it," she replied, gravely and gently. "You think of me still as little Madge; I am no longer little Madge, even to myself. A woman's instincts are usually right, Graydon."

"Oh, thank you! I am glad I am still 'Graydon.' Why do you not call me 'Mr. Muir?'"

"Because I am perfectly rational. Because I regard you as almost the best friend I have."

"Break up that confabulation," cried Mr. Muir to the young people, who had paused and were confronting each other at the further end of the piazza. "If you think Madge can explain herself in a moment or a week you are mistaken. Come to supper."

"My brother is right—you are indeed an enigma," he said, discontentedly.

"An enigma, am I?" she responded, smiling. "Please remember that most of the world's enigmas were slowly found out because so simple."

As they passed from the dusky piazza to the large, brilliantly lighted supper-room, with nearly all its tables occupied, he was curious to observe how she would meet the many critical eyes turned toward her. Again he was puzzled as well as surprised. She walked at his side as though the room were empty. There was no affectation of indifference, no trace of embarrassed or of pleased self-consciousness. From the friendly glances and smiles that she received it was also apparent that she had already made acquaintances. She moved with the easy, graceful step of perfect good breeding and assured confidence, and was as self-possessed as himself. Was this the little ghost who had once been afraid of her own shadow, which was scarcely less substantial than herself?

They had been seated but a moment when Miss Wildmere entered alone. To Graydon this appeared pathetic. He did not know that her mother was so worn out from the journey, and so embarrassed by unaided efforts to get settled while still caring for her half-sick child, that she had decided to make a slight and hasty repast in her own room. Miss Wildmere cared little for what took place behind the scenes, but was usually superb before the footlights. Nothing could have been more charming or better calculated to win general good-will than her advance down the long room. In external beauty she was more striking at first than Madge. She did not in the least regret that she must enter alone, for she was not proud of her mother, and nothing drew attention from herself. She assumed, however, a slight and charming trace of embarrassment and perplexity, which to Graydon was perfectly irresistible, and he mentally resolved that she should not much longer want a devoted escort. Madge saw his glance of sympathy and strong admiration, his smile and low bow as she passed, ushered forward by the obsequious headwaiter, and her heart sank. In spite of all she had attempted and achieved, the old cynical assurance came back to her—"You are nothing to Graydon, and never can be anything to him." She was pale enough now, but her eyes burned with the resolution not to yield until all hope was slain. She talked freely, and was most friendly toward Graydon, but there was a slight constraint in his manner. The beautiful and self-possessed girl who sat opposite him was not little Madge whom it had been his pleasure to pet and humor. She evidently no longer regarded herself as his sister, but rather as a charming young woman abundantly able to take care of herself. She had indeed changed marvellously in more respects than one, and he felt aggrieved that he had been kept in ignorance of her progress. He believed that she had grown away from him and the past, as well as grown up, according to her declaration. He recalled her apparent disinclination for correspondence, and now thought it due to indifference, rather than an indolent shrinking from effort. The surprise she had given him seemed a little thing—an act due possibly to vanity—compared with the sisterly accounts she might have written of her improvement. She had achieved the wonder without aid from him, and so of course had not felt the need of his help in any way. In remembrance of the past he felt that he had not deserved to be so ignored. Her profession of friendship was all well enough—there could scarcely be less than that—but the Madge he had looked forward to meeting again as of old no longer existed.

Oh, yes, she should have admiration and exclamation points to her heart's content, but he had come from his long exile hungry for something more and better than young lady friends. He had long since had a surfeit of these semi-Platonic affinities. The girl who apparently had been refusing scores of men for his sake was more to his taste. His brother's repugnance only irritated and incited him, and he thought, "I'll carry out his business policy to the utmost, but away from the office I am my own man."

As these thoughts passed through his mind, they began to impart to his manner a tinge of gallantry, the beginning of a departure from his old fraternal and affectionate ways. He was too well-bred to show pique openly, or to reveal a sense of injury during the first hours of reunion, but he already felt absolved from being very attentive to a girl who not only had proved so conclusively that she could manage admirably for herself, but who also had been so indifferent that she had not needed his sympathy in her efforts or thought it worth while to gladden him with a knowledge of her progress. He had loved her as a sister, and had given ample proof of this. He had maintained his affection for the Madge that he remembered. "But I have been told," he thought, bitterly, "that the young lady before me is a 'friend.' She has been a rather distant friend, if the logic of events counts for anything. Not satisfied with the thousands of miles that separated us, she has also withheld her confidence in regard to changes that would have interested even a casual acquaintance."

Madge soon detected the changing expression of his eyes, the lessening of simple, loving truth in his words, and while she was pained she feared that all this and more would necessarily result from the breaking up of their old relations. Her task was a difficult one at best—perhaps it was impossible—nor had she set about it in calculating policy.

Their old relations could not be maintained on her part. Even the touch of his hand had the mysterious power to send a thrill to her very heart. Therefore she must surround herself at once with the viewless yet impassable barriers which a woman can interpose even by a glance.

As they rose, Graydon remarked, "I have helped you at supper, and yet one of my illusions has not vanished. The air at Santa Barbara must have been very nourishing if your appetite was no better there than here. Your strange 'sea-change' on that distant coast is still marvellous to me."

"Mary can tell you how ravenous I usually am. I do not meet friends every day from whom I have been separated so long."

"It is a very ordinary thing for me to meet 'friends,'" he replied, *sotto voce*, "for I have many. I had hopes that I should meet one who would be far more than a friend. I'm half inclined to go out to Santa Barbara and see if my little sister Madge is not still there."

"Do you think me a fraud?"

"Oh, no, only so changed that I scarcely know how to get acquainted with you."

"Even if I granted so much, which I do not, I might suggest that one must be uninteresting indeed if she inspires no desire for acquaintance. But such talk is absurd between us, Graydon."

"Of course it is. You are so changed for the better that I can scarcely believe my eyes or ears, and my heart not at all. Of course your wishes shall be my law, and my wishes will lead me to seek your acquaintance with deep and undisguised interest. You see the trouble with me is that I have not changed, and it will require a little time for me to adapt myself to the new order of things. I am now somewhat stunned and paralyzed. In this imbecile state I am both stupid and selfish. I ought to congratulate you, and so I do with all the shattered forces of my mind and reason. You have improved amazingly. You are destined to become a belle *par excellence*, and probably are one now—I know so little of what has occurred since we parted."

"You are changed also, Graydon. You used to be kind in the old days;" and she spoke sadly.

"In some respects I am changed," he said, earnestly; "and my affection for you is of such long standing and so deep that it prompts me to make another protest." (They had strolled out upon the grounds and were now alone.) "I have changed in this respect; I am no longer so young as I was, and am losing my zest for general society. I was weary of residence abroad, where I could have scarcely the semblance of a home, and, while I had many acquaintances and friends, I had no kindred. I'm sorry to say that the word 'friend,' in its reference to young ladies, does not mean very much to me; or, rather, I have learned from experience just what it does mean. A few years since I was proud of my host of young lady friends, and some I thought would continue to be such through life. Bah! They are nearly all married or engaged; their lives have drifted completely away from mine, as it was natural and inevitable that they should. We are good friends still, but what does it amount to? I rarely think of them; they never of me, I imagine. We exert no influence on each other's lives, and add nothing to them. I never had a sister, but I had learned to love you as if you were one, and when I heard that you were to be of our family again, the resumption of our old relations was one of my dearest expectations. It hurt me cruelly, Madge, when you laughed at the idea as preposterous, and told me that I had forgotten myself when following the most natural impulse of my heart. It seemed to me the result of prudishness, rather than womanly delicacy, unless you have changed in heart as greatly as in externals. You could be so much to me as a sister. It is a relationship that I have always craved—a sister not far removed from me in age; and such a tie, it appears to me, might form the basis of a sympathy and confidence that would be as frank as unselfish and helpful. That is what I looked forward to in you, Madge. Why on earth can it not be?"

She was painfully embarrassed, and was glad that his words were spoken under the cover of night. She trembled, for his question probed deep. How could she explain that what was so natural for him was impossible for her? He mistook her hesitation for a sign of acquiescence, and continued: "Wherein have I failed to act like a brother? During the years we were together was I not reasonably kind and considerate? You did not think of yourself then as one of my young lady friends. Why should you now? I have not changed, and, as I have said, I have returned hungry for kindred and the quieter pleasures of home. It is time that I was considering the more serious questions of life, and of course the supreme question with a man of my years is that of a home of his own. I have never been able to think of such a home and not associate you with it. I can invite my sister to it and make her a part of it, but I cannot invite young lady friends. A sister can be such a help to a fellow; and it seems to me that I could be of no little aid to you. I know the world and the men you will meet in society. Unless you seclude yourself, you will be as great a belle as Miss Wildmere. You also have a fine property of your own. Will it be nothing to have a brother at your side to whom you can speak frankly of those who seek your favor? Come, Madge, be simple and rational. I have not changed; my frank words and pleadings prove that I have not. If we do not go back to the hotel brother and sister it will be because you have changed;" and he attempted to put his arm around her and draw her to him.

She sprang aloof. "Well, then, I have changed," she said, in a low, concentrated voice. "Think me a prude if you will. I know I am not. You are unjust to me, for you give me, in effect, no alternative. You say, 'Think of me as a brother; feel and act as if you were my sister,' when I am not your sister. It's like declaring that there is nothing in blood—that such relations are questions of choice and will. I said in downright sincerity that I regarded you as almost the best friend I had, and I have not so many friends that the word means nothing to me. I do remember all your kindness in the past—when have I forgotten it for an hour?—but that does not change the essential instincts of my womanhood, and since we parted I've grown to womanhood. You in one sense have not changed, and I still am in your mind the invalid child you used to indulge and fondle. It is not just to me now to ask that I act and feel as if there were a natural tie between us. The fact ever remains that there is not. Why should I deceive you by pretending to what is impossible? Nature is stronger than even your wishes, Graydon, and cannot be ignored."

She spoke hesitatingly, feeling her way across most difficult and dangerous ground, but her decision was unmistakable, and he said, quietly, "I am answered. See, we have wandered far from the house. Had we not better return?"

After a few moments of silence she asked, "Are you so rich in friends that you have no place for me?"

"Why, certainly, Madge," he replied, in cordial, offhand tones, "we are friends. There's nothing else for us to be. I don't pretend to understand your scruples. Even if a woman refused to be my wife I should be none the less friendly, unless she had trifled with me. To my man's reason a natural tie does not count for so much as the years we spent together. I remember what you were to me then, and what I seemed to you. I tried to keep up the old feeling by correspondence. The West is a world of wonders, and you have come from it the greatest wonder of all."

"I hope I shall not prove to you a monstrosity, Graydon. I will try not to be one if you will give me a chance."

"Oh, no, indeed; you promise to be one of the most charming young ladies I ever met."

"I don't promise anything of the kind," she replied, with a laugh that was chiefly the expression of her intense nervous tension. It jarred upon his feelings, and confirmed him in the belief that their long separation had broken up their old relations completely, and that she, in the new career which her beauty opened before her, wished for no embarrassing relations of any kind.

"Well," he said, with an answering laugh, "I suppose I must take you for what you are and propose to be—that is, if I ever find out."

In a few moments more, after some light badinage, he left her with Mr. and Mrs. Muir on the piazza, and went to claim his waltz with Miss Wildmere.

CHAPTER XI

"I FEAR I SHALL FAIL"

The band had been discoursing lively strains for some time, and Miss Wildmere had at last dragged her mother down for a chaperon—the only available one as yet. The anxious mother was eager to return to her fretting child, and her daughter was much inclined to resent Graydon's prolonged absence. "If it were politic, and I had other acquaintances, I would punish him," she thought. It was a new experience for her to sit in a corner of the parlor, apparently neglected, while others were dancing. There were plenty who looked wistfully toward her; but there was no one to introduce her, and Graydon's absence left the ice unbroken.

She ignored the inevitable isolation of a new-comer, however, and when he appeared shook her finger at him as she said, "Here I am, constancy itself, waiting to give you my first dance, as I promised."

"I shall try to prove worthy," he said, earnestly. "You must remember, in extenuation, that I have not seen the ladies of our family for a long time."

"You use the plural, and are Dot at all singular in your prolonged absence with the charming Miss Alden. You certainly cannot look upon her as an invalid any longer, however else you may regard her," she added, with an arch look.

"You shall now have my entire regard as long as you will permit it."

"That will depend a little upon yourself. Mamma is tired, and I'm of no account compared with that infant upstairs; therefore I can't keep her as a chaperon this evening, and I will go to my room as soon as you are tired of me."

"Not till then?"

"Not unless I go before."

"At some time in the indefinite future, Mrs. Wildmere, you may hope to see your daughter again."

The poor lady smiled encouragingly and gratefully. She would be most happy to have Graydon take the brilliant creature for better or worse as soon as possible. She liked him, as did all women, for she saw that he had a large, kindly nature. She now stole meekly away, while he with his fair partner glided out upon the floor. All eyes followed them, and even the veterans of society remarked that they had never seen more graceful dancing.

From her seat on the piazza Madge also watched the couple. The struggle to which she had looked forward so long had indeed begun, and most inauspiciously. Her rival had every advantage. The mood in which Graydon had returned predisposed him to prompt action, while she had lost her influence for the present by a course that seemed to him so unnatural as to be prudish. Miss Wildmere's manner gave all the encouragement that a man could wish for, and it was hard to view with charity the smiling, triumphant belle. Madge suddenly became conscious that Mr. Muir was observing her, and she remarked, quietly: "I never saw better dancing than that. It's grace itself. Miss Wildmere waltzes superbly."

"Not better than you, Miss Alden," said Mr. Henderson, a young man who prided himself on his skill in the accomplishment under consideration, and with whom she had danced several times. "I've been looking for you, in the hope that you would favor me this evening."

She rose and passed with him through the open window. The waltz was drawing to a close; the majority had grown weary and sat down; and soon Madge and Miss Wildmere were the only ladies on the floor. Opinion was divided, some declaring that the former was the more graceful and lovely, while perhaps a larger number gave their verdict for the latter.

The strains ceased, and left the couples near each other. Graydon immediately introduced Miss Wildmere. The girls bowed a little too profoundly to indicate cordiality. Madge also presented Mr. Henderson, hoping that he might become a partner for Miss Wildmere, and give Graydon an opportunity to dance with her. He resolved to break the ice at once so far as his relatives were concerned, and he conducted Miss Wildmere to Mrs. Muir, and gave her a seat beside that lady. The girl of his choice should have not only a gallant for the evening, but also a chaperon. He was not one to enter on timid, half-way measures; and he determined that his brother's prejudice should count for nothing in this case. His preference was entitled to respect, and must be respected. Of course the group chatted courteously, as well-bred people do in public, but Miss Wildmere felt that the atmosphere was chilly. She was much too politic to permit the slightest tinge of coldness in her manner toward those with whom she meditated such close relations should the barring "if" melt out of the way.

The people were forming for the lancers, and Mr. Henderson asked Madge to help make up a set. She complied without hesitation. Nor was she unmindful of the fact that Graydon sat in a position which commanded a view of the floor. He had seen her glide out in the waltz with a grace second only to that of Miss Wildmere, even in his prejudiced eyes. Now he again observed her curiously, and his disappointment and bitterness at heart increased, even while she compelled his wondering admiration. He saw that, though she lacked Miss Wildmere's conventional finish, she had a natural grace of her own. He admitted that he had never seen so perfect a physical embodiment of womanhood. She was slightly taller than her rival in his thoughts, and her costume gave an impression of additional height. Apparently she was in the best of spirits, laughing often with her partner and an elderly gentleman who danced opposite to her, and who was full of old-time flourishes and jollity. At last Graydon thought, resentfully, "She is indeed changed. That's the style of life she is looking forward to, and she wishes no embarrassment or advice from me. That dancing-jack, Henderson, and others of his sort are to be her 'friends' also, no doubt. Very well, I know how to console myself;" and he turned his eyes resolutely to Miss Wildmere.

In the galop that followed he naturally danced with his quondam sister, and Mr. Henderson with Miss Wildmere. Graydon was the last one to show feeling in public or do anything to cause remark. Now that Madge possessed in her partner the same advantage that Miss Wildmere had enjoyed, the admiring lookers-on were at a loss to decide which of the two girls bore the palm; and Graydon acknowledged that the former invalid's step had a lightness and an elasticity which he had never known to be surpassed, and that she kept time with him as if his volition were hers. She showed no sign of weariness, even after he began to grow fatigued. As he danced he remembered how he had carried "the little ghost" on his arm, then tossed her, breathless from scarce an effort, on the lounge, whence she looked at him in laughing affection. This strong, superb creature was indeed another and an alien being, and needed no aid from him. Before he was conscious of flagging in his step, she said, quietly, "You are growing tired, Graydon. Suppose we return to the piazza."

"Yes," he said, a trifle bitterly, "you are the stronger now. The 'little ghost' has vanished utterly."

"A woman is better than a ghost," was her reply.

He and Miss Wildmere strolled away down the same path on which Madge had told him that she could not be his sister. Mr. Muir was tired, and went to his room in no very amiable humor. Mrs. Muir waited for Graydon's return, feeling that, although the office of chaperon had in a sense been forced upon her, she could not depart without seeing Miss Wildmere again. The young lady at last appeared, and, believing that she had made all the points she cared for that night, did not tax Mrs. Muir's patience beyond a few moments. While she lingered she looked curiously at Madge, who was going through a Virginia reel as if she fully shared in the decided and almost romping spirit with which it was danced. She was uncertain whether or not she saw a possible rival in Graydon's thoughts, but she knew well that she had found a competitor for sovereignty in all social circles where they might appear together. This fact in itself was sufficient to secure the arrogant girl's ill-will and jealousy. A scarcely perceptible smile, that boded no good for poor Madge, passed over her face, and then she took a cordial leave of

Graydon, and retired with Mrs. Muir.

He remained at the window watching, with a satirical smile, the scene within. People of almost every age, from elderly men and matrons down to boys and girls, were participating in the old-fashioned dance. The air was resonant with laughter and music. In the rollicking fun Madge appeared to have found her element. No step was lighter or quicker than hers, and merriment rippled away before her as if she were the genius of mirth. Her dark eyes were singularly brilliant, and burned as with a suppressed excitement.

"She is bound to have her fling like the rest, I suppose," he muttered; "and that romp is more to her than the offer of a brother's love and help—an offer half forgotten already, no doubt. Yet she puzzles one. She never was a weak girl mentally. She was always a little odd, and now she is decidedly so. Well, I will let her gang her ain gate, and I shall go mine."

He little dreamed that she was seeking weariness, action that would exhaust, and that the expression of her eyes, so far from being caused by excitement, was produced by feelings deeper than he had ever known. When the music ceased he sauntered up and told her that her sister had retired.

"I had better follow her example," she said.

"Would you not like a brief stroll on the piazza? After exertions that, in you, seem almost superhuman, you must be warm."

"Why more superhuman in me than in others?"

"Simply because of my old and preconceived notions."

"I fear I am disappointing you in every respect. I had hoped to give you pleasure."

"Oh, well, Madge, I see we must let the past go and begin again."

"Begin fairly, then, and not in prejudice."

"Does it matter very much to you how I begin?"

"I shall not answer such questions."

"I am glad to see that you can enjoy yourself so thoroughly. You can now look forward to a long career of happiness, Madge, since you can obtain so much from a reel."

"You do not know what I am looking forward to."

"Why?"

"Because you are not acquainted with me."

"I thought I was at one time."

"I became discontented with that time, and have tried to be different."

"And you must have succeeded beyond your wildest dreams."

"Oh, no, I've only made a beginning. I should be conceit embodied if I thought myself finished."

"What is your supreme ambition, then?"

"I am trying to be a woman, Graydon. There, I'm cool now.

Good-night."

"Very cool, Madge."

He lighted a cigar and continued his walk, more perturbed than he cared to admit even to himself. Indeed, he found that he was decidedly annoyed, and there seemed no earthly reason why there should have been any occasion for such vexation. Of course he was glad that Madge had become strong and beautiful. This would have added a complete charm to their old relations. Why must she also become a mystery, or, rather, seek to appear one? Well, there was no necessity for solving the mystery, granting its existence. "Possibly she would prefer a flirtation to fraternal regard; possibly—Oh, confound it! I don't know what to think, and don't much care. She is trying to become a woman! Who can fathom some women's whims and fancies? She thinks her immature ideas, imbibed in an out-of-the-way corner of the world, the immutable laws of nature. Of one thing at least she is absolutely certain—she can get on without me. I must be kept at too great a distance to be officious."

This point settled, his own course became clear. He would be courtesy itself and mind his own business.

"I fear I shall fail," murmured poor Madge, hiding her face in her pillow, while suppressed sobs shook her frame.

CHAPTER XII

THE PROMPTINGS OF MISS WILDMERE'S HEART

Graydon slept very late the following morning. He found out that he was tired, and resolved to indulge his craving for rest so far as his suit to Miss Wildmere would permit. When he could do nothing to promote his advantage he proposed to be indolence itself. He found that his vexation had quite vanished, and, in cynical good-nature, he was inclined to laugh at the state of affairs. "Let Madge indulge her whims," he thought; "I may be the more free to pursue my purposes. Her sister, of course, shares in Henry's prejudices against the Wildmeres, and they would influence Madge adversely. All handsome girls are jealous of each other, and, perhaps, if what I had so naturally hoped and expected had proved true, I should have had more sisterly counsel and opposition than would have been agreeable. Objections now would be in poor taste, to say the least. If I'm not much mistaken I can speak my mind to Stella Wildmere before many days pass; and, woman-nature being such as it is, it may be just as well that I am not too intimate with a sister who, after all, is not my sister. Stella might not see it in the light that I should;" and so he came down at last, prepared to adapt himself very philosophically to the new order of things.

"The world moves and changes," he soliloquized, smilingly,

"and we must move on and change with it."

He found Mr. and Mrs. Muir, with Madge and the children, ready for church, and told them, laughingly, to "remember him if they did not think him past praying for." During his breakfast he recalled the fact that Madge was uncommonly well dressed. "She hasn't in externals," he thought, "the provincial air that one might expect, although her ideas are not only provincial, but prim, obtained, no doubt, from some goody-good books that she has read in the remote region wherein she has developed so remarkably. She has some stilted ideal of womanhood which she is seeking to attain, and the more unnatural the ideal, the more attractive, no doubt, it appears to her."

It did not occur to him that he was explaining Madge on more theories than one, and that they were not exactly harmonious. Having finished his meal, he sought for Miss Wildmere, and soon found her in a shady corner, reading a light, semi-philosophical work, thus distinguishing and honoring the day in her choice of literature. He proposed to read to her, but the book was soon forgotten in animated talk on his part. She could skilfully play the role of a good listener when she chose, and could, therefore, be a delightful companion. Her color came and went under words and compliments that at times were rather ardent and pronounced. He soon observed, however, that she led the way promptly from delicate ground. This might result from maidenly reserve or from the fact that she was not quite ready for decisive words. He still believed that he had all needed encouragement—that the expression of her eyes often answered his, and he knew well what his meant. When, in response to his invitation, she promised to drive with him in the afternoon, all seemed to be going as he wished.

Graydon felt that during dinner and thereafter for a time he should be devoted to his party, to preclude criticism on his course in the late afternoon and in the evening, when he proposed to seek society which promised more than theirs. He began to discover that, except as her intelligence was larger, in one respect Madge had not changed from her old self. She responded appreciatively to his thought and fancy, and gave him back in kind with interest. She began to question him about a place in Europe with which he was familiar, and showed such unusual knowledge of the locality that he asked, "You haven't slipped over there unknown to me, I trust?"

"You might think of an easier explanation than that. You kindly sent me books, some of which were rather realistic."

"Did you read them all?"

"Certainly. It would have been a poor return if I had not."

"What an inordinate sense of duty you must have had!"

"I did not read them from a sense of duty. You have perhaps forgotten that I am fond of books."

"Not all of the books were novels."

"Many that were not proved the most interesting."

"Oh, indeed; another evidence of change," he said, laughing.

"And of sense, too, I think. Mr. Wayland, who is a student, had a splendid library, and he gave me some ideas as to reading."

"Can you part with any of them?"

"That depends," she replied, with a manner as brusque as his own.

"On what?"

"The inducements and natural opportunities. I'm not going to recite a lesson like a schoolgirl."

"One would think you had been to school."

"I have, where much is taught and learned thoroughly."

"Now, that is enigmatical again."

"The best of the books you sent me left some room for the imagination."

"Ha, ha, ha, Madge! you are scoring points right along. I told you, Graydon, that you couldn't understand her in a moment or in a week."

"I never regarded your imagination as rampant, Henry. Have you fathomed all her mystery?"

"Far from it; nor do I expect to, and yet you will grant to me some degree of penetration."

"Well, to think that I should have come home to find a sphinx instead of little Madge!"

"Thank you. A sphinx is usually portrayed with at least the head of a woman."

"In this case she has one that would inspire a Greek sculptor. Perhaps in time I may discover a heart also."

"That's doubtful."

"Indeed."

"Yes, indeed."

"What far-fetched nonsense!" said Mrs. Muir, sententiously. "Madge has come back one of the best and most sensible girls in the world. Men and poets are always imagining that women are mysteries. The fact is, they are as transparent as glass when they know their own minds; when they don't, who else should know them?"

"Who indeed?" said Graydon, laughing. "Your saving clause, Mary, is as boundless as space."

"How absurd! I understand Madge perfectly, and so does Henry."

"You said last evening that the change in her was a miracle. Once in the realm of the supernatural, what may not one expect?"

"You knew what I meant. I referred to Madge's health and appearance and accomplishments and all that. She has not changed in heart and feeling any more than I have, and I'm sure I'm not a sphinx."

"No, Mary; you are a sensible and excellent wife and my very dear sister. You suggest no mystery. Madge certainly does, for you have, in addition to all the rest, announced an indefinite list of accomplishments."

"If I remain the subject of conversation I shall complain that your remarks are personal," said Madge, her brows contracting with a little vexation.

"That is what makes our talk so interesting. Personals are always read first. In drawing Mary and Henry out, I am getting acquainted with you."

"It's not a good way. You like it merely because it teases me and saves trouble. If you must gossip and surmise about me, wait till I'm absent."

"There, Madge, you know I'm nine-tenths in fun," said he, laughing.

"That leaves a small margin for kindly interest in an old acquaintance," was her reply as they rose from the table, and he saw that her feelings were hurt.

"Confound it!" he thought, with irritation, "it's all so uncalled-for and unnatural! Nothing is as it used to be. Well, then, I'll talk about books and matters as impersonal as if we were disembodied spirits."

They had scarcely seated themselves on the piazza before Miss Wildmere came forward and introduced her mother. The young lady was determined to prepare the way for a family party. Graydon had a confident, opulent air, which led to the belief that her father's fears were groundless, and that before many weeks should elapse the Muirs would have to acknowledge her openly. It would save embarrassment if this came about naturally and gradually, and she believed that she could be so charming as to make them covet the alliance. Miss Alden might not like it, and the more she disliked it the better.

Mrs. Muir's thoughts were somewhat akin. "If Graydon will marry this girl, it's wise that we should begin on good terms. This is a matter that Henry can't control, and there's no use in our yielding to prejudice."

Therefore she was talkative, courteous, and rapidly softened toward the people whom her husband found so distasteful. Graydon employed all his skill and tact to make the conversation general and agreeable, but the cloud did not wholly pass from Madge's brow. From the moment of her first cold, curious stare, years since, Miss Wildmere had antagonized every fibre of the young girl's soul and body, and she had resolved never to be more than polite to her. She did not look forward to future relationship, as was the case with Mrs. Muir, but rather to entire separation, should Graydon become Miss Wildmere's accepted suitor. Now, with the instinct of self-defence, she was more cordial to her rival than to Graydon, until, at the solicitation of the children, she stole away. Mr. Muir remarked that he was going to take a nap, and soon followed her.

Their departure was a relief to Graydon, for it rendered the carrying out of his plan less embarrassing. In his eagerness to be alone with the object of his hopes, he soon obtained a carriage, and with Miss Wildmere drove away. Mrs. Muir and Mrs. Wildmere compared maternal and domestic notes sometime longer, and then the former went to her room quite reconciled to what now appeared inevitable.

"I think you are prejudiced, Henry," she remarked to her husband, who was tossing restlessly on the bed.

"Least said soonest mended," was his only response, and then he changed the subject.

Graydon came back with the hope—nay, almost the certainty—of happiness glowing in his eyes. He had spoken confidently of his business plans and prospects, and had touched upon the weariness of his exile and his longing for more satisfactory pleasures than those of general society. His companion had listened with an attention and interest that promised more than sympathy. The wild, rugged scenes through which they had passed had made her delicate beauty more exquisite from contrast. It was as if a rare tropical bird had followed the wake of summer and graced for a time a region from which it must fly with the first breath of autumn. In distinction from all they saw and met she appeared so fragile, such a charming exotic, that he felt an overpowering impulse to cherish and shelter her from every rude thing in the world. With a nice blending of reserve and complaisance she appeared to yield to his mood and yet to withhold herself. To a man of Graydon's poise and knowledge of society such skilful tactics served their purpose perfectly. They gave her an additional charm in his eyes, and furnished another proof of the fineness of her nature. She could not only feel, but manifest the nicest shades of preference. If not fully satisfied as to her own heart, what could be more refined and graceful than the slight restraint she imposed upon him? and how fine the compliment she paid him in acting on the belief that he was too well bred and self-controlled to precipitate matters!

"She has the tact and intuition to see," he thought, "that she can show me all the regard she feels and yet incur no danger of premature and incoherent words. She will one day yield with all the quiet grace that she shows when rising to accept my invitation to waltz."

Therefore, as he approached the hotel he was complacency itself until he saw Mr. Arnault on the piazza, and then his face darkened with the heaviest of frowns.

"Why, what is the matter?" Miss Wildmere asked.

"I had hoped that this perfect afternoon might be followed by a more delightful evening, but from the manner in which that gentleman is approaching you, it is evident that he expects to claim you."

"Claim me? I do not think any one has that right just yet. Mr. Arnault certainly has not."

"Then I may still hope for your society this evening?"

"Have I not permitted you to be with me nearly all day? You must be more reasonable. Good-evening, Mr. Arnault. Did you drop from the clouds?"

"There are none, and were there I should forget them in this pleasure. Mr. Muir, I congratulate you. We have both been on the road this afternoon, but you have had the advantage of me."

"And mean to keep it, confound you!" thought Graydon. "Ah, good-evening, Mr. Arnault. You are right; I have found rough roads preferable to smooth rails and a palace car."

"How well you are looking, Miss Stella! but that's chronic with you. This is perfectly heavenly" (looking directly into her eyes) "after the heat of the city and my dusty journey."

"You are a fine one to talk about things heavenly after fracturing the Sabbath-day. What would have happened to you in Connecticut a hundred years ago?"

"I should have been ridden on one rail instead of two, probably. I'm more concerned about what will happen to me to-day, and that depends not on blue laws, but blue blood. I saw your father this morning, and he intrusted me with a letter for you."

Mr. Arnault manifested not a particle of jealousy or apprehension, and Graydon felt himself shouldered out of the way by a courtesy to which he could take no exception. He saw that only Miss Wildmere herself could check his rival's resolute and easy assurance. This he now felt sure she would do if it passed a certain point, and he went to his room, annoyed merely, and without solicitude. "She must let the fellow down easily, I suppose," he thought; "and after to-day I need have few fears. If she had wanted *him* she could have taken him long ago."

Miss Wildmere also went to her room and read her father's letter. It contained these few and significant words: "In speaking of possible relations with Mr. M. I emphasized a small but important word—'if.' I now commend it to you still more emphatically. You know I prefer Mr. M. Therefore you will do well to heed my caution. Mr. M. may lose everything within a brief time."

Miss Wildmere frowned and bit her lip with vexation. Then her white face took on hard, resolute lines. "I came near making a fool of myself this afternoon," she muttered. "I was more than once tempted to let Graydon speak. Heavens! I'd like to be engaged to him for awhile. Mr. Arnault plays a bold, steady hand, but he's the kind of man that might throw up the game if one put tricks on him. My original policy is the best. I must pit one against the other in a fair and open suit till I can take my choice. Now that it is clear that Graydon cares little for that hideous thing he calls his sister, my plan is safe."

"What a lovely color you have, Madge!" Graydon remarked, as they met at supper. "You are unequalled in your choice of cosmetics."

"Not to be surpassed, at any rate."

"Where did you get it?"

"Up at Grand View."

"What, have you climbed that mountain?"

"It's not much of a mountain."

"It's a tremendous mountain," cried little Harry. "Aunt Madge's been teaching us to climb, and she lifted us up and down the steep places as if we were feathers, and she told us stories about the squirrels and birds we saw up there. Oh, didn't we have a lovely time, Jennie?"

"Now I understand," said Graydon. "The glow in your face comes from the consciousness of good deeds."

"It comes from exertion. Are you not making too much effort to be satirical?"

"Therefore my face should be suffused with the hue of shame. You see I have changed also, and have become a cynic and a heathen from long residence in Europe."

"Please be a noble savage, then."

"That's not the style of heathen they develop abroad."

"Madge told us about the savages that used to live in these mountains, and how bad they were treated," piped Jennie.

"Poor Lo! No wonder he went to the bad," said Graydon, significantly. "He was never recognized as a man and a brother."

"And he was unsurpassed in retaliation," Madge added.

"Considering his total depravity and general innocence, that was to be expected."

"It turned out to be bad policy."

"In so far as he was a man he hadn't any policy."

"I shall not depreciate the Indians for the sake of argument. They rarely followed the wrong trail, however."

"What on earth are you and Madge driving at?" exclaimed Mrs. Muir.

"It matters little at what, but Madge appears to be the better driver," chuckled Mr. Muir.

"You have a stanch champion in Henry," said Graydon.

"You wouldn't have him take sides against a woman?"

"Oh, no, but you have become so abundantly able to take care of yourself that he might remain neutral."

"When you all begin to talk English again I'll join in, and now merely remark that I am grateful to you, Madge, for taking care of the children. Jack was good with the nurse, too, and I've had a splendid nap."

"I'm evidently the delinquent," laughed Graydon, "and have led the way in a conversation that has been as bad as whispering in company. What will become of me? You are not going to church to-night, Madge?"

"I did not expect to. If your conscience needs soothing—"

"Oh, no, no. My conscience has been seared with a hot iron—a cold one, I mean. The effects are just the same."

At the supper-room door they were met by Dr. Sommers, with a world of comical trouble in his face, and he drew Madge aside.

"What's a man to do?" he began. "Here's our choir-leader sick, and the rest won't chirp without him. I can't sing any more than I can dance. You can—sing, I mean—both, for that matter. I'd give the best cast of a fly I ever had to take you out in a reel. Well, here's the trouble. It's nearly meeting-time, and what's a meeting without music? You can sing—I'm sure you can. I've heard you twice in the chapel. Now, it isn't imposing on good-nature, is it, to ask you to come over and start the tunes for us to-night? Come now, go with me. It will be a great favor, and I'll get even with you before the summer is over."

Madge hesitated a moment. She had hoped for a chat with Graydon that evening, which might lead to a better understanding, and end their tendency to rather thorny badinage. But she heard him chatting gayly with Miss Wildmere and Mr. Arnault in the distance; therefore she said, quietly, "It is time for me to get even with you first. To refuse would not be nice after the lovely drive you took us the other day."

"Oh, you made that square as you went along. Well, now, this is famous. What a meeting we'll have!"

"You explain to Mrs. Muir, and I'll get my hat."

"I'm in luck," the doctor began, joining the Muirs on the piazza.

"Of course you are. You are always in luck," said Mrs. Muir.

"Oh, no, oh, no. Draw it milder than that. I've fished many a bad day. I'm in luck to-night . What do you think? You can't guess."

"You and Madge had your heads together, and so something will happen. Are you going to capture a mountain?"

"Yes, a brace of 'em before long. Well, as good luck would have it, our choir-leader is sick. I thought it was bad luck at first, and meant to give him an awful dose for being so inopportune. It has turned out famously. 'All-things work together for good,' you know. That text required faith once when I had hooked a three-pound trout, and in my eagerness tumbled in where the fish was. Oh, here you are, Miss Alden. We'll go right along, for it's about time."

"But you haven't explained," cried Mrs. Muir.

"We will when we come back," said the doctor.

"Oh, I'm merely going over to the chapel to help the doctor out with the singing," said Madge, carelessly. "Good-by."

"Well," remarked Mr. Muir, *sotto voce*, "if I were a young fellow, there's a trail I'd follow, and not that will-o'-the-wisp yonder."

"What did you say, Henry?" asked his wife.

"It will be hot in town to-morrow, Mary. It's growing confoundedly hot in Wall Street."

"Nothing serious, Henry?"

"It's always serious there."

"Oh, well, you'll come out all right. It's a way you have."

Mr. Muir looked grim and troubled, but the piazza was dusky. "She can't help me," he thought, "and if she was worrying she might hinder me. Things are no worse, and they may soon be better. If I had fifty thousand for a month, though, the strain would be over. She'd be nagging me to take a lot of her money, and I'd see Wall Street sunk first. Well, well, Wildmere and I may land together in the same ditch."

For a few moments Graydon and Mr. Arnault sat on either side of the broker's daughter, each seeking the advantage. The young lady enjoyed the situation immensely, and for a time had the art to entertain both. Arnault at last boldly and frankly took the initiative, saying, "Please take a walk with me, Miss Wildmere. I have come all the way from New York for the pleasure of an evening in your society. You will excuse us, Mr. Muir. You have had to-day and will have to-morrow, for I must take an early train."

Miss Wildmere laughed, and said: "I must go with you surely, or you will think you have made a bad 'put' in railroad tickets, as well as shares, for you are like the rest, I suppose;" and with a smiling glance backward at Graydon she disappeared.

"You are mistaken," he said; "we foresaw this 'squeeze' in the market, and have money to lend if the security is ample. We were never doing better."

"Poor papa!" she sighed, "his securities are lacking, I suppose. He does not write very cheerfully."

"His security is the best in the city, in my estimation. I'd take this little hand in preference to government bonds."

"Oh, don't lend papa anything on that basis, for you would

surely manage to claim the collateral, or whatever you call it in your Wall Street jargon."

"You are infinitely better off than the majority in these hard times."

"How so?"

"By one word you can make three rich, yourself included. Your father only needs to be tided over a few months."

"Come, come, Mr. Arnault, this is Sunday, and you must not talk business."

"My fault leans to virtue's side for once."

"I'm not just sure to which side it leans," was her laughing reply.

"Are you going to accept Muir?"

"I'm not going to accept any one at present—certainly not Mr. Muir before he asks me."

"He will ask you."

"Has he taken you into his confidence?"

"Oh, he's as patent as a country borrower."

"Mr. Arnault, we must change the subject; such questions and remarks are not in good taste, to say the least. I appreciate your friendship, but it does not give you the right to forget that I am a free girl, or to ignore my assurance that I propose to remain free for the present."

"That is all the assurance that I require just now," he answered. "I have been a frank, devoted suitor, Stella. If you do not act precipitately you will act wisely in the end. I shall not be guilty of the folly of depreciating Muir—he's a good fellow in his way—but you will soon be convinced that you cannot afford to marry him."

"I think I can afford not to marry any one until my heart prompts me to the act," she replied, with well-assumed dignity. Her swift thought was, "He also knows that the Muirs are embarrassed. How is it that Graydon speaks and acts in the assured confidence of continued wealth? Is he deceiving me?"

Mr. Arnault changed the subject, and none could do this with more adroitness than he, or be a more entertaining gallant if he so chose. At the same time he maintained a subtle observance, in spite of his vaunted frankness, and he soon believed he had reason to hope that Miss Wildmere had been influenced by his words. Almost imperceptibly she permitted additional favor to come into her manner, and when she said good-night and good-by also, in view of his early start for the city, it was at the foot of the stairway, she casually remarking that she would not come down again.

"My brief visit has not been in vain," he thought. "I have delayed matters, and that now means a great deal. She will marry the survivor of this financial gale, and in every man's philosophy the survival of the fittest is always the survival of the *ego*."

CHAPTER XIII

"YOU WILL BE DISAPPOINTED"

Graydon felt that it was scarcely possible to resent Mr. Arnault's tactics or to blame Miss Wildmere. The former certainly had as good a right to be a suitor as himself, and even to his prejudiced mind it would have been ungracious in the lady had she not given some reward for his rival's long journey. It was natural that Mr. Arnault, an old friend of the Wildmeres, should sit at their table and receive the consideration that he enjoyed. Graydon had little cause for complaint or vexation, since his rival would depart in the morning, and, judging from to-day, his own suit was approaching a successful termination. The coast would be clear on the morrow, and he determined to make the most of opportunities. He now even regretted that Madge and his relatives were at the house, for in some degree they trammelled his movements by a watchful attention, which he believed was not very friendly. It would not be well to ignore them beyond a certain point, for it was his wish to carry out his purposes with the least possible friction. Madge's course had compelled a revision of his plans and expectations, but his intimate relations with his brother in business made harmony and peace very essential. He felt keenly, however, the spur of Mr. Arnault's open and aggressive rivalry, and determined to enter upon an equally vigorous campaign.

Having reached this definite conclusion, he joined Mr. and Mrs. Muir on the piazza, and after some desultory talk asked, "Where is Madge?"

Mrs. Muir explained, adding, "I think you might go over to the chapel and accompany her home."

"I'll be there by the time service is over," he replied.

There was sacred music in the hotel parlor, but it seemed to him neither very sacred nor very attractive. Then he strolled toward the chapel. As the service was not over, he stood and watched the great moonlit mountains, with their light and shade. The scene and hour fostered the feelings to which he had given himself up. In revery he went over the hours he had spent with Miss Wildmere since his return, and hope grew strong. In view of it all—and vividly his memory retained everything, even to the droop of her eyelids or the tone in which some ordinary words had been spoken—there could scarcely be a doubtful conclusion. Thoughts of him had kept her free, and now that they had met again she was seeking to discover if her old impressions had been true, and in their confirmation was surely yielding to his suit.

He started. Through the open windows of the adjacent chapel came the opening notes of a hymn, sung with a sweetness and power that in the still summer night seemed almost divine. Then other voices joined, and partially obscured the melody; but above all floated a voice that to his trained ear had some of the rarest qualities of music.

"That's Madge," he muttered, and strode rapidly to the door. Again, in the second stanza, the rich, pure voice thrilled his every nerve, gaining rather than losing in its effect by his approach.

Unconsciously the poor girl had yielded to the old habit of self-expression in music. Her heart had been heavy, and now was sad indeed. Earthly hope had been growing dim, but the words of faith she had heard had not been without sustaining influence. With the deep longing of her woman's nature for love—divine love, if earthly love must be denied—her voice in its pathos was unconsciously an appeal, full of entreaty. She half forgot her surroundings; they were nothing in her present mood. The little audience of strangers gave a sense of solitude.

The quaint old tune was rich in plaintive harmony. It had survived the winnowing process of time, and had endeared itself to the popular heart because expressive of the heart's unrest and desire for something unpossessed. Along this old, well-worn musical channel Madge poured the full tide of her feeling, which had both the solemnity and the pathos inseparable from all deep and sacred emotion. Graydon was now sure that he must dismiss one of his impressions of Madge, and finally. No one could sing like that and be trivial at heart. "I don't understand her," he muttered, gloomily, "but I appreciate one thing. She has withheld from me her confidence, she does not wish to keep her old place in my affection, and has deposed herself from it. She appears to be under the influence of a brood of sentimental aspirations. I shall remain my old self, nor shall I gratify her by admiring wonder. The one thing that would make life a burden to me is an intense, aesthetical, rapturously devotional woman, with her mental eye fixed on a vague ideal. In such society I should feel much like a man compelled to walk on stilts all the time. The idea of going back to the hotel, smoking a cigar, and talking of the ordinary affairs of life, after such music as that!"

"It was very kind of you to come over for me," said Madge, as she came out. "Thank you, doctor; no, there is no need of your going back with me. Good-night."

"Thanks to you, Miss Alden, thanks, thanks. The sermon was good, but that last hymn rounded up Sunday for me. I was going up to the house, but I'll go home and keep that music in my ears. If they had known, they wouldn't have spared you from the hotel music to-night."

"Please say nothing about it—that is all I ask," she said, as she took Graydon's arm.

"Yes, Madge," he began, quietly, "you sung well. You had the rudiments of a fine voice years ago. In gaining strength you have also won the power to sing."

"Yes," she said, simply.

"Do you sing much?"

"I do not wish to sing at all in the hotel. I did not study music in order to be conspicuous."

"Have you studied it very carefully?"

"Please leave out the word 'very.' I studied it as a young girl studies, not scientifically. I had a good master, and he did his best for me. Poor Herr Brachmann! he was sorry to have me come away. Perhaps in time I can make progress that will satisfy him better. I could see that he was often dissatisfied."

"You don't mean to suggest that you are going back to Santa Barbara?"

"Why not?"

"True enough, 'why not?' It was a foolish question. You

doubtless have strong attachments there."

"I have, indeed."

"And it's natural to go where our attachments are strongest."

"Yes; you have proved that to-day."

"You evidently share in my brother's disapproval. Mary would soon become quite reconciled."

"I? I have no right to feel either approval or disapproval, while you have an undoubted right to please yourself."

"Indeed! are you so indifferent? If you think Miss Wildmere objectionable you should disapprove."

"If you find her altogether charming, if she realizes your ideal, is not that sufficient? Everything is very much what it seems to us. If I as a girl would please myself, you, surely, as a man have a right to do so."

"Do you propose to please yourself?"

"Indeed I do."

"You will be disappointed. You have formed a passion for ideals. I imagine, though, that you are somewhat different from other girls whose future husbands must be ideal men, but who are content themselves to remain very much what their milliners, dressmakers, and fashion make them."

"I can at least say that I am not content; and I am also guilty of the enormity of cherishing ideals."

"Oh, I've found that out, if nothing else. Ideals among men

are as thick as blackberries, you know. Jack Henderson dances superbly."

"Yes; he quite meets my ideal in that respect."

"Perhaps you left some one in Santa Barbara who meets your ideal in all respects?"

"There was one gentleman there who approached it nearly."

"How could you leave him?"

"He came on with me—Mr. Wayland."

"Pshaw! He's old enough to be your father."

"And very like a father he was to me. I owe him an immense deal, for he helped me so much!"

"You did not let me help you?"

"Yes; I did. I wrote to you for books, and read all you sent me; some parts of them several times."

"You know that is not what I meant. I am learning to understand you somewhat, Madge. I hope you may realize all your ideals, and find some young fellow who is the embodiment of the higher life, aspirations, and all that, you know."

Her laugh rang out musically. Mrs. Muir heard it, and remarked to her husband: "Madge and Graydon are getting on better. They have seemed to me to clash a little to-day."

Mr. Muir made no reply, and Graydon, as he mounted the steps, whispered, hurriedly, "What you said about Miss

Wildmere was at least just and fair. I wish you liked her, and would influence Henry to like her, for I see that you have influence with him."

She made no response by word or sign.

The ladies soon retired, and Graydon waited in vain for another interview with Miss Wildmere. While he was looking for her on the piazza she passed in and disappeared. He at last discovered Mr. Arnault, who was smoking and making some memoranda, and, turning on his heel, he strode away. "She might have said good-night, at least," he thought, discontentedly, "and that fellow Arnault did not look like a man who had received his *conge."*

That this gentleman did not regard himself as out of the race was proved by his tactics the next morning. Before reaching the city he joined Mr. Muir in the smoking section of a parlor car, and easily directed their talk to the peculiar condition of business. Mr. Muir knew little in favor of his companion, and not much against him, but devoutly hoped that he would be the winning man in the contest for Miss Wildmere. He also knew that the firm to which Mr. Arnault belonged had held their heads well up in the fluctuations of the street. Both gentlemen deplored the present state of affairs, and hoped that there might soon be more confidence. "By the way, Mr. Muir," Mr. Arnault remarked, casually, "if you need accommodation we have some money lying idle for a short time, which we would like to put out as a call loan, and would be glad to place it in good conservative hands, like yours."

"Thank you," said Mr. Muir, with some cordiality.

He went to his office and looked matters over carefully. He was convinced that a crisis was approaching. More money was required immediately, since the securities in which he had invested had declined still further. He had not lost his faith in them at all, knowing that they had a solid basis, and would be among the first to rise in value with returning confidence. He had gone so far and held on so long that it was a terrible thing to give up now. Comparatively little money would probably carry him over to perfect safety, but his means were tied up, the banks stringent, and he had already strained his credit somewhat. Mr. Arnault's proffer occurred to him again, and at last, much as he disliked the expedient, he called upon the broker, who was affable, off-hand, and business-like.

"Yes, Mr. Muir," he said, "I can let you have thirty thousand just as well as not; as the times are, I would like some security, however."

"Certainly, here are bonds marketable to-day, although depressed unnaturally. You are aware that they will be among the first to appreciate."

"In ordinary times one would think so."

"How soon do you think you may call in this loan?"

"Well, the probabilities are, that you may keep it as long as you wish, at the rates named. They are stiff, I know, but not above the market."

Mr. Muir had thought it over. If he failed he was satisfied that his assets would eventually make good every dollar he owed, with interest, while, on the other hand, even the small sum named promised to preserve his fortune and add very largely to his wealth. The transaction was soon completed.

Mr. Arnault was equally satisfied that he also took but slight risk. The loan, however, was made from his own means, and was not wholly a business affair. He had made up his mind to win Stella Wildmere, and would not swerve from the purpose unless she engaged herself to another. Then, even though she might be willing to break the tie through stress of circumstances, he would stand aloof. There was only one thing greater than his persistency—his pride. She was the belle who, in his set, had been admired most generally, and his god was success—success in everything on which he placed his heart, or, rather, mind. For her to become engaged to Graydon, and then, because of his poverty, to be willing to renounce him for a more fortunate man, would not answer at all. He must appear to the world to have won her in fair competition with all others, and the girl had an instinctive knowledge of this fact. The events of the previous day, with her father's note, therefore confirmed her purpose to keep both men in abeyance until the scale should turn.

CHAPTER XIV

MISS WILDMERE'S STRATEGY

As we have seen, Madge could not resume her old relations with Graydon Muir. Indeed, the turning-point in her life had been the impulse and decision to escape them by going away. She was also right in thinking that this inability would rather help than hinder her cause. If he had come back and realized his expectations, he would have bestowed unstintedly the placid affection of a brother, given her his confidence, his aid, anything she wished, except his thoughts. While she lost much else, she retained these in a way that puzzled and even provoked him, in view of his devotion to Miss Wildmere. The very fact that he resented the way in which he had been treated by Madge made him think of her, although admitting to himself that it might all turn out for the best. He would have soon accepted changes in externals, and her added accomplishments, but there were other and more subtle changes which he could not grasp. It began to pique him that he had already been forced to abandon more than one impression in regard to her character. It was somewhat humiliating that he, who had seen the world, especially in its social aspects, should be perplexed by a young girl scarcely twenty, and that this girl of all others should be little Madge. He had intimated that she had become imbued with sentimentality and aspirations after ideals, and was hoping to meet a male embodiment of these traits, which he regarded as prominently lackadaisical. Her merry and half ironical laugh was not the natural response of a woman of the intense and aesthetic type.

"I don't understand her yet," he admitted; and he again assured himself that it was not necessary that he should. She had not merely drifted away from him, but had deliberately chosen that others should guide and help in the new development. The thing for him to do now was to secure the girl of his heart, who was not shrouded in mystery. It was evident that Mr. Arnault had been an urgent suitor, and that she was not already engaged to him proved, as he believed, that she had been under the influence of a restraint readily explained by her more than manner toward himself. "She will have to choose between us soon," he thought. "She understands us both, and her heart will soon give its final verdict, if it has not already done so."

Miss Wildmere's heart would have slight voice in the verdict. Indeed, it never had been permitted to say very much, and was approaching the condition of a mute. She had her preference, however, and still hoped to be able to follow it. She smiled upon Graydon almost as sweetly as ever during the next two days, but he felt that she had grown more elusive. She lured him on unmistakably, but permitted no near approach. With consummate art, she increased the spell of her fascinations, and added to the glamour which dazzled him. He might look his admiration, and, more, he might compliment indefinitely; but when he spoke too plainly, or sought stronger indications of her regard, she was on the wing instantly, and he was too fine in his perceptions to push matters against her will. One thing appeared hopeful to him—she seemed possessed by a carefully veiled jealousy of Madge. In his downright earnestness, he determined to give her no cause for this, and treated Madge much as he did Mrs.

Muir, allowing for difference in age and relation. He determined that Miss Wildmere should discover no ambiguity in his course or intentions. If thoughts of him had kept her waiting through years, he would justify those thoughts by all the means in his power. Casting about with a lover's ingenuity for an explanation of her tantalizing allurement, yet elusiveness, it occurred to him that she was unwilling to yield readily and easily, from very fear that he might surmise the cause of her freedom—that she had given him her love before it had been asked. Therefore, it was not impossible that she now proposed for him a somewhat thorny probation as an open suitor. She would not appear to be easily won, and perhaps she thought that, since this was to be the last wooing she could enjoy, she would make the most of it. He also resolved to make the most of this phase of life, and to enjoy to the utmost all of her shy witchery, her airy, hovering nearness to the thought uppermost in his mind, as if she were both fascinated by it and afraid. He little dreamed that her feminine grace and *finesse* were but the practical carrying out of her father's suggestion, to "keep him well in hand."

Madge felt herself neglected and partially forgotten. She saw that Miss Wildmere's spell grew stronger upon Graydon every day. It was not in her nature to seek to attract his attention or in the slightest degree to enter the lists openly against her rival. During the first three days of the week, her chief effort was to be so active and cheerful that her deep despondency should be hidden from all. She was the life of every little group of which she formed a part. Wherever she appeared, mirth and laughter soon followed. The young girls in the house began to acknowledge her as a natural leader, the boyish young fellows to adore her, and the maturer men to discover that she could hold her own with them in conversation, while another class learned, to their chagrin, that she would not flirt. For every walking expedition started she was ready with her alpenstock, and the experts in the bowling alley found a strong, supple competitor, with eye and hand equally true. Graydon, as far as his preoccupation permitted, saw all this with renewed perplexity. She now appeared to him as a beautiful, vigorous girl, with healthful instincts and a large appetite for enjoyment.

Wednesday morning was cool and cloudy, and a large party was forming to climb to Spy Rock. Graydon was longing for more activity, and since the day was so propitious, Miss Wildmere consented to go. Of course Madge was in readiness, and in charming costume for a walk. The moment they were on the steep path he had to admit that she appeared the superior of Miss Wildmere. The one owed her bloom to artificial and metropolitan life; the other had gone to nature, and now acted as if her foot were on her native heath. Her step was light, yet never uncertain. Her progress was easy, and, although different, was quite as graceful as if she were promenading the piazza, proving that she was an adept in mountain-climbing. It was evident, however, that to Miss Wildmere a mountain was a *terra incognita.* She trod uncertainly, her feet turned on loose stones that hurt her, and before the first steep ascent was passed, she panted and was glad to sit down with others, more or less exhausted.

Madge's breathing was only slightly quickened, and color was beginning to come in her usually pale face, yet she had lent a helping hand more than once.

"How easily you climb, Miss Alden!" gasped Miss Wildmere. "Have you taken lessons?"

"Yes," she replied, smiling sweetly, "and from a master."

Miss Wildmere also was beginning to discover a problem in Madge; she could not patronize, snub, or apparently touch her with shafts of satire. The young girl treated her with cordial indifference, as one-of the guests of the house. She appeared to be capable of enjoying herself thoroughly, with scarcely a consciousness of the belle's existence, unless, as in the present case, she was addressed. Then she would reply with perfect courtesy, but in some such ambiguous way. It soon became evident to Graydon that the two girls were hostile, and this both amused and vexed him. He was beginning to learn that Madge was the more skilful opponent. She was never aggressive, yet seemed clad in polished armor when attacked, and her quick replies flashed back under the light of her smile. By acting, however, as if Miss Wildmere were never in her thoughts, except when in some way obtruded upon them, she gave the keenest wound. The flattered girl enjoyed being envied, hated, and even detested by her own sex, but to be politely ignored was a new and unwelcome experience, and she chafed under it, not so secretly but that Graydon observed her annoyance.

After a rest they started on again, he with Miss Wildmere falling to the rear. Before Madge passed around a curve in the path she saw a lily on a bank above her, and with the aid of her alpenstock sprang upon the mossy shelf, plucked the flower, and leaped down with an effort so quick and agile that it seemed like the impulse of a bird to get something and pass on. She put the flower in her belt, and a moment later was hidden from view.

"I hope you observed that feat," Miss Wildmere remarked. "Indeed, Miss Alden appears inclined to call attention to her feet this morning."

"I hope the ladies will observe them," he replied; "the gentlemen will, for they are pretty. Did you not note that her boots are adapted to walking? You could climb with twice the ease if your heels were not so high. For mountain scrambling a lady needs short skirts, and boots like those that Miss Alden wears. You should see the English girls walking in the Alps. It's my good-fortune, however, that you are partially disabled this morning. Here's a steep place. Take my arm and put all the weight upon it you can—the more the better. Lean on me as if you trusted me."

There was a slight frown on her brow, as he began his speech, but it soon passed, and she said, softly, as she still lingered, "Well, I'm not an athlete. I should value more a man's strong arm than strength of my own."

"You know that the arm of one man is ever at your service."

"'Ever' implies more patience than any man possesses."

"I should think so; yet you will find me reasonably patient."

"Everything is a matter of reason with men."

"Our reason assures us that certain things are a matter of the heart with women. Therefore we hope."

"Men are much too exacting. They reason a thing out and make up their minds. If they base any hopes on women's hearts, they should remember what unreasoning organs they are—full of hesitations, doubts, absurd fears, and more absurd confidence at times. Have you ever seen a bird hovering in the air, not knowing where to alight? Give it time, and it makes its selection and swiftly follows its choice. No good hunter rushes at it in the hope of capturing it during the moment of indecision."

"Indeed, Miss Wildmere, if I understand your little parable, I think Mr. Arnault errs egregiously, yet he does not frighten the bird into a very distant flight."

"You do not know how distant it is."

"No; I only see that he goes straight for the bird the moment he sees her."

"He might have found a more considerate policy wiser." Then she added, gravely, with a little reproach in her voice: "Mr. Arnault is an old friend and a friend of papa's, whom he often favors in business. I think my manner toward you should prove that I am not inclined to be disloyal toward old friends. You have just defended Miss Alden against a little feminine spite on my part. That was nice. In the same way I defend Mr. Arnault, whom, for reasons equally absurd, you do not altogether like. I'm only a woman, you know, and a little spite is one of our prerogatives. After all, it doesn't amount to anything. I would do as much for Miss Alden as for any one in the house." (Quite true, which was nothing.) "You know how girls are."

"Certainly, especially when both are reigning belles."

"The men are always the rulers sooner or later; and I shall give my allegiance to those gentlemen friends who are the least like myself—tolerant, patient, you know. Mr. Arnault is coming to-night to spend the Fourth. I must give him more or less of my time—I should be ungrateful if I did not—but I don't wish you to feel toward me or him as I should toward you and Miss Alden if I saw that you were together a great deal. How you see how frank I am, and what a compliment I pay to your masculine superiority."

"Miss Wildmere, I think I understand you; I hope I do. Your manner of greeting me on my return from long absence proved that you were not disloyal to one old friend. If you could keep me in mind for years, I can hope I am not forgotten during the hours when others have claims upon you. I have ever kept you in mind, and I might say more. If women have a little natural spite, men in some situations are endowed with enormous selfishness, and the bump of appropriation grows almost into a deformity."

"I never expect to see deformities of any kind in Graydon Muir," she said, laughing. "Now that we understand each other so well, give me your hand and pull me up this steep place before which we have stood so long, while getting over another little steep place that lay in our path. I'm glad the others have all gone on, for now you can help me all you choose, and I shan't care."

He did help her, with a touch and freedom that grew into something like caresses. He felt that he had revealed himself almost as completely as if he had spoken his love, and that he had received and was receiving more than encouragement. She did not rebuke his manner, which was that of a lover. There was no committal in that, nothing that could bind her. She permitted the avowal of his hope, that he had been in her thoughts during his long absence, and the natural inference that her hand was still free because of his hold upon her heart. This belief filled him with gratitude, and inspired him, as she intended it should, with generous thoughts and impulses toward her. What if she did prefer to maintain a little longer the delicate half reserve that precedes a positive engagement? It only insured that the cup of happiness should be sipped and enjoyed more leisurely. She had seen too much of life, and enjoyed too many of its pleasures, to act with precipitation now. She understood him, and yet loved him well enough to be jealous of one whom she believed that he regarded as a sister. With amusement he thought: "She is not even that to me now. Hanged if I know what she is to me beyond a pretty, vexatious puzzle!"

Miss Wildmere's strategy had accomplished one thing,

however. Believing that he was absolved by Madge's course from everything beyond cordial politeness, he had resolved to carry out her rival's wishes. It was no great cross to forego Madge's society, and if Miss Wildmere saw that he was not consoling himself during the hours she spent with Arnault, she would shorten them in his behalf.

After reaching a certain point he suggested: "Instead of scaling that rocky height after the rest of the party, suppose we follow this grassy wood-road to parts unknown. It will be easier for you than climbing, and you are better society than a crowd."

She assented smilingly, and Madge did not see Graydon again until they met at dinner.

She was pale, and looked weary. "Oh," she thought, "perhaps my hopes are already vain! They have been alone all the morning. He may have spoken; he looks so happy and content that he must have spoken and received the answer he craved. If so, I shall soon join the Waylands in my native village, for I can't keep up much longer without a little hope."

"You are tired, Madge," he said, not unkindly.

"A little," she replied, carelessly. "A short nap this afternoon will insure my being ready for the hop to-night."

CHAPTER XV

PERPLEXED AND BEGUILED

Madge was so discouraged that she contented herself with a manner of listless apathy during dinner, and then retired to her room. Graydon was giving her so little thought that there was slight occasion for disguise, and less incentive for effort to interest him.

"The struggle promises to be short and decisive," she moaned. "Perhaps it has been already decided. I had no chance after all. He came here fully committed in his own thoughts to Miss Wildmere. I have merely lost my old place in his affection, and have had and shall have no opportunity to win his love. If this is to be my fate it is well to discover it so speedily, and not after weeks of torturing hope and fear. I'll learn the truth with absolute certainty as soon as possible, and then find a pretext to join the Waylands."

At last the fatigue of the morning brought the respite of sleep, and when she waked she found late evening shadows in her room, and learned that Mr. Muir had arrived, it being his purpose to spend the Fourth and the remainder of the week with his family.

Weariness and despondency are near akin, and in banishing

one Madge found herself better able to cope with the other. At any rate, she determined to show no weakness. If Graydon would never love her he should at least be compelled to respect and admire her, and he should never have cause to surmise the heart-poverty to which she was doomed. Still less would she give her proud rival a chance to wound her again. Miss Wildmere might make Graydon's devotion as ostentatious as she pleased, but should never again detect on Madge's face a look of pained surprise and solicitude.

She made a careful toilet for the evening, telling Mr. Muir and her sister not to wait for her, as she had overslept herself.

"Where is Madge?" Graydon asked, at the supper-table.

"She did not wake up in time to come down with us," Mrs. Muir replied. "What does it matter? Miss Wildmere so fills your eyes that you see no one else. When is it to be, Graydon?"

"Madge evidently sees quite as much of me as she cares to," he replied, somewhat irritably. "I have not asked when it's to be or whether it's to be at all. I suppose," he added, satirically, "that in consideration of my extreme youth I should obtain permission from my family before venturing to ask anything."

"That remark is absurd and uncalled for," Mr. Muir replied, gravely. "Of course you will please yourself, as I did, and we shall make the best of it. But you have no right to expect that we shall see the lady with your eyes. I cannot help seeing her as she is. I do not like her, but if you choose to marry her, rest assured I shall give neither of you cause for complaint. Now, according to my custom, I've had my say. You could not expect me, as your brother, to be indifferent; still less could I pretend an approval that I don't feel; but I recognize that you are as free as I was when Mary's suitor, and I do not think you can reasonably ask more. Our relations are too intimate for misunderstanding. You know that, in my present plans and hopes, I looked forward to receiving you as a partner at no distant time, if such purposes are carried out our interests must always be identical."

"Pardon me, Henry," said Graydon, warmly, "and do not misunderstand my hasty words. I know you have my best welfare at heart—you have ever proved that—but you misjudge my choice. Even Mary begins to see that you do, and woman's insight is keener than man's. You attribute to the daughter the qualities you dislike in the father. Is it nothing that she has waited for me during my long absence, when she could pick and choose from so many?"

"I'm not sure she has been waiting for you; her manner toward Mr. Arnault yonder suggests that she may still pick and choose."

"Bah! I'm not afraid of him. She could have taken him long since had she so wished."

Others who had seats at the table now approached, and prevented further interchange of words on so delicate a subject. Nevertheless Mr. Muir's arrow had not flown wide of the mark, and Graydon thought that Miss Wildmere was unnecessarily cordial toward his rival, and that Mr. Wildmere, who had also come from the city, was decidedly complacent over the fact.

Graydon's furtive observation was now cut short by the entrance of Madge, and even he was dazzled by a beauty that attracted many eyes. It was not merely a lovely woman who was advancing toward him, but a woman whose nature was profoundly excited. What though she moved in quiet, well-bred grace, and greeted Mr. Muir with natural cordiality? The aroused spiritual element was not wanting in the expression of her face or in the dignity of her carriage. Her deep, suppressed feeling, which bordered on despair; her womanly pride, which would disguise all suffering at every cost, gave to her presence a subtle power, felt none the less because intangible. It was evident that she neither saw nor cared for the strangers who were looking their curiosity and admiration; and Graydon understood her barely well enough to think, "Something, whatever it may be, makes her unlike other girls. She was languidly indifferent at dinner; now she is superbly indifferent. This morning and yesterday she was a gay young girl, eager for a mountain scramble or a frolic of any kind. How many more phases will she exhibit before the week is over?"

Poor Madge could not have answered that question herself. She was under the control of one of the chief inspirations of feeling and action. Moods of which she had never dreamed would become inevitable; thoughts which nothing external could suggest would arise in her own heart and determine her manner.

In ceasing to hope one also ceases to fear, and Graydon admitted to himself that he had never before felt the change in Madge so deeply. The weak, timid little girl he had once known now looked as if she could quietly face anything. The crowded room, the stare of strangers, were simply as if they were not; the approach of a thunder-gust in the sultry evening was unheeded; when a loud peal drowned her voice, she simply waited till she could be heard again, and then went on without a tremor in her tones, while all around her people were nervous, starting, and exclaiming. There was not the faintest suggestion of high tragedy in her manner. To a casual observer it was merely the somewhat proud and cold reserve of a lady in a public place, while under the eyes of a strange and miscellaneous assemblage. Graydon imagined that it might veil some resentment because he had been so remiss in his attentions. He could scarcely maintain this view, however, for she was as cordial to him as to any one, while at the same time giving the impression that he was scarcely in her thoughts at all.

Mr. Muir was perplexed also, and watched her with furtive admiration. "If she cares for Graydon's neglect she's a superb actress," he thought. "Great Scott! what an idiot he is, that he cannot see the difference between this grand woman and yonder white-faced speculator! She actually quickens the blood in my veins to-night when she fixes her great black eyes on me."

Graydon felt her power, but believed that there was nothing in it gentle or conciliatory toward himself. Probably her mood resulted from a proud consciousness of her beauty and the triumphs that awaited her. She had been young and gay heretofore with the other young people, but now that a number of mature men, like Arnault, had appeared upon the scene, she proposed to make a different impression. The embodiment of her ideal might be among them. "At any rate," he concluded, "she has the skill to make me feel that I have little place in either her imaginings or hopes, and that for all she cares I may capture Miss Wildmere as soon as I can. Both of us probably are so far beneath her ideals of womanhood and manhood that she can never be friendly to one and is fast losing her interest in the other. She has already virtually said, 'Our relations are accidental, and if you marry Stella Wildmere you need not hope that I shall accept her with open arms as inseparable from one of my best friends.' 'Best friend,' indeed! Even that amount of regard was a lingering sentiment of the past. Now that we have met again she realizes that we have grown to be comparative strangers, and that our tastes and interests lie apart."

Thus day after day he had some new and perturbed theory as to Madge, in which pique, infused with cynical philosophy and utter misapprehension, led to widely varying conclusions. Ardent and impatient lover of another woman as he was, one thing remained true—he could neither forget nor placidly ignore the girl who had ceased to be his sister, and who yet was not very successful in playing the part of a young lady friend.

When the dancing began, the storm was approaching its culmination. More vivid than the light from the chandeliers, the electric flashes dazzled startled eyes with increasing frequency. Miss Wildmere at first tried to show cool indifference in the spirit of bravado, and maintained her place upon the floor with Mr. Arnault and a few others. She soon succumbed, with visible agitation, as a thunderous peal echoed along the sky. Madge danced on with Graydon as if nothing had occurred. He only felt that her form grew a little more tense, and saw that her eyes glowed with suppressed excitement.

"Are you not afraid?" he asked, as soon as his voice could be heard. "See, the ladies are scattering or huddling together, while many look as if the world were coming to an end."

"The world is coming to an end to some every day," she replied.

"That remark is as tragic as it is trite, Madge. What could have suggested it?"

"Trite remarks cannot have serious causes."

"Account for the tragic phase, then."

"I'm in no mood for tragedy, and commonplace does not need explanation."

"What kind of mood are you in to-night, Madge? You puzzle me;" and he looked directly into her eyes. At the moment she was facing a window, and a flash of strange brilliancy made every feature luminous. It seemed to him that he saw her very soul, the spirit she might become, for it is hard to imagine existence without form—form that is in harmony with character. The crash that followed was so terrific that they paused and stood confronting each other. The music ceased; cries of terror resounded; but the momentary transfiguration of the girl before him had been so strange and so impressive that Graydon forgot all else, and still gazed at her with something like awe in his face. Her lip trembled, for the nervous tension was growing too severe. "Why do you look at me so?" she faltered. "What has happened? Is there danger?"

"What *has* happened, Madge, that I cannot understand you? The electric gleam made you look like an angel of light. Your face seemed light itself. Are you so true and good, Madge, that such vivid radiance brings out no stain or fear? What is it that makes you unlike others?" Instinctively he looked toward Miss Wildmere. Her face was buried in her hands, and Mr. Arnault was bending over her with reassuring words.

Madge felt her self-control departing. "Mary is afraid in a thunderstorm," she said, in a low tone. "I'll go to her. She does not find me so puzzling;" and she hastened away, yet not so swiftly but that he saw her quivering lip and look of trouble.

He took a few impulsive steps in pursuit, then hesitated and walked irresolutely down a hallway, that he might have a chance for further thought. The alarm and confusion were so great that the little episode had been unnoted. It had made an impression on Graydon, however, that he could not shake off readily.

Emotion, if forced, has little power except to repel, but even a glimpse of deep, suppressed feeling haunts the memory, especially if its cause is half in mystery.

Madge had set her heart on one thing, had worked long and patiently for its attainment, had hoped and prayed for it, and within the last few hours was feeling the bitterness of defeat. The event she so dreaded seemed inevitable, even if it had not already occurred. The expression on Graydon's face when she had first met him after his long ramble with Miss Wildmere had been that of a tranquilly happy lover, whose heart was at rest in glad certainty. Why should he not have spoken? what greater encouragement could he ask than the favor she herself had seen? During his long absence another girl had apparently been waiting for him also, "But not working for him," she sighed, "and keeping herself aloof from all and everything that would render her less worthy. While I sought to train heart, body, and soul to be a fit bride, she has dallied with every admirer she met, and now wins him without one hour of self-denial or effort. It is more bitter than death to me. It is cruelty to him, for that selfish girl will never make him happy. Even after he marries her he will be only one among many, and the ballroom glare will be more to her than the light of her own hearth."

Such thoughts had been in Madge's mind, and self-control had been no easy matter. When to all had been added the excitement of the storm and his unexpected words, her overstrained nerves gave way. She was too desperately unhappy for the common fear which temporarily overwhelmed many—the greater swallows up the less—but the storm had led to words that both wounded and alarmed her. Why did she so perplex him? What had the lightning's gleam revealed, to be understood when he should think it all over? Could the truth of her love, of which she was so conscious, be detected in spite of her efforts and disguises? Was she doomed, not only to failure and an impoverished life, but also to the humiliation of receiving a lifelong, yet somewhat complacent pity from Graydon, and possibly the triumphant scorn of her rival?

With these thoughts surging in her mind she locked herself in her room and sobbed like the broken-hearted girl she felt herself to be. The passing storm was nothing to her. A heavier storm was raging in her soul, nor had it ceased when the skies without grew cloudless and serene. She at last felt that she must do something to maintain her disguise. Hearing little Jack crying and Mrs. Muir trying to hush him, she washed her eyes and went to the partially darkened room where the child was, and said, "Let me take him, Mary, and you go down and see Henry."

"It's awfully good of you, Madge. The children have been so frightened that I've been up here all the evening. You seem to have better luck in quieting Jack than any of us."

"He'll be good with me. Go down at once, and don't worry. You have hardly had a chance to see Henry."

"You will come down again after Jack goes to sleep?"

"Yes, if I feel like it."

Graydon soon discovered Mrs. Muir after she had joined her husband, and asked, "Where is Madge?"

"She has kindly taken the baby so that I can spend a little time with Henry. The children have been frightened, and Jack is very fretful. I'm tired out, and don't know what I should do if it wasn't for Madge."

"Why can't the nurse take him?"

"He won't go to her in these bad moods. Madge can quiet him even better than I. What's the matter that you are so anxious to see Madge? You have seemed abundantly able to amuse yourself without her the last few days. Is Mr. Arnault in the way to-night?"

"As if I cared a rap for him!" said Graydon, turning irritably away.

He did care, however, and felt that Miss Wildmere was making too much use of the liberty she had provided for. She, like many others, could be half hysterical while the violence of the storm lasted, and yet, when quiet was restored, was capable of making a jest of her fears and the most of a delightful conjunction of affairs, which placed two eligible men at her beck, to either of whom she could become engaged before she slept. The arrival of her father had turned the scale decidedly in favor of Mr. Arnault, for the latter, without revealing his transaction with Mr. Muir, had whispered to Mr. Wildmere his conviction that Henry Muir was borrowing at ruinous interest. This information accorded with the broker's previous knowledge, and he was eager that his daughter should decide for Arnault at once.

This, however, the wilful girl would not do. She enjoyed the present condition of affairs too well, and was not without hope, also, that her father was mistaken; for she felt sure, from Graydon's manner, that he was not aware of his brother's financial peril, and this fact inclined her to doubt its existence. She was actuated by the feeling that she had given much time and encouragement to Graydon, and that now Arnault should have his turn. Madge had been invisible since the storm, and there was nothing to indicate that Graydon was disposed to give her much thought. Miss Wildmere's natural supposition was that he and Madge had been like brother and sister once, and that the form of the relation still existed, but that in their long separation they had grown somewhat indifferent toward each other. She believed that the solicitude she had seen in Madge's face, on the evening so memorable in the latter's experience, was due to the jealousy of an immature, sickly girl, who had been so humored as to feel that Graydon belonged to her. She naturally believed that if there had been anything beyond this, it would have been developed by correspondence, or else indifference on both sides would not now be so palpable. She disliked Madge chiefly as a rival in beauty and admiration. Nothing could be more clear than that Graydon was completely under the spell of her own fascination, and that Madge was receiving even scant fraternal regard. All she feared was, that during the process of keep him "well in hand" he might become more conscious of Madge's attractions, which she recognized, however much she decried them openly. Even if compelled by circumstances to accept Arnault, she proposed to herself the triumph of rejecting Graydon, and thought she could do this so skilfully as to give the idea that he had made a deep impression on her heart, and so eventually win him again as one of her devoted followers in the future. This product of fashionable society had not the slightest intention of giving up her career as a belle for the sake of Mr. Arnault or any one else. She had more liking and less fear for Graydon than for Arnault. The latter was an open, resolute suitor, but she knew that he was controlled more by ambition than by affection—that he would yield everything and submit to anything up to a certain point. The moment she jeopardized his prestige before the world, or interfered with his scheme of success, she would meet rock-like obduracy, both before and after marriage. She knew that Graydon had a sincere affection for her, and a faith in her which, even in her egotism, she was aware was unmerited—that he had a larger, gentler, and more tolerant nature, and would be easier to manage than Arnault.

Her fear of the latter proved his best ally. There was a resolution in his eye since his return this evening that, even while it angered her somewhat, convinced her that he would not be trifled with. His suit was that of a man who had an advantage which she dared not ignore, and her father's manner increased this impression. She felt that her game was becoming delicate and hazardous, but she would not forego its delicious excitement, or abandon the hope that Graydon might still be in a position to warrant her preference. Therefore she proposed to yield to Arnault as far as she could without alienating Muir, hoping that the former would soon return to town again, and thus more time be secured for her final decision.

Before the first evening of his rivals advent had passed, Graydon felt that he must appear to the people in the house as supplanted, and his pride was beginning to be touched. Mrs. Muir's words had added to his irritation. The episode with Madge had left a decidedly unpleasant impression. He felt not only that he had failed to understand her, but that he might be treating her with a neglect which she had a right to resent. Her appearance and manner during the storm had almost startled him; her abrupt departure had caused sudden and strong compunction; and he had wished that they might come to a better understanding; but thoughts of her had soon given place to anxiety in regard to Miss Wildmere. It began to seem strange that the girl who had apparently waited for him so long, and who had permitted such unequivocal words and manner on his part that day, should now, before his very eyes, be accepting attentions even more unmistakable from another man. She had tried to explain and prepare him for all this, but there was more than he was prepared for. She not only danced oftener with Arnault than with any one else, but also strolled with him on the dusky piazza, which, by reason of the dampness due to the storm, was almost deserted. Graydon had permitted his brow to become clouded, and was so perturbed by the events of the evening that he had not disguised his vexation by gallantries to others. At last he detected smiles and whispered surmises on the part of some who had seen his devotion before the arrival of Mr. Arnault. This almost angered him, and he felt that Miss Wildmere had imposed a role that would be difficult to maintain.

He had lingered conspicuously near, intent on proving his loyalty, and had hoped every moment that his opportunity would come. He felt that she should at least divide her time evenly with him and Mr. Arnault, but the evening was drawing to a close, and the latter had received the lion's share. After noting that others were observing his desolation, he went resolutely out on the piazza, with the intention of asking Miss Wildmere to give him the last waltz. Its wide space was deserted. He waited a few moments, thinking that the object of his thoughts would turn the corner in her promenade with his rival. Time passed, and she did not come. He looked through a parlor window, thinking that she might have entered by some other means of ingress; and while he was standing there steps slowly approached from a part of the piazza which was usually in utter darkness, and which was known as the "lovers' retreat." As the figures passed a lighted window he recognized them, and was also observed. He was too angry and jealous now to carry out his purpose, and returned to the general hallway.

Here he was joined a moment later by Miss Wildmere and

Mr. Arnault, and the former began to chat with him in imperturbable ease, while the gentleman bowed and sought another partner for the waltz that was about to be danced. Graydon would not show his chagrin under the many eyes directed toward them, but she nevertheless saw his anger in the cold expression of his eyes, and realized her danger. She ignored everything with inimitable skill and sweetness, and there was nothing for him to do but take her out with the others. Indeed, it almost instantly became his policy to convince observers that their surmises were without foundation. He determined that the girl should show him all the favor his rival had enjoyed, or else—A sudden flash of his eyes indicated to his observant companion that all her skill would be required. She was graciousness itself, and when Arnault could not observe her, stole swift and almost pleading glances into her partner's eyes.

Another observed her, however. Madge did come down at last, for she had concluded that the memorable day should not close until she had had one more glimpse of the problem which had grown so dark and hopeless. Graydon soon observed her standing in the doorway, but then she was talking and laughing with a lady friend. A moment later she glided out on the floor with one of a half dozen who had been waiting for the favor. Graydon sought to catch her eye, but did not succeed. Again she made upon his mind the impression of troubled perplexity, but his purpose was uppermost, and he was bent on carrying it out.

"Come," he said to Miss Wildmere, in quiet tones, "I should enjoy a stroll on the piazza, the room has grown so warm and close."

Feeling that she must yield, she did so with ready grace and apparent willingness, and Graydon led her out through the main entrance, that it might be observed that he received no less favor than had been given to another.

"She is playing them both pretty strong," whispered one of the committee, before referred to, that sits perpetually on the phases of life at such resorts.

"I feared you would not be very patient," said Miss Wildmere, in a low tone.

"I said I would be reasonably patient," was the reply.

"Reason again."

"Yes, Miss Wildmere; I think I can justly say that I am endowed with both heart and reason. There are some questions in life that demand both."

"Please do not speak so coldly. You do not understand."

"I wish I did."

"Be patient and you will. After maintaining friendship true and strong for years, it hurts me to be misjudged now."

"But, Miss Wildmere—" he began, impetuously.

"Hush," she said, hastily; then added, a little coldly, "if I am not worthy of a little trust I am not worthy of anything."

Graydon was touched to the quick. Honorable himself, he felt that he was acting meanly and suspiciously—that his jealousy and irritation were leading him to unmanly conduct. There was some reason for her course, which would be explained eventually, and he ought not to ask a woman to be his wife at all unless he could trust her. Therefore he said, humbly. "I beg your pardon. In my heart I believe you worthy of all trust. I will wait and be as patient as you desire, since I know that you cannot have failed to understand me." Then he added, with a deprecating laugh, "There are times, I suppose, when all men are a little blind and unreasonable."

"Heaven keep him blind!" she thought, yet she winced under his honest words in their contrast with herself.

"I hope some day to prove worthy of your trust," she breathed, softly, and looked in dread into the darkness lest in some way her words should reach Arnault. "Come, please," she added, with a gentle pressure on his arm, "let us return, or the hotel may be closed upon us."

"Please give me all the time you can," pleaded Graydon, as they paused at the door.

Looking within, she saw Arnault with his back toward them, and said, hastily, and as if impulsively, "I will—all that I can. Possibly my regret will be deeper than yours that I cannot give you more."

"You should know that that is not possible," he said, in low, earnest tones. Then he added, in a whisper, as she was entering, "I can trust you now and wait."

"My good fortune is still in the ascendant," was her thought; "I can still keep him in hand, in spite of papa and Mr. Arnault."

"Her father's relations with Mr. Arnault must give him some hold upon her," he thought, "and for her father's sake she cannot yield to me at once, but she will eventually."

Mr. Arnault came forward with smiling lips, light words, yet resolute eyes. Graydon felt that he had received all the assurance that he needed—that she was under some necessity of keeping his rival in good-humor—so he smiled significantly into her eyes, and bowed himself away.

"Muir looked as if he had received all the comfort that he required," Arnault said, as they strolled across the parlor, now deserted.

"Did he? Well, he did not require very much."

"How much?"

"You had better ask him."

"Stella," he said, and there was a suggestion of menace in his tone, "I'm in earnest now. You will soon have to choose between us."

"Shall I?" she replied, bending upon him an arch, bewildering smile. "Then please don't speak as if I had no choice at all;" and she was going.

"Wait," he said. "Will you drive with me to-morrow?"

"Yes. Is there anything else your lordship would like?"

He seized her hand, and held it in both his. "This," he said.

"Is that all?" was her laughing reply, as she withdrew it. "I wish you had more of Mr. Muir's diffidence;" and she vanished before he could speak again.

Graydon found that Madge had retired, so that there was no chance for him to speak to her that night; but his mind was in too happy a tumult to give her much thought.

CHAPTER XVI

DECLARATION OF INDEPENDENCE

Mrs. Muir came into Madge's room for a bit of the gossip that she dearly loved, but, as usual, obtained little information or surmise from the young girl. "I'm glad you came down," she said, "if only to prove to Graydon that you were not moping upstairs."

"Why should I mope upstairs?" Madge asked, with a keen look at her sister.

"No reason that I know of, only Graydon has been slightly spoiled by his success among ladies, and society men are always imagining that girls are languishing for them."

"Have I given him or anyone such an impression?" Madge again inquired, indignantly.

"Oh, no, indeed! On the contrary, you seem so indifferent as not to be quite natural. Even Graydon feels it, and is perplexed and troubled. He was inquiring for you during the evening, and I told him you were kindly caring for Jack, so that I might have a little fresh air with Henry on the piazza."

"There it is again—perplexed and troubled. I'm sick of being misunderstood so ridiculously. The scraps of time that he gives me when Miss Wildmere does not fill his eyes and thoughts are employed in criticism. Why should I perplex and trouble him? I have told him to please himself with Miss Wildmere—that I should certainly please myself in my choice of friends, and that he as a man assuredly had a right to do the same. He will soon be engaged to her, and probably is already, but he has no right to demand that I should receive this girl with open arms. She already detests me, and I do not admire her. It's none of my business, but if I were a man I wouldn't stand her flirtation with Mr. Arnault. Even the people in the house are observing it with significant smiles. He must get over the impression that I'm the weak, limp child in mind or body that he left. I'm an independent woman, and have as much right to my thoughts and ways as he to his. If he wants my society, let him treat me with natural friendliness. If he's afraid to do it—if Miss Wildmere won't let him—rest assured I won't receive any furtive, deprecatory attentions. I am abundantly able to take care of myself in my own way."

"Oh, Madge, you have so changed! Before you went away the sun seemed to rise and set in Graydon."

"Well, the sun now rises in the west and sets in the east—What am I saying? Well, perhaps, it's true for me, after all. In the West I gained the power to live a strong, resolute life of my own choosing, and he may as well recognize the truth first as last. Let him give all his thoughts to Miss Wildmere. From what I see and have heard she will keep them busy before and after marriage."

"He's not engaged to her yet; he said so positively."

"Oh, well," Madge replied, with well-assumed indifference, although her heart bounded at the tidings, "it's only a question of time. There, we've talked enough about *her*. Of course I remember Graydon's old kindness, and all that; and if he would treat me with frank and sensible friendliness, I should enjoy his society. Why not?"

"I thought he regarded you as his sister."

"Sister, indeed! I'm Henry's sister, not his. I'm only an object of criticism, of perplexity, a sphinx, and all that kind of nonsense. He was bent on seeing a 'little ghost,' as he used to call me. I'm not a bit of a ghost, and have as much proud blood in my veins as he has."

"Well, Madge, I'm glad you feel that you are Henry's sister. He likes and admires you so much that I'm half jealous."

"Henry and I understand each other. He thinks I'm sensible, and I certainly think he is. Good-night, now, dear. It's after twelve, and I wish you a merry Fourth of July; I mean to have one."

Graydon had not found himself in a sleeping mood until the shadows of night were almost ready to depart, and so came down very late. Mrs. Wildmere, who was on the piazza with her child, informed him, with a deprecatory smile, that Stella had gone to drive with Mr. Arnault. He bit his lip, and went to make a leisurely breakfast. By the time he had finished, Madge came in with a party of young people who had been on a ramble. Her greeting was friendly, but nothing more, and having received a long letter from Mrs. Wayland, she took it to a small summer-house. Graydon soon strayed after her in a listless way, and in no very amiable humor. The greater anxiety had swallowed up the less, and his perturbed thoughts about Madge were now following a light carriage on some wild mountain road. His generous glow of feeling of the night before had passed somewhat, and he was inclined to think that Miss Wildmere's relations to Arnault, whatever they were, placed him, a committed lover, in a rather anomalous position. Since she was absent, however, he would while away an hour with Madge, and try to solve the riddle she had become.

She greeted him with a slight smile, and went on with her letter. He watched her curiously and with contracting brow.

"Will you ever finish?" he soon asked.

"I can read it some other time," she said, laying it down.

"Oh, that is asking far too much!"

"Is it?"

"Confound it, Madge! Why is it that we are drifting further and further apart every day?"

"I am not drifting," she said, quietly, "nor do you give that impression. I am just where you found me on your return. Since we are so far apart you must be doing the journeying."

"Well, Heaven knows I found you distant enough!"

"I beg your pardon; Heaven knows nothing of the kind! It's not my fault that you value friendship so lightly."

"You know I wished for so much more."

"You thought you did at first, Graydon," she replied, with a quiet smile, "but I imagine that you soon became quite reconciled to my view of the case. The relation would surely prove embarrassing to you. Haven't you since thought that it might?" she asked, with sweet directness.

He colored visibly, and was provoked with himself that he did. "If you persist in being at swords' points with Miss Wildmere—" he began, hesitatingly.

"I persist in being simply myself, and true to my own perceptions. Wherein have I failed in courtesy toward Miss Wildmere?"

"But you dislike her most cordially."

"And you like her most cordially and more. Have I not granted your perfect right to do so?"

"If you were even the friend you claim to be, you would not be so indifferent."

"I have not said I was indifferent. Miss Wildmere is far from indifferent to me. What have I done to gain her ill-will?"

"Much, as human nature goes. You have made yourself her rival in beauty and attractiveness."

"Is that human nature? If that is the cause of her hostility I should say it is Miss Wildmere's nature."

"Let us change the subject," said Graydon, a little irritably. "We shall not agree on this point, I fear; you share in Henry's prejudices."

"I did not introduce the subject, Graydon, and I think for myself."

"Hang it all, Madge! you are so changed I scarcely know you. Every time we meet I find you more of a conundrum. Friend, indeed! You certainly have been a distant one in every sense. If I had been the friend you say I was, you would have written me about the marvellous transformation you were accomplishing."

She sprang up, and her dark eyes flashed indignantly. "I am beginning to think that you are changed more than I," she said, impetuously. "You know, or might, if you took the trouble, that I did not tell Mary, my own sister, of my progress toward health and strength. My wish to give you all a pleasant surprise may seem a little thing to you, or you may give some sinister, unnatural meaning to the act. It was not a little thing to go away 'a ghost, a wraith,' as you were wont to call me—it was not a little thing to go away alone, perhaps to die, as I then felt. Nor was it a little thing to battle for weary months with weakness of mind and body, morbid timidity, indolence, ignorance, and everything that was contrary to my ideal of womanhood. I can say thus much in self-defence. Was there harm in my adding some incentive to a hard sense of duty? I felt that if I could change for the better and keep my secret I could give you all a glad surprise. I had almost a child's pleasure in the thought. Mary and Henry rewarded me, but you are spoiling it all. You at once make an impossible demand, and discover, within twenty-four hours, how awkward my compliance would have been. I did not know you so long without gaining the power of guessing your thoughts. I suggested a simple, natural relation, and as the result I have become a 'conundrum.' A charming title, truly! I shall remain a simple, natural girl, and when you are through with your riddle theories perhaps you will treat me as I think you might in view of old times;" and she started swiftly toward the house.

"Madge!" cried Graydon, springing up and following her.

At that moment Miss Wildmere approached, and Madge gained the piazza and disappeared, leaving Graydon ill disposed toward himself and all the world, even including

Miss Wildmere; for she had a charming color, and appeared not in the least a victim to *ennui* because of forced association with an objectionable party. She came smilingly toward him, saying, "It's too bad to interrupt your hot pursuit of another lady, but girls have not much conscience in such matters."

"As long as you have conscience in other matters, it does not signify," he answered, meaningly.

"Not conscience, but another organ, controls our action chiefly, I imagine," she replied, with a glance that gave emphasis to her words of the previous evening, and she passed smilingly on.

Arnault soon followed her, spoke pleasantly to Graydon, and, having obtained a morning paper, was at once absorbed in its contents.

"He does not appear like a baffled suitor who has enjoyed only a veiled tolerance," was Graydon's thought. "Things will come out all right in the end, I suppose, but they certainly are not proceeding as I expected. Stella will be mine eventually—it were treason to think otherwise—but she is carrying it off rather boldly to keep Arnault so complacent at the same time. As far as Madge is concerned, I've been a fool and made a mess of it. How in the mischief has she been able to divine my very thoughts! She is wrong in one respect, however. If she had felt and acted toward me like a sister I would have been loyal to her, and would have compelled even Miss Wildmere to recognize her rights. I am not so far gone but that I can act in a straightforward, honorable way. My acceptance of her action was an afterthought, a philosophical way I have of making the best of everything. I now believe that it has turned out for the best, but I have been guilty of no coldblooded calculation.

Very well, I'll treat her as a simple, natural girl and my very good friend, and see how this course works. Not that she is a simple girl. I've met too many of that kind, and of those also who enshroud themselves in a cloud of little feminine mysteries, all transparent enough to one of experience; but Madge does puzzle me. She has not explained herself with her fine burst of indignation. Jove! how handsome she was! She ever gives the impression that there is something back of all she says and does. Even Henry feels it in his dim way, but that lightning flash made it clear that it is something of which she need not be ashamed. Since she has learned to read me so understandingly, I will try to fathom her thoughts. Perhaps friendship does mean more to her than to others. If so, I'll be as true a friend to her as she to me. If I grant Stella such broad privileges with Arnault, she must admit mine with one of whom it would be absurd to be jealous;" and, with cogitations like the above, he also pretended to read his paper, and finished his cigar.

CHAPTER XVII

NOT STRONG IN VAIN

Graydon dreaded embarrassment when meeting Madge at dinner, but was agreeably disappointed. There was nothing in the young girl's manner which suggested a vexed consciousness of their recent interview, neither were there covert overtures, even in tones, toward more friendly relations. He saw that if any were made he must make them. Madge was merely too well bred to show anger in public, or occasion surmises that would require explanations. During the meal she spoke of missing her horseback exercise, and said that she meant to ask Dr. Sommers if he did not know of a good animal that might be hired for a few weeks. Graydon at once resolved to make a propitiatory offering, and to go out with Madge when Miss Wildmere was unattainable. For the time he was content to imitate Madge's tactics, and acted as if he intended to follow the course that she had suggested. The fact that Arnault was so evidently enjoying his dinner and the Wildmere smiles did not detract from his purpose to prove that he also was not without resources. Moreover, he felt that he had not treated Madge fairly; he had been truly fond of her, and now was conscious of a growing respect. As she had said, it was not a little thing that she had attempted and accomplished, and there had been small ground for his discontent. After dinner, however, he found a chance to ensconce himself by Miss Wildmere on the piazza, and he was fully resolved to lose no such opportunities.

Madge, with the Muir children, passed him on the way to a small lake on which she had promised to give the little people a row. He took off his hat in cordial courtesy, and she recognized him with a brief smile, in which Miss Wildmere could detect no apprehension.

"I hope that 'sister Madge,' as you call her, does not resent my enjoyment of your society."

"Not in the least. I feel, however, that I have been neglecting her shamefully, and propose to make amends."

"Indeed; has she brought you to a sense of your short-comings? This scarcely bears out your first remark."

"It is nothing against its truth. Miss Aldeu makes it very clear that she is not dependent on me or any one for enjoyment; but in view of the past I have been scarcely courteous. Therefore," he added, with a laugh, "when Arnault monopolizes you I shall console myself with Madge."

"And therefore I shall feel the less compunction. Thank you."

"I am glad to take the least thorn from the roses of your life," was his smiling answer.

She veiled close scrutiny under her reply: "I fear the brilliant Miss Alden will cause my society to appear commonplace in contrast."

"I do not see how you can fear anything of the kind," was his prompt answer; "I trust you, and you must trust me."

"I do trust you, Mr. Muir," she said, softly.

Before he could speak again nurses and children came streaming and screaming from the lake toward the house. "Nellie Wilder is drowned," was the burden of their dire message.

Graydon sprang down the steps, and rushed with the fleetness of the wind toward the lake.

As Madge, with Jennie and Harry Muir, approached the water, they saw a party of children playing carelessly in a boat, and a moment later a little girl fell overboard. The boat was in motion toward the shore, and when she rose it had passed beyond her reach. Her companions gave way to wild panic, and, instead of trying to save her, screamed and pulled for land. No one was present except nurses and other children, and they all joined in the wild, helpless chorus of alarm, and began a stampede toward the hotel.

Madge saw that if the child was saved she must act promptly and wisely. To the Muir children she said, authoritatively, "Sit down where you are and don't move." Then she rushed forward and unfastened a skiff. As she did so the child rose for the last time and sunk again with a gurgling cry. Keeping her eyes fixed on the spot, and with an oar in her hand, Madge pushed away from the shore vigorously with her feet, and with the impetus sprang upon the narrow stern-sheets, then crept forward toward the bow, at the same time ever keeping her eyes fixed unwaveringly on the spot where the child had sunk, from which widening circles were eddying. The nurses and children who had not started for the house, seeing that a rescue was attempted, looked on with breathless dread and suspense.

When the impetus that Madge had first given to the skiff ceased, she kept the little craft in motion by paddling, first on one side, then on the other, her eyes still fixed on one point in the dark water. At last this point seemed almost beneath her; she dropped the oar, stooped, and peered over the side of the boat. After a moment's hesitation she appeared to those on shore to have lost her balance, fallen overboard, and sunk. Renewed screams of terror resounded, and the Muir children fled toward the hotel, crying, "Aunt Madge is drowned."

"What do you mean?" Graydon gasped, seizing Harry by the arm.

"Oh, Uncle Graydon! run quick. Aunt Madge fell out of a boat under water."

A moment later he saw the young girl rise to the surface with a child in her grasp. With one headlong plunge, and a few strong strokes, he was at her side, exclaiming, "Great God, Madge! what does this mean?"

"Take her to the shore, quick; no matter about me;" and she pushed the limp and apparently lifeless form into his arms.

"But, Madge—" he began.

"Haste! haste! and the child may be saved. Don't think of me; I can swim as well as you;" and she struck out toward the shore.

Wondering and thrilled with admiration, in spite of the confusion of his thoughts, he did as directed, and took the child to land at once.

Madge was there as soon as he, crying, even before she left the water, "Run for Dr. Sommers, and if not at home ride after him."

Meanwhile gentlemen and employes of the house were arriving, and some turned back in search of the physician.

The awful tidings had come upon poor Mrs. Wilder, the mother of the child, like a bolt out of a clear sky, and she had run screaming and moaning toward the scene of disaster. Mother love had given her almost superhuman strength; but when she saw the pale little face on the ground, with the hue of death upon it, she crouched beside it in speechless agony, and watched the efforts that were made to bring back consciousness.

Madge led and directed these efforts. In truth, she did as much to save the child on land as when it had lain submerged on the muddy bottom of the pond. Graydon, seeing that she was coming up the bank, had paused a moment irresolutely, and then was about to start for the hotel with his burden. Madge caught his arm, and took the child from him.

"Graydon, take off your coat and give it to me," she said, imperatively, as she laid the child down on its back; "your handkerchief, also," she added.

She forced open the pale lips, and wiped out the mouth with marvellous celerity, paying no heed to the clamorous voices around her. "Some one give me a sharp knife," she cried, "and don't crowd so near."

Lifting the child's clothing at the throat, she cut it down ward to the waist, then down each arm, leaving the lovely little form exposed and free. Dropping the knife, she next rolled the coat into a bundle, turned the child over so that her abdomen should rest upon it; then with hands pressed rather strongly on each side of the little back, Madge sought to expel the water that might have been swallowed. Turning the child over on her back again, the bundle made by the coat was placed under the small of her back, so as to raise the chest. Then, catching the little tongue that had awakened merry echoes but a few moments before, she drew it out of the mouth to one side by the aid of the handkerchief, and said to Graydon, "Hold it, so."

All now saw that they were witnessing skilled efforts. Discordant advice ceased, and they looked on with breathless interest.

"Has any one smelling salts?" Madge asked. There was no response. She snatched a bit of grass and tickled the child's nose, saying, at the same time, "Bring water." This, after a few seconds, she dashed over the face and exposed chest, waited an instant, then gave her patient a slap over the pit of the stomach.

Graydon, kneeling before her, looked on with silent amazement. Her glorious eyes shone with an absorbed and merciful purpose; she was oblivious of her own strange appearance, the masses of her loosening hair falling over and veiling the lovely form outlined clearly by the wet and clinging drapery of her summer dress. Others looked on in wonder, too, and with a respect akin to awe. Among them were her sister and Henry Muir, Mr. Arnault, and Miss Wildmere—her feelings divided between envy and commiseration for the child and its stricken mother.

These first simple efforts having no apparent effect, Madge said, quietly, "We must try artificial respiration. Move a little more to one side, Graydon."

Kneeling behind the child, she lifted the little arms quickly but steadily up, over and down, until they lay upon the ground behind the wet golden curls. This motion drew the ribs up, expanded the chest and permitted air to enter it. After two or three seconds Madge reversed the motion and pressed the arms firmly against the chest, to expel the air. This alternate motion was kept up regularly at about the rate of sixteen times a minute, until the sound of a galloping horse was heard, and the crowd parted for Dr. Sommers. He took in the situation with his quick eye, and said, "Miss Alden, let me take your place."

"Oh, thank God, you are here!" she exclaimed. "Let me hold her tongue, Graydon; I must do something."

"Yes, Mr. Muir," added the physician; "let her help me; she knows just what to do. How long was the child under water?"

"I don't know exactly; not long."

"Not more than four or five minutes?"

"I think not."

"There should be hope, then."

"We must save her!" cried Madge. "I once saw people work over an hour before there were signs of life."

"Oh, God bless your brave heart!" murmured the poor mother. "You won't leave my child—you won't let them give her up, will you?"

"No, Mrs. Wilder, not for one hour or two. I believe that your little girl will be saved."

"Have some brandy ready," said Dr. Sommers.

A flask was produced, and Graydon again knelt near, to have it in readiness, while the doctor kept up his monotonous effort, pressing the arms against the lungs, then lifting them above the head and back to the ground, with regular and mechanical iteration.

The child's eyelids began to tremble. "Ah!" exclaimed the doctor; a moment later there was a slight choking cough, and a glad cry went up from the throng.

"The brandy," said the doctor.

Madge now gave up the case to him and Graydon, and slipped down beside the mother, who was swaying from side to side. "Don't faint," she said; "your child will need you as soon as she is conscious."

"Oh, Heaven bless you! Heaven bless you!" cried the mother; "you have saved my only, my darling."

"Yes, madam, you are right. It's all plain sailing now," the doctor added.

Then Madge became guilty of her first useless act. In strong revulsion she fainted dead away. In a moment her head was on Mrs. Muir's lap, and Henry Muir was at her side.

"Poor girl! no wonder. There's not a woman in a hundred thousand who could do what she has done. There, don't worry about her. Put her in my carriage with Mrs. Muir, and take her to her room; I'll be there soon. She'll come out all right; such girls always do."

Meanwhile Mr. Muir and Graydon were carrying out the

doctor's directions, and the unconscious girl was borne rapidly to her apartment, where, under her sister's ministrations, she soon revived.

Almost her first conscious words, after being assured that the child was safe, were, "Oh, Mary! what a guy I must have appeared! What will Graydon—I mean all who saw me—think?"

"They'll think things that might well turn any girl's head. As for Graydon, he is waiting outside now, half crazy with anxiety to receive a message from you."

"Tell him I made a fool of myself, and he must not speak about it again on the pain of my displeasure."

"Well, you have come to," said Mrs. Muir, and then she went and laughingly delivered the message verbatim, adding, "Go and put on dry clothes. You'll catch your death with those wet things on, and you look like a scarecrow."

He departed, more puzzled over Madge Alden than ever, but admitting to himself that she had earned the right to be anything she pleased.

Dr. Sommers continued his efforts in behalf of the little girl, chafing her wrists and body with the brandy, and occasionally giving a few drops until circulation was well restored; and then, at her mother's side, carried the child to her room, and gave directions to those who were waiting to assist.

When he entered Madge's apartment, she greeted him with the words, "What a silly thing I did!"

"Not at all, not at all. You made your exit gracefully, and

escaped the plaudits which a brave girl like you wouldn't enjoy. I take off my hat to you, as we country-folks say. You are a heroine—as good a doctor as I on shore and a better one in the water. Where did you learn it all?"

"Nonsense!" said Madge, "nothing would vex me more than to have a time made over the affair. It's all as simple as a, b, c. What's that little pond to one who has been used to swimming in the Pacific! As I said, I saw a girl restored once, and Mr. Wayland has explained to me again and again just what to do."

"Oh, yes, it's all simple enough if you know how, but that's just the trouble. In all that crowd I don't believe there was one who would not have done the wrong thing. Well, well, I can manage now if I'm obeyed. You've had a good deal of a shock, and you must keep quiet till to-morrow. Then I'll see."

Madge laughingly protested that nothing would please her better than a good supper and a good book. "Please give out also," she said, "that any reference to the affair will have a very injurious influence on me."

In spite of the doctor, messages and flowers poured in. At last Mrs. Wilder came and said to Mrs. Muir, "I must see her, if it is safe."

"It's safe enough," Mrs. Muir began, "only Madge doesn't like so much made of it."

"I won't say much," pleaded the mother. She did not say anything, but put her arms around Madge and pressed her tear-stained face upon the young girl's bosom in long, passionate embrace, the hastened back to her restored treasure, who was sleeping quietly. Madge's eyes were wet also, and she turned her face to the wall and breathed softly to herself, "Whatever happens now—and it's plain enough what will happen—I did not get strong in vain. Graydon can never think me altogether weak and lackadaisical again, and I have saved one woman's heart from anguish, however my own may ache."

CHAPTER XVIII

MAKE YOUR TERMS

Graydon's uppermost thought now was to make his peace with Madge. He dismissed all his former theories about her as absurd, and felt that, whether he understood her or not, she had become a splendid woman, of whose friendship he might well be proud, and accept it on any terms that pleased her. He also was sure that Miss Wildmere's prejudices would be banished at once and forever by Madge's heroism, believing that the girl's hostile feeling was due only to the natural jealousy of social rivals. "If Stella does not regard Madge's action with generous enthusiasm, I shall think the worse of her," was his masculine conclusion.

The wily girl was not so obtuse as to be unaware of this, and when he came down she said all he could wish in praise of Madge, but took pains to enlarge upon his own courage. At this he pooh-poohed emphatically. "What was that duck-pond of a lake to a man!" he said. "Madge herself has become an expert ocean-swimmer, I am told. She wasn't afraid of the water. It was her skill in finding the child beneath it, and in resuscitation afterward, that chiefly commands my admiration."

"Oh, dear!" cried the girl, "what can I do to command

your admiration?"

"You know well, Miss Wildmere, that you command much more."

She blushed, smiled, and looked around a little apprehensively.

"Don't be alarmed," he added; "I have such confidence in you that I will bide your time."

"Thank you, Graydon," she whispered, and hastened away, leaving him supremely happy. It was the first time she had called him "Graydon."

Seeing Dr. Sommers emerging from the hotel, he hastened after him, bent on procuring a peace-offering for Madge—the finest horse that could be had in the region.

"I know of one a few miles from here," said the doctor. "He's a splendid animal, but a high and mighty stepper. I don't believe that even she could manage him."

"I'll break him in for her, never fear. Of course I won't let her take any risks."

"Well, leave it to me, then. I can manage it. He's awfully headstrong, though. I give you fair warning."

"Take me to see him as soon as you can; the horse, I mean, or, rather, both man and horse."

"To-morrow morning, then. I have patients out that way."

At supper and during the evening Madge and her exploit were the themes of conversation. Some tried to give Graydon a part of the credit, but he laughed so contemptuously at the idea that he was let alone. Henry Muir did not say much, but looked a great deal, and with Graydon listened attentively as his wife explained how it was that Madge had proved equal to the emergency.

"Why don't more people follow her example?" said the practical man, "and learn how to do something definite? As she explains the rescue, there was nothing remarkable in it. If she could swim and dive in the ocean for sport, she would not be much afraid to do the same in that so-called lake, to save life. As to her action on shore, the knowledge she used is given in books and manuals. What's more, she had seen it done. But most people are so pointless and shiftless that they never know just what to do in an emergency, no matter what their opportunities for information may have been."

"Now you hit me," Graydon remarked, ruefully, "Left to myself I should have finished the young one, for I was about to run to the hotel with her, a course that I now see would have been as fatal as idiotic."

"Madge says," Mrs. Muir continued, "that they used to bathe a great deal, and that Mr. Wayland explained just what should be done in all the possible emergencies of their outdoor life at Santa Barbara."

"Wayland in a level-headed man. If he is bookish, he's not a dreamer with his head in the clouds. Madge was in good hands with them, and proves it every day."

"I think she shows the influence of Mrs. Wayland even more than that of her husband. Fanny is a very accomplished woman, and saw a great deal of society in her younger days."

"Confound it all! Why didn't you tell me that Madge had

been living with two paragons?" said Graydon.

"Oh, you have been so occupied with another paragon that there has not been much chance to tell you anything," was Mrs. Muir's consoling reply.

"Madge has not been made what she is by paragons," Mr. Muir remarked, dryly. "She made herself. They only helped her, and couldn't have helped a silly woman."

"It's time you were jealous, Mary," said Graydon, laughing.

"Mary isn't a silly woman. I should hope that no Muir would marry one."

"I see no prospect of it," was the rather cold reply.

"I fear I see a worse prospect," was his brother's thought. "Of what use are his eyes or senses after what he has seen to-day?"

Mrs. Muir had explained to some lady friends about Madge, and the information was passing into general circulation—the ladies rapidly coming to the conclusion that the young girl's action was not so remarkable after all, which was true enough. The men, however, retained their enthusiastic admiration, although it must be admitted that its inspiration was due largely to Madge's beauty.

"Of course women have done braver things," said one man, with sporting tendencies, "but it was the neat, gamy way in which she did it that took my eye. Her method was as complete and rounded out as herself. Jove! as she bent over that child she was a nymph that would turn the head of a Greek."

"She has evidently turned the head of a Cyprian," laughed one of his friends.

"Come, that's putting it too strong," said the man, with a frown. "I'll affect no airs, though. I'm not a saint, as you all know, but the aspect of that girl, in her self-forgetful effort, might well make me wish I were one. She is as good and pure-hearted as the child she saved. If there had been a flaw in the white marble of her nature she would have been self-conscious. An angel from heaven couldn't have been more absorbed in the one impulse to save."

Graydon had approached the group unobserved, and heard these words. He walked away, smiling, with the thought, "My sentiments, clearly expressed."

The night was warm, and he saw Miss Wildmere and Arnault going out for a stroll. Following a half-defined inclination, he bent his steps toward the lake. The moon was mirrored in its glassy surface, the place silent and deserted. With slight effort of fancy he called up the scene again. He saw in the moonlight the fairy form of the child, and what even others had regarded as the embodiment of human loveliness and truth bending over it.

"And she was the little ghost that once haunted me," he thought, "and seemed all eyes and affection. How those eyes used to welcome and turn to me, as if in some subtle way she drew from me the power to exist at all. I wish I could follow the processes of her change from the hour of our parting, and see how I passed from what I was to her to what I am now. She does not seem to forget or ignore the past. She is not conventional, and never was; hence, friendship may not mean what it does to so many of her sex and age—a little moony sentiment blended with calculation as to a fellow's usefulness. If we could enjoy something of the good-comradeship that obtains between man and man, she is the one woman of the world with whom I should covet the relation. Stella, in herself, is all that I could ask for a wife, but I don't like her family much better than Henry does. Confound the father! Why should he so mix his daughter up in his speculation that she dare not dismiss Arnault at once and follow her heart? If I were not a good-natured man I wouldn't submit to it. As it is, since I am sure of the girl, I suppose I should give *paterfamilias* a chance to turn himself. She has appealed to me as delicately, yet as openly, as she can, and has given me to understand by everything except plain words that she is mine. Probably that is all she can do without bringing black ruin upon them all. Well, I suppose I should imitate her self-sacrificing spirit; but I hate this jumbling of Wall Street with affairs of the heart. It angers me that she must play with that fellow for financial reasons, and that he, conscious of power, may use language which she would not dare to resent. I can't imagine Madge in such a position. Yet, who knows? As the French say, 'It is the unexpected that happens,' and this has proved true enough in my experience. I'll go and see how Madge is now, and be as penitent as she requires. I don't mind being tyrannized over a little by such a girl;" and he returned.

As he approached Mrs. Muir's door he heard the sound of voices and laughter, and plainly those of his brother and Madge. In response to his knock Mrs. Muir opened the door a little way, and he caught a glimpse of Henry.

"Well?" said Mrs. Muir.

"It's not well at all," he began, in an aggrieved tone. "Here's a family party, and I'm shut out in outer darkness. What have I done to be banished from Rome?"

"'What's banished but set free?'" trilled out Madge. "Oh,

Graydon, I'm not fit to be seen!"

"How can I know that unless I see you?"

"Nonsense, Madge!" expostulated her sister, "you look charming. Why put on airs? As he says, it's a family party. Let him join in our fun;" and, without waiting for further objections, she brought him in and gave him a chair.

"Now this warms an exile's heart," he began. "If you had shut the door on me I should have asked Henry to send me back to Europe. Mary's right, Madge; you do look charming."

And so she did, blushing and laughing in her dainty wrapper, with her long hair falling over her shoulders and fastened by a ribbon.

"How comes it that you are in such a deserted and disconsolate condition?" cried Mary.

"I am not in such a condition. Since crossing your threshold I have become contentment itself. Indeed, I regard myself as the most favored man in the house, for I, first of all, am able to lay my homage at Madge's feet."

"Let me warn you from the start that it will prove a stumbling-block in both our paths," said the girl. "Did you not receive my message? But, then, it's stupid to think you will ever consider me."

"I have been considering you a great deal more than you think, especially since you metaphorically boxed my ears this morning, and took away my breath generally this afternoon."

"You seem to have plenty left."

"Oh, I'm recovering. Reason is trying to scramble back on her throne. I've been out to the lake alone in the moonlight, and have had the whole scene over again, to assure myself that it was real."

"What! You have not been in the water?"

"No; I was content to moon it out on the shore; but it seemed to me that I saw you as clearly there as here."

"Little wonder! I must have been the most extraordinary looking creature that ever prowled in these wilds."

"You were; only lookers-on did all the devouring. I wouldn't dare tell you the compliments I have heard."

"You had better not, if your reason is even within sight of her throne. When the danger was all over I caught a mental glimpse of myself, and fell over as if shot;" and a slow, deep crimson stole into her face.

"Madge," said Graydon, gravely and almost rebukingly, "do you think there was a man present who did not reverence you? I was proud even of your acquaintance."

Her face softened under his words, but she did not look at him. "We were partners in misery," she said, laughing softly; "I have a vague remembrance that you were as great a guy as I was."

"I shall be glad to be a guy with you in any circumstances you can imagine, if you will let me make my peace, and will forgive my general stupidity. Be reasonable also, as well as merciful. If it took you over two years to make such changes, you should give me a few days to rub my eyes and get them focused on the result."

Madge was now laughing heartily. "I don't believe a man could ever eat the whole of a humble pie," she said. "He ever insists that the donor, especially if she be a woman, should have a piece also."

"There, now," cried Graydon, ruefully; "give me all of it, and make your terms."

"Solomon himself couldn't have advised you better," said Madge, while Henry leaned back in his chair and laughed as if immensely amused, while Mary improved the occasion by remarking, "When will men ever learn that that is the way to get the best terms possible from a woman?"

"Indeed!" said Graydon. "How you enlighten me! Well, Madge, I'm the more eager now to learn your terms."

She felt that it was a critical moment—that there was, under their badinage, a substratum of truth and feeling—and that she had now a chance to establish relations that would favor her hope, if it had a right to exist at all, and render future companionship free from surmise on the part of her family.

"Come, Graydon," she said, "we have jested long enough, and there is no occasion for misunderstanding. I have not forgotten the past any more than you have, nor all your unstinted kindness for years. As Mary says, this is a family party. I'm not your sister, and embarrassment always accompanies an unnatural relation. The common-sense thing to do is to recognize the relation that does exist. As I intimated at first, I see no reason why we should not be the best of friends, and then, imitating the stiff-necked Hebrews, do what seemeth good in our eyes."

"And these are your terms, Madge?"

"As far as I have any, yes. I don't insist on anything, but warn you that I shall follow my eyes, and consult a very wilful little will of my own."

"Will your wilful will permit you to accept of a horse that I am going after in the morning? Dr. Sommers told me about him, and I had proposed to make him a peace-offering."

Madge clapped her hands with the delight of a child.

"Oh, Graydon, that's splendid of you! I've been sighing, 'My kingdom for a horse,' ever since I came here. But he's no peace-offering. I forgave you when I saw your headlong plunge into the lake. You went into it like a man, while I flopped in so awkwardly that all said I had fallen overboard."

"Shake hands, then."

She sprang up and joined hands with him in frank and cordial grasp, saying, "It's all right now, and Mary and Henry will understand us as well as we do ourselves."

"One condition: you will let me ride with you?"

"When you are disengaged, yes," was her arch reply, "and I'll prove that on horseback I can be as good a comrade as a man."

"Well, if something I've dreamt of is true I never saw such acting," thought Henry Muir. Then he said, quietly, "Madge, how did you find the child so surely and quickly?"

"That accounts for my awkwardness somewhat," she replied, laughing. ("How happy she looks!" he thought.) "I never took my eyes from the spot where I had last seen the child sink, and I had to do everything as if my head was in a vise.

Don't let us talk about it any more."

"No, nor about anything else," said Mary, rising. "I'm proving a fine nurse, and am likely to be lectured by the doctor to-morrow. You men must walk. Here is Madge flushed, feverish, and excited about a horse. Brain-fever will be the next symptom."

An hour later Madge was sleeping quietly, but the happy flush and smile had not left her face. She felt that she had at last scored one point. Oh, that she could have more time!

"Jupiter!" muttered Graydon, as he descended the stairs, "her talk makes a fellow's blood tingle."

Miss Wildmere had just entered with Arnault, and Graydon asked, "Are you not going to give me one dance this evening?"

"Yes, two, if you wish," she replied, sweetly.

He took her at her word, and was as devoted as ever. He had no thought of being anything else. Arnault secured the last word, however, and Graydon made no effort to prevent this. He had accepted the disagreeable situation, and proposed, although with increasing reluctance and discontent, to let the girl have a clear field and manage the affair as she thought wise under the circumstances. He was too proud to have maintained a jostling and open pursuit with Arnault in any event, and now, believing that he understood the lady better, felt that there was no occasion for it He had indicated to her just where he stood, and just where she could ever find him. When her diplomacy with Arnault should cease to be essential to her father's safety, the final words could be spoken.

He acted on this policy so quietly that she was somewhat troubled, and feared that Madge might be taking too large a place in his thoughts. Therefore, when Arnault ventured to make a somewhat humorous reference to the young girl's appearance, her spite found utterance. "I never saw such a looking creature in my life. She had the appearance of a crazy woman, with her hair dishevelled, and her wet, muddy clothes sticking to her as if glued. She ought at least to have slipped away when the doctor came. But instead of that she fainted—all put on, I believe, to attract attention."

"She perhaps felt that she must put on something," chuckled Arnault. "The two Muirs looked as if she were too precious and sacred for mortal gaze."

"Well," concluded Miss Wildmere, "I like to see a lady who never forgets herself;" and she was an example of the type.

"I like to see one lady, whom, having seen, no one can forget," was his gallant reply.

CHAPTER XIX

AN OBJECT FOR SYMPATHY

Miss Wildmere's indignant virtue was not soothed on the following morning, when, as she returned from a drive with Arnault, Graydon galloped up on a superb bay horse, and Madge so far forgot herself again as to rush to meet him with unaffected pleasure. The champion of propriety paused in the distance to take an observation, for she thought she saw a cloud in the sky.

"What a beauty! what a grand arch of the neck he has! Oh, I'm just wild to be on him! Don't bribe me with horses, Graydon; I can resist anything else."

"I am glad of the information. A volume of thanks would not be worth half so much."

"I thought the thanks were in my tone and manner."

"So I thought, and am more than content; but, Madge, I am troubled about your riding him. I fear he is a very Satan of a horse."

"Nonsense! Wait till you see me mounted, and your fears will vanish. People don't walk at Santa Barbara; they ride;

every one rides. If the horse don't tumble, there'll be no tumbling on my part. Oh, he is such a splendid fellow! What shall I call him?"

"Better call him 'Go.' There is more go in him than in any horse I ever bestrode."

"All the better. I shall give him another name, however. It will come to me sometime;" and she patted the proud neck, and fondled the tossing head, in a way to excite the envy of observers from the piazza. "Oh, Graydon, what shall I do for a saddle? Do you think there is one to be had in this region? I'm impatient for a gallop."

"I telegraphed, early this morning, for equipments; and they should be here this afternoon."

"That was considerate kindness itself. You must let me pay for all this. You know I can."

"So can I."

"But there's reason in all things."

"Therefore, a little in me. Please, Madge, don't make me feel that I am almost a stranger to you. If we had remained together, I should have paid out more than this for candy, flowers, and nonsense. I have yielded everything, haven't I? and, as Mary says, I do wish to feel a little like one of the family."

"Well, then," she said, laughing and blushing, "as from one of the family—"

"And from your deceased brother," he interrupted.

She put her finger to her lips. "That's past," she said. "No more allusions. We began sensibly last night, and I certainly am very lenient now in taking gifts that I should protest against even from Henry. I wish to prove to you that I am the Madge of old times as far as I can be."

"Rest assured I'm the same fellow, and ever shall be."

He had dismounted, and they were walking slowly toward the stable. "Bless me!" cried Madge, "where am I going with no better protection than a sunshade? I'm always a little off when a horse like that is at hand. I say, Graydon," she added, in a wheedling tone, "mount and put him through his paces. I can't resist the fun, no matter what the dowagers say."

He vaulted lightly into the saddle, and the horse reared and dashed toward the stable, but was soon pulled up. Then Graydon made him prance, curvet, and trot, Madge looking on with parted lips, and eyes glowing with delicious anticipation. If a close observer had been present he might have seen that the rider, with his fine easy grace and mastery, was, after all, the chief attraction.

She walked back to the house, thinking, "I'll have some bright hours before the skies grow gray. Oh, kindly fate! prosper Mr. Arnault here and in Wall Street, too, for all I care."

"Oh, Mr. Muir, teach me to ride," said Miss Wildmere, when he joined her in the deserted parlor. "You have such a superb horse! and you sat on him as if you were a part of him."

"I will teach you with pleasure," said Graydon. "Nothing would give me more enjoyment, for I am very fond of riding, and we could explore the mountain roads far and near."

"Can I ride your horse?"

"That was not my horse. He belongs to Miss Alden."

"Oh, indeed," began Miss Wildmere, hastily, yet coldly; "I wouldn't think of it, then."

"She would lend him to you readily, if it were safe; but only an expert should ride that horse. As it is, I shall run him four or five miles before I let her mount him. He is awfully high-strung and a little vicious. I'll get you a quiet, safe lady's horse, suitable for a beginner. You will soon acquire confidence and skill. I wouldn't have you incur any risks for all the world."

"Wouldn't you?" she asked, with a fascinating and incredulous smile.

"You know well that I would not."

"I shall scarcely know what I know when I see you galloping away with Miss Alden."

"Come, Miss Stella, we may as well get through with that phase of the question at once. Madge Alden came into our family when I was scarcely more than a boy, and she but a child. She is still one of the family. The idea of your being concerned about her makes me smile audibly. I only wish you girls would be good friends. It would save awkwardness and embarrassment. Madge is a sister to me in everything but name, and ever will be. I'm proud of her, as I ought to be, and a distant manner would be absurd toward a member of our household. Why should I affect it when I'm truly fond of her jolly good company? Don't you think I am setting you a good example? I'm patient over your good times with Mr. Arnault, who is an open suitor."

"I have not said they were good times."

"Nor have you said they were not. He evidently enjoys them, and little wonder. You can make any fellow have a good time without trying. I don't pretend to understand the necessity of your being so friendly, or tolerant, or what you will, with him; neither do I pry or question. My regard for you makes trust imperative. I do trust you as readily as you should trust me. What else can we do till times are better?"

"What do you mean by saying, 'till times are better?'" she asked, in gentle solicitude. "Are you having a hard time in town, like poor papa?"

"Oh, bless you! no. I don't suppose Henry is making much. He's the kind of man to take in sail in times like these. I'm not in the firm yet, you know, but shall be soon. My foreign department of the business is all right. I left it snug and safe. Of course, I don't know much about things on this side of the water yet. Mr. Muir is not the kind of man to speak to any one about his affairs unless it is essential, but if anything were amiss he would have told me. I know the times are dismal, and I am better off on my assured salary than if in the firm now. No one but 'bears' are making anything."

"I hope your brother isn't in anxiety, like papa," she said, warmly.

His quick commercial instinct took alarm, and he asked, "What, have you heard anything?"

"Oh, no indeed. Papa says that Mr. Muir is one of the most conservative of men; but he also says that there is scarcely a chance now for any honest man, and that investments which once seemed as solid as these mountains are sinking out of sight. If it wasn't so we shouldn't be so worried. He wouldn't like it if he knew I was talking to you in this way; but then I know it will go no further, and naturally my mind dwells on the subject of his anxieties. What wouldn't I do to help him!" she concluded, with a fine enthusiasm.

"I think you are doing a great deal to help him, Stella," he said, gravely and gently; "and, believe me, it involves no little sacrifice on my part also."

"But you have promised to be patient, Graydon."

"I have, but you cannot think that I like it or approve of the diplomacy you are compelled to practice, even though your motive be unselfish and filial. I don't think you ought to be placed in such a position, and would that it were in my power to relieve you from it!"

Tears of self-commiseration came into her eyes, and they appeared to him exceedingly pathetic. She made as if she would speak but could not, then retreated hastily to her room. Once in seclusion she dashed the drops away, her eyes glittered with anger, and she stamped her foot on the floor and muttered: "It is indeed an abominable position. I might accept Graydon any day, any hour, now, and dare not. Yet if he gets an inkling of my real attitude he'll be off forever. He is as proud as Lucifer about some things, and would be quick as a flash if his suspicions were aroused. Even the belief that I am humoring Arnault for papa's sake tests his loyalty greatly. If I have to refuse him at last I shall be placed in an odious light. The idiots! why can't they find out whether Henry Muir is going to fail or not! That horrid Madge Alden is not his sister, and knows it, and she is gaining time to make impressions. I know how she felt years ago, when she was a perfect spook. I don't believe she's changed. With all her impulsive ways she's as deep as perdition, and she'd flirt with him to spite me, if nothing more. Papa said last night that I had better accept Arnault. I won't accept him till I must, and he'll rue his success if he wins it." Then the mirror reflected a lovely creature dissolved in tears.

Again she soliloquized: "I can't accept a horse from Graydon; Arnault would never submit to it. The receiving of such a present would compromise me at once. It does not matter so much what I say or look in private; this proves nothing to the world, and I see more and more clearly that Arnault will not permit his pride to be humiliated. He will endure what he calls a fair, open suit philosophically, but the expression of his eyes makes me shiver sometimes. Was ever a girl placed in such a mean and horrible position! I won't endure this shilly-shally much longer. If they can't prove something more definite against the Muirs, I'll accept Graydon. Papa is just horrid! Why can't he make more in Wall Street? There must be ways, and any way is as respectable as the one I may be compelled to take. Well, if I do have to accept Arnault I'll make Graydon think that I had to do so for papa's sake, and we'll become good friends again before long. Perhaps this would be the best way in the end, for papa looked wildly, and spoke of a tenement-house last night. Tenement! Great heavens! I'd sooner die."

CHAPTER XX

"VEILED WOOING"

"Graydon, when do you think I can have my first ride?" Madge asked at dinner, with sparkling eyes.

"At about five this afternoon. I have found a saddle that I can borrow in case yours does not come till the late train."

"Oh, I'm so glad that I've lost my appetite! You can't know how much a horse means to me. It was after I began to ride that I grew strong enough to hope."

"Why, Madge, were you so discouraged as that?" he asked, feelingly.

"I had reason to be discouraged," she replied, in a low tone. Then she threw back her head, proudly. "You men little know," she continued, half defiantly. "You think weakness one of our prerogatives, and like us almost the better for it. We are meekly to accept our fate, and from soft couches lift our languid eyes in pious resignation. I won't do it; and when a powerful horse is beneath me, carrying me like the wind, I feel that his strength is mine, and that I need not succumb to feminine imbecility or helplessness in any form."

"Brava, Madge!" cried Henry Muir.

"You were born a knight," added Graydon, "and have already made more and better conquests than many celebrated in prose and poetry."

"Oh, no," cried Madge, lifting her eyebrows in comic distress. "I was born a woman to my finger-tips, and never could conquer even myself. I have an awful temper. Graydon, you have already found that out."

"I have found that I had better accept just what you please to be, and fully admit your right to be just what you please," he answered, ruefully.

"What a lovely and reasonable frame of mind!" Mrs. Muir remarked. "Truly, Miss Wildmere is to be congratulated. You have only to stick to such a disposition, and peace will last longer than the moon."

"Oh, Miss Wildmere will prove a rose without a thorn," Madge added, laughing, while under Mr. Muir's eye her face paled perceptibly. "There will never be anything problematical in her single-minded devotion. She has been well and discreetly brought up, and finished by the best society, while poor me!—I had to fly in the face of fate like a virago, and scramble up the best I could in Western wilds. Oh, well, Graydon, don't be alarmed. I'll be a good fellow if you'll take me out riding occasionally."

He began to laugh, and she continued: "I saw you frown when I began my wicked speech. We'll tick off tabooed subjects, and make an *index expurgatorius*, and then we'll get on famously."

"No need of that," he said. "As far as *I* am concerned, please consider *me* fair game."

"Consider you fair game?" she said, with her head archly on one side. "That would be arrant poaching. Don't fear, Graydon, I shall never regard any man as game, not even if I should become a fat dowager with a bevy of plain daughters and a dull market."

Grave and silent Mr. Muir leaned back in his chair and laughed so heartily that he attracted attention at the Wildmere table across the room.

"That man doesn't act as if on the brink of failure," thought Miss Wildmere. "It's all a conspiracy of Arnault with papa."

"You are making game of me in one sense very successfully," Graydon admitted, laughing a little uneasily.

"Oh, in that sense, all men are legitimate game, and I shall chaff as many as possible, out of spite that I was not a man."

"You would make a good one—you are so devoid of sentiment and so independent."

"And yet within a week I think a certain gentleman was inclined to think me sentimental, aesthetic, intense, a victim of ideals and devotional rhapsodies."

"Oh, ye gods! Here, waiter, bring me my dessert, and let me escape," cried Graydon.

"Did you say I was to be ready at five?" she asked, sweetly.

"Yes, and bring down articles of a truce, and we'll sign them in red ink."

An hour later she heard the gallop of a horse, and saw him riding away. "She shan't mount the animal," he had thought, "till I learn more about him and give him all the running he wants to-day. She has a heavy enough score against me as it is, and I'll not employ another brute to make things worse."

He learned more fully what he had discovered before, that she would have her hands full in managing the horse, and he gave him a run that covered him with foam and tested his breathing. At four he galloped back to the station to see if the saddle had arrived, but found that even his skill and strength were not sufficient to make the animal approach the engine. Shouting to the baggage-man to bring the expected articles to the stable, he was soon there and made another experiment. A hostler brought him a blanket, which he strapped around his waist, and mounted again in a lady's style. It was at once evident that the horse had never been ridden by a woman. He reared, kicked, and plunged around frightfully, and Graydon had to clutch the mane often to keep his seat. Madge had speedily joined him, and looked with absorbed interest, at times laughing, and again imploring Graydon to dismount. This he at last he did, the perspiration pouring from his face. Resigning the trembling and wearied horse to a stable-boy, he came toward the young girl, mopping his brow and exclaiming: "It will never do at all. He is ugly as sin. No woman should ride him, not even a squaw."

"Bah, Graydon! he did not throw you, although he had you at every disadvantage. I'm not in the least afraid. Has the saddle come?"

"Yes; but I protest, Madge. Here, Dr. Sommers" (who was approaching), "lay your commands on this rash girl."

"If Dr. Sommers says I'm rash he doesn't understand my case, and I refuse to employ him," cried Madge. Then she added, sweetly: "If I break any bones, doctor, I'll be your very humble and obedient servant. It's half-past four, and I'll be ready as soon as you are, Graydon. No backing out. You might as well warn me against the peril of a rocking-chair;" and she went to put on her habit.

"Heaven help us!" said Graydon to the doctor. "We're in a scrape. She's so resolute that I believe she would go alone. What would you do? Hang it all! the people of the house have got an inkling of what's up; some are gathering near, and the windows are full of heads."

"Put the saddle on one of the quiet livery horses, and you ride this brute," said the doctor.

"You don't know her. She wouldn't stand that at all."

"Then give her her head. After yesterday I believe she can do what she undertakes. You have tired the horse out pretty thoroughly, and I guess she'll manage him."

Leaving orders to have Madge's horse sponged off and dried, and the best animal in the stable prepared for himself, he said, "Well then, doctor, be on hand to repair damages," and went to his room to change his dress.

The doctor did more. He saw that Madge's horse was saddled carefully, meanwhile admiring the beautiful equipment that Graydon had ordered. He also insured that Graydon had a good mount.

When at last the young man tapped at Madge's door she came out looking most beautiful in her close-fitting habit and low beaver, with its drooping feather. Mary followed her, protesting and half crying, and Mr. Muir looked very grave.

"Madge," said Graydon, earnestly, "I should never forgive myself if any harm came to you. That horse is not fit for you to ride."

"Good people, see here," said Madge, turning upon them; "I am not a reckless child, nor am I making a rash experiment. Even if I did not fear broken bones, do you think I would give you needless anxiety? Graydon has kindly obtained for me a fine horse, and I must make a beginning to show you and him that I can ride. If Mr. and Mrs. Wayland were here they would laugh at you. Don't come out to see me off, Mary. Others would follow, and I don't want to be conspicuous. I do wish people would mind their own business."

"No danger of my coming out. I don't want to see you break your neck," cried Mary, re-entering her room.

"You must let me go, Madge," said Mr. Muir, firmly. "I may have to interpose my authority."

"Yes, do come, for Heaven's sake!" said Graydon.

"Very well," laughed Madge. "If I once get on, you and the horse may both find it hard to get me off. Where are the horses?" she asked, upon reaching the door.

"You must yield one point and mount near the stable," said Graydon, resolutely.

"Oh, certainly, I'll yield everything except my ride."

Madge's horse stood pawing the ground, showing how obdurate and untamable was his spirit. She exclaimed at the beauty of the saddle and its housings, and said, "Thank you, Graydon," so charmingly that he anathematized himself for giving her a brute instead of a horse. "I should have satisfied myself better about him," he thought, "and have looked further."

In a moment she had the animal by the head, and was patting his neck, while he turned an eye of fire down upon her, and showed no relenting in his chafed and excited mood. Graydon meanwhile examined everything carefully, and saw that the bridle had a powerful curb.

"Well," said he, ruefully, "if you will, you will."

"Yes; in no other way can I satisfy you," was her quiet reply.

"Let us get away, then; spectators are gathering. You should be able to hold him with this rein. Come."

She put her foot in his hand, and was mounted in a second, the reins well in hand. The horse reared, but a sharp downward pull to the right brought him to his feet again. Then he plunged and kicked, but she sat as if a part of him, meanwhile speaking to him in firm, gentle tones. His next unexpected freak was to run backward in a way that sent the neighboring group flying. Instantly Madge gave him a stinging blow over the hind quarters, and he fairly sprang into the air.

"Get off, Madge," cried Mr. Muir, authoritatively, but the horse was speeding down the road toward the house, and Graydon, who had looked on breathlessly, followed. Before they reached the hotel she had brought him up with the powerful curb, and prancing, curvetting, straining side-wise first in one direction, then in the other, meanwhile trembling half with anger, half with terror, the mastered brute passed the piazza with its admiring groups. Graydon was at her side. He did not see Miss Wildmere frowning with vexation and envy, or Arnault's complacent observance. With sternly compressed lips and steady eye he watched Madge, that, whatever emergency occurred, he might do all that was possible. The young girl herself was a presence not soon to be forgotten. Her lips were slightly parted, her eye glowing with a joyous sense of power, and her pose, flexible to the eccentric motions of the horse, grace itself. They passed on down the winding carriage-drive, out upon the main street, and then she turned, waved her handkerchief to Mr. Muir, and with her companion galloped away.

Several of Mr. Muir's acquaintances came forward, offering congratulations, which he accepted with his quiet smile, and then went up to reassure his wife, who, in spite of her words to the contrary, had kept her eyes fastened upon Madge as long as she was in sight.

"Well," she exclaimed, "did you ever see anything equal to that?"

"No," said her husband, "but I have seen nothing wonderful or unnatural; she did not do a thing that she had not been trained and taught to do, and all her acts were familiar by much usage."

"I think she's a prodigy," exclaimed Mrs. Muir.

"Nothing of the kind. She is a handsome girl, with good abilities, who has had the sense to make the most and best of herself instead of dawdling."

After an easy gallop of a mile, in which Madge showed complete power to keep her horse from breaking into a mad run, she drew rein and looked at Graydon with a smile. He took off his hat and bowed, laughingly.

"Oh, Graydon," she said, "it was nice of you to let me have

my own way!"

"I didn't do it very graciously. I have seldom been more worried in my life."

"I'm glad you were a little worried," she said. "It recalls your look and tone at the time of our parting, when you said, 'Oh, Madge, do get well and strong!' Haven't I complied with your wish?"

"Had my wish anything to do with your compliance?"

"Why not?"

"What an idiot I've been! I fear I have been misjudging you absurdly. I've had no end of ridiculous thoughts and theories about you."

"Indeed! Apparently I had slight place in your thoughts at all, but I made great allowances for a man in your condition."

"That was kind, but you were mistaken. Why, Madge, we were almost brought up together, and I couldn't reconcile the past and the present. The years you spent in the far West, and their result, are more wonderful than a fairytale. I wish you would tell me about them."

"I will. Friends should be reasonably frank. What's more, I wish to show you how natural and probable the result, as you call it, has been. Your wondering perplexity vexes me. You know what I was when we parted."

"No, I don't believe I do, or you couldn't be what you are now."

"Well, I can tell you: I had weak lungs, a weak body, and a

weak, uncultured mind. I was weak in all respects, but I discovered that I had a will, and I had sense enough, as Henry says, to know that if I was ever going to be more than a ghost it was time I set about it. I knew of Mrs. Wayland's restoration to health in the climate of Santa Barbara, and I determined to try it myself. I couldn't have had better friends or advantages than the place afforded. But oh, Graydon, I was so weak and used up when I reached there that I could scarcely do more than breathe. But I had made up my mind either to get well or to die. I rested for days, until I could make a beginning, and then, one step at a time, as it were, I went forward. Take two things that you have seen me do, for example. One can bathe in the sea at Santa Barbara almost throughout the year. At first I was as timid as a child, and scarcely dared to wet my feet; but Mr. Wayland was a sensible instructor, and led me step by step. The water was usually still, and I gradually acquired the absolute confidence of one who can swim, and swims almost every day. So with a horse. I could hardly sit on one that was standing still, I was so weak and frightened; but with muscle and health came stronger nerves and higher courage. After a few months I thought nothing of a ten-mile gallop on the beach or out to the canons. I took up music in the same way, and had a thoroughly good teacher. He did the best he could for me, which wasn't so very much. I never could become a scientist in anything, but I was determined to be no sham within my limitations. I have tried to do some things as well as I could and let the rest go. Now you see how easily I can explain myself, and I only seem wonderful because of contrast with what I was."

"But where do I come in?" he asked, eagerly.

"Did you not say, 'Please get well and strong?' I thought it would gratify you and Mary and Henry. You used to call me a ghost, and I did not want to be a ghost any longer. I saw that you enjoyed your vigorous life fully, and felt that I might enjoy life also; and as I grew strong I did enjoy everything more and more. Two things besides, and I can say, 'All present or accounted for.' Mr. Wayland is a student, and has a splendid library. He coached me—that was your old college jargon—on books, and Mrs. Wayland coached me on society. So here I am, weighing a hundred and twenty pounds, more or less, and ready for another gallop;" and away she went, the embodiment of beautiful life.

"One more question, Madge," he said, as they slackened pace again. "Why wouldn't you write to me oftener?"

"I don't like to write letters. Mine to Mary were scarcely more than notes. Ask her. Are you satisfied now? Am I a sphinx—a conundrum—any longer?"

"No; and at last I am more than content that you are not little Madge."

"Why, this is famous, as Dr. Sommers says. When was a man ever known to change his mind before?"

"I've changed mine so often of late that I'm fairly dizzy. You are setting me straight at last."

Madge laughed outright, and after a moment said, "Now account for yourself. What places did you visit abroad?"

He began to tell her, and she to ask questions that surprised him, showing that she had some idea of even the topography and color of the region, and a better knowledge of the history and antiquities than himself. At last he expressed his wonder. "What nonsense!" she exclaimed. "You don't remember the little I did write you. As I said before, did you not at my request—very kindly and liberally, too, Graydon—send me books about the places you expected to see? A child could have read them and so have gained the information that surprises you."

They talked on, one thing leading to another, until he had a conscious glow of mental excitement. She knew so much that he knew, only in a different way, and her thoughts came rippling forth in piquant, musical words. Her eyes were so often full of laughter that he saw that she was happy, and he remembered after their return that she had not said an ill-natured word about any one. It was another of their old-time, breezy talks, only larger, fuller, complete with her rich womanhood. He found himself alive in every fibre of his body and faculty of his mind.

As they turned homeward the evening shadows were gathering, and at last the dusky twilight passed into a soft radiance under the rays of the full-orbed moon.

"Oh, don't let us hasten home," pleaded poor Madge, who felt that this might be her only chance to throw about him the gossamer threads which would draw the cord and cable that could bind him to her. "What is supper to the witchery of such a night as this?"

"What would anything be to the witchery of such a girl as this, if one were not fortified?" he thought. "This is not the comradeship of a good fellow, as she promised. It is the society of a charming woman, who is feminine in even her thoughts and modes of expression—who is often strangely, bewilderingly beautiful in this changing light. When we pass under the shadow of a tree her eyes shine like stars; when the rays of the moon are full upon her face it is almost as pure and white as when it was illumined by the electric flash. Did I not love another woman, I could easily imagine myself learning to love her. Confound it! I wish Stella had more of

Madge's simple loftiness of character. She would compel different business methods in her father. She would work for him, suffer for him, but would not play diplomat. I like that Arnault business to-night less than ever."

Mr. and Mrs. Muir were anxiously awaiting them on the piazza as they trotted smartly up the avenue. "It's all right," cried Graydon. "The horse has learned to know his mistress, and will give no more trouble."

"I wish you had as much sense," growled Muir, in his mustache; then added, aloud, "Come to supper. Mary could not eat anything till assured of your safety."

"Yes, Henry, I won't keep you waiting a moment, but go in with my habit on. I suppose the rest are all through, and I'm as ravenous as a wolf."

They were soon having the merriest little supper, full of laughing reminiscence, and Henry rubbed his hands under the table as he thought, "Arnault is off mooning with the speculator, and Graydon doesn't look as if the green-eyed monster had much of a grip upon him."

Miss Wildmere's solicitude would not permit her to prolong her walk with Arnault, and she returned to the parlor comparatively early in the evening. She found Graydon awaiting her, and he was as quietly devoted as ever. She looked at him a little questioningly, but he met her eyes with his quiet and assured look. When she danced with Arnault and other gentlemen he sought a partner in Madge or some other lady; and once, while they were walking on the piazza, and Miss Wildmere said, "You must have enjoyed yourself immensely with Miss Alden to have been out so long," he replied, "I did. I hope you passed your time as agreeably."

She saw that her relations with Arnault gave him an advantage and a freedom which he proposed to use—that she had no ground on which to find fault—and that he was too proud to permit censure for a course less open to criticism than her own.

Before she slept she thought long and deeply, at last concluding that perhaps affairs were taking the right turn for her purpose. Graydon was tolerating as a disagreeable necessity what he regarded as her filial diplomacy with Arnault. He was loyally and quietly waiting until this necessity should cease, and was so doing because he supposed it to be her wish. If she could keep him in just this attitude it would leave her less embarrassed, give her more time, than if he were an ardent and jealous suitor. She was scarcely capable of love, but she admired him more than ever each day. She saw that he was the superior of Arnault in every way, and was so recognized by all in the house; therefore one of her strongest traits—vanity—was enlisted in his behalf. She saw, also, that he represented a higher type of manhood than she had been accustomed to, and she was beginning to stand in awe of him also, but for reasons differing widely from those which caused her fear of Arnault. She dreaded the latter's pride, the resolute selfishness of his scheme of life, which would lead him to drop her should she interfere with it. She was learning to dread even more Graydon's high-toned sense of honor, the final decisions he reached from motives which had slight influence with her. What if she should permit both men to slip from her grasp, while she hesitated? She fairly turned cold with horror at the thought of this and of the poverty which might result.

Thus, from widely differing motives, two girls were sighing for time; and Graydon Muir, strong, confident, proud of his knowledge of society and ability to take care of himself, was walking blindly on, the victim of one woman's guile, the object of another woman's pure, unselfish love, and liable at any hour to be blasted for life by the fulfilment of his hope and the consummation of his happiness.

Sweet Madge Alden, hiding your infinite treasure, deceiving all and yet so true, may you have time!

CHAPTER XXI

SUGGESTIVE TONES

Miss Wildmere had promised to drive with Graydon on the following morning, but Madge felt as if heaven had interfered in her behalf, for the skies were clouded, and the rain fell unceasingly. People were at a loss to beguile the hours. Graydon, Miss Wildmere, and Mr. Arnault played pool together, while Mr. Muir, his wife, and Madge bowled for an hour, the last winning most of the games. Mr. Arnault had a certain rude sense of fair play, and it appeared to him that Graydon's course had become all that he could ask—more than he could naturally expect. The lady was apparently left wholly free to make her choice between them, and all protest, even by manner, against her companionship with him had ceased. He could drive, walk, or dance with her at his will; then Graydon would quietly put in an appearance and make the most of his opportunity. Arnault was not deceived, however. He knew that his present rival was the most dangerous one that he had ever encountered—that Stella might accept him at any time and was much inclined to do so speedily. Indeed, he was about driven to the belief that she would do so at once but for the fear that the Muirs were in financial peril. He hoped that this fear and the pressure of her father's need might lead her to decide in his favor, without the necessity of his being the immediate and active agent in breaking down the Muirs. As a business man, he shrunk from this course, and all the more because Graydon was acting so fairly. Nevertheless, he would play his principal card if he must. It was his nature to win in every game of life, and it had become a passion with him to secure the beautiful girl that he had sought so long and vainly. If it could appear to the world that he had fairly won her, he would not scruple at anything in the accomplishment of his purpose, and would feel that he had scored the most brilliant success in his life. If he could do this without ruining them, he would be glad, and his good-will was enhanced by Graydon's course this morning. The former had sauntered into the billiard-room, but, seeing Graydon with Miss Wildmere, had been about to depart, when Muir had said, cordially, "Come, Arnault, take a cue with us," and had quite disarmed him by frank courtesy.

At last the sound of music and laughter lured them to the main hall, and there they found Madge surrounded by children and young people, little Nellie Wilder clinging to her side the most closely, with Mr. and Mrs. Wilder looking at the young girl with a world of grateful good-will in their eyes.

"Oh, Miss Alden, sing us another song," clamored a dozen voices.

"Yes," cried Jennie Muir; "the funny one you sang for us in the woods."

Madge smilingly complied, and the children fairly danced in their delight at the comical strains, abrupt pauses, droll sentiment, and interlarded words of explanation. The more elderly guests were attracted, and the audience grew apace. Having finished her little musical comedy, Madge arose, and Mr. Arnault, aware of Stella Wildmere's ability to sing selections from opera, said, "Since the children have been so well entertained, I suggest that we who have the misfortune to be grown have our turn, and that Miss Wildmere give us some grown-up music."

Madge flushed slightly, and Miss Wildmere, after a little charming hesitation, seated herself at the piano, and sang almost faultlessly a selection from an opera. It was evident that she had been well and carefully trained, and that within her limitations, which she thoughtfully remembered, she gave little occasion for criticism. Both her suitors were delighted. They applauded so heartily, and urged so earnestly with others, that she sang again and again, to the unaffected pleasure of the throng who had now gathered. At last she pleaded fatigue, and rose from the instrument, flushing proudly amid vociferous encores. Graydon was about to ask Madge to sing again, when an old gentleman who had listened to the children's ditties, and had detected unusual sweetness and power in Madge's tones, said, promptly, "I may be mistaken, but I have an impression that Miss Alden can give us some grown-up music, if she will."

Instantly his suggestion was seconded by general entreaty, in which not only Graydon joined from sincere good-will, but also Mr. Arnault, in the hope of giving Stella a triumph, for he believed that the best her social rival could do would be to render some ballad fairly well.

Madge's brow contracted, as though she were irresolute and troubled.

"Truly, Miss Alden," said Stella, who was standing near, "I have done my part to beguile the dismal day; I think you might favor us, also. There are no critics here, I hope. We should enjoy a simple song if you cannot now recall anything else."

"Very well, then, I will give you a little German song that my old teacher loved well;" but Graydon saw the same slight flush and a resolute expression take the place of her hesitancy.

After a brief prelude, which, to his trained ear, revealed her perfect touch, her voice rose with a sweet, resonant power that held those near spellbound, and swelled in volume until people in distant parts of the house paused and listened as if held by a viewless hand. Connoisseurs felt that they were listening to an artist and not an amateur; plain men and women, and the children, knew simply that they were enjoying music that entranced them, that set their nerves thrilling and vibrating. Madge hoped only that her voice might penetrate the barriers between herself and one man's heart. She did not desire to sing on the present occasion. She did not wish to annoy him by the contrast between her song and Miss Wildmere's performance, feeling that he would naturally take sides in his thoughts with the woman outvied; nor had she any desire to inflict upon her rival the disparagement that must follow; but something in Miss Wildmere's self-satisfied and patronizing tone had touched her quick spirit, and the arrogant girl should receive the lesson she had invited. But, as Madge sang, the noble art soon lifted her above all lower thoughts, and she forgot everything but Graydon and the hope of her heart. She sang for him alone, as she had learned to sing for him alone.

In spite of her explanations he looked at her with the same old wonder and perplexity of which he had been conscious from the first. If she had merely sung with correctness and taste, like Miss Wildmere, there would have been nothing to disturb his complacent admiration; but now he almost felt like springing to her side with the words, "What is it, Madge? Tell me all."

As the last lovely notes ceased, only the unthinking children applauded. From the others there was entreaty.

"Please sing again, Miss Alden," said the gentleman who had first asked her. "I am an old man, and can't hope for many more such rich pleasures. I am not an amateur, and know only the music that reaches my heart."

"Sing something from 'Lohengrin,' Madge," said Henry Muir, quietly. She glanced at him, and there was a humorous twinkle in his eyes.

Herr Brachmann had trained her thoroughly in some of Wagner's difficult music, and she gave them a selection which so far surpassed the easy melodies of Verdi, which Miss Wildmere had sung, that the latter sat pale and incensed, yet not daring to show her chagrin. This music was received with unbounded applause, and then a little voice piped, "The big folks have had more'n their turn; now give us a reg'lar Mother Goose."

This request was received with acclamations, and soon ripples of laughter broke over the crowd in all directions, and then one of the adoring boys who were usually worshipping near cried out, "A reel, Miss Alden, a reel, and let us finish up with a high old dance before dinner."

Graydon seized Miss Wildmere's hand, boys made profound bows to their mothers, husbands dragged their protesting wives out upon the floor. Soon nearly all ages and heights were in the two long lines, many feet already keeping time to Madge's rollicking strains. Never had such a dance been known before in the house, for the very genius and inspiration of mirth seemed to be in the piano. The people were laughing half the time at the odd medley of tunes and improvisations that Madge invoked, and gray-bearded men indulged in some of the antics that they had thought forgotten a quarter of a century before. As the last couple at the head of the lines was glancing down the archway of raised and clasped hands, the lively strains ceased, and the dancers swarmed out, with thanks and congratulations upon their lips, only to see Madge flying up the stairway.

"Madge," said Graydon, at dinner, "I suppose you will tell me you have practiced over and over again every note you sang this morning."

"Certainly; some of the more difficult ones hours and hours and months and months. Herr Brachmann was an amiable dragon in music, and insisted on your knowing what you did know."

"I thought you would say all this, but it doesn't account for your singing."

"What do you mean?"

"I don't know exactly. There is something you did not get from Herr Brachmann—scarcely from nature. It suggests what artists call feeling, and more."

"Oh, every one has his own method," said Madge, carelessly, and yet with a visible increase of color.

"'Method,' do you call it? I'm half inclined to think that it might be akin to madness were you very unhappy. The human voice often has a strange power over me, and I have a theory that it may reveal character more than people imagine. Why shouldn't it? It is the chief medium of our expression, and we may even unconsciously reveal ourselves in our tones."

"When were you so fanciful before? What does a professional reveal?"

"Chiefly that she is a trained professional, and yet even the most blase among them give hints as to the compass of their woman-nature. I think their characters are often suggested quite definitely by their tones. Indeed, I even find myself judging people by their voices. Henry's tones indicate many of his chief traits accurately—as, for instance, self-reliance, reserve, quiet and unswerving purpose."

"Well," asked Mrs. Muir, who was a little obtuse on delicate points, "what did Miss Wildmere's tones indicate?"

Graydon was slightly taken aback, and suddenly found that he did not like his theory so well as he had thought. "Miss Wildmere's tones," he began, hesitatingly, "suggested this morning little more than a desire to render well the music she sang, and to give pleasure to her listeners."

"I thought they suggested some self-complacency, which was lost before the morning was over," added Mr. Muir, dryly.

"Miss Wildmere sang admirably," exclaimed Madge, warmly, "and could sing much better if she had been trained in a better method and gave more time to the art. I sang hours every day for nearly two years. Nothing will take the place of practice, Graydon. One must develop voice like muscle."

"You are a generous, sensible critic, Madge," he said, quietly, although there was a flush of resentment on his face at his brother's words. "In the main you are right, but I still hold to my theory. At least, I believe that in all great music there is a subtle individuality and *motif.* Love may be blind, but it is not deaf. Miss Wildmere gave us good music, not great music."

Mr. Muir began talking about the weather as if it were the only subject in his mind, and soon afterward Madge went to her room with bowed head and downcast heart.

"I have no chance," she sighed. "He loves her, and that ends all. He is loyal to her, and will be loyal, even though she breaks his heart eventually, as I fear. It's his nature."

CHAPTER XXII

DISHEARTENING CONFIDENCES

Under a renewed impulse of loyalty Graydon intercepted Miss Wildmere as she was going to her room, and said: "The clouds in the west are all breaking away—they ever do, you know, if one has patience. We can still have our drive and enjoy it all the more from hope deferred."

"I'm so sorry," she began, in some embarrassment. "Of course I couldn't know last night that it would rain in the morning, and so promised Mr. Arnault this afternoon."

"It seems as if it would ever be hope deferred to me, Miss Wildmere," he said, gravely.

"But, Graydon, you must see how it is—"

"No, I don't see, but I yield, as usual."

"I promise you Sunday afternoon or the first clear day," she exclaimed, eagerly.

"Very well," he replied, brightening. "Remember I shall be a Shylock with this bond." But he was irritated, nevertheless, and went out on the piazza to try the soothing influence of a cigar.

The skies cleared rapidly. So did his brow; and before long he muttered: "I'll console myself by another gallop with Madge. There goes my inamorata, smiling upon another fellow. How long is this going to last? Not all summer, by Jupiter! Her father must not insist on her playing that game too long, even though she does play it so well."

Madge was sitting in her room in dreary apathy and spiritless reaction from the strain of the morning, when she was aroused by a knock on her door. "Madge," called a voice that sent the blood to her face, "what say you to another ride? I know the roads are muddy, but—"

"But I'll go with you," she cried. "Why use adversatives in the same breath with 'ride'? The mud's nothing. What won't rub off can stay on. How soon shall I be ready?"

"That's a good live girl. In half an hour."

When they were a mile or two away Madge asked, as if with sudden compunction, "Graydon, are you sure you were disengaged?"

He laughed outright. "That question comes much too late," he said.

She braced herself as if to receive a deadly blow, and was pale and rigid with the effort as she asked, with an air of curiosity merely, "Are you truly engaged to Miss Wildmere, Graydon?"

"In one sense I am, Madge," he replied, gravely. "I have given her my loyalty, and, to a certain extent, my word; but I have not bound her. Since you have proved so true and generous a friend to me I do not hesitate to let you know the truth. I am sorry you do not like her altogether, and that you have some cause for your feeling; but you are both right at heart. She spoke most enthusiastically of your rescue of the child. You ladies amuse me with your emphasis of little piques; but when it comes to anything large or fine you do justice to one another. Henry had no right to say what he did at dinner, for Stella applauded you as you had her; but Henry's prejudices are inveterate. Why should I not be loyal to her, Madge? I believe she remained free for my sake during the years of my absence."

"I think your feelings are very natural. They are what I should expect of you. You have always seemed to me the soul of honor when once you obtain your bearings," she added, with a wan smile.

"How pale you are, Madge!" he said, anxiously.

"I am not feeling very well to-day, and then I am suffering from the reaction of this morning. I never can get over my old timidity and dislike to do anything in public. I can do what I will, but it often costs me dear. I was led on unexpectedly this morning. I only anticipated singing a ditty for the children when I first went to the piano at their request."

"I saw that, Madge. Any other woman with your power of song would have made it known long before this."

"And, believe me, Graydon, I did not want to sing in rivalry with Miss Wildmere. I'm sorry I did."

"I saw that too," he replied, laughing. "Stella drew that little experience down upon herself."

"I'm sorry now that I sang," she said, in a low tone. "I didn't want to do anything to hurt the feelings of so good a friend as you are."

"You didn't hurt my feelings in the least. Just the contrary. You gave much pleasure, and made me all the more proud of you. It will do Stella no harm to have her self-complacency jostled a little. Slight wonder that her head is somewhat giddy from the immense amount of attention she has received. I'm not perfect, Madge; why should I demand perfection? It's delightful to be talking in this way—like old times. I used to talk to you about Stella years ago. If I have the substance I can forego the shadow, and I do feel that I can say to you all that I could to a sensible and loving sister. Believe me, Madge, I can never get over my old feeling for you, and I'm just as proud of you as if your name was Madge Muir. I think your brave effort and achievement at Santa Barbara simply magnificent. You have long had the affection that I would give to a sister, and now that I understand you, I feel for you all the respect that I could give to any woman."

"Those are kind, generous words, Graydon. I knew that you misunderstood me, and I was only provoked at you, not angry."

"You had good reason to be provoked and much more. If you and Stella understood each other in the same way, and—well—if she were only out of that atmosphere in which she has been brought up, I could ask nothing more."

"What atmosphere?"

"Wall Street atmosphere transferred to the domestic and social circle. You have too much delicacy, Madge, to refer to what I know puzzles you, and I admit that I do not fully understand it all, though I know Stella's motive clearly enough. Her motive is worthy of all commendation, but not her method. She is not so much to blame for this as her father, and perhaps her mother, who appears a weak, spiritless woman, a faint echo of her husband. It is here that the infernal Wall Street atmosphere comes in that she has breathed all her life. Does it not puzzle you, in view of my relations to her, that she should be out driving with Arnault?"

"Yes, Graydon, it does."

"Well, Arnault is a money-lender, and I am satisfied that in some way he has her father in his power. Many of these brokers are like cats. They will hold on to anything by one nail, and the first thing you know they are on their feet again all right. As soon as Wildmere makes a lucky strike in the stock-market he will extricate himself and his daughter at the same time. Of course these things are not formulated in words, in a cold-blooded way, I suppose. Arnault has long been a suitor that would take no rebuff. I am satisfied that she has refused him more than once, but he simply persists, and gives her to understand that he will take his chances. This was the state of affairs when I came home, and she, no doubt, feels that if she can save her father, and keep a home for her mother and the little one, she ought to retain her hold on Arnault. After all, it is not so bad. Many women marry for money outright, and all poor Stella proposes is to be complaisant toward a man who would not continue his business support to one whose daughter had just refused him."

Madge was silent.

"You wouldn't do such a thing, I suppose."

"I couldn't, Graydon," she said, simply. "If I should ever love a man I think I could suffer a great deal for his sake, but there are some things I couldn't do."

"I thought you would feel so."

"Why don't you help her father out?" Madge faltered.

"I don't think I have sufficient means. I have never been over-thrifty in saving, and have not laid by many thousands. I have merely a good salary and very good prospects. You can't imagine how slow and conservative Henry is. In business matters he treats me just as if I were a stranger, and I must prove myself worthy of trust at every point, and by long apprenticeship, before he will give me a voice in affairs. He says coming forward too fast is the ruination of young men in our day. Nothing would tempt him to have dealings with Mr. Wildmere, and I couldn't damage myself more than by any transactions on my own account. But even if I were rich I wouldn't interfere. I don't like her father any better than Henry does, and if I began in this way it would make a bad precedent. What's more, I won't introduce money influences into an affair of this kind. If it comes to the point, Stella must decide for me, ignoring all other considerations. If she does, I won't permit her family to suffer, but I propose to know that she chooses me absolutely in spite of everything. I am also resolved that she shall be separated from her family as far as is right, for there is a tone about them that I don't like."

"I thank you for your confidence, Graydon," said Madge, quietly. "You are acting just as I should suppose you would. No one in the world wishes you happiness more earnestly than I do. Come, let us take this level place like the wind."

She was unusually gay during the remainder of their ride, but seemed bent almost on running her horse to death. "To-morrow is Sunday," she explained, "and I must crowd two rides into one."

"Wouldn't you ride to-morrow?"

"No; I have some old-fashioned notions about Sunday. You have been abroad too long, perhaps, to appreciate them."

"I appreciate fidelity to conscience, Madge."

They had their supper together again as on the evening before, but Madge was carelessly languid and fitful in her mirthful sallies, and complained of over-fatigue. "I won't come down again to-night," she said to Graydon as they passed out of the supper-room. "Good-night."

"Good-night, Madge," he replied, taking her hand in both his own. "I understand you now, and know that you have gone beyond even your superb strength to-day. Sleep the sleep of the justest and truest little woman that ever breathed. I can't tell you how much you have added to my happiness during the past two days."

"He understands me!" she muttered, as she closed the door of her room. "I am almost tempted to doubt whether a merciful God understands me. Why was this immeasurable love put into my heart to be so cruelly thwarted? Why must he go blindly on to so cruel a fate? Of course she'll renounce everything for him. Whatever else she may be, she is not an idiot."

Henry Muir's quiet eyes had observed Madge closely, and from a little distance he had seen the parting between her and his brother. Then he saw Graydon seek Miss Wildmere and resume a manner which he had learned to detest, and the self-contained man went out upon the grounds, and said, through clinched teeth: "To think that there should have been such a fool bearing the name of Muir! He's been gushing to Madge about that speculator, and we shall yet have to take her as we would an infection."

CHAPTER XXIII

THE FILIAL MARTYR

Miss Wildmere appeared in one of her most brilliant moods that evening. There was a dash of excitement, almost recklessness, in her gray eyes. She and Mr. Arnault had been deputed to lead the German, but she took Graydon out so often as to produce in Mr. Arnault's eyes an expression which the observant Mr. Wildmere did not like at all. He had just returned from dreary, half-deserted Wall Street, which was as dead and hopeless as only that region of galvanic life can be at times. He had neither sold nor bought stock, but had moused around, with the skill of an old *habitue*, for information concerning the eligibility of the two men who were seeking his daughter's hand. In the midsummer dullness and holiday stagnation the impending operation in the Catskills was the only one that promised anything whatever. He became more fully satisfied that Arnault's firm was prospering. They had been persistent "bears" on a market that had long been declining, and had reaped a golden harvest from the miseries of others. On the other hand, he learned that Henry Muir was barely holding his own, and that he had strained his credit dangerously to do this. He knew about the enterprise which had absorbed the banker's capital, and while he believed it would respond promptly to the returning flow of the financial tide, it now seemed stranded among more hopeless ventures. There was no escaping the conviction that Muir was in a perilous position, and that a little thing might push him over the brink. Therefore, he had returned fully beat upon using all his influence in behalf of Arnault, and was spurred to this effort by the fact that his finances, but not his expenses, were running low. His wife could give but a dubious account of Stella's conduct.

"In short," said Mr. Wildmere, irritably, "she is dallying with both, and may lose both by her hesitating folly."

His daughter's greeting was brief and formal. A sort of matter-of-course kiss had been given, and then he had been left to eat his supper alone, since his wife could not just then be absent from her child. At last he lounged out on the piazza, sat down before one of the parlor windows, glanced at the gay scene within, and smoked in silence. Before the German began, Graydon passed him several times, regarding him curiously and with a growing sense of repulsion. He disliked to think that the relation between this man and the girl he would marry was so close.

Before the evening was over, Mr. Wildmere saw that his daughter was in truth pursuing a difficult policy. The angry light in Arnault's eyes and the grave expression on Graydon's face proved how fraught with peril it was to his hopes. Neither of her suitors liked Stella's manner that evening, for it suggested traits which promised ill for the future. Graydon, who understood her the less, was the more lenient judge.

"Not only Arnault," he thought, "but her father also, has been pressing her toward a course from which she revolts, and she is half reckless in consequence."

He endeavored by his quiet and observant attention, by the

grave and gentle expression of his eyes, to assure her once more that she could find a refuge in him the moment that she would decide absolutely in his favor. She understood him well, and was enraged that she could not that night go out with him into the moonlight, put her hand in his, and end her suspense.

Her father had whispered, significantly, when they met, "Stella, I must see you before you give Mr. Muir further encouragement;" and she, feeling that it might be among her last chances, for the present, of showing Graydon favor, was lavish of it. But it was not the preference of strong, true, womanly choice; it was rather the half-defiant aspect with which forbidden fruit might be regarded.

As the great clock was about to chime the hour of midnight the dancing ceased. Arnault seemed determined to have the last word, and Graydon interposed no obstacle. The former walked on the piazza by Stella's side for a few turns in moody silence. Her father still sat at his post of observation. Mrs. Wildmere had been with him part of the time, but he had not had much to say to her.

"Mr. Arnault," said Stella, satirically, at last, "I will not tax your remarkable power for entertainment any longer. I will now join papa, and retire."

"Very well, Stella," was the quiet reply; "but before we part I shall speak more to the point than if I had talked hours. By this time another week the question must be decided."

She bowed, and made no other answer.

"Stella," said her father when they were alone and he had regarded for some moments her averted and half-sullen face, "what do you propose to do?" There was no answer.

After another pause he continued: "In settling the question, represent your mother and myself by a cipher. That is all we are, if the logic of your past action counts for anything. Again I ask, What do you propose to do? No matter how pretty and flattered a girl may be, she cannot alter gravitation. There are other facts just as inexorable. Shutting your eyes to them, or any other phase of folly, will not make the slightest difference."

"I think it's a horrid fact that I must marry a man that I don't love."

"That is not one of the facts at all. Stock-gambler as I am, and in almost desperate straits, I require nothing of the kind. Knowing you as I do, I advise you to accept Arnault at once; but I do not demand it; I do not even urge it. If you loved me, if you would say, 'Give up this feverish life of risk; I will help you and suffer with you in your poverty; I will marry Graydon Muir and share his poverty,' I would leave Wall Street at once and forever. It's a maelstrom in which men of my calibre and means are sucked down sooner or later. The prospects now are that it will be sooner, unless I am helped through this crisis."

"I believe you are mistaken about the Muirs being in financial danger."

"I am not mistaken. They may have to suspend daring the coming week."

"I know that Graydon Muir has no suspicion of trouble."

"He is but a clerk in his brother's employ, and has just returned from a long absence. Mr. Muir is one of the most reticent of men. I have invested in the same dead stock that is swamping him, and so know whereof I speak. Should this stock decline further—should it even remain where it is much longer—he can't maintain himself. I know, for I have taken pains to obtain information since I last went to town."

"But if the stock rises," she said, with the natural hope of a speculator's daughter, "he is safe."

"Yes, *if*."

"How much time will you give me?" she asked, the lines of her face growing hard and resolute.

"This is to be your choice, not mine," said her father, coldly. "You shall not be able to say that I sold you or tried to sell you. Of course it would be terribly hard for me to lose my footing and fall, and I feel that I should not rise again. Arnault worships success and worldly prestige. You are a part of his ambitious scheme. If you helped him parry it out he would do almost anything you wished, and he could throw business enough in my way to put me speedily on my feet. You must make your choice in view of the following facts: You can go on living here, just as you are, two or three weeks longer, dallying with opportunity. By that time, unless I get relief and help, I shall reach the end of my resources, and creditors will take everything. The Muirs cannot help me, and I don't believe they would in any event. I am not on good terms with Henry Muir. If they go down now they will be thoroughly cleaned out. Arnault has long been devoted to you, and you could have unbounded influence over him if you acted in the line of his ruling passion. It would gratify his pride and add to the world's good opinion of him if I prospered also. In plain English, we may all be in a tenement house in a month, or I on safe ground and you the affianced wife of a rich man."

"Well," said Stella, coldly, "you have given me facts enough.

It's a pity you couldn't have brought me something better from Wall Street after all these years."

"What have you brought to me during these past years," he demanded, sternly, "but constant requests for money, and the necessity for incessant effort to meet new phases of extravagance? You have not asked what was kind, merciful, and true, but what was the latest style. Few days pass but that I am reminded of you by a bill for some frippery or other; but how often am I reminded of you by acts of filial thoughtfulness, by words of sympathy in my hard battle of life when I am present, or by genial letters when absent? I have spent three hot days in the city seeking chiefly your interest, and a more mechanical, perfunctory thing never existed than your kiss of greeting to-night. There was as much feeling in it as in the quarter that I handed to the stage-driver. I have spent thousands on your education, but you don't sing for me, you don't read to me, you never think of soothing my overtaxed nerves by cheerful, hopeful talk. Were I a steel automaton, supplying your wants, I should answer just as well, and in that case you might remember the laws of matter and apply a little oil occasionally. What are the motives of your life but dress, admiration, excitement, a rapid succession of men to pass under your baleful fascination, and then to pass on crippled in soul for having known you? Unless you can give Graydon Muir a loving woman's heart, and mean to cling to him for worse as well as better, you will commit a crime before God and man if you accept him. With Arnault it is different. In mind you are near enough of kin to marry. As long as you complied with fashionable and worldly proprieties, he would be content; but a man with a heart and soul in his body would perish in the desert of a home that your selfishness would create."

"It's awful for you to talk to me in this way!" she whined, wincing and crying under his arraignment.

"It's awful that I have to speak to you in this way, either to make you realize what deformities your beauty hides, so that you may apply the remedy, or else, if you will not, to promote your union with a man content to take for a wife a belle, and not a woman.

"I suppose I am chiefly to blame, though, or you would be different," he added, with a dark, introspective look. "I was proud of you as a beautiful child, and tried to win your love by indulgence. Heaven knows, I would like to be a different man, but it's all a breathless hurry after bubbles that vanish when grasped! Well, what do you propose to do? You see that you can't hesitate much longer."

"I will decide soon," she answered, sullenly. Although her conscience echoed his words, and she felt their justice, her pride prevailed, and she permitted him to depart without another word.

CHAPTER XXIV

"I'LL SEE HOW YOU BEHAVE"

The dawn of the following sacred day was bright, beautiful, and serene, bringing to the world a new wealth of opportunity. Miss Wildmere began its hours depressed and undecided. Her conscience and better angel were pleading; she felt vaguely that her life and its motives were wrong, and was uncomfortable over the consciousness. Her phase of character, however, was one of the most hopeless. It was true that her vanity had grown to the proportions of a disease, but even this might be overcome. Her father's stern words had wounded it terribly, and she had experienced twinges of self-disgust. But another trait had become inwrought, by long habit, with every fibre of her soul—selfishness. It was almost impossible to give up her own way and wishes. Graydon Muir pleased her fancy, and she was bent on marrying him. Her father's assurance that she would bring him disappointment, not happiness, weighed little. Too many men had told her that she was essential to their happiness to permit qualms on this score. Her conscience did shrink, to some extent, from a loveless, business-like marriage, and her preference for Graydon made such a union all the more repugnant; but she was incapable of feeling that she would do him a wrong by giving him the pretty jewelled hand for which so many had asked. Indeed, the question now was, Could she be so self-sacrificing as to think of it under the circumstances? If that stock would only rise, if in some way she could be assured that the Muirs would be sustained, and so pass on to the wealth sure to flow in upon them in prosperous times, she would decide the question at once, whether they would do anything for her father or not. He could scramble on in some way, as he had done in the past. What she desired most was the assurance that there should be no long and doubtful interregnum of poverty and privation—that she might continue to be a queen in society during the period of youth and beauty.

This remained the chief consideration amid the chaos of her conflicting feelings and interests, for she had lived this life so long that she could imagine no other as endurable. She had, moreover, the persistence of a small nature, and longed to humiliate the Muir pride, and to spite Madge Alden, who she half believed cherished more than a sisterly regard for Graydon. As for her father, she did little more than resent his words and the humiliating disquietude they had caused. They had sorely wounded her vanity, and presented a painful alternative.

As the day passed, and old habits of mind resumed sway, she began to concentrate her thoughts on three questions: Should she accept Graydon and take her chances with him? Should she accept Mr. Arnault, with his wealth, and be safe? or should she hesitate a little longer, in the hope that she could secure Graydon and wealth also? The persistence of a will that had always had its own way decided finally in favor of the last course of action. She would not give Graydon up unless she must, and not until she must. Accustomed to consult self-interest, she believed that her father was doing the same, that he was favoring Arnault because the latter would be more useful to him, and that for this reason he was exaggerating the Muirs' peril, if not inventing it. She dismissed his words about leaving Wall Street with scarcely a thought; he always talked in this way when the times were bad or his ventures unlucky. They had been on the eve of ruin so many times, that the cry of "wolf" was not so alarming as formerly.

"I suppose I must decide before this week is over," she thought. "Arnault has practically given me this length of time, and I shall take him at his word." Therefore, she was very sweet to him during the morning hours, and prepared him to submit to her drive with Graydon in the afternoon.

Arnault felt that he had given his ultimatum, and was resolved to abide by it. At the same time he knew that it would be a terrible wrench to give up the girl. The very difficulty of winning her had stimulated to the utmost his passion for attainment. She was the best that existed in his superficial world, and fulfilled his ideal. Her delicate yet somewhat voluptuous beauty completely intoxicated him.

He too thought, and made his decision during the day. If he won her at all it must be speedily, and it should be done by promises of devotion and wealth if possible, and by breaking the Muirs down if this should become necessary. The time had come for decisive action. It was evident that her father was in sore straits; the man's appearance confirmed this belief. Arnault was almost certain that Henry Muir was in his power. He would not play the latter card unless he must, but he would watch so vigilantly as to be promptly aware of the necessity. He decided to spend several days of the present week in the mountains and so keep himself informed how the game went here, and while in the city he would not only be observant, but would also drop a few words to weaken Mr. Muir's credit. One thing, however, was settled—the problematical issue of his matrimonial scheme must soon be made known, and he rather relished its congenial elements of speculative uncertainty, being conscious that so much depended upon his skill and power to pull unseen wires.

Seeing that Arnault was at Miss Wildmere's side, Graydon accompanied his relatives to church, and soon found himself looking over the same hymn-book with Madge. The choir were present, and she now merely delighted Graydon with her rich alto; and so rich and true was it that he often felt his nerves thrilling at her tones. He did not become absorbed in the service or sermon, but thought a little wonderingly: "Here is a faith ever finding expression all over the world, while I ignore it. How much truth does it represent? It's evidently a reality to Madge, although she makes so little parade of the fact. I don't believe she would do anything contrary to its teachings as she understands them. We men may think what we please, but we have confidence in a woman who looks as she does now. She is not in the least inclined to devotional rhapsodies or to subserviency to priestcraft, like so many women abroad. She merely appears to recognize a divine power as she accepts nature, only more reverently and consciously. I suppose I am an agnostic as much as anything, yet I should only be too glad to have Stella at my side with such an expression on her face. I wonder if she will go with me this afternoon. I will submit to this diplomacy a few days longer, and shall then end the matter. There is an increasing revulsion of my whole being from such tactics in my future wife. Beyond a certain point she shall not be a partner in her father's gambling operations, and I would have brought the affair to an end at once, were it not for that limp little woman, his wife, and her child. But I can't sacrifice my self-respect and Stella's character for them. I must get her out of that atmosphere, so that her true nature may develop. Sweet Madge Alden, with your eyes so serious and true, and again so full of mirth and spirit, what a treasure you will prove some day if there is a man worthy of you!"

In his deep preoccupation, he forgot his intent regard, until reminded of it by the slow deepening of her color, which so enhanced her beauty that he could not at once withdraw his gaze. Suddenly she turned on him with a half-angry, half-mirthful flash in her eyes, and whispered, "Looking at girls in church is not good form; but, if you will do it, look at some other girl."

He was delighted at this little unexpected prick, and replied, "St. Paul never would have complained of such a thorn." Then he saw Dr. Sommers looking ominously at him. This factotum of the chapel sat where he could oversee the miscellaneous little assemblage, and his eyes instantly pounced upon any offender. Graydon pushed his insubordination no further than making an irreverent face at the doctor, and then addressed himself to the minister during the remainder of the hour.

"We'll arrange it differently next Sunday, Miss Alden," said the doctor, as Madge passed out; "I'll have Mr. Muir sit with me."

"Try it," whispered Graydon, "and if you don't fall from grace before meeting is over I'll give you a new trout-pole. Miss Alden can manage me better than you can."

"No doubt, no doubt. A man must be in a bad way if she couldn't make a saint of him if she undertook it," was the doctor's laughing reply.

Greatly amused, Graydon repeated the words to Madge. "She won't undertake it in this case," was her brusque comment. "I have no ambition to enlighten continental heathen, with their superior tolerance of a faith good enough for women and children."

"My charming rose has not only a thorn but a theological stiletto in her belt."

"It is evident you have never had trouble, Graydon."

"Why is it evident?"

"Because you are content with the surface-tide of life."

"And you are not?"

"One rarely is when fearing to sink."

"What has that to do with faith?"

"Faith can sustain; that's all."

"And your faith sustained you?"

"What else was there to sustain when day after day brought, not a choice of pleasures, but the question, Shall I live or die?"

"Poor Madge! Dear Madge! And you didn't let me know. I don't suppose I could have helped you, though."

"No; not then."

"Madge," he said, earnestly, "won't you promise me one thing? If you ever should have trouble of any kind again, won't you let me help you, or at least try to?"

"I'll see how you behave," she said, laughing. "Besides, it's not women's place to make trouble for men. The idea! Our mission is to soothe and console you superior beings."

"Women do make a power of trouble for men. Mother Eve began wrong, and—"

"And Adam laid all his misdeeds on her weak shoulders."

"The upshot of all this talk is, I suppose, that your shoulders are so strong, and your spirit so high, that you can at least take care of your own troubles."

"I hope so," she again laughed, "and be ready also to give you a lift. When you successful men do get a tumble in life, you are the most helpless of mortals."

"Well, well, well, to think that I am talking to little Madge, who could not say good-by to me without fainting away!"

"Good-by meant more to me than to you. You were going away to new and pleasant activity. I doubted whether I should see you again—or indeed any one long," she added, hastily.

"Don't imagine that I did not feel awfully that night, dear Madge. Tears do not come into my eyes easily, but I added a little salt water to the ocean as I leaned over the taffrail and saw the city that contained you fade from view."

"Did you truly, Graydon?" she asked, turning away.

"I did, indeed."

In her averted face and quickened respiration he thought he saw traces of more than passing feeling, but she turned on him in sudden gayety, and said: "Whenever I see the ocean I'll remember how its tides have been increased. Graydon, I've a secret to tell you, which, for an intense, aesthetic, and vaguely devotional woman, is a most humiliating confession:

I'm awfully hungry. When will dinner be ready?"

"I have a secret to tell you also," he replied, with a half-vexed flash in his eyes: "There is a girl in this house who explains herself more or less every day, and who yet remains the most charming conundrum that ever kept a man awake from perplexity."

"Oh, dear!" cried Madge, "is Miss Wildmere so bad as that? Poor, pale victim of insomnia! By the way, do you and Mr. Arnault keep a ledger account of the time you receive? or do you roughly go on the principle of 'share and share alike'?" and with eyes flashing back laughter at his reddening face, she ran up the steps and disappeared.

"That was a Parthian arrow," he muttered. "If we go smoothly on the sharing principle at present, we shall soon go roughly enough, or cease to go at all."

But the lady in question was putting forth all her resources, which were not slight when enlisted in her own behalf, to keep the two men *in statu quo* until more time, with its chances, should pass.

Arnault smiled grimly when he saw her departing with Graydon. She had been evasive, but very friendly, during the day thus far, and after what he had said the preceding night he felt that he was committed to her moods for a week if he could not bring her to a decision before. Seeing Mr. Wildmere walking restlessly up and down the piazza, he joined him, and offering a superb cigar, said, "Suppose we go out to the lake and see where the little kid was so nearly drowned."

Soon after they were smoking in the shade, the thoughts of both reverting to kindred anxieties. Arnault decided to make one move before the final one. Perhaps only this would be required; perhaps it might prepare the way for more serious action. They talked over business. Arnault, permitting the other to see through a veiled distinctness of language that he was prospering, remarked, "By the way, I have a little transaction which I wish you would carry out for us," and mentioned an affair of ordinary brokerage, concluding, in off-hand tones, "from what you said some days since I infer that you may find a little money handy at present. I can let you have a check for five hundred or a thousand just as well as not. I know how dull times are now, and you will soon make it up by commissions."

The hard-pressed man could scarcely disguise the relief which these words brought. He began a grateful acknowledgment of the kindness, when Arnault interrupted him by saying, "Oh, that's nothing—mere matter of business. I will write you a check to-night for a thousand. It's only an advance, you know," and then changed the subject.

"Will you go to town to-morrow?" Mr. Wildmere asked.

"No, not to-morrow. I'll run down Tuesday or Wednesday. In spite of the times business doesn't give us much leeway this summer, but I've arranged to be away more or less at present." Then he added, with what was meant to be a frank, deprecatory laugh, "I suppose you see how it is. It's some time since I asked permission to pay my addresses to your daughter. I don't think I've been neglectful of opportunities, but I don't get on as fast as I would like, and now feel that if I would keep any chance at all I must be on hand. Muir is a formidable rival."

"You know that you have my consent and more, Mr. Arnault."

"It's the lady's consent that I must obtain," was the reply. "Muir is a fine fellow, and I cannot wonder that she hesitates—that is, if she does hesitate. I may be wasting my time here and adding to the bitterness of my disappointment, for of course it must become greater if I see Miss Wildmere every day and still fail."

There was a covert question in this remark, and after a moment or two Mr. Wildmere said, hesitatingly: "I do not think you are wasting your time. I think Stella is in honest doubt as to her choice. At least, that is my impression. You know that young ladies in our free land do not take much counsel of parents, and Stella has ever been very independent in her views. When once she makes up her mind you will find her very decided and loyal. Of course I have my strong preference in this case, and have a right also to make it known to her, as I shall. I should be very sorry to see her engaged to a man whose fortunes are dependent on a brother in such financial straits as Mr. Muir is undoubtedly in."

"Do you think Henry Muir is in very great danger?"

"I do indeed."

"Hum!" ejaculated Arnault, looking serious.

"What! would he involve you?"

"Oh, no, a mere trifle; but then—Well, please make some inquiries to-morrow, and I'll see you during the week."

"I'll do anything I can to oblige you, Mr. Arnault. I wouldn't like my questions, however, to hurt Muir's credit, you understand."

"Of course not, nor would I wish this; but as one of our

brokers you can pick up some information, like enough. I knew, as did others, that Muir was having a rather hard time of it, but if there is pressing danger I may have to take some action."

"In that case of course you can command me."

"I only wish to do what is fair and considerate among business men. We'll lunch together when I come to town, and perhaps the case will be clearer then."

During his drive with Miss Wildmere, Graydon simply adhered to the tactics which he had adopted, and she saw that he was waiting until the Arnault phase of the problem should be eliminated. When, however, she took occasion to bewail the dismal prospects of her "poor papa," and to open the way for him to speak naturally of his own and his brother's affairs, he was gravely silent. She didn't like this, for it tended to confirm her father's belief that they were in trouble, or else it looked like suspicion of her motive. The trait of reticence which Graydon at times shared with his brother was not agreeable, for it suggested hidden processes of thought which might develop into very decisive action. She came back satisfied that Graydon was still thoroughly "in hand," and that she must obtain information in some other way, if possible.

There was sacred music in the parlor during the evening, but neither Miss Wildmere nor Madge would sing in solo. Graydon good-naturedly tried to arrange a duet between the two girls. The former declined instantly, yet took off the edge of her refusal by saying, "I would gladly sing for you if I could, but do not care to permit all these strangers to institute comparisons."

Therefore, the guests sang in chorus as usual, a professional playing the accompaniments. There were few, however, who did not recognize the strong, sweet alto which ran through each melody like a minor key. Graydon's acute ear for music heard little else, and he said to Madge "I shall be glad when this hotel life is over. What delicious evenings I shall have this fall! By the way, I'm going to have your piano tuned when I go to town."

"Perhaps."

"Perhaps what? Perhaps I shall remember about the tuner? You'll see."

"I may go back with the Waylands. I'm not at all sure that I shall not spend my winter on the Pacific."

"Why, Madge! With your health you could spend it in Greenland."

"That's what I may do. We always have a lovely green land in that climate."

"I must investigate Santa Barbara. You have left some one or something there which has powerful attractions."

"Yes, memories; as well as skies so bright that you can't help smiling back at them."

"I supposed you were going to enter society this fall and create a *furore*."

"Oh, bah!" Then she began to laugh, and said, "A certain gentleman in this house thought I was so bent on having my fling in society that I didn't wish to be embarrassed by even a little fraternal counsel."

"A certain fellow in this house finds himself embarrassed by a black-eyed clairvoyant, who reads his thoughts as if they were sign-boards, but remains inscrutable herself."

"Such an objectionable and inconvenient creature should certainly be banished to wilds of the West"

"As one of the Muir family I'll never consent."

"You'll soon be engrossed by cares of your own," she concluded, laughing. "Good-night."

"Stay," said Graydon, eagerly; "one so gifted with second-sight should be able to read the thoughts of others."

"Whose?" Madge asked, demurely.

"Whose indeed? As if you did not know! Miss Wildmere's."

"What! Reveal a woman's thoughts? I won't speak to you again to-night;" and she left him with his tranquillity not a little disturbed.

CHAPTER XXV

GOSSAMER THREADS

Mr. Muir was to depart on the early train the following morning, and was pleased when Madge opened her door at the same time and said, "I'm going to see that you have a good breakfast and a good send-off."

She chattered merrily with him during the meal, ignoring his somewhat wistful and questioning glances. "When shall we see you again, Henry?" she asked.

"Friday evening, I hope."

"Don't work and worry too much."

"I defy fate now. You've given me your luck."

"Heaven forbid! Well, good-by."

A little later she and two of her boys, as she called them, were off on the hills. Mrs. Muir and Graydon breakfasted long after, and the latter observed with a frown that Arnault was still at the Wildmere table, with all the serenity of one *en famille*.

"Doctor," he said, a little later, "how much will you take—the money to be given to your chapel—to go trouting with me for a day?"

"A good round sum," Dr. Sommers replied.

"All right. When can you go?"

"Wednesday, I guess, if I can leave my patients."

"Oh, come now; go and give your patients a chance to get well."

"Wait till I catch you sick, and I'll pay you up for that."

"You'll stand a better chance of catching trout."

The day passed much as usual, only Arnault appeared in the ascendant.

"He is going to town in a day or two," pleaded the diplomat, after dinner.

"And I'm going trouting," Graydon replied.

"When?"

"Soon."

"Only for a day, I suppose."

"It depends on my luck. You will get on better when I'm away."

"It's cruel for you to speak like that," she replied, her eyes moistening.

"I suppose it is," was his rueful reply; "but I can be more patient, I imagine, back in the mountains than here."

"But how about poor me?"

"That is a question that I often ask myself, Miss Wildmere, but you alone can answer it. As far as I am able to judge, you can meet the problem in your mind, whatever it is, as well, if not better, in my absence. You must understand me, and I have promised to be reasonably patient."

"Very well, Mr. Muir," she replied, in apparent sadness, "I will try not to tax your patience beyond what you well term reason."

"Something far beyond reason, and—I may add—pride also, permits you to tax it all. I would rather not revert to this topic again. It is embarrassing to us both. I cannot help saying, however, that it is essential to my happiness that the present state of affairs should soon cease."

"If it were only present happiness that one had to consider—" she began, and then hastened away.

Thus she played upon his sympathy, and held him by the generous side of his nature.

But he determined not to give Arnault the pleasure of seeing him wait for the crumbs of time that fell from his table, and he delighted Madge, having sought her out on the piazza, by remarking: "It is so cool to-day I do not see why we cannot start at once. I shall not find the time too long, for you can talk as well as ride."

She made good his words, and gave wings to the hours. Among the scenes through which they passed, she reminded him, not of an exotic or a stray tropical bird, but rather of the ideal mountain nymph humanized, developed into modern life, the strong original forces of nature harmonized into perfect womanhood, yet unimpaired. Her smiles, her piquant words, and, above all, the changing expression of her lovely eyes, affected him subtilely, and again imparted a rising exhilaration. Her thoughts came not like the emptying of a cup, but rippled forth like a sparkling rill from some deep and exhaustless supply. And what reservoir is more inexhaustible than the love of a heart like hers?—a love born as naturally and unconsciously as life itself—that, when discovered, changes existence by a sudden kaleidoscopic turn, compelling all within and without to pass at once into new arrangement and combination—that inspires heroic, patient effort, self-denial, and even self-sacrifice.

She had prepared herself for this opportunity by years of training and thought, but his presence brought her an inspiration beyond all that she had gained from books or study. He was the magician who unconsciously had the power to waken and kindle her whole nature, to set the blood flowing in her veins like wine, and to arouse a rapidity and versatility of thought that was surprising even to herself. With the pure genius of love she threw about his mind gossamer threads, drew the filaments together, and held them in her heart. The pulses of life grew stronger within him, his fancy kindled, the lore of books long since forgotten, as he supposed, flashed into memory, and out into happy allusion and suggestion. Still his wonder increased that her knowledge coincided so fully with his own, and that their lines of reading had been so closely parallel. It was hard for him to find a terra incognita of thought into which she had not made some slight explorations. In his own natural domains she skilfully appeared to know enough to follow, but not to lead with mortifying superiority. She also had her own preserves of thought and fancy, of which she gave him tantalizing glimpses, then let fall the screening boughs; and he, who fain would see more, was content to pass on, assured that another vista would soon be revealed. It was the reserve of this frank girl that most charmed and incited him, the feeling, more or less defined, that while she appeared to manifest herself by every word and smile, something richer and rarer still was hidden.

"No one will ever have a chance to understand her fully but the man she loves," he thought. "To him she would give the clew to all her treasures, or else show them with sweet abandon, and it would require a lifetime for the task. She has a beauty and a character that would never pall, for the reason that she draws her life so directly from nature. I have never met a woman that affected me as she does."

He sighed again. In spite of the loyalty to which he believed himself fully committed, Stella Wildmere, with her Wall Street complications, her variegated experience as to adorers, and her present questionable diplomacy, seemed rather faded beside this girl, upon whose heart the dew still rested.

For the first time the thought passed consciously through his mind, "Stella has never made me so happy as I have been the last few hours. More than that, she never gave life an aspect so rich, sweet, and full of noble possibility. Madge makes blase, shallow cynicism impossible in a fellow."

As he danced with Miss Wildmere that evening, or sauntered with her on the piazza or through secluded paths, the same tendency to comparisons tormented him. He could not make himself believe that Miss Wildmere's words were like the flow of a clear, bubbling spring, pure and sweet. There was in them a sediment, the product of a life which had passed through channels more and more distasteful to contemplate.

The next day he went to town to look after some business matters, and returned by the latest train. To his surprise he found Madge absent, and was immediately conscious of a vague sense of disappointment.

CHAPTER XXVI

MRS. MUIR'S ACCOUNT

After a light supper Graydon went in search of Stella, but she was nowhere to be found, nor had the warm evening lured Mrs. Wildmere from her room. He had learned that Arnault was still at the house, and he inferred, from the surpassing beauty of the moonlit evening, that his rival would not let such witching hours pass without an effort to turn them to account. With a frown he retreated from the music, dancing, and gayety of a full house, and went up to Mrs. Muir's room.

That lady was found writing to her husband, but she welcomed Graydon, and began volubly: "I'm very glad you have come; I'm so full and overflowing about Madge that I had to write to Henry."

"It certainly does seem an odd proceeding on her part—this remaining all night at a farmhouse among strangers," was his discontented reply.

"It would be odd in any one but Madge. I do not think there are many girls in this house who would be guilty of such eccentricities—certainly not Miss Wildmere," she added, with a rather malicious twinkle in her eyes. "If I were a man, I wouldn't stand it. I've been on the alert somewhat to-day, for I don't wish to see you made a fool of. That Mr. Arnault has been at her side the livelong time, and he's out driving with her now."

"I understand all about that," said Graydon, impatiently; "tell me about Madge."

"Perhaps you do, and perhaps you don't. It's certainly beyond my comprehension," continued Mrs. Muir, determined to free her mind. "If she is anything to you, or wishes to be, her performances are as unique as those of Madge, although in a different style. We Alden girls were not brought up in that way. Pardon me; I know it's your affair, but you are my brother, and have been a good one, too. I can't wonder that Henry dislikes her. Well, well, I see you are getting nettled, and I won't say anything more, but tell you about Madge. It has been an awfully hot day, you know, and I did not order a carriage till five. Madge was restless, and had sighed for a gallop more than once, so I proposed to do the best for her I could. As we were starting for our drive Dr. Sommers appeared, and I asked him to go with us.

"'I will,' he said, 'if you will take me to see one of my patients—one that will make Miss Alden contented till she has some imaginary trouble of her own. My horse is nearly used up from the long drive I've had in the heat.'"

"'Oh, do take me to see some one in trouble!' exclaimed Madge."

"'Yes,' replied the doctor, laughing, 'that will be a novelty. To see you young ladies dancing and promenading, one would think you had never heard of trouble.'"

"After a lovely drive through a wild valley we came to a little gray farmhouse, innocent of paint since the memory of man. The mountain rose steeply behind it with overhanging rocks, cropping out through the forest here and there. An orchard shaded the dwelling, and beyond the narrow roadway in front brawled a trout-stream. To the eastward were rough, stony fields, that sloped up, at what seemed an angle of forty-five degrees, to other wooded mountains. It was the roughest, wildest-looking place I ever saw. How strange and lonely it must look now in the moonlight, with not another dwelling in sight!"

"Too lonely for Madge to be there," exclaimed Graydon. "I don't like it, and I should not have expected such imprudence from you, Mary."

"Oh, Madge is safe enough! Wait till you know all. Well, the farmer and his wife were at their early supper when we arrived. I went in with Madge and the doctor, for I wanted to see how such people lived, and also thought I could do something for them. I hadn't been in the room five minutes, however, before I gave up all thought of offering assistance. The people were plainly and even poorly dressed. The man was in his shirt-sleeves, but he put on his coat immediately. He had a kind of natural, quiet dignity and a subdued manner—the result of his trouble, no doubt. We were in their little sitting-room or parlor, but the door into the kitchen, where they had been taking their meal, was open. The room we were in was very plainly furnished, but perfectly neat, and I was at once struck by the number of books that it contained. Would you believe it? one of the leading magazines lay on the table. The mother, a pale, gaunt woman, who looked utterly worn out, went with the doctor to the adjoining sick-room, and the husband's eyes followed them anxiously.

"'Your place seems rather lonely,' I said to him, 'but you evidently know how to find society in books.'"

"'Yes,' he answered, 'I s'pose this region seems lonesome to you, but not to us who were brought up here. It all depends on what you're used to, especially when you're a-growin' up. I'm not much of a reader myself, but Tilly was'; and he heaved a great sigh. 'She took to readin' almost as soon as to walkin',' he continued, 'and used to read aloud to us. I s'pose I soon dozed off, but her mother took it all in, and durin' the long winter evenin's they kinder roamed all over the world together. I suspicion Tilly had more books than was good for her, but she was our only child, and I couldn't say no to her. She edicated herself to be a teacher, and stood high, and we was proud of her, sure enough, but I'm afeared all that study and readin' wasn't good for her;' and then came another of his deep sighs."

"Madge's great eyes meanwhile were more and more full of trouble, and there was a deal of pathos suggested by the man's simple story. Indeed, I felt my own throat swelling at the poor man's last sigh, it was so deep and natural, and seemed to express a great sorrow, for which there were no words in his homely vernacular."

"What selfish egotists we are over our picayune vexations!" Graydon muttered.

"Well, the mother and the doctor now appeared. The latter looked grave; and when he looks grave things are serious indeed."

"'Ain't she no better?' the father asked, with entreaty in his tone."

"'I wish she was,' said the doctor, in his blunt way, which nevertheless expressed more sympathy than a lot of fine phrases. Then he said to the mother: 'You're all worn out, and yet she'll need close watching to-night. Isn't there some neighbor—'"

"'Oh, please let me stay!' began Madge, in a low, eager tone, speaking for the first time. 'I'm strong, and I'll follow your directions in everything. Do, please. I've been ill myself, and think I know how to nurse.'"

"The woman hesitated, and looked doubtfully, wonderingly, at the doctor. Madge sprang up, and taking the mother's hand, continued: 'Indeed, madam, you do look worn out; you will be ill yourself. For your daughter's sake, as well as mine, let me stay.'"

"'For your sake, miss?'"

"'Yes, for my sake. Why should I not bear a little of this heavy burden? It will do me good. Doctor, say I can stay. My strength should not be wasted in amusement only.'"

"'Well,' he replied, 'if Mrs. Muir consents, there's no one I'd trust sooner.'"

"'Then it's settled, Mary,' she said, in her decisive way. 'It's perfectly proper for me to stay under the protection of these good people.'"

"'But you haven't had your supper,' I began."

"A little color came into the woman's face at my foolish speech, and she said, 'If the young lady will take what we can offer—'"

"'Of course I will,' interrupted Madge, with a smile that would have propitiated a dragon; 'a little bread and milk would suit me best.'"

"'She shall have a chicken broiled as nice as she ever tasted at the hotel,' said the man, impulsively. 'Heaven bless your kind heart, and perhaps you can coax Tilly to take a bit!'"

"'The young lady's name is Miss Alden,' said the doctor, 'and this is Mrs. Muir, Mr. and Mrs. Wendall, ladies; I should have introduced you before, but my mind was on my patient. Well, well, well, what a world it is! Some very good streaks run through it, though.'"

"'I'll come for you in the morning,' I said to Madge, who had thrown off her hat, looking so resolute and absorbed in her purpose that I knew there was nothing more to be said. So I shook hands with the poor people, and came away with the doctor."

"I'm going for Madge in the morning," said Graydon, decisively.

"I thought you were going trouting with the doctor."

"Not till I've told Madge what I think of her," he said, gravely.

"I'm sure her impulse and motives were good."

"They were more than good—they were divine, and just like Madge Alden as she now is. She keeps one's blood tingling with surprises; but I've not become such a cynic that I do not understand her. When you come to think of it, what is more natural than that one girl with her superb health should lend her strength to another who, perhaps, is dying; but you may well ask, Who in the house would think of doing this?"

"Yes; the doctor said she was dying—that she couldn't last much longer."

"Well, I never had a sister, but I'm just as proud of Madge, and just as fond of her, as if she were my own flesh and blood. She shall never lack what a brother can do for her while I live."

"I'm glad you feel so," said Mrs. Muir. Then she sighed, and thought, "A plague upon him! Why will he keep following up the other white-faced thing, when he might win Madge if he tried hard enough. It's plain that she don't care for him now except as she used to. And she does care for him just as she did before she went away, in spite of all her prudishness about the words brother and sister. I'm not blind. She has grown so pretty, however, that I suppose Graydon would wish to kiss her too often. She is just as fond of him as he is of her, and in just the same way; but if I had his chance I'd soon have it a different way;" and the good lady was complacency itself over her penetration, as she bade Graydon good-night. No one could see and report the surface of affairs more accurately than she.

As he descended to the hall, Arnault and Miss Wildmere entered. The latter hastened forward and gave him her hand most cordially, saying, "Why, Mr. Muir, I'm ever so glad to see you; you have been away an age."

"A day, Miss Wildmere. Your appearance indicates that you have survived admirably."

"The moon is so bright that we could drive fast, and I'm always happy when in rapid motion."

"You have had the advantage of me then; yet I've been in rapid motion a good part of the day on express trains."

"I feared you were not going to return to-day," she said, as she strolled out with him on the piazza.

"Feared?"

"Yes, why not?"

"It strikes me that I might ask, Why?"

"Surely you would not have me lose such an evening as this, Mr. Muir?" she said, a little reproachfully.

"I would have you follow your own heart."

"I shall follow it as soon as possible," she replied, so earnestly that he was disarmed—especially as the glance which accompanied the words was full of soft allurement and appeal. Of her own accord she put her hand on his arm, and spoke in low, contented tones, as if she had at last found rest and refuge. The moon poured around her a flood of radiance, which gave her an ethereal aspect. Her white drapery enhanced and spiritualized her remarkable beauty, making her appear all that lover or poet could ask. His own words grew kinder and gentler; his heart went out to her as never before; she seemed so fair, delicate, and pure in that witching light that he longed to rescue her at once from her surroundings. Why should he not? She had never manifested a more gentle and yielding mood. He directed her steps from the piazza to a somewhat distant summer-house, and her reluctance was a shy half revolt, which only emphasized the natural meaning of her unspoken consent.

Mrs. Muir was still keeping her eyes open, and from her window saw them pass under the shadow of the trees.

At last they were sitting alone in the summer night. Graydon felt that words were scarcely needed—that his manner had spoken unequivocally, and that hers had granted all; but he took her hand and looked earnestly into her downcast face.

"Oh, Stella—" he began.

A twig snapped in the adjacent grove. She sprang up. "Hush, Graydon," she whispered; "not yet. Please trust me. Oh, what am I thinking of to be out so late!—but could not resist. Come;" and she started for the house.

As they passed in at the door he said, in a low, deep tone, "You cannot put me off much longer, Stella."

"No, Graydon," she whispered, hurriedly, and hastened to her room.

In his deep feeling he had not heard the suspicious sound in the grove, and Miss Wildmere's manner was only another expression of the strong constraint which he believed to be imposed upon her by her father's financial peril. He felt bitterly disappointed, however. Although irritated, he was yet rendered more than forgiving by the apparent truth that she had almost yielded to the impulses of her heart, in spite of grave considerations—and promises perhaps—to the contrary.

He was at a loss what to do, yet felt that the present condition of affairs was becoming intolerable. Almost immediately upon his return from Europe he had written to Mr. Wildmere for permission to pay his addresses, and had received a brief and courteous reply. The thought of again appealing to the father occurred to him, but was speedily dismissed with unconquerable repugnance. The very fact that this man compelled his daughter to take such a course made Graydon wish never to speak to him again. "No," he muttered; "the girl must yield to me, and cut loose from all her father's shifty ways and associations."

The night was so beautiful, and his thoughts kept him so

wakeful, that he sat in a shadow and watched the moonlight transfiguring the world into beauty. Before long he heard a step, and a man came from that end of the piazza which was nearest the summer-house. As he passed in, Graydon saw that it was Arnault. The quick suspicion came into his mind, "Could he have been watching?" Then flashed another thought, "Could she have become aware of his presence, and was this the cause of her abrupt flight?"

The latter supposition was dismissed indignantly and at once. The affair was taking on an aspect, however, so intensely disagreeable that he resolved to write to Miss Wildmere that he would absent himself until Arnault should disappear below the horizon. He would then go trouting or take a trip to some other resort. This course he believed would bring her to a decision, and after their recent interview he could scarcely doubt its nature.

Before he was aware of it, his thoughts returned to Madge. In fancy he saw the gray farmhouse on the lonely mountain-side, with a sweet face at the window, the dark, sympathetic eyes now looking out on the silent, moonlit landscape, and again at the thin, white face of a dying girl. "Poor, poor child!" he thought, reverting to the patient. "Well, for once, at least, she has had a good angel watching over her. I would like to see Madge's face framed by the open window in this witching light. Would to Heaven that Stella was more like her! Yet Stella was beautiful as a dream to-night, and it seemed that my vision of happiness was on the very eve of fulfilment."

CHAPTER XXVII

MADGE'S STORY

Early in the beautiful morning of the following day Graydon was out securing a light carriage, for he reasoned that after watching all night Madge would be too weary to enjoy horseback exercise. He first called on the doctor, and obtained careful directions as to the locality of Madge's sojourn. "The best I can do is to go with you as guide this afternoon to the trout-stream, and then drive back by moonlight," the doctor added.

Within an hour Graydon reached the cottage, and Madge ran out to welcome him. "Now, this is kind and thoughtful of you," she said, and there was unmistakable gladness in her face.

"Dear Madge, you have had a long, dismal night, I fear. I can see it from the lines under your eyes."

"It has been a sad night, Graydon, yet I am very glad I came, and you have now rewarded me. The poor girl is sleeping, and I can slip away."

Mr. and Mrs. Wendall parted from her feelingly and gratefully. Madge promised to come again soon.

For a few moments they drove in silence, and then Madge sighed: "How young, fresh, and full of beautiful life the world seems this morning! The contrast with that poor, suffering, dying girl is too great. Nature often appears strangely indifferent."

"I am not indifferent, Madge. I kept a sort of watch with you for an hour or two last night in the wee, sma' hours, and tried to imagine you sitting in just such an open window as I saw there, with the moonlight on your face; and I thought that the poor girl had one good angel watching over her. You know I am a man of the world, but an act of ministry like this touches me closely."

"No, Graydon; not a good angel, but a very human creature was the watcher."

"Tell me about it—that is, continue the story from the point where Mary left off;" and he explained about Mrs. Muir's account of the previous evening.

"Well, you know what a wilful creature I am?" she began, with the glimmer of a smile.

"Oh, yes; I've learned to understand that feature of your royal womanhood. You are trying to be a woman, Madge. Well, you are one—the kind I believe in. See how much faith I have—I believe, yet don't understand."

"No jesting or compliments this morning, please; I'm too heavy-hearted for them now."

"You ought to be serene and happy after so kind and good a deed."

"No," she said, decisively; "that sympathy must be superficial which can pass almost immediately into self-complacency. Oh, Graydon, it is all so sad, yet not sad; so passing strange, yet as natural and true as life and death! I did sit for hours just as you imagined, looking out on the great, still mountains. Never did they seem so vast and stable, and our life so vapor-like, as when I heard that poor fluttering breath come and go at my side. There was a time when this truth grew oppressive; but later on that feeble life, which seemed but a breath, came to mean something greater and more real than the mountains themselves. But I am anticipating. As soon as Mary departed I became as imperious as I dared to be. I saw that the poor mother had reached about the limit of her endurance, and I arranged the lounge in the sitting-room, so that she could lie down at once, saying: 'I am a stranger, and young, and it's not natural that you should be willing to give up to me too much, nor do I wish you to be far away; yet I can see just how sorely in need of rest you are. You must finish your supper, give me your directions, and then lie down and get every bit of rest you can. I can easily keep awake, and promise to call you whenever you are needed.'

"'Nancy,' her husband added, 'Miss Alden is right. I see by the way she takes hold that she'll do everything, and you're jest beat out.' So between us we had our way."

"'Bless you, miss,' said the man, trying to smile in a way that almost made me cry, 'I'm as handy as a woman 'bout a kitchen;' and he soon proved that he was handier than I could have been, for in a few minutes he pulled up from the well a pail, took out a dressed chicken, and broiled it to perfection. I made his wife eat some of it, and saved a little of the breast for poor Tilly, as they call her."

"Did you take any yourself?" interrupted Graydon.

"Oh, yes, indeed! I'm one of those prosaic creatures whose

appetite never fails. If the world were coming to an end to-day I should insist on having my breakfast."

"Madge," said Graydon, ruefully, "I might as well tell you, for I'm sure to be found out: I once called you 'lackadaisical.'"

"Oh, I knew that over two years ago! What's more, you were right."

"No; I was not right," he answered, positively. "I should have recognized the possibilities of your nature then. I did in regard to your beauty, but not those higher qualities which bid fair to make you my patron saint."

"Oh, hush, Graydon. Such words only pain me. I don't want your compliments, and if any man made a patron saint of me I should be so exasperated that I should probably box his ears. Let us stick to what is simple, natural, and true, in all our talk."

"You may say what you please, Madge, I see it more clearly every day, and reproach myself that I did not understand you. I was content to amuse and pet you, and you naturally did not think me capable of doing anything more. You went away alone to make as brave a fight as was ever battled out in this world, and I had no part in helping you. Mr. and Mrs. Wayland were worth a wilderness of superficial society-fellows like me. I now know why you did not care to correspond with me while making your noble effort."

"Truly, Graydon, your memory and penetration are phenomenal."

"You may disclaim out of kindness now, but I know I am right. You make my life appear shallow and trivial. What have I done in the last two years but attend carefully, from habit, to the details of business, and then amuse myself? And when I wrote I merely sought to amuse you. What were my flippant letters worth to one who was in earnest?"

"Graydon," said Madge, looking into his eyes with gentle dignity, "you may do yourself injustice if you will, but you shall not misjudge me. I have acquired a little of the art of taking care of myself, and you are doing me a wrong which I cannot permit. I remember everything, from the time that your kind eyes rested on the pallid, shrinking child that crept down to the dining-room when we first met, and from that day to this you have been kind and helpful to me. I said that I regarded you as one of the best friends I had in the world. Do you think me insincere? Do you think I forget how kind you were when society would not have tolerated the ghost I was? I am not one who forgets and ignores the past—who can go on to new friends with a frigid shoulder for old ones. Let us end these misunderstandings. Before the year is out you will probably be engaged, perhaps married. Our lives will be widely separated. That is inevitable from the nature of things. But distance and absence can cause no such separation as results from misunderstanding. If we should not meet again in twenty years I should be the same loyal friend. Now I've said it, and don't vex me again by speaking as if I had not said and meant it."

"I can scarcely tell whether your words make me more glad or sad. Each feeling is deeper than you will ever believe. You certainly give me the impression that if I marry Stella Wildmere our lives will be separated."

"You don't take nature, especially woman-nature, into consideration at all. I am not congenial to Miss Wildmere; she does not like me. It is nothing against her, but some people are antagonistic. This is especially true among women, and in this case it is not strange. Our experiences have been very different. She has ever been a beautiful, brilliant society-girl. With her at your side you would always be an object of envy in circles congenial to you, for admiration would follow her as the light follows day. In the past, you know, I have not been influenced by society considerations, and in the future they shall be very secondary. Therefore we of necessity are unlike, and could never be much company for each other. There is never any use in trying to ignore the old law of 'like unto like.' I say this in explanation of what you know is true all the world over. Even the close ties of kindred often count for little where tastes, occupations, and habits of thought are diverse. All this is nothing against your perfect right to please yourself. In this land, thank Heaven! families and friends cannot yoke people together to pull forward general and miscellaneous interests."

"You speak as if it were a slight thing when the woman whom a man marries is merely accepted, tolerated, by his kindred."

"I have not said that, Graydon; I have only said again what I said before—that a man has a right to please himself. The truth is trite enough; why recur to it?"

"Gravitation is trite enough, but it often has an acute bearing on one's experience. You do not like Stella—"

"And she does not like me."

"Very well; but you try to be just to her, and when she has lived a while in different associations you will find her greatly changed. I think you can be her close friend in the future. But Henry detests her, and he is so quietly and obstinately tenacious in his views that the fact annoys me exceedingly."

"Very well; you can't help that. You will live in different houses, and your domestic life will be quite removed from business interests."

"Oh, confound Henry! He married to suit himself, so shall I. But, Madge, dear Madge, you will try to love her—to help her to be more like you, for my sake?"

At last Madge's laugh rang out merrily. "For mercy's sake, Graydon, don't ask me to be a missionary to your wife," she cried. "If I escaped with my eyes I should be lucky. You must think your wife perfection, and make her think you do. Woe be unto you if you introduce a female friend and suggest that she should be imitated, even to the arch of an eyebrow. Oh, no, I thank you! That's a sphere in which I shouldn't shine at all, and I wouldn't dare attempt it with any feminine saint in the calendar. Oh, Graydon, what a dear old goose you are!" and she laughed till the tears came into her eyes. He joined her in a half vexed way, protesting that she was still as uncanny as a ghost, although she had lost the aspect of one.

Suddenly she stopped, and tears of sorrow filled her eyes. "Here I am, laughing at our absurd talk," she said, "when I have just left the side of a poor girl, no older than myself, who is ghostly indeed in her flickering life. Is it heartless to seem to forget so soon? Oh, Graydon, you don't know what trouble is! You have only had vexations thus far. Let me tell you what happened last night, if only to make you grateful for your strong, prosperous life."

"Tell me anything you wish. I always have better thoughts and impulses after being with you."

"Please don't regard me as egotistical, or offend me by thinking I am trying to be better than others. Why shouldn't I help that poor girl? We often dance all night for fun; why can't we watch occasionally for pity? And in simple truth it will be a long time before the ache for that poor creature will go out of my heart. It came very close home, Graydon—very close. It brought to mind another girl, who was once scarcely stronger or better than Tilly Wendall is to-day, but God was kind. Tilly also has great black eyes, and they do look so large and pathetic in the wan little face! At first they did not notice me much. I was only another of the watchers who had come to aid her mother. It's astonishing how kind these plain country people are to one another in trouble, and many a housewife in this region has toiled all day and then sat up with the poor child the livelong night.

"For the first few hours I could do little more than help her move in her weak restlessness, and give remedies to relieve her incessant cough. The poor thing seemed neither more nor less than a victim of disease, that with a cruelty almost malign had tortured her. I can't explain how this awful impression grew upon me. It was as if viewless, brutal hands had racked the emaciated form until intelligence was gone, and then, not content, would continue their vindictive work while breath remained in the body. As my watch was prolonged this impression grew into a nightmare of horror. The still house, the silent, white, beautiful world without, and that frail young girl tortured hour after hour under my eyes by fever and a convulsive, incessant, remorseless cough."

She buried her face in her hands, and for a moment or two her voice was choked with sobs.

"Oh, Madge," cried Graydon, almost fiercely, "you anger me! I would strangle a man who harmed a hair of such a child's head. How can I worship a God who sends or permits such a thing? You are braver than I. I could see a man shot, but I couldn't look upon what you have described. Yet the picture brings back the moment when we parted—when you struggled feebly in my arms with a premonition of your almost mortal weakness, and then sank back white and deathlike. If you had not made so wise and brave an effort you might have lingered on in torture like this poor girl. You stood in just that peril, did you not?"

"I suppose I did."

"Oh, what a clod I was! I used to hear you cough night after night, and I would mutter, 'Poor Madge!' and go to sleep. To think that you might have suffered as this girl is suffering! I never realized it before, yet I thought I did. I can't tell you how my whole nature rebels at it all, and pious talk about resignation in the presence of such scenes fairly makes me grind my teeth;" and his brow blackened like night in his mental revolt, and his eyes were sternly fixed in honest, indignant arraignment of the Power he did not scruple to defy, though so impotent to resist.

Madge brushed away her tears, and watched him earnestly for a moment. In that confused instant she exulted in the strong, generous, kindly manhood that would not cringe even to omnipotence when apparently cruel. She said, gently, "Graydon, you are condemning God."

"I can't help it," he began, impetuously, "that is, such a God—"

She put her hand over his mouth.

"I like you better for your words," she continued, "but please don't talk so any more. Let what you have said apply to 'such a God—' I know what you mean, but there is no such being in existence. Let me finish my story. We have had too many interruptions, and this secluded road has an end. I won't try to explain my faith. What happened may make it clearer to you. Well, Tilly gradually grew quieter, and at last slept. The tired mother was sleeping also, and I sat at the window just as you imagined, my thoughts sad and questioning, to say the least At last I saw that Tilly was awake, and looking at me with something like interest and curiosity. I went to her and asked if I could do anything.

"She said, in her slow, feeble way, 'I thought I knew every one about here, but I don't remember to have seen you before.'"

"Then I told her who I was, and that her mother was in the next room."

"'You are very kind,' she said. 'And you are from the hotel. Isn't it a little strange?'"

"'It should not be,' I replied, and explained how I came to stay, adding, 'Don't talk any more. You are not strong enough.'"

"With a quiet smile that astonished me, she said, 'It won't make any difference, Miss Alden; I shall never be any better, or, rather, I shall soon be well. My mind seems growing clearer, and I'd like to talk a little. It is strange to see a young girl here. Are you strong and well?'"

"'Yes, very strong, and very glad to help your mother take care of you. I was once almost as ill as you are, yet I got well. Cheer up, and let us nurse you back to health.'"

"She shook her head. 'No, that's now impossible. You come and cheer poor mother and father, Miss Alden. I am more than cheerful, I am happy.'"

"I made her call me Madge, and said: 'Tell me then in a few words how you can be happy. My heart has just been aching for you ever since I came.'"

"Perhaps she saw tears in my eyes, for she said, 'Sit down by me.' Then she took my hand, leaned her cheek upon it, and looked at me with such a lovely sympathy in her beautiful dark eyes!"

"'Yes,' she said, 'I see you are young and strong, and you probably have wealth and many friends; still I think I am better off than you are. I am almost home, and you may have long, weary journeying before you yet. You ask me why I am happy. I'll just give you the negative reasons: think how much they mean to me—"And there shall be no more death, neither sorrow, nor crying, neither shall there be any more pain." All these may be taken from my life any hour. Think of what will be added to it. You believe all this, Madge?'"

"'Yes.'"

"'Then you must know why I am happy, and why I may be better off than you are. It will be very hard for father and mother—there will be more pain for them here in consequence—but soon it will all end forever; in a little while we shall be together again. So you know nearly all about poor little me,' she said, with another of her smiles, which were the sweetest, yet most unearthly things I ever saw. 'And now tell me about yourself. I'm not able to talk much more for the present. I'd like to know something about the friend who helped me through the last few steps of my journey. I can think about you in heaven, you know,' she said, with the sweetest little laugh. 'Don't look so sad, Madge. They'll tell you I'm gone soon. "Gone where?" ask yourself, and never grieve a moment.'"

"Oh, Graydon, she made it all seem so real, talking there alone in the night! And it is just as she says or it isn't anything. When you said, 'Such a God,' you had in mind a theological phantom, and I don't wonder you felt as you did; but this girl believes in a God who 'so loved the world'—who so loved her—and I do also. Her pain, her thwarted young life, I don't understand any more than I do other phases of evil, but I can give my allegiance to One who came to take away the evil of the world. That's about all the religion I have, and you mustn't ever say a word against it.

"Well, there is but little more to tell. Tilly spoke in quiet, broken sentences as her cough permitted, and I told her a little about myself and sang to her some hymns that mother sang to me when I was a child. With the dawn her mother came in, and was frightened at having slept so long, but Tilly laughed and said it was just splendid."

"She was evidently a very intelligent girl, and must have been a pretty one, too. She certainly has read a great deal, and has taught in public schools. There didn't seem to be a trace of morbidness in her mind or feeling. She was simply trying to make the best of everything, and her best certainly is *the* best. She has helped and comforted me more than I could her."

"Comforted you, Madge?"

"Oh, well," was the somewhat confused reply. "I've had trouble, and shall have again. Who is without it long in this world?"

"It's almost hard to see how serious trouble can reach you hereafter, you are so strong, so fortified. No, Madge; I'll never say a word against your faith or that of your new friend. Would to Heaven I had it myself! I wouldn't have missed this talk with you for the world, and you can't know how I appreciate the friendship which has led you to speak to me frankly of what is so sacred. All the whirl and pressure of coming life and business shall never blot from my memory the words you have spoken this morning or the scenes you have made so real."

If this were true, how infinitely deeper would have been his impression if he could have seen the beautiful girl, now smiling into his eyes, bowed in agony at that sick-bed, while she acknowledged with stifled sobs that the dying girl *was* better off—far happier than she who had to face almost the certainty of lifelong disappointment. Poor Madge had not told Graydon all her story. She would have died rather than have her secret known on earth, but she had not feared to breathe it to one on the threshold of heaven.

CHAPTER XXVIII

DISPASSIONATE LOVERS

During the last moments of their drive Madge and Graydon were comparatively silent. They were passing dwellings, meeting strangers, and they could not, with the readiness of natures less finely organized, descend to commonplaces. Each had abundant food for thought, while even Graydon now believed that he so truly understood Madge, and had so much in common with her, that words were no longer needed for companionship.

As they approached the piazza, they saw that Arnault was still Miss Wildmere's devoted attendant. His presence meant hope for Madge, and Graydon was slightly surprised at his own indifference. He felt that the girl to whom he regarded himself as bound belonged to a different world, a lower plane of life than that of which he had been given a glimpse. The best elements of his nature had been profoundly moved, and brought to the surface, and he found them alien to the pair on the piazza. He was even self-reproachful that he saw with so little resentment Stella's present companionship.

"While I don't like her course at all," he thought, "I must believe that she is acting from the most self-sacrificing motives. What troubles me most now is that I have a growing sense of the narrowness of her nature."

He had never come from her presence with his manhood aroused to its depths. It was her beauty that he dwelt upon; her piquant, alluring tones and gestures. Madge was not an ill-natured critic of the girl who threatened to destroy her future, but, by being simply what she was, she made the other shrink and grow common by contrast.

To Graydon such comparisons were odious indeed, and he would not willingly permit them; but, in conformity to mental laws and the force of circumstances, they would present themselves. Each day had found him in the society of the two girls, and even an hour like one of those just passed compelled him to feel the superiority of Madge. His best hope already for Stella was that she would change when surrounded by better influences—that her faultless taste in externals would eventually create repugnance to modes of thought and action unsuitable in a higher plane of life. He did not question his love for her, but he felt this morning that it was a love which was becoming disenchanted early, and into which the elements of patience and tolerance might have to enter largely. Should he marry her to-day he could not, as Madge had said, and with the first glow of affection, believe her perfect. He even sighed as he thought of the future.

His heart was very tender toward Madge, but it was with an affection that seemed to him partly fraternal, and partly a regard for one different, better, purer than himself. He proved the essential fineness, the capabilities of his nature, by his appreciation of some of her higher traits. Her ministry to the dying girl had given her a sacredness in his eyes. For the time she was becoming a sort of religion to him. He revealed this attitude of mind to her by a gentle manner, and a tone of respect and consideration in the least thing he said.

"Oh," thought the poor girl, "he could be so much to me and I to him! His touch, even in thought, would never be coarse and unfeeling; and I have seen again and again that I can inspire him, move him, and make him happy. Why must a wretched blunder thwart and blight two lives?"

Before they had finished their breakfast the beautiful languor of sleep was again in his companion's eyes, and he said: "Dear Madge, promise me you will take a long rest. Before we part I want to tell you what an illumined page you have put in my memory this morning. Some of the shadows in the picture are very dark, but there is also a light in it that 'never was on sea or land.' When you wake I shall be on my way to the trout-stream to which Dr. Sommers will guide me; and, do you know? I feel as if my memories will be in accord with the scene of my camping-ground. As I sit in my tent-door to-night I shall think over all you have said and described."

Her only answer was a smile, that for some reason quickened his pulse.

Much occurred before they met again.

He went to his room, wrote some letters, and made other preparations. Then, feeling that he should give the remaining time before his departure to Miss Wildmere, he sought her. She appeared to be waiting for him on the piazza, and there was reproach in her tone, as she said, "I half feared you were going without bidding me good-by."

"Such fears were scarcely just to me."

"I did not know but that you had so greatly enjoyed your morning drive as to go away in a fit of absent-mindedness. I have been sitting here alone an hour."

"I could not know that. When I drove up I saw that I should be *de trop*," he replied, as they sauntered to an adjacent grove.

"Now, Graydon, you know that is never true, so far as I am concerned."

"The trouble is, Miss Wildmere, others are concerned in such a way that the only resource left me is to keep my distance."

"Mr. Arnault has returned to the city," she said, with what appeared a great sigh of relief. "I am perfectly free now."

"Till Mr. Arnault returns."

"I cannot help his return."

"Oh, no. I do not question his right to come back, or even to buy this hotel and turn us all out."

"Please don't talk about him any more. I'm doing the best I can."

"I believe you think so, but I cannot think it will prove the best for any one. It is not what I expected or even imagined. You are acting from a mistaken sense of duty, and I am more sorry every day that you can commit such an error. Look at it in its true light, Stella. I cannot believe you are deceiving me: you must be leading Mr. Arnault to entertain a false hope."

"Graydon, I have refused Mr. Arnault, and he will take no refusal."

"You can refuse him in such a way that he must take it at once and forever."

"You don't know—" she began, tears coming into her eyes.

"No; you have only led me to surmise a great deal by implication."

"What would become of mamma and my little sister if papa should fail utterly?" and tears came faster. No one could be more pathetic than Miss Wildmere when she chose.

"Can you not trust me for them as well as for yourself?"

"Oh, Mr. Muir, I know you mean most generously and kindly, but papa is so anxious and fearful! He tries to keep up before others, but I know how he feels, and it's terrible. He is past middle age, and business success means very much to him. How can I do anything to harm him? I know so little about business and its perils, while papa thinks there may be terrible dangers ahead for every one. You might have the good-will to help us and yet soon be scarcely able to help yourself. I have been made to feel that the best I could do through these troublous times was to try to aid papa as far as possible, and then I shouldn't have anything with which to reproach myself."

Graydon was perplexed. Apparently she was doing wrong in the most self-sacrificing spirit, and believed that doing right, which would end her abnegation, was wrong and selfish.

While he hesitated, she resumed: "You see, Graydon, papa has the same as said that Mr. Arnault was tiding him over until he could realize on securities now of little value. Of course there has been no compromising understanding in words—do not think us capable of that. It would cut me to the heart to have you misjudge me or condemn me. I will give you the highest proof I can of my—my—esteem by being frank on a delicate subject, so that you can see how I am placed. I don't think many young ladies would do as much. Of course what I say is sacred between us. Mr. Arnault offered himself long since, and I promptly declined the honor, but he laughingly told me he would take no refusal, and chatted through the rest of the evening as pleasantly as if nothing had happened. I have virtually refused him several times since, but he persists, declaring that he will remain an agreeable friend until I change my mind. Surely, I am not misleading him. I do like him as a friend, and he knows that I have for him no other regard, and never had. Before you came he had begun to help papa, and to throw business in his way, and just now he is rendering him very great service. He may do this in the hope of influencing me, but he gives his aid without conditions. Yet I know him well enough to be sure that he would withdraw this business help should I now harshly dismiss him or engage myself to another. While I do show him that I appreciate his kindness, I do nothing to indicate that my feeling is changed. He must know that I regard him in the same light as in the past. If he is content with this, I have asked myself why I should be precipitate—why alienate him now in the very crisis of papa's affairs. Of course if I had only myself to think of—I've been foolish enough to think that I might help papa and still be happy in the end. Am I so very naughty, Graydon?"

He was at a loss how to answer her, but felt that he must at once disabuse her mind of one expectation.

"I admit, Stella," he said, thoughtfully, "that you are peculiarly placed, and I thank you for making clearer what I had partially surmised. While I admire and respect the motive, I must still repeat that I regret beyond all words such action in one who is so much to me. It is right also that I should define my own position more clearly. I will imitate your generous frankness. You know how greatly I admired you before I first went abroad; and while I felt that there was little chance for me, you being sought by so many, I did not give up hope. This hope was strengthened by my visit last summer, and when I returned and found you free a few weeks since I determined to win you if I could. You know I would have spoken before had you permitted. I have for some little time felt myself irrevocably bound by what has passed between us. I also believed that you would eventually give me a full explanation in regard to Mr. Arnault, and that his attentions would cease. As to my not being able to take care of you, that is absurd. I am not wealthy yet, but few young men in the city have better prospects. My brother's business is large and profitable, and I am soon to share in it. I could not, from the nature of things, enter into business relations with your father—I should not be at the head of the firm—but neither you nor yours should ever want. As to my brother, he is in no financial danger whatever. He has a large fortune, and is conservatism itself. If you are placed in an embarrassing position, I am also. Arnault's manner is not that of a friend. Others misjudge you and me also. It looks to the people here, and to my own family, as if you were playing with us both.

"Moreover," he continued, after a moment's thought, "you are drifting into a false relation with Arnault, although you may not be conscious of it. Before these troubles began you simply tolerated his attentions good-naturedly, and without any special motive. Now you have a definite motive and purpose, and—pardon me, Stella—they are misleading him. He would not continue his attentions an hour, did he believe they were utterly hopeless. To Arnault and all others you appear undecided between him and myself. Such an experiment as you are trying cannot work well. If he has any other power beyond that of your maidenly preference, he will not hesitate to increase it, and may make your father more utterly dependent upon him while appearing helpful."

"Yes; I have thought of that," she said, musingly.

"There seems to me but one straightforward, high-toned thing for you to do, Stella, and that is to follow your heart."

He was almost frightened at himself that he spoke with so little eagerness and longing. His words seemed but the honorable and logical sequence of what had gone before. For some reason this girl in the broad light of day did not appear to be the same as when she had fascinated him in the witching moonlight the evening before. It was not that her beauty had gone with the glamour of the night, but he had been breathing a different and a purer atmosphere. Madge had been revealing what to him seemed ideal womanhood.

In regard to Stella his illusion had so far passed that he thought, consciously, "Even at her best she is presenting Wildmere traits; her very self-sacrifice takes on a Wildmere form, and there is a flavor of Wall Street in it all."

But he still believed that he loved her, and that, if she was equal to such great though mistaken self-sacrifice for her father, she would, under his influence, throw off certain imperfections and gain a better tone.

That such thoughts were passing through his mind was a bad omen for the continuance of Miss Wildmere's power, and yet the opportunity of her life was still hers. She had simply to put her hand into his with a look of trust, and abide by the act, to secure a loyalty that would always have tried to promote her best interests. That she was strongly tempted to do this was proved by her manner, in spite of the fact that she had promised Arnault not to decide against him before Saturday.

It was a moment of indecision. His strong assurance that he

was abundantly able to take care of her, that Mr. Muir was wealthy and free from financial embarrassment, almost turned the scale. She felt that both Arnault and her father were deceiving her for their own purposes, and she had little hesitation in acting for herself without regard to them. Graydon's suggestion that her action was not high-toned, although delicately made, touched her pride to the quick, and she was compelled to feel during this interview, as never before, the superiority of the man who addressed her. She longed to force Henry Muir to acknowledge the daughter of the man he shunned in business; and not the least among her incentives was the thought of triumphing over Madge as a possible rival.

"At any rate," she had thought, "if I become engaged to Graydon he will have to be very much less fraternal. As to his not aiding papa," she concluded, "I can't help that. When once married I could make him do all he could afford, and papa and mamma have no right to expect anything more."

To the potency of all these considerations was added a sentiment for the man who awaited her answer, and who chafed inwardly that it was so long in coming.

"Truly," he thought, "this is a strange wooing. Henry himself could not more carefully weigh the *pros* and *cons* than does she apparently, nor am I in feverish suspense. I had hoped for something different in my mating."

A glimmering perception that her manner was not calculated to inspire a lover at last dawned on Miss Wildmere, and with it came a faltering purpose to decide in favor of Graydon at once; but as she turned toward him, to speak with what was meant to be a bewildering smile of joy, a messenger from the office said, "A telegram, miss."

Graydon frowned, and then laughed outright. She stopped in the very act of tearing open the envelope, and looked at him inquiringly.

"Oh, nothing," he said, lightly. "The opportuneness of that fellow's coming was phenomenal. How much longer am I to wait for your decision, Stella? Were the world in our secret, I should be known as St. Graydon the patient."

She flushed, but adopted his apparently light mood as the least embarrassing. "My memory is good, and I shall know how to reward you," she smilingly replied. "Please let me satisfy my mind about papa, for I'm sure it's from him."

"Oh, satisfy your *mind* fully about everything, Miss Wildmere."

She tore open the envelope with a strong gesture of impatience, and read, with a suddenly paling cheek, "Unless you choose the immediate certainty of absolute loss, wait till I see you. Will come soon. Wildmere."

She crushed the telegram in her hand, and turned away with a half-tragic air which at the moment struck Graydon as a little "stagy," and then he condemned himself for the thought. As she did not speak for a moment, he said, sympathetically, "Your tidings are bad?"

She tried to think, but was confused, and felt that she was in a cruel dilemma. Could Graydon be deceiving her? or was he as ignorant as he seemed of his brother's peril? Was her father in league with Arnault after all? and were they uniting to separate her from Graydon? She could not tell. She must gain more time. She would see her father, charge him with duplicity, and wring the truth from him.

When she turned to Graydon her eyes were full of tears again, and she faltered: "You may despise me if you will, but my father has made an appeal to me, and is coming to see me. I must hear what he has to say. I must tell him that I can't endure—that I can't go on this way any longer. I would gladly help him, save him, but after what you have said it's impossible to—Oh, was ever a girl placed in such wretched straits! Graydon, can you be patient a little longer?"

"There is nothing else for me to do, Stella. I only stipulate that your decision be made speedily, and that Arnault be given to understand what my rights are. I shall have no difficulty in enforcing them."

"I shall decide speedily. It is not right that I should be placed in such a torturing, humiliating position."

"Now I agree with you perfectly. When does your father come?"

"He says 'soon.'"

"Very well; I will return on Saturday."

"I wish you wouldn't go away now," she entreated.

"I think it is best," replied Graydon, decisively, yet kindly. "I have said all that is possible to an honorable man. By remaining I am placed in an anomalous position which my self-respect does not permit any longer."

"I suppose," she sighed, "that I should not ask too much. Well, so be it, then."

They walked back to the house in silence. At the door of a side entrance she turned to him, her face flushing at the admission, and said, hastily, "I waited a long time for you, Graydon," and then fled to her room.

"Oh, confound it!" he muttered, as he walked away. "What a muddle it all is! I ought to feel like strangling myself for permitting this doubting, cynical spirit to creep over me. Curse it all! her words and manner haven't the ring of absolute truth. It seems as if I heard a voice in the very depths of my soul, saying, 'Beware!' Am I becoming an imbecile? I doubted and misjudged Madge. Thank Heaven that is past forever! Now I am doubting and misjudging the woman I have asked to be my wife. I must be misjudging her—the alternative is horrible. I can't escape one conviction, however. It is turning out just as I expected and told her it would. Arnault's aid to her father has been delusive, and Wildmere is deeper in the mire than ever. This is a fine ending of my social career! The girl of my choice puts me off until she can end this Wall Street business more satisfactorily. She must wait and hear her father's reasons for further diplomacy before she can answer me. If Henry knew all this—But Madge, crystal Madge, won't repeat what I said. I must risk the loss of her society also. Has her keen insight into character enabled her to detect these Wildmere traits, and is this the cause of her antipathy? How simply she said 'I couldn't do'—what Stella has accomplished with so much skill that the gossips in the house are in honest doubt as to her choice, or whether, indeed, she proposes to accept either Arnault or myself. Well, well, I'll wait till she has had this interview with her father, and then she must either decide for me and against such tactics forever, or else she can wear my scalp in her belt with those of the other unfortunates."

In an hour he was on the road with Dr. Sommers to a wild and secluded valley.

CHAPTER XXIX

THE ENEMIES' PLANS

It has been shown that Arnault believed the decisive period to have come that would see the success or failure of his "operation" in the Catskills. Keen, penetrating, he had comprehended the situation clearly. He knew that Stella wished to accept Graydon, and was held in check by financial considerations only. He had seen her manner during the preceding moonlight evening, and with intense anger had observed from a neighboring grove the episode in the summer-house. The twig had not casually parted under his step, but had been snapped between his fingers. Stella's quick alarm and flight had revealed the continuance of his hold upon her fears, if not her heart. From that moment he dismissed all indecision. In bitterness he realized that his prolonged stay in the mountains had not advanced his interests. He had hoped to win the girl by devotion, keeping financial pressure in the background; she had been only suave, agreeable, and elusive. He had told her that he expected her decision by Saturday evening; she had merely bowed in a non-committal way. Meanwhile it was evident that if the Muirs kept up, apparently retaining the power to pass unscathed to better times, she would prolong her hesitancy, and in the end accept Graydon. He determined, therefore, to see her first, then her father, and to call in his loan immediately.

While Graydon and Madge were returning next morning from the lonely farmhouse Arnault was breakfasting at the hotel. He appeared in excellent spirits. Miss Wildmere's alert observation could not detect from his manner his knowledge of the fact that she had been on the point of yielding to Graydon the evening before. He was full of gallant courtesy toward her, and every glance and word expressed admiration. This was always the breath of life to her, and while it had ceased to give positive pleasure, its absence was like uncomfortable weather.

After the meal was over he led her to the same summer-house in which Graydon had almost spoken words endowed with a lover's warmth and eagerness.

"Stella," he said, "I shall go to town on the ten-o'clock train."

"I supposed you had concluded to remain all the week," she replied.

"No; very important interests call me to the city, much to my regret. You only bowed when I requested that I should receive a final answer before the close of this week. I shall return Saturday. Will you end my suspense within this time?"

She was silent.

"Will you make me another promise, then? Will you remain free this week? If you will not bind yourself to me, will you promise that no one else shall have a claim upon you until the time specified expires?"

After some hesitation she said, "Yes, I will promise that."

"Please do so, and you will not regret it," was his quiet response.

"I am not so eager to be bound that I cannot promise so much."

"Very well then, I am content for the present;" and he changed the subject.

They soon returned to the piazza, and Arnault employed his utmost effort to be agreeable during the brief time remaining.

Earlier in the week he had written Mr. Wildmere a letter, in consequence of which the momentous telegram had restrained the daughter at the critical moment already mentioned.

When Madge came down to a late dinner she saw that Arnault had disappeared from the Wildmere table, and that the belle was already a victim of *ennui* in the absence of both gentlemen. During the afternoon Mrs. Muir was eager to gossip a little over the aspect of affairs, but soon found that Madge would do scarcely more than listen.

"I don't understand that Miss Wildmere at all," said the elder sister; "late last evening she went to yonder summer-house, hanging on Graydon's arm as if they were engaged or married, and now he's gone to be absent several days. This morning she was there again with Arnault, and he wasn't talking about the weather, either. Now he's gone also. Before Graydon went she had another long interview with him while you were asleep. Good gracious! what is she aiming at? Young men were not so patient in my day or in our village; and quiet as Henry appears, he wouldn't play second string to a bow as Graydon does. When Miss Wildmere first came I thought it was about settled, and I tried to be polite to one whom I thought we should soon have to receive. Now it's a sort of neck-and-neck race between the two men. If Graydon wins, how shall you treat Miss Wildmere?"

"Politely for Graydon's sake, of course."

"Whose chances are best?"

"Graydon's."

"Do you think she loves him?"

"Yes, as far as she can love any one.'"

"Why, Madge, what do you mean?"

"She could not love as we should; she doesn't know what the word means. If she did she wouldn't hesitate."

"You think Henry's opinion of her is correct, then?"

"I think he's right usually. Miss Wildmere is devoted to one being—herself."

"Why, Madge, it would be dreadful to have Graydon marry such a girl!"

"Graydon is not Harry Muir. He attained his majority some years since."

"He certainly is old enough to show more spirit. Well, I don't understand her tactics, but such belles, I suppose, are a law unto themselves."

"Don't let us gossip about her any more. If Graydon becomes engaged there is only one thing for us to do. Miss Wildmere has made herself disagreeable to me in many little nameless ways, and we never could be friends, but I shall not give Graydon cause for just complaint. If he asks me to see her with his eyes, I shall laugh at him and decline."

"They shall never live with us," said Mrs. Muir, emphatically. "I know I'm not a brilliant and accomplished woman, but I have always made home a place of rest and comfort for Henry, and I intend it always shall be just such a refuge. He is nervous and uncomfortable whenever that girl comes near him. Some people can't get on together at all. I am so glad that he likes you! He says you are one that a man could depend upon in all sorts of weather."

"We'll see; but I like Santa Barbara weather, which is usually serene."

"Oh, Madge, you'll not go there again?"

"Yes, I shall probably make it my home. I should never keep my health in the East, and I should dread a winter in New York more than I can tell you."

"Well," said Mrs. Muir, discontentedly, "I suppose you will have your own way in everything hereafter; but I think you might at least try to spend a winter with us."

"If there were cause I would, Mary, but you are happy in your home, and I am not greatly needed. In my Western home I feel I can get the most out of life, just as you are getting the most out of yours. I should suffer from my old troubles in New York." This statement was true enough to both ladies, although a very prosaic impression was conveyed to Mrs. Muir's mind.

To Madge, Graydon's absence contained a strong element of hope. He would not have gone away if all had been settled between him and Miss Wildmere, and, as Mary had said, there appeared stronger evidence of uncertainty now than at first. Graydon had seen Miss Wildmere, and she evidently had not finally dismissed Arnault.

Madge indulged in no idle brooding, however, and by activity every hour in the day, passed the time bravely. One of her boy admirers had a horse, and became her escort on long excursions; and with Mrs. Muir she went to see Tilly Wendall again on Friday morning. The poor girl was very weak indeed, and could do little more than smile her welcome. Madge promised to spend Sunday night with her. She would have come before, but Graydon had told her that he might return Friday evening, and as a storm was threatening she thought it probable that he would hasten back to avoid it. She believed that there was still hope for her, and determined that she should never have cause in the future to reproach herself with lost opportunities. There was no imperative call of duty to her sick friend, for Mrs. Wendall said that two or three neighbors had lately offered their services.

Mrs. Muir was gladdened on her return to the hotel by a telegram from her husband, saying that he would arrive on the late train and spend Saturday with her. She and Madge sat down to dinner in a cheerful mood, which evidently was not shared by Miss Wildmere.

That brilliant young woman, although she made herself the centre of all things as far as possible, was a victim of poverty when thrown upon her own resources. Madge detected her in suppressed yawns, and had noted that she had apparently done little else than read novels since parting with the two men who were metaphorically at her feet. Since the telegram she had not received a word from her father or any one, and was inwardly chafing at the dead calm that had followed her exciting experiences. She did not misinterpret the deceptive peace, however, and knew that on the morrow she must decide what even she regarded as the most momentous question of life. Persons under the dominion of pure selfishness escape many perplexities, however, and she was prone to take short cuts to desired ends. Ready to practice deceit herself, she became more strongly impressed that her father and Arnault were misleading her. Therefore she impatiently awaited the former's appearance, that she might tax him with duplicity. Unless he had something stronger than vague surmises to offer, she intended on the morrow to promise Graydon Muir to be his wife.

As has been seen, Wildmere had too much conscience to try to sell his daughter outright, but since she was in a mood for a bargain he had insured the possibility of one remarkably good in his estimation, and was now on his way with very definite offers and statements indeed.

In the late afternoon Madge was speaking about a book to an acquaintance who said, "Go up to my room and get it."

Madge was not sure whether she cared to read the book or not, and sat down to examine it. Suddenly she heard distinctly the words, "I don't believe Henry Muir is in danger of failure. Graydon scouted the idea. You and Arnault are seeking to mislead me."

Madge then remembered that the next room was occupied by Miss Wildmere, and her first impulse was to make a noise, that the proximity of some one might be known, but like a flash came the thought, "Chance may have put me in the way of getting information of vital importance to Henry;" and the next sentence spoken assured her that this was true, for she heard a voice which she recognized as Mr. Wildmere's say:

"In all human probability Muir will be compelled to suspend to-morrow. Mr. Arnault has placed in his hands a call loan. You know what that is. Arnault is so alarmed about Muir's condition that he will demand the money in the morning, and I am perfectly satisfied that Muir can't raise it. You know enough about business to be aware of what will happen if he cannot. Such is the market now that if Muir goes down he will be cleaned out utterly, and Graydon will have to begin at the bottom like any other young man without resources. Of course, Arnault cannot afford to lose the money, and must act like any other business man.

"But he did not send me here to tell you this. As his broker I know about it, and tell you of my own accord. This is what he did authorize me to say to you. Had not business interests, which have already suffered from his devotion to you, prevented, he would be here now to make the offer in person. He says that he will settle upon you one hundred thousand dollars in your own right the day you marry him, and also give you an elegant home in the city. Now what is your answer?"

"When Henry Muir fails I'll believe all this," was the sullen reply.

"Be careful, Stella. Devoted as Arnault is he is not a man to be trifled with. He has made you a munificent offer, but if you show this kind of spirit he is just the one to withdraw at once and forever. If you love Graydon Muir well enough to share his poverty, I have not another word to say, although I shall be homeless myself in consequence."

"Nonsense, papa! You have been on the eve of ruin more times than I can remember. Graydon assured me that he was abundantly able to take care of me, and that his brother was in no danger. I can have all the elegance I want and still follow my own inclination. If Henry Muir fails, of course that ends the matter; and if he is to fail to-morrow it will be time enough to give Mr. Arnault my answer to-morrow night, as he asked that I would. If I give him a favorable one I prefer to do it in person, for I don't wish to appear mercenary. You, I hope, have the sense to keep this phase out of view."

"Oh, certainly. Such high-minded people as we are should not be misjudged," was the bitter reply.

"One has to take the world as it is, and one soon learns that all are looking after their own interests," was the cynical reply.

"A beautiful sentiment for one so young! Well, I must return to the city to-night, and I cannot take your acceptance of Mr. Arnault's offer?"

"No. I will give my answer in person to-morrow night. I can either accede in a way that will please him, or decline in a manner that will keep his friendship. I suppose you believe what you say about Mr. Muir, but I am sure you are mistaken, and I have set my heart on marrying Graydon."

"Your heart?" satirically.

She made no answer.

"You are taking no slight risk," he resumed, after a moment.

"Either Arnault is misleading you, or Graydon is deceiving me, and I would believe him in preference to Arnault any day. I won't be duped."

"But I tell you, Stella, that under the circumstances Graydon's ignorance is not at all strange. He has been absent; he is not in the firm; and what is swamping Muir is an investment outside of his regular business."

"You yourself said within a month that if Henry Muir went through this business crisis he would represent one of the strongest and wealthiest houses in the country. If he is in the danger you assert, the fact will soon be manifested. Mr. Arnault has requested my answer to-morrow night. I have not promised to give it; I have only promised him not to accept Graydon in the meantime."

"The fact that Mr. Arnault is helping me so greatly counts for nothing, I suppose."

"Oh, yes; I appreciate it very much, but not enough to marry him unless I must. I am literally following your advice—to choose between these two men. I shall convey to Mr. Arnault the impression that I am deeply moved by the generosity of his offer. I am. Girls don't get such offers every day. You can show him that the very fact of my hesitation proves that I am not mercenary; or I can, when I see him. At the same time I am not at all satisfied that Graydon Muir's offer is not a better one, and it is certainly more to my mind—if you don't like the word heart. This fact, however, may as well not be mentioned."

After some moments' hesitation he said, slowly: "Very well, then. You are my daughter, although a strange one, and I shall do as well for you as I can."

"Yes, please. I parted with sentiment long ago, but I can do well by those who do well by me. I shall soon be off your hands, and then you won't have me to worry about."

He made no response, and Madge heard his step pass into his

wife's room. A moment later Miss Wildmere also departed, and her voice was soon heard on the piazza. The conversation had been carried on in a comparatively low tone, and some words had been lost, but those heard made the sense given above. Circumstances had favored Madge. The open window at which she was sitting was near the next window in Miss Wildmere's room, and within two or three feet there was the customary thin-panelled door which enables the proprietor to throw rooms together, as required, for the accommodation of families. Therefore, without moving or volition on her part information vital to her relatives had been brought to her knowledge. She was perfectly overwhelmed at first, and sat as if stunned, her cheeks scarlet with shame for the act of listening, even while she felt that for the sake of the innocent and unsuspecting, to whom she owed loyalty and love, it was right. Soon, however, came the impulse to seek the refuge of her own room and think of what must be done. She stepped lightly to the outer door; there was no sound in the corridor, and with all the composure she could assume she passed quietly out and gained her own apartment unobserved.

CHAPTER XXX

THE STRONG MAN UNMANNED

Madge locked her doors, bathed her hot face, then paced her room in great agitation, feeling that not only her own happiness was in peril, but Graydon's also. Her mental distress was greatly enhanced by a feeling that in order to save her relatives she herself had been guilty of what to her sensitive nature appeared almost like a crime. "Was it right?" she asked herself again and again, and at last reached the conclusion that the fealty she owed to her relatives and to the man she loved justified her course—that she should shield them even at such cost to herself. "It was not curiosity that kept me passive," she thought, "but the hope, the chance to save Henry from financial ruin and Graydon from far worse disaster." It would indeed be "horrible" for any true man to marry such a girl; and to permit the man she loved to make such a fatal blunder was simply monstrous. Yet how could she prevent it without doing violence to every maidenly principle of her nature?

Should she tell her sister? This impulse passed almost instantly. Mary had not the tact, nerve, or reticence to meet such an emergency. It seemed, however, that if something was not done almost immediately this callous, selfish girl would cause lifelong wretchedness to Graydon as certainly as to Madge herself. Such a nature could not long maintain its disguise, and probably would not be at pains to do so after marriage. The self-sacrifice that she had led Graydon to believe in was all deceit. It was self with her, first and last; it would be self always. Madge knew Graydon well enough to be sure that to him, when his illusions were dissipated, the marriage vow would become a chain growing heavier with time.

This absolutely certain phase of the danger was so terrible that at first it almost completely dominated her thoughts. "Oh," she moaned, "I could see him marry a woman who would make him happy, and yet survive, but this would be worse than death!"

As she became more calm and could think connectedly, her mind reverted to what had been said about Henry's financial peril; and while she was inclined to take the same view as Miss Wildmere, she soon began to see that her brother-in-law should be informed of all references to him. Then the impression grew upon her that it would be wisest to tell him all, and let him save his brother, if possible, from a fate infinitely worse than lifelong poverty. Would this involve the disclosure to Mr. Muir of her secret? Sometimes she thought that he half suspected her already, and she feared that she could scarcely speak of a subject that touched her heart's interests so closely without revealing to those keen gray eyes more than she would have them see. But the risk must be taken to save Graydon.

"Can it be?" she said, after musing awhile, "that Henry is in any such danger as that man asserted, or was it a trumped-up scheme to influence the girl? Still, he did say that if she would choose Graydon and poverty he would not interpose. Poverty! I would welcome bondage and chains with Graydon. I would almost welcome Henry's failure, that I might prove to them my devotion. Every penny of my fortune should be theirs. Henry has looked very anxious and troubled sometimes when thinking himself unobserved. He keeps everything to himself so—"

Suddenly she sprang up with a flash of joy in her face, and whispered to herself, excitedly: "Suppose there is truth in what was said by those speculators. I have a fortune, and it's my own. Henry said it was so left to me that I could control it after I was eighteen. I can lend Henry the money to pay Arnault. I will give him every penny I possess to carry him safely through. Oh, I am so glad he is coming to-night!"

"Come down to supper," called Mrs. Muir.

"Why, Madge," exclaimed the lady, as they sat down under the light of the chandelier, "how flushed you are! And your eyes fairly beam with excitement. I half believe you are feverish."

"Nonsense! No doses for me now; milk and beefsteak are my remedies. I've been dwelling on some scenes partly imaginary, and you know how wrought-up I get."

"Oh, yes; now I remember, you asked Miss Thompson for a book, and went for it to her room. Of course that was the last seen of you. I never could get so carried away by a story."

"I haven't your even disposition, Mary."

"Miss Wildmere looks brilliant to-night, also. And if there isn't her father! This is the first time I've seen him up during the week. Well, I'm glad to see that his daughter can wake up a little for his sake, a well as for some other man."

Madge looked at her with mingled curiosity and repugnance.

"Horrid little monster!" she thought. "Now she is performing her filial act. As her father said, 'such high-toned people should not be misjudged.'"

"I think you dislike her worse than Henry does," said Mrs. Muir, with a low laugh. "You look at her as if she were a snake."

"She is not a girl after my heart," Madge replied, carelessly; then added, under her breath, "She's a vampire, but she shan't drain Graydon's life-blood."

Miss Wildmere was certainly in a genial mood. The munificent offer received from Mr. Arnault had enhanced her self-appreciation, and she felt that she had met it with rare nerve and sagacity. She had not shown herself dazzled like a village girl, and eager to grasp the prize. Moreover, she had thought, with proud complacency: "The man who can offer so much is not going to give me up, even should I keep him waiting months longer. I still believe that Graydon can give me all I want at present, and at the same time a position in society which Arnault could never attain, though worth millions. Arnault is on top of the wave now, but he is a speculator, like papa, and I'm sick of these Wall Street ups and downs. I believe in Henry Muir's conservatism. Because he is keeping quiet now they think he is going to fail. He is just the kind of man to be five times as rich as people think. Graydon will succeed to his business and business methods, and will not only make an immense fortune, but keep it. Papa has given me the test of all these gloomy warnings. If Henry Muir does not fail to-morrow, I won't believe a word of all that's been said. If he does, I'll do the next best thing, and take Arnault. No tenement-house for me, thank you. I've not been in society so long as not to make the most of my chances;" and under the inspiration of thoughts like these Miss Wildmere condescended to be affable to her parents, and to smile upon the world in general.

Madge Alden was an exception, however, and for her she had only a frown as she looked across the room at the young girl and saw the admiration and friendly regard that were so freely bestowed upon her. As was inevitable, the selfish spirit of one girl had repelled and the kindly nature of the other had attracted good-will. Human instinct is quick to recognize the tax-gatherers of society—the people who are ever exacting, yet give little except slights, wounds, and criticism.

"Oh," thought Miss Wildmere, "if I can only marry Graydon and snub that girl unmercifully I shall be perfectly happy!"

The late train would not arrive before nine o'clock, and Madge determined to go down in the stage to meet Mr. Muir. In the meantime her quick mind was coping with the emergency. She had often heard it said that in times of financial uncertainty an air of the utmost confidence should be maintained. Therefore she drew her sister into the parlor, and managed to place her in a lively and congenial group of ladies. Mrs. Muir herself was happy in the thought of soon seeing her husband, and appeared cheerfulness embodied.

Miss Wildmere saw her laughing and chatting with such unforced geniality that she muttered: "It's perfectly absurd to imagine that her husband is on the eve of bankruptcy. Even if he tried he couldn't keep such trouble utterly from his wife, and I've seen enough of people to be sure she does not dream of danger. The best people of the house are ever around her and that Madge Alden. Unless papa returns to-morrow night with predictions confirmed, the Muirs will have to admit me hereafter into their charmed circle. 'Sister Madge' looks also as if something keyed her up tremendously. Perhaps she is thinking that Graydon will return to-morrow to be her escort on long rides again. I'll soon put a spoke in that wheel, my proud minx. In a few hours you may wear a very different expression."

When the two girls met, however, they were scrupulously polite; but Madge took such pains to make these occasions rare that Miss Wildmere perceived the avoidance, and her vindictive feeling was intensified. Madge saw one or two of her dark looks, but only thought, "I shall now take a part in your cruel game, and it may not end as you imagine." She danced and laughed as if not a care weighed upon her mind.

When the hour arrived for the stage to meet the train she slipped away, wrapped herself in a cloak, and said to the driver that she was going to meet a relative. The train, was on time, and Mr. Muir, with others who were strangers, entered the stage.

"Why, Madge!" he exclaimed; "you here? This certainly is very kind."

They sat a little apart, and she whispered: "Don't show any surprise at this or anything else to-night. I have something to tell you, and you must manage to give me a private interview without any one knowing it—not even Mary at present."

"It's about Graydon," he said, anxiously.

"It's chiefly about yourself. I've heard something." She took his hand in the darkness, and felt it tremble. "You know how to keep cool and disguise your feelings," she resumed. "We can beat them yet. I left Mary in the parlor, the merriest of a merry group. She is happy in the thought that you are coming, and doesn't suspect anything. I am sure you will know just what to do when I tell you all, and you can avert all danger. Greet Mary as usual, and make the people in the house think you have no trouble on your mind."

"All right, Madge. As soon as I've had a little supper, you come to my room."

"No, you must take a walk with me outside. I want no walls with ears around."

"Is it so very serious?"

"You will know best when I have told you everything."

A few moments later Mr. Muir walked into the parlor the picture of serene confidence, and smiling pleasure at meeting his wife, who sprang up, exclaiming: "I declare, I was so enjoying myself that I did not realize it was time for you to be here. Come, I've ordered a splendid supper for you."

"I shall reward your thoughtfulness abundantly," he replied, "for I am ravenous." He then greeted Mrs. Muir's friends cordially, said some pleasant words, and even bowed, when retiring, very politely to Mrs. Wildmere, who in her meek, deprecating way sat near the door.

Two or three gentlemen sought Madge's hand for the next dance, and she was out upon the floor again, her absence not having been commented upon.

Not a feature of this by-play had been lost on Miss Wildmere, and she smiled satirically. "They thought to dupe me with delusions about Mr. Muir. He has no more idea of failing than I have, and before very long he shall be Brother Henry to me as well as to Madge Alden."

After a little while Madge excused herself and joined her relatives in the dining-room. She found her sister happy in giving all the details of what had occurred in her husband's absence, and he was listening with his usual quiet interest, while deliberately prolonging his meal to give the impression that his appetite made good his words. But Madge saw that he was pale and at times preoccupied.

At last he rose from the table, and Mrs. Muir said, "I will go and have a look at the children, and then join you on the piazza."

"Very well, Mary, I'll be there soon. I've sat so long in the cars that I want to walk a little for a change, so don't hasten or worry if I'm gone a little longer than usual. After such a splendid supper as you have secured for me I need a little exercise, and will smoke my cigar on my feet. The fact is, I don't get exercise enough. Come, Madge, you'd walk all day if you had a chance."

Mrs. Muir thought the idea very sensible. Mr. Muir and Madge passed out through a side door. The former lighted his cigar leisurely, and they strolled away as if for no other purpose than to enjoy the warm evening. The storm had not come, but clouds were flying wildly across the disk of the moon, and the hurry-skurry in the sky was akin to the thoughts of the quiet saunterers.

"Where shall we go?" he asked.

"Not far away. There is an open walk near, where we could see any one approach us."

"Now, Madge," Mr. Muir began, after reaching the spot, "I have followed your suggestions, for I have great confidence in your good sense. Your words have worried me exceedingly."

"There is reason for it, Henry, even though there is probably no truth in what has been said about your financial peril."

"Great God!" he exclaimed, starting, "is that subject talked about?"

"Do you owe money to Mr. Arnault?"

"Yes," with a groan.

"Would it hurt you should he demand it to-morrow?"

"Oh, Madge, this is dreadful!" and she saw that he was trembling.

"Now, Henry, take heart, and be your cool, brave self."

"Give me a little time, Madge. I've been carrying a heavy load, but thought the worst was over. I believe things have touched bottom, and I was beginning to see my way to safety in a short time. Even now the tide is turning, and I can realize on some things in a few days. But if this money is demanded to-morrow—Saturday, too, when nearly all my friends are out of town—it is very doubtful whether I could raise it."

"Would it cause your failure?"

"Yes, yes, indeed. A man may be worth a million but if he can't get hold of ready money at the moment it is needed, everything may be swept away. Oh, Madge, this is cruel I With just a little more time I could be safe and rich."

"Why have you not told us this?"

"Because I wouldn't touch your money and Mary's under any

circumstances, and I know that you both would have given me no peace, through trying to persuade me to borrow from you."

"That's just like you, Henry. How much do you owe Mr. Arnault?"

"Madge, I'm not going to borrow your money."

"Of course not, Henry. Please tell me."

"You will take no action without my consent?"

"Certainly not."

"Well, the paltry sum of thirty thousand, if demanded to-morrow, may involve the loss of my fortune. Of course if I could not pay this at once all the rest would be down on me. How in the world did you gain any knowledge of this affair?"

"Thank God, and take courage. I believe good is going to come out of this evil, and I believe you will think so too when you have heard my story;" and she told him everything.

"And Graydon has, to all intents and purposes, engaged himself to this—speculator," said Mr. Muir, grinding his teeth. "He's no brother of mine if he does not break with her; and, as it is, I feel as if I could never trust him with my affairs again."

Henry Muir was a man not easily moved, but now his concentrated passion was terrible to witness. His hands worked convulsively; his respiration was quick and irregular. His business and his commercial standing were his idols, and to think that a selfish, scheming girl had caused the jeopardy of both to further her own petty ambition, and that his brother should be one of her tools, enraged him beyond measure.

"Now," he hissed, "I understand why that plausible scamp offered to lend me money. He and his confederate Wildmere have been watching and biding their time. I had to be ruined in order to bring that speculator's daughter to a decision, and Graydon has been doing his level best to further these schemes."

"Henry, Henry, do be calm. You are not ruined, and shall not be."

"It's no use, Madge; I'm foully caught in their devilish toils."

Madge grasped his arm with a force that compelled his attention.

"Henry Muir," she said, in low and almost stern tones, "you shall listen to me. Ignorant girl as I am, I know better, and I demand that you meet this emergency, not in impotent anger, but with your whole manhood. I demand it for the sake of my sister and your children, for your own sake and Graydon's. You explained to me before we left town that I had sixty thousand dollars in United States bonds, first mortgage, and other good securities. You also explained that by the provisions of my father's will I had control of this money after I was eighteen. You have been so scrupulous that you have not even thought of asking for the use of it, but I demand of you, as an honest man, what right have you to prevent me from doing what I please with it?"

"You cannot make me take it, Madge."

"I can and will. I shall go to the city with you by the earliest train, and when Arnault asks for his money you shall quietly give it to him, and no one but ourselves shall know anything about the matter. If you pay this money promptly, will it not help your credit at once?"

"Certainly, Madge, but—"

"Oh, Henry," she cried, "why will you cloud all our lives by scruples that are now not only absurd but almost criminal? Think of the loss you will inflict on Graydon, your children, and your wife, by such senseless refusal. Have you not said that a little time will insure safety and fortune? And there is my money lying idle, when with to-morrow's sun it could buy me more happiness than could millions at another time. I trust to your business judgment fully. Suppose the money was lost—suppose my whole fortune was lost—do you think I would care a jot compared with being denied at this critical moment? I should hate the money you saved for me in this way, and I should never forgive you for saving it." She stood aloof and faced him proudly, as she continued: "Do you imagine I fear poverty? Believe me, Henry Muir, I have brain and muscle to take care of myself and others too if need be." Then, in swift alternation of mood, she clasped her hands caressingly upon his arm, and added: "But I have a woman's heart, and there are troubles worse than poverty. To see you lose the results of your lifework, and to see Graydon's prospects blighted, would be more than I could bear. You can give me all the security you wish, if that will satisfy you better; but if you deny me now, I shall lose confidence in you, and feel that you have failed me in the most desperate emergency of my life."

"The most desperate emergency of *your* life, Madge?"

"Yes; of *my* life," she replied, her voice choking with sobs, for the strain was growing too great for her nerve-force to resist. "You give way to senseless anger; you inveigh against Graydon, when he has only acted honorably, and has been deceived; you refuse to do the one simple, rational thing that will avert this trouble and bring safety to us all."

"Why, Madge, if I fail, this speculator will drop Graydon at once. Scott! this fact alone would be large compensation."

"If you were cool—if you were yourself—you could save Graydon in every way. I want to see him go on in life, prosperous and happy, not thwarted and disheartened almost at its beginning. Oh, why won't you? Why *won't* you?" and she wrung her hands in distress.

"Is Graydon so very much to you, Madge?" he asked, in a wondering tone.

"Hush!" she said, imperiously; "there are things which no man or woman shall know or appear to know unless I reveal them. It's enough that I am trying to save you all, and my own peace of mind. Henry Muir, I will not be denied. There are moments when a woman feels and *knows* what is right, while a man, with his narrow, cast-iron rules, would ruin everything. You *must* carry out my wish, and Graydon must know *nothing* about it. Oh, God! that I were a man!"

"Thank God, you are a woman! Child as you are, compared with my years and experience, you shall have your own way. I will this once put my lifelong principle under my feet, and if the future house of Muir & Brother is saved, you shall save it."

"Oh, thank you, thank you, Henry! Now see how happy I am. I have but one stipulation—the 'brother' must not know it. We shall go on the first train, shall we not?"

"Yes. You can say you want to do some shopping. Come, we have been away from Mary too long already. Oh, Madge, Madge, would that there were more girls like you!"

CHAPTER XXXI

CHECKMATE

"Well," exclaimed Mrs. Muir, when they appeared at last; "I thought you and Madge had eloped!"

"We are going to to-morrow by first train," said the young girl. "Henry says he must return to town for the day, and I shall accompany him to do some shopping."

"Now, Henry, this is too bad, and I've scarcely seen you this evening."

"I'm truly sorry, Mary; I did look forward to a good quiet day with you, but there is an important matter which I neglected to see to to-day, and which must be attended to. Graydon will soon be ready to relieve me a great deal."

"Well, I shall be glad when he can do something besides waiting on Mr. Arnault's convenience for the privilege of seeing Miss Wildmere. It will be a terribly long, fatiguing day for you, Madge—for you both, indeed!"

"Oh, I shan't mind it in the least! It won't be half so fatiguing as one of my long rides. You spoke of wanting some things, and I can shop for you, too."

Mrs. Muir had long since given up the idea of objecting seriously to anything for which business was the alleged reason. The chance to do some shopping by proxy soon occupied her mind, and when Miss Wildmere took occasion to pass and repass, the only apparent topic of interest in the Muir group was the prospect of purchasing some expensive goods.

Madge retired early to prepare for her journey. Mrs. Muir soon followed, and her husband remarked that he would merely remain down long enough to write a note to Graydon. This missive was brief, but was charged with dynamite.

On the morrow, long before Miss Wildmere waked from the golden dreams which that day should realize, Madge and Mr. Muir were on their way to the city. The young girl had said: "Don't let us do anything by halves. I have read that in the crisis of a battle timid measures are often fatal. Let me give you everything that you can use as collateral. How much is there?"

"Sixty thousand available at once. As I have said, you shall have your own way."

"Well, for once a woman is wiser than Solomon."

They went immediately to the trust company which had her property in keeping, and, having complied with the forms, obtained the entire sum, then parted on Broadway, to rendezvous at the train. Mr. Muir gave the radiant girl a look which she valued more than the money. He then went to his bank. The official whom he accosted had been rather cold and shy of late, but when he received the securities he grew perceptibly urbane.

On reaching his office Mr. Muir found that a transaction

which had been greatly delayed was now consummated, and that another ten thousand in cash was available. This also was sent to the bank at once. Several business men were present when a confidential clerk from Arnault appeared, and asked for a private interview.

"Well, really you must excuse me to-day. I'm very busy, and expect to leave town in an hour or two. Please state what you have to say in few words, or else I will see you next week."

"Mr. Arnault," began the clerk, in a metallic tone, "says that he is compelled to call in the loan he recently made you."

"Oh, certainly, certainly! Have you the securities I gave him as collateral?"

"No, sir, but I can get them," said the man.

"Do so, and I will give you my check. Thank Mr. Arnault for the accommodation, and say I have thirty or forty thousand to spare should he be hard pressed. Be quick."

The Wall Street men present looked at one another significantly, and one of them remarked, "You are forehanded for these times, Muir."

"If this absurd lack of confidence would only pass," was the careless reply, "I should have more money on hand than I could invest profitably;" and then he appeared absorbed in other matters.

Arnault received the message from his clerk with something like dismay, and turning on Mr. Wildmere, who was present, he said, almost savagely, "You have been misleading me."

"Indeed I have not, sir—not intentionally. I can't understand it."

"Well, I can. Muir is an old fox in business. I was a fool to think that a paltry thirty thousand would trouble him. Well, there is nothing to do but to close the matter up."

"What, in regard to my daughter?" said Mr. Wildmere, inadvertently.

"Oh, no; confound it! What has she got to do with this affair?" replied Arnault, with an irritation that he could not disguise. "I certainly have made Miss Wildmere a fair offer; some would regard it as more. I shall go up to-night and receive her answer, as I promised. I am one who never fails in a promise to man or woman, and I am ready to make good all that I have authorized you to say to your daughter, and more."

"Let me add," said Mr. Wildmere, with some assumption of dignity, "that as far as I have influence it is absolutely yours. I have ever prided myself on my fidelity to those who trust me."

"Thanks," replied Arnault, with a little menacing coldness in his tone. "I hope I shall have proof of the fact this evening. If so, all shall go swimmingly."

Poor Wildmere bowed himself out with trepidation at heart, and Arnault followed him with a dark look, muttering, "Let them both beware."

Mr. Muir met Madge at the depot, and was quietly jubilant. Both laughed heartily over the experiences of the day.

"You are a blessed little woman, Madge. I was never so off my balance before in my life as I was last night. When confused and upset, it is one of my impulses to stick to some principle of right, like a mule. Bless you, I think I have secured you twice over! I have given you a lien on property worth two hundred thousand in ordinary times."

"You have taught me to lean on you once more, Henry, and that is worth more than all your other liens."

Mr. Arnault now appeared, and came affably forward, saying, "I am glad my enforced action did not incommode you to-day."

"Thank you. I trust you are not in trouble, Mr. Arnault;" and there was a world of quiet satire in the remark.

"Oh, no—only a temporary need, I assure you," was the hasty reply.

"So I supposed;" and as Arnault turned away, the speaker gave Madge a humorous glance, which made her look of demure innocence difficult to maintain.

* * * * *

Graydon had enjoyed fair success in fishing, and yet had not been supremely happy. He found, with the venerated Izaak Walton, that the "gentle art" was conducive to contemplation; but there were certain phases in his situation that were not agreeable to contemplate. As he followed the trout-stream amid the solitudes of nature, the artificial and conventional in life grew less attractive. In spite of his efforts to the contrary, Miss Wildmere seemed to represent just these phases. He recalled critically and dispassionately all the details of their past acquaintance, and found, with something like dismay, that she had exhibited only the traits of a society belle—that he could recall no new ideas or inspiring thoughts received from her. The apparent self-sacrifice for her father, which he had so unequivocally condemned, was, after all, about the best thing he knew of her. The glamour of her beauty had been upon his eyes, and he had credited her with corresponding graces of heart and mind. What evidence had he of their existence?

The more he thought of it, the more his pride, also, rebelled at the ignominious position in the background that he was compelled to take while the Wall Street diplomacy was prolonged. At last, in anger and disgust, he resolved that, if he found Arnault in his old position by Stella's side, he would withdraw at once and forever.

After all, although he was as yet unconscious of it, the secret of his clarified vision was the influence of Madge upon his mind. She seemed in harmony with every beautiful aspect of nature—true and satisfying, while ever changing. Madge was right: the mountains, streams, rocks, and trees became her allies, suggesting her and not Miss Wildmere. He would have returned, for the pleasure of her society, but for his purpose not to appear again until Arnault should have time to arrive from the city and resume his attentions. If they were received as in the past, he would write to Miss Wildmere his withdrawal of further claims upon her thoughts.

It was with something like bitter cynicism that he saw his illusions in regard to Miss Wildmere fade, and when he drove up to the hotel after nightfall on Saturday, he was not sure that he cared much what her answer might be, so apathetic had he become. The force of his old regard was not wholly spent; but in his thoughts of her, much that was repugnant to his feelings and ideals had presented itself to his mind, and he felt that the giving up of his dream of lifelong companionship with her would almost bring a sense of relief. Without pausing to analyze the reason of his eagerness to see Madge and hear of her welfare, he ran up at once to Mrs. Muir's room.

"Madge went to New York!" he echoed, in surprise at Mrs. Muir's information.

"Yes; why not? She went to do some shopping for herself and me. Miss Wildmere's here, and, for a wonder, Mr. Arnault is not. What more could you ask?"

"Hang Mr. Arnault—" He had come near mentioning both in his irritation.

"When will Madge and Henry arrive?"

"Soon now—on the nine-o'clock train. Oh, by the way, Henry left a note for you!"

"Very well. I'll go to my room, dress, and meet them."

"He is asking after Madge rather often, it seems to me. She doesn't compare so very unfavorably with the speculator, after all, even in his eyes."

On reaching his room he threw himself wearily into a chair, and carelessly tore open his brother's note. Instantly he bounded to his feet, approached the light more closely, and saw in his brother's unmistakable hand the following significant words:

"Read this letter carefully and thoughtfully; then destroy it. Show your knowledge of its contents by neither word nor sign. Be on your guard, and permit no one to suspect financial anxieties. Arnault and Wildmere have struck me a heavy blow. The former has lent me money. I must raise a large sum in town, but think I can do it, even in the brief time permitted. If I cannot we lose everything. If I don't have to suspend to-morrow Miss Wildmere will accept you in the evening. She has been waiting till those two precious confederates, her father and Arnault, did their worst, so that she could go over to the winning side. You are of course your own master, but permit me, as your brother, affectionately and solemnly to warn you. Stella Wildmere will never bring you a day's happiness or peace. She loves herself infinitely more than you, her father, or any one else. Be true to me, and you shall share my fortunes. If you follow some insane notion of being true to her, you will soon find you have been false to yourself. Again I warn you. Speak to no one of all this, and give no sign of your knowledge. HENRY."

Graydon read this twice, then crushed the paper in his hand as he muttered, "Fool, dupe, idiot! Now at last I understand her game and allusions. She was made to fear that Henry was about to fail, and she would not accept me until satisfied on this point. Great God! my infatuation for her has been inciting Arnault in these critical times to break my brother down, and her father has been aiding and abetting, in order that I might be removed out of the way. She was so false herself that she suspected her own father, also Arnault, of deceiving her, and so kept putting me off, that she might learn the truth of their predictions or the result of their efforts. How clear it all becomes, now that I have the key! Well, I should be worse than a heathen if I did not thank God for such an escape."

CHAPTER XXXII

MADGE IS MATTER-OF-FACT

"Well, I have come back to civilization and all its miseries," thought Graydon. "I was among scenes that know not Wildmeres or Arnaults. 'Oh, my prophetic soul!' I felt that there was something wrong, in spite of her superb acting. Sweet Madge, dear sister Madge, as you ever will be to me, the more I think of it the more clearly I see that you are the one who first began to shatter my delusion. Since that morning when I brought you home from your long vigil, and you revealed to me your true, brave heart Stella Wildmere has never seemed the same, and the revolt of my nature has been growing ever since."

His wish now was to avoid seeing every one until he had met his brother. While the thought of his escape was uppermost in his mind, he was consumed with anxiety to learn the result of Henry's efforts in town. His commercial instincts were also very strong, and the thought of what might happen fairly made him tremble.

He slipped down a back stairway and out into the darkness, then bent his rapid steps to the depot, at which he arrived half an hour before the train was due. Remembering that excited pacing up and down there would not be very intelligent obedience to his brother's injunctions, he started down a country road in the direction from which the train would come, and paced to and fro in his strong excitement. At last the train arrived, and his first glimpse of Henry's face and Madge's was reassuring. The moment the former saw him he called out, "Hello, Graydon! Have you a trout supper for us?"

"Yes," was the hearty response; and he hastened forward and shook hands cordially, saying, in an aside, "Oh, Madge! I am so glad to see you again!"

"You are! Tell that to the marines. The length of your stay proves it to be a fish story."

"Here, Madge, we'll put you in the stage. I'll rest myself by walking to the house with Graydon."

"Henry, you are all right?" said Graydon, eagerly, as soon as they were out of earshot.

"Yes," was the quiet reply; "I raised the money, paid Arnault in full, and have a good surplus in the bank."

"Thank Heaven! How did you raise it? How has all this knowledge reached—"

"Patience, Graydon, patience. As soon as you are in the firm I shall have no secrets from you. Until you are, you must let me manage in my old way."

"I have indeed little claim on your confidence. I have been deceived, and have acted like a fool. But it's all over now. Henry, you may not believe me, but my nonsense would have ended to-night if I hadn't received your letter, and all this had not occurred. I had been disgusted with this Arnault business for some time, and had let Miss Wildmere know my views. As I thought it over while away it all grew so detestable to me that I resolved, if Arnault appeared again and renewed his attentions, I would never renew mine. He's here again, as you may have seen."

"Oh, yes; and I have talked with him. Please show no resentment. I obtained my information in a way unknown to him, and there is nothing unusual in our transaction on its face. How was it that you began to grow critical toward Miss Wildmere?"

"Well, I don't mind telling you. There was not a ring of truth or a stamp of nobility about her words and manner, and I have been associating with a girl who is truth itself and twice as clever and accomplished. Miss Wildmere was growing commonplace in contrast. I learned to love Madge as a sister before she went away, and now no man ever admired and loved a sister more."

Mr. Muir smiled broadly to himself in the darkness, and said: "Truly, Graydon, you are giving satisfactory proofs of returning sanity. We may as well conclude with the old saying, 'All's well that ends well.'"

"I think I had better go to town Monday and resume business. It's time I did something to retrieve myself."

"No, Graydon, not yet. I have everything in hand now, and believe the tide has turned. I realized ten thousand to-day on a transaction that I will tell you about. I am not doing much business now, only watching things and waiting. It was the suddenness of Arnault's demand that worried me—on Saturday, too, you know. He had about the same as said that I might have the money as long as I wanted it, and I should not have needed it much longer. In ordinary times I wouldn't have given it a thought.

"You can help me more up here. It's growing warm, and Jack isn't improving as I would like. After what has occurred I don't wish Mary and Madge to meet these Wildmeres any longer, so I propose that you and Madge go to the Kaaterskill Hotel on Monday and explore. If you like the place, then you can take Mary and the children there. I've had a little scare in town, and propose to realize on some more property and make myself perfectly safe. By going to a higher-priced hotel we increase our credit also, and add to the impression I made to-day, that we are in no danger."

As the stage drew near the piazza Graydon hastened forward to help Madge out. In doing so he saw Miss Wildmere greeting Arnault cordially. As he passed up the steps with Madge, he caught Stella's swift, appealing look at him. He only bowed politely and passed on. It was Madge's triumphal entry now by the same door at which she had seen him enter with Miss Wildmere but a few weeks before. How complete her triumph was, even Madge did not yet know. While she went to her room he sought the office and ordered some of the trout he had caught to be prepared for supper. As he stood there Miss Wildmere left Arnault's side, and said, "Mr. Muir, are you not going to shake hands with me?"

"Why, certainly, Miss Wildmere;" but there was little more than politeness in his tone and manner. As there were many coming and going, she drew away with a reproachful glance. "So long as Arnault is with me, he will not be cordial," was her thought.

She looked around for her father, but he, nervous and apprehensive, had disappeared. He felt that if he should be compelled to disclose the failure of his predictions, she would pass into one of her sullen, unmanageable moods. He feared that things were beyond his control, and decided to let the young men manage for themselves. He was not, however, exceedingly solicitous. He hoped that Arnault, aided by the influence of his munificent offer, would have the skill to push his suit to a prompt conclusion; but he believed that, if this suitor should be dismissed, Graydon would not fail his daughter, and that all might yet end well for her, and perhaps for himself.

The supper-room was again occupied by the late comers, many of whom were accompanied by their families and friends. Mr. Muir's quiet eyes fairly beamed over the group gathered at his table, and he felt that but few moments of his life compared with those now passing. Twenty four hours before he had seen himself drifting helplessly on a lee shore, but a little hand had taken the helm when he had been paralyzed, and now he saw clear sea-room stretching away indefinitely, with a turning tide and favoring gales. The terrible evils threatening him and his had been averted. The results of his lifework would not be swept away, his idolized commercial standing could now be maintained, his wife's brow remain unclouded by care, his children be amply provided for, Graydon saved from a worse fate than financial disaster, and, last but not least, the young fellow would be cured by Madge of all future tendencies toward the Wildmere type. He never could think of this hope without smiling to himself. He had at last obtained the explanation of Madge's effort and success. By the superb result he measured the strength of the love which had led to it. "Great Scott!"—his favorite expletive—he had thought; "what a compass there is in her nature! I had long suspected her secret, but when I touched upon it last night she made my blood tingle by her magnificent resentment. I would sooner have trifled with an enraged empress. Look at her now, smiling, serene, and, although not in the least artful, keeping all her secrets with consummate art. Who would imagine that she was capable of such a volcanic outburst? If Graydon does not lay siege to her now, the name of the future firm should be Henry Muir and idiot."

That sagacious young man did not appear at all blighted by the wreck of the hope he had cherished. He turned no wistful glances toward the girl who had so long satisfied his eyes, and, as he had believed, his heart. He felt much the same as if he had been imposed upon by a cunning disguise. Unknown to her, he had caught a glimpse of what the mask concealed, and his soul was shuddering at the deformities to which he had so nearly allied himself. Her very beauty, with its false promise, had become hateful to him.

"She is indeed a speculator," he thought, "and I'm a little curious to see how she will continue her game." It afforded him vindictive amusement that she often, yet furtively, turned her eyes toward him as if he were still a factor in it.

She never looked once in Graydon's direction but that Arnault was aware of the act. There was no longer any menace in his deportment toward her—he was as devoted as the place and time would permit—but in his eyes dwelt a vigilance and a resolution which should have given her warning.

After supper Mr. and Mrs. Muir found a comfortable nook on the piazza, and the banker smoked his cigar with ineffable content.

"Do you feel too tired for a waltz, Madge?" Graydon asked.

"The idea! when I've rested in the cars half a day."

"Oh, Madge!" he whispered; "dear, sweet little friend—you know I mean sister, only I dare not say it—I'm so glad to be with you again! What makes you look so radiant to-night? You look as though you had a world of happy thoughts behind those sparkling eyes."

"Nonsense, Graydon! You are always imagining things. I have youth, good health, have had my supper—a trout supper, too—and I like to dance, just as a bird enjoys flying."

"You seem a bird-of-paradise. Happy the man who coaxes you into his cage! Brother or not, when your beaux become too attentive they will find me a perfect dragon of a critic."

"When I meet my ideal, you shall have nothing to say."

"I suppose not. I am at a loss to know where you will find him."

"I shan't find him; he must find me."

"He will be an idiot if he doesn't. Pardon me if I don't dance any more to-night. I have had a long tramp over mountain paths, followed by a long, rough ride in a farmer's wagon, and now have a very important act to perform before I sleep. As a proof of my fraternal—I mean friendly—confidence, I will tell you what it is, if you wish."

"I don't propose to fail in any friendly obligations, Graydon," she replied, laughing, as they strolled out into the summer night, followed by Miss Wildmere's half-desperate eyes.

As they walked down a path, Graydon said, "Take my arm; the pavement is a little rough. Dear Madge, you look divine to night. Every time I see you my wonder increases at what you accomplished out on the Pacific coast. That great, boundless, sparkling ocean has given you something of its own nature."

"Graydon, you must be more sensible. When a fellow takes your arm you don't squeeze it against your side and say, 'Dear Tom,' 'Sweet Dick,' or 'Divine Harry,' no matter how good friends they may be. Friends don't indulge in sentimental, far-fetched compliments."

"I certainly never did with any friends of mine. On this very walk you told me that you were not my sister, and added, 'There is no use in trying to ignore nature.' See how true this last assertion is proving, now that I am again under your influence, and so enjoy your society that I cannot ignore nature. During all those years when you were growing from childhood to womanhood I treated you as a sister, thought of you as such. It was nature, or rather the accord of two natures, that formed and cemented the tie, and not an accident of birth. Even when you were an invalid, and I was stupid enough to call you 'lackadaisical,' your presence always gave me pleasure. Often when I had been out all the evening I would say, with vexation, 'I wish I had stayed at home with the little ghost.' How you used to order me about and tyrannize over me from your sofa when you were half child and half woman! I can say honestly, Madge, it was never a bore to me, for you had an odd, piquant way of saying and doing things that always amused me; your very weakness was an appeal to my strength, and a claim upon it. You always appeared to have a sister's affection for me, and your words and manner proved that I brought some degree of brightness into your shadowed life. In learning to love you as a sister in all those years, wherein did I ignore nature? During my absence my feelings did not change in the least, as I proved by my attempts at correspondence, by my greeting when we met. Then you perplexed and worried me more than you would believe, and I imagined all sorts of ridiculous things about you; but on that drive, after your vigil with that poor, dying girl, I felt that I understood you fully at last. Indeed, ever since your rescue of the little Wilder child from drowning my old feelings have been coming back with tenfold force. I can't help thinking of you, of being proud of you. I give you my confidence to-night just as naturally and unhesitatingly as if we had been rocked in the same cradle. I am not wearying you with this long explanation and preamble?"

"No, Graydon," she replied, in a low tone.

"I am very glad. I don't think well of myself to-night at all, and I have a very humiliating confession to make—one that I could make only to such a sister as you are, or rather would have been, were there a natural tie between us. I would not tell any Tom, Dick, and Harry friends in the world what I shall now make known to you. If I didn't trust you so, I wouldn't speak of it, for what I shall say involves Henry as well as myself. Madge, I've been duped, I've been made both a fool and a tool, and the consequences might have been grave indeed. Henry, who has so much quiet sagacity, has in some way obtained information that proved of immense importance to him, and absolutely vital to me. I shudder when I think of what might have happened, and I am overwhelmed with gratitude when I think of my escape. I told you that Miss Wildmere was humoring that fellow Arnault to save her father, and consequently her mother and the child. This impression, which was given me so skilfully, and at last confirmed by plain words, was utterly false. Henry has been in financial danger; Wildmere knew it, and he also knew that Arnault had lent Henry money, which to-day was called in with the hope of breaking him down. They would have succeeded, too, had he not had resources of which they knew nothing. You, of course, can't realize how essential a little ready money sometimes is in a period of financial depression; but Henry left a note which gave me an awful shock, while, at the same time, it made clear Miss Wildmere's scheme. She had simply put me off, that she might hear from Wall Street. If Henry had failed she would have decided for Arnault, and I believe my attentions led to his tricky transaction—that he loaned the money and called it in when he believed that Henry could not meet his demand. I must be put out of his way, for he reasoned justly that the girl would drop me if impoverished. Thus indirectly I might have caused Henry's failure—a blow from which I should never have recovered. Henry is safe now, he assures me; and, oh, Madge, thank God, I have found her out before it was too late! I had fully resolved while oft trouting that I would break with her finally if I found Arnault at her side again. Now he may marry her, for all I care, and I wish him no worse punishment. I shall go to my room now and write to her that everything is over between us. The fact is, Madge, you spoiled Miss Wildmere for me on that morning drive the other day. After leaving your society and going into hers I felt the difference keenly, and while I should then have fulfilled the obligations which I had so stupidly incurred, I had little heart in the affair. Her acting was consummate, but a true woman's nature had been revealed to me, and the glamour was gone from the false one. Now you see what absolute confidence I repose in you, and how heavily this strange story bears against myself. Could I have given it to any one for whom I had not a brother's love, and in whom I did not hope to find a sister's gentle charity? I show you how unspent is the force of all those years when we had scarcely a thought which we could not tell each other. I have little claim, though, to be a protecting brother, when I have been making such an egregious fool of myself. You have grown wiser and stronger than I. You won't think very harshly of me, will you, Madge?"

"No, Graydon."

"And you won't condemn my fraternal affection as contrary to nature?"

She was sorely at a loss. She had listened with quickened breath, a fluttering pulse, and in a growing tumult of hope and fear, to this undisguised revelation of his attitude toward her. She almost thought that she detected between the lines, as it were, the beginning of a different regard. He believed that he had been frankness itself, and his words proved that he looked upon his fraternal affection and confidence as the natural, the almost inevitable, sequence of the past. She could not meet him on the fraternal ground that he was taking again, nor did she wish him to occupy it in his own mind. To maintain the attitude which she had adopted would require as much delicacy as firmness of action, or he would begin to query why she could not go back to their old relations as readily as he could. She had listened to the twice-told tale of the events of the past few days with almost breathless interest, because his words revealed the workings of his own mind, and she had not the least intention of permitting him to settle down into the tranquil affection of a brother.

While she hesitated, he asked, gently, "Don't you feel a little of your old sisterly love for me?"

"No, Graydon, I do not," she replied, boldly. "I suppose you will think me awfully matter-of-fact. I love Mary as my sister, I have the strongest esteem and affection for Henry as my brother-in-law, and I like you for just what you are to me, neither more nor less. The truth is, Graydon, when I woke up from my old limp, shadowy life I had to look at everything just as it was, and I have formed the habit of so doing. I think it is the best way. You did not see Miss Wildmere as she was, but as you imagined her to be, and you blame yourself too severely because you acted as you naturally would toward a girl for whom you had so high a regard. When we stick to the actual, we escape mistakes and embarrassment. Every one knows that we are not brother and sister; every one would admit our right to be very good friends. I have listened to you with the deep and honest sympathy that is perfectly natural to our relations. I think the better of you for what you have told me, but I'm too dreadfully matter-of-fact," she concluded beginning to laugh, "to do anything more."

He sighed deeply.

"Now, there is no occasion for that sigh, Graydon. Recall that morning drive to which you have alluded. What franker, truer friendship could you ask than I gave evidence of then? Come now, be sensible. You live too much in the present moment, and yield to your impulses. Miss Wildmere was a delusion and a snare, but there are plenty of true women in the world. Some day you will meet the right one. She won't object to your friends, but she probably would to sisters who are not sisters."

Graydon laughed a little bitterly as he said, "So you imagine that after my recent experience I shall soon be making love to another girl?"

"Why not? Because Miss Wildmere is a fraud do you intend to spite yourself by letting some fair, true girl pass by unheeded? That might be to permit the fraud to injure you almost as much as if she had married you."

He burst out laughing, as he exclaimed, "Well, your head is level."

"Certainly it is. My head is all right, even though I have not much heart, as you believe. I told you I could be a good fellow, and I don't propose to indulge you in sentiment about what is past and gone—natural and true as it was at the time—or in cynicism for the future. I shall dance at your wedding, and you won't be gray, either. Come; the music has ceased, and it must be almost Sunday morning."

"Very well. On the day when you rightly boxed my ears, and I asked you to make your own terms of peace, I resolved to submit to everything and anything."

"You don't 'stay put,' is the trouble. Did I look and act so very cross that morning?"

"You looked magnificent, and you spoke with such just eloquent indignation that you made my blood tingle. No, my brave, true friend—I may say that, mayn't I?—it was not a little thing for you to go away alone to fight so heroic a battle and achieve such a victory; and, Madge, I honor you with the best homage of my heart. You have taught me how to meet trouble when it comes."

As they went up the steps, Arnault, with a pale, stern face, and looking neither to the right nor to the left, passed them and strode away.

CHAPTER XXXIII

THE END OF DIPLOMACY

Mr. Arnault's manner as he passed struck both Graydon and Madge as indicating strong feeling and stern purpose. In order to account for his action, it is necessary to go back in our history for a short period. While Madge was receiving such rich compensation for having become simply what she was, Miss Wildmere had been gathering the rewards of diplomacy. As we have seen, she had reached the final conclusion that if Mr. Muir did not fail that day she would accept Graydon at once; and, during its earlier hours, she had been complacency itself, feeling that everything was now in her own hands. Mr. Muir's appearance and manner the previous evening had nearly convinced her that he was in no financial difficulties whatever—that her father and Mr. Arnault were either mistaken or else were deceiving her. "If the latter is the case," she had thought, "they have so bungled as to enable me to test the truth of their words within twenty-four hours.

"I am virtually certain," she said, with an exultant smile, "that I shall be engaged to Graydon Muir before I sleep to-night."

In the afternoon it began to trouble her that Graydon had not appeared. As the hours passed she grew anxious, and with the shadow of night there fell a chill on her heart and hope. This passed into alarm when at last Graydon arrived with his brother and Madge, and greeted her with the cold recognition that has been described. She had met Mr. Arnault cordially at first, because there were still possibilities in his favor; but when her father promptly disappeared, with the evident purpose to avoid questions, and Mr. Muir and his family at supper gave evidence of superb spirits instead of trouble, she saw that she had been duped, or, in any case, misled. Her anger and worry increased momentarily, especially since Graydon, beyond a little furtive observation, completely ignored her. She naturally ascribed his course to resentment at her first greeting of Arnault, his continued presence at her side, and the almost deferential manner with which he was treated by her father, who had joined his family at supper, when no queries could be made.

"I'll prove to Graydon by my manner that I am for him," was her thought; but he either did not or would not see her increasing coldness toward Arnault.

Her purpose and tactics were all observed and thoroughly understood by the latter, however, but he gave few obvious signs of the fact. In his words, tones, compliments he proved that he was making good all that he had promised; but the changing expression in his eyes grew so ominous that Mr. Wildmere saw his suppressed anger with alarm.

Miss Wildmere felt sure that before the evening was over she could convey to Graydon her decision, and chafed every moment over the leisurely supper that Mr. Arnault persisted in making, especially as she saw that it was not his appetite that detained him. The Muir group had passed out, and to leave him and her father would not only be an act of rudeness, but also would appear like open pursuit of

Graydon. When at last she reached the parlor, to decline Arnault's invitation to dance would be scarcely less than an insult; yet, with intensifying anger and fear, she saw that circumstances were compelling her to appear as if she had disregarded Graydon's warnings and expectations. So far from being dismissed, Arnault was the one whom she had first greeted and to whom she was now giving the evening.

While she was dancing with Arnault, Graydon, with Madge, appeared upon the floor. She was almost reckless in her efforts to secure his attention. In this endeavor she did not fail, but she failed signally in winning any recognition, and the ill-concealed importunity of her eyes hastened Graydon's departure with Madge, and gave time for the long interview described in the previous chapter. She grew cold with dread. It was the impulse of her self-pleasing nature to want that most which seemed the most denied, and she reasoned, "He is angry because Arnault is at my side as usual, in spite of all he said. He is determined to bring me to a decision, and won't approach me at Arnault's side. Yet I dare not openly shake Arnault off, and he's so attentive that I must do it openly if at all. Graydon's manner was so very strange and cold that I feel that I should do something to conciliate him at once; and yet how can I when Arnault is bent upon monopolizing the whole evening? He gives me no chance to leave him unless I am guilty of the shameful rudeness of telling him to leave me. Oh, if I could only see Graydon alone, even for a moment!"

Arnault was indeed a curious study, and yet he was acting characteristically. He had virtually given up hope of ever winning Stella Wildmere. He had wooed devotedly, offered wealth, and played his final card, and in each had failed. When he left the city he still had hope that his promise of immediate wealth and Mr. Wildmere's necessity and influence might turn the scale in his favor; and he believed that having secured her decision she, as a woman of the world, would grow content and happy in the future that he could provide for her. But, be his fate what it might, both his pride and his peculiar sense of honor made it imperative that he should be her suitor until the time stipulated for his answer should expire. Up to twelve o'clock that night he would not give her the slightest cause for resentment or even complaint. Then his obligation to her ceased utterly, and she knew that it would.

He had been irritated and despondent ever since Mr. Muir, through Madge's aid, had so signally checkmated him. But Stella's greeting had reassured him, and Graydon's manner toward her gave the impression that she had not been extending encouragement to him. This promising aspect of affairs speedily began to pass away, however, when he saw her step to Graydon's side and ask if he was not going to shake hands with her. He knew how proud the girl was, and by this high standard measured the strength of the regard which impelled to this advance. He had since noted every effort that she had made to secure Graydon's attention, and the truth became perfectly clear. She had utterly lost faith in his and her father's predictions of financial disaster to Henry Muir, and would accept Graydon at the earliest opportunity. He saw that his defeat in Wall Street insured his defeat in the Catskills, and feared that Graydon had guessed his strategy, and, therefore, would not approach the girl while he was at her side. There was no use in his playing lover any longer—he had no desire to do so—for even he now so clearly recognized the mercenary spirit which might have brought her to his arms, that such manhood as he had revolted at it. If she had given him her hand it would have been secured purely through a financial trick, and even his Wall Street soul experienced a revulsion of disgust at the thought of a wife thus obtained. If he could have detected a little sentiment toward him, some kindly regret that she could not reward his long-continued and unstinted devotion, he would have parted from her more in sorrow than in anger; but now he knew that she was wild to escape from him, that she would instantly break her promise not to accept Muir before the close of the week, and, to his punctilious business mind, the week did not end until twelve o'clock Saturday night.

With a sort of grim vindictiveness he had muttered, "She shall keep her promise. Neither she nor Muir shall be happy till my time has expired."

Later in the evening, Graydon not returning, the thought occurred to Arnault, "Perhaps he too has recognized the sharp game she has played—perhaps Henry Muir has said to him, 'She has been putting you off to see the result of the sudden calling in of Arnault's loan,' and now young Muir proposes to console himself with that handsome Miss Alden;" and a gleam of pleasure at the prospect illumined his face for a moment. Meanwhile he maintained his mask before the world so admirably that even Miss Wildmere little guessed the depth of his revolt. He was the last one to reveal his bitter disappointment and humiliating defeat to the vigilant gossips of the house. Those who saw his smiling face and gallantries, and heard his breezy, half-cynical words, little guessed the storm within. He had been taught in the best school in the world how to say and look one thing and mean another.

At last an acquaintance approached, and said, "Pardon me, Mr. Arnault, but I don't propose to permit you to monopolize Miss Wildmere all the evening;" and then asked for the next dance.

Stella complied instantly, thinking, "Graydon may return now at any moment, and if he sees that I am not with Arnault will come to me, as usual."

Arnault bowed politely, looked at his watch, and invited another lady to dance. Stella had been on the floor but a few moments when not Graydon, but her father came and said to her partner, "Excuse me, sir. I wish to speak to my daughter."

Requesting her companion to wait, she followed Mr. Wildmere through an open window, and when on the piazza he took her hand and put it within his arm with a firmness that permitted no resistance. Arnault noted the proceeding with a cynical smile.

"Stella," said her father, in a low, stern tone, "did you not promise Mr. Arnault his answer this evening?"

"Answer my question first," she replied, bitterly. "Did Henry Muir fail to-day? Of course he did not. You have been deceiving me."

"I did not deceive you—I was mistaken myself. But I warn you. Graydon Muir is not at your side. He may not return. Arnault is waiting to give you wealth and me safety, but he may not wait much longer. You are taking worse risks than I ever incurred in the Street, and your loss may be greater than any I have met with."

"Bah!" she replied, in anger. "I might have been engaged to Graydon Muir this moment had I not listened to your croakings. I'll manage for myself now;" and she broke away and joined her partner again.

After the dance was over she said, "Suppose we walk on the piazza; I'm warm." She was cold and trembling. Arnault took his stand in the main hall, where he and she could see the clock should she approach him again. The last hour was rapidly passing. Miss Wildmere and her attendant strolled leisurely the whole length of the piazza, but Graydon was not to be seen. Then she led him through a hall whence she could glance into the reception and reading rooms. The quest was futile, and she passed Arnault unheedingly into the parlor, saying that she was tired, and with her companion sat down where they could be seen from the doorway and windows. But he thought her singularly *distraite* in her effort to maintain conversation.

"Oh," she thought, "he will come soon—he must come soon! I must—I *must* see him before I retire!"

Arnault meantime maintained his position in the hall, chatting and laughing with an acquaintance. She could see him, and there was little in his manner to excite apprehension. He occasionally looked toward her, but she tried to appear absorbed in conversation with the man whom she puzzled by her random words. Arnault also saw that her eyes rested in swift, eager scrutiny on every one who entered from without, and that the two hands of the clock were pointing closely toward midnight.

The parlor was becoming deserted. Those whom the beauty of the night had lured without were straggling in, the man at her side was growing curious and interested, and he determined to maintain his position as long as she would.

He was detained but little longer. The clock soon chimed midnight. Arnault gave her a brief, cold look, turned on his heel and went out, passing Graydon and Madge, who were at that moment ascending the steps.

"Oh, pardon me," said Miss Wildmere, fairly trembling with dread; "I had no idea it was so late!" and she bowed her companion away instantly. At that moment she saw Graydon entering, and she went to the parlor door; but he passed her without apparent notice, and bade Madge a cordial good-night at the foot of the stairs. As he was turning away Miss Wildmere was at his side.

"Mr. Muir—Graydon," she said, in an eager tone, "I wish to speak with you."

He bowed very politely, and answered, in a voice that she alone could hear, "You will receive a note from me at your room within half an hour." Then, bowing again, he walked rapidly away.

She saw from his grave face and unsympathetic eyes that she had lost him.

Half desperate, and with the instinct of self-preservation, she passed out on the piazza to bid Arnault good-night, as she tried to assure herself, with pallid lips, but ready then at last to take any terms from him. Arnault was not to be seen. After a moment her father stepped to her side and said:

"Stella, it is late. You had better retire."

"I wish to say good-night to Mr. Arnault," she faltered.

"Mr. Arnault has gone."

"Gone where?" she gasped.

"I don't know. As the clock struck twelve he came rapidly out and walked away. He passed by me, but would not answer when I spoke to him. Come, let me take you to your room."

With a chill at heart almost like that of death she went with him, and sat down pale and speechless.

In a few moments a note was brought to Mr. Wildmere's door, and he took it to his daughter. She could scarcely open it with her nerveless fingers, and when she read the brief words—

> "MISS WILDMERE—You must permit me to renounce all claims upon you now and forever. Memory and your own thoughts will reveal to you the obvious reasons for my action, GRAYDON MUIR,"

she found a brief respite from the results of her diplomacy in unconsciousness.

CHAPTER XXXIV

BROKEN LIGHTS AND SHADOWS

Mr. Wildmere looked almost ten years older when he came down to what he supposed would be a solitary breakfast; but something like hope and gladness reappeared on his haggard face when he saw Arnault at his table as usual. He scarcely knew how he would be received, but Arnault was as affable and courteous as he would have been months previous, and no one in the breakfast-room would have imagined that anything had occurred to disturb the relations between the two gentlemen. He inquired politely after the ladies, expressed regret that they were indisposed, and changed the subject in a tone and manner natural to a mere acquaintance.

Although his courtesy would appear faultless to observers, it made Wildmere shiver.

"Mr. Arnault," Mr. Wildmere said, a little nervously, as they left the breakfast-room, "may I speak with you?"

"Certainly," replied Arnault, with cool politeness, and he followed Mr. Wildmere to a deserted part of the piazza.

"You made a very kind and liberal offer to my daughter," the latter began.

"And received my final answer last night," was the cold, decisive reply. "It would be impossible to imagine more definite assurance that Miss Wildmere has no regard for me than was given within the time I stipulated. I have accepted such assurance as final. Good-morning, sir," and with a polite bow he turned on his heel and went to his room.

Mr. Wildmere afterward learned that he took the first train to New York.

"Arnault has a clear field now," Graydon had thought, cynically, while at breakfast. "I can scarcely wish him anything worse than success;" and then he looked complacently around the family group to which he belonged, and felicitated himself that Wildmere traits were conspicuously absent. His eyes dwelt oftenest on Madge. At this early meal she always made him think of a flower with the morning dew upon it. Even her evening costumes were characterized by quiet elegance; but during the earlier hours of the day she dressed with a simplicity that was almost severe, and yet with such good taste, such harmony with herself, that the eye of the observer was always rested and satisfied. Gentlemen who saw her would rarely fail to speak about her afterward; few would ever mention her dress. Miss Wildmere affected daintiness and style; Madge sought in the most quiet and modest way to emphasize her own individuality. As far as possible she wished to be valued for what she actually was. The very fact that there was so much in her life that must be hidden led to a strong distaste for all that was misleading in non-essentials.

"I am going to church with you to-day," said Graydon, "and I shall try to behave."

"Try to! You cannot sit with me unless you promise to behave."

"That is the way to talk to men," said Mrs. Muir, who was completely under her husband's thumb. "They like you all the better for showing some spirit."

"I am not trying to make Graydon like me better, but only to insure that he spends Sunday as should a good American."

"There is no longer any 'better' about my liking for Madge. It's all best. I admit, however, that she has so much spirit that she inspires unaffected awe."

"A roundabout way of calling me awful."

"Since you won't ride or drive with me to-day, are you too 'awfully good,' as Harry says, to take a walk after dinner?"

"It depends on how you behave in church."

They spent the afternoon in a very different manner, however, for soon after breakfast Dr. Sommers told them that Tilly Wendall was at rest, and that the funeral would be that afternoon.

With Dr. Sommers's tidings Graydon saw that a shadow had fallen on Madge's face, and his manner at once became gravely and gently considerate. There were allusions to the dead girl in the service at the chapel, where she had been an attendant, and Graydon saw half-shed tears in Madge's eyes more than once.

She drove out with him in the lovely summer afternoon to the gray old farmhouse. The thoughts of each were busy—they had not much to say to each other—and Madge was grateful, for his quiet consideration for her mood. It was another proof that the man she loved had not a shallow, coarse-fibred nature. With all his strength he could be a gentle, sympathetic presence—thinking of her first, thoughtfully respecting her unspoken wishes, and not a garrulous egotist.

He in turn wondered at his own deep content and at the strange and unexpected turn that his affairs had taken. He not only dwelt on what had happened, but on what might have happened—what he had hoped for and sought to attain. He remembered with shame that he had even wished that Madge had not been at the resort, so that he might be less embarrassed in his suit to Miss Wildmere. From his first waking moment in the morning he had been conscious of an immeasurable sense of relief at his escape. He felt now that he had never deeply loved Miss Wildmere—that she had never touched the best feelings of his heart, because not capable of doing so. But he had admired her. He had been a devotee of society, and she had been to him the beautiful culmination of that phase of life. He saw he had endowed her with the womanly qualities which would make her the light of a home as well as of the ballroom, but he had also seen that the woman which his fancy had created did not exist. There is a love which is the result of admiration and illusion, and this will often cling to its imperfect object to the end. Such was not the case with Graydon, however. His first motive had been little more than an ambition to seek the most brilliant of social gems with which to crown a successful life; but he was too much of a man to marry a belle as such and be content. He must love her as a woman also, and he had loved what he imagined Stella Wildmere to be. Now he felt, however, like a lapidary who, while gloating over a precious stone, is suddenly shown that it is worthless paste. He may have valued it highly an hour before; now he throws it away in angry disgust. But this simile only in part explains Graydon's feelings. He not only recognized Miss Wildmere's mercenary character and selfish spirit, but also the power she would have had to thwart his life and alienate him from his brother and Madge. While she was not the pearl for which he might give all, she could easily have become the active poison of his life.

"Oh," he thought, "how blessed is this content with sweet sister Madge—sister in spite of all she says—compared with brief, feverish pleasure in an engagement with such a sham of a woman, or the mad chaos of financial disaster which my suit might have brought about!" and he unconsciously gave a profound sigh of satisfaction.

"Oh, Graydon, what a sigh!" Madge exclaimed. "Is your regret so great? You were indeed thinking very deeply."

"So were you, Madge—so you have been during the last half hour. My sigh was one of boundless relief and gratitude. If you will permit me, I will tell you the thoughts that occasioned it as a proof of my friendly confidence. May I tell you?"

"Yes, if you think it right," she said, with slightly heightened color.

"It seems to me both right and natural that I should tell you;" and he put the thoughts which preceded his sigh into words.

"Yes," she replied, gravely; "I think you have escaped much that you would regret. Please don't talk about it any more."

"What were you thinking about, Madge?" he asked, looking into her flushed and lovely face.

"I have thought a great deal about Tilly and what passed between us. That is the house there, and it will always remain in my mind as a distinct memory."

Farm wagons and vehicles of all descriptions were gathering at the dwelling. They were driven by men with faces as rugged and weather-beaten as the mountains around them. By their sides were plain-featured matrons, whose rustic beauty had early faded under the stress of life's toil, and apple-cheeked boys and girls, with faces composed into the most unnatural and portentous gravity. There was a sprinkling of young men, with visages so burned by the sun that they might pass for civilized Indians. They were accompanied by young women who, in their remote rural homes, had obtained hints from the world of fashion, and after the manner of American girls had arrayed themselves with a neatness and taste that was surprising; and the fresh pink and white of their complexions made a pleasing contrast with their swains. Although the occasion was one of solemnity, it was not without its pleasurable excitement. They all knew about poor Tilly, and to-day was the culmination of the little drama of her illness, the details of which had been discussed for weeks among the neighbors—not in callous curiosity, but with that strange blending of gossip and sympathy which is found in rural districts. The conclusion of all such talk had been a sigh and the words, "She is prepared to go."

The people as yet were gathered without the door and in groups under the trees. Tilly's remains were still in her own little room, Mrs. Wendall taking her farewell look with hollow, tearless eyes. A few favored ones, chiefly the watchers who had aided the stricken mother, were admitted to this retreat of sorrow.

When Dr. Sommers saw Madge and Graydon he came to them and said, "Mrs. Wendall requested that when you came you and whoever accompanied you should be brought to her. Tilly, before she died, expressed the wish that you should sit with her mother during the funeral. No, no, Mr. Muir, Mrs.

Wendall would have no objection to any of Miss Alden's friends. I can give you a seat here by this window. The other rooms will be very crowded with those who are strangers to you."

Graydon found himself by the same window at which Madge had sat in her long vigil. The bed had been removed, and in its place was a plain yet tasteful casket. Mr. Wendall, with his head bowed down, sat at its foot, wiping away tears from time to time with a bandana handkerchief. Two or three stanch friends and helpers sat also in the room, for it would appear that the Wendalls had no relatives in the vicinity.

As Madge sat down by Mrs. Wendall, so intent was the mother's gaze upon her dead child that she did not at first notice the young girl's presence. Madge took a thin, toil-worn hand caressingly in both her own, and then the tearless eyes were turned upon her, and the light of recognition came slowly into them, as if she were recalling her thoughts from an immense distance.

"I'm glad you've come," she said, in a loud, strange whisper. "She wanted you to be with me. She said you had trouble, and would know how to sustain me. She left a message for you. She said, 'Tell dear Madge that the dying sometimes have clear vision—tell her I've prayed for her ever since, and she'll be happy yet, even in this world. Tell her that I only saw her a little while, but she belongs to those I shall wait for to welcome.' You'll stay by me till it's all over, won't you?"

Madge was deeply agitated, but she managed to say distinctly, "Tilly also said something to me, and I want you to think of her words through all that is to come. She said, 'Think where I have gone, and don't grieve a moment.'"

"Yes, I'll come to that by and by; but now I can think of only one thing—they are going to take away my baby;" and she laid her head on the still bosom with a yearning in her face which only God, who created the mother's heart, could understand.

What followed need not be dwelt upon. The mother and father took their last farewell, the casket was carried to the outer room, the simple service was soon over, the tearful tributes paid, and then the slow procession took its way to a little graveyard on a hillside among the mountains.

"I can't go and see Tilly buried," said Mrs. Wendall, in the same unnatural whisper. "I will go to her grave some day, but not yet. I am trying to keep up, but I don't feel that I could stand on my feet a minute now."

"I'll stay with you till they come back," Madge answered, tenderly; and at last she was left alone in the house, holding the tearless mother's hand. She soon bowed her young head upon it, bedewing it with her tears. The poor woman's deep absorption began to pass away. The warm tears upon her hand, the head upon her lap, began to waken the instincts of womanhood to help and console another. She stroked the dark hair and murmured, "Poor child, poor child! Tilly was right. Trouble makes us near of kin."

"You loved Tilly, Mrs. Wendall," Madge sobbed. "Think of where she's gone. No more tears; no more pain; no more death."

Her touch of sympathy broke the stony paralysis; her hot tears melted those which seemed to have congealed in the breaking heart, and the mother took Madge in her arms and cried till her strength was gone.

When Mr. Wendall returned with some of the neighbors,

Madge met him at the door and held up a warning finger. The overwrought woman had been soothed into the blessed oblivion of restoring sleep, the first she had for many hours. A motherly-looking woman whispered her intention of remaining with Mrs. Wendall all night. Mr. Wendall took Madge's hand in both his own, and looked at her with eyes dim with tears. Twice he essayed to speak, then turned away, faltering, "When I meet you where Tilly is, perhaps I can tell you."

She went down the little path bordered by flowers which the dead girl had loved and tended, and gathered a few of them. Then Graydon drove her away, his only greeting being a warm pressure of her hand.

At last Madge breathed softly, "Think where I have gone. Where is heaven? What is it?"

His eyes were moist as he turned toward her. "I don't know, Madge," he said. "I know one thing, however, I shall never, as you asked, say a word against your faith. I've seen its fruits to-day."

CHAPTER XXXV

A NEW EXPERIMENT

Stella Wildmere would not leave the seclusion of her room. As the hours passed the more overwhelming grew her disappointment and humiliation, and her chief impulse now was to get away from a place that had grown hateful to her. She had bitterly reproached her father as the cause of her desolation, but thus far he had made no reply whatever. She had passed almost a sleepless night, and since had shut herself up in her room, looking at the past with a fixed stare and rigid face, over which at times would pass a crimson hue of shame.

Mrs. Wildmere went down to dinner with her husband, and then learned that Mr. Arnault had breakfasted with him. This fact she told Stella on her return, and the girl sent for her father immediately.

"Why did you not tell me that Mr. Arnault was here this morning?" she asked, harshly.

He looked at her steadily, but made no reply.

"Why don't you answer me?" she resumed, springing up in her impatience and taking a step toward him.

He still maintained the same steadfast, earnest look, which began to grow embarrassing, for it emphasized the consciousness which she could not stifle, that she alone was to blame.

She turned irritably away, and sat down on the opposite side of the room.

"It's just part and parcel of your past folly," she began. "If I had known he was here, and could have seen him or written to him—"

She still encountered the same searching eyes that appeared to be looking into her very soul.

"Oh, well, if you have nothing to say—"

"I have a great deal to say," answered her father, quietly, "but you are not ready to hear it yet."

"More lecturing and fault-finding," said Stella, sullenly.

"I have not lectured or found fault. I have warned you and tried to make you see the truth and to help you."

"And with your usual success. When can we leave this house?"

"We *must* leave it to-morrow. I will speak in kindness and truth when you are ready to listen. I know the past; I have little left now but memory."

He waited some moments, but there was no relenting on her part, and he passed out.

All the afternoon conscience waged war with anger, shame,

pride and fear—fear for the future, fear of her father, for she had never before seen him look as he had since he had met her on the piazza the evening before. He had manifested none of his usual traits of irritability alternating with a coldness corresponding to her own. He seemed to have passed beyond these surface indications of trouble to the condition of one who sees evils that he cannot avert and who rallies sufficient manhood to meet them with a dignity that bordered on despair.

As Stella grew calmer she had a growing perception of this truth. He no longer indulged in vague, half-sincere predictions of disaster. His aspect was that of a man who was looking at fate.

A cold dread began to creep over her. What was in prospect? Was he, not Henry Muir, to lose everything? After all, he was her father, her protector, her only hope for the future. As reason found chance to be heard, she saw how senseless was her revolt at him. She could not go on ignoring him any longer. Perhaps it would be best to hear what he had to say.

This feeling was intensified by her mother, who at last came in and said, in a weak, half-desperate way, "Stella, there is no use of your going on in this style any longer. Distressed and worried as I am, I can see that we can't help matters now by just wringing our hands. Your father says we must leave as early as possible to-morrow. I can't do everything to get ready. I'm so unnerved I can scarcely stand now. Do come down to supper with us, or else let a good supper be brought to you, and then let us act as if we had not lost our senses utterly. Your father looks and is so strange that I scarcely know him."

"I'll not go down again. Nothing would tempt me to meet Graydon Muir and the curious stare of the people. I suppose they are full of surmises. If you will have a supper sent to me I will take it and do all the packing myself. Please tell papa that I wish to see him after supper."

She then made a toilet suitable for her task, and waited impatiently. Her father soon appeared with a dainty and inviting supper. As soon as they were alone Stella began:

"Now, papa, tell me the worst—not what you fear, but just what is before us."

"Eat your supper first."

"No; I wish to learn the absolute truth. You said you had a great deal to say to me. I'm calm now, and I suppose I've acted like a fool long enough."

"I have much to say, but not many words. *I* must begin again, Heaven only knows how or where. I am about at the end of my resources. I shall not do anything rash or silly. I shall do my best while I have power to do anything. I do not propose to reproach you for the past. It's gone now, and can't be helped. My proposal to you is that *you* begin also. You have tried pleasing yourself and thinking of self first pretty thoroughly. You know what it is to be a belle. Now, why not try the experiment of being a true, earnest, unselfish woman, whose first effort is to do right. Believe me, Stella, there is a God in heaven who thwarts selfishness and punishes it in ways often least expected. The people with whom we associate soon recognize the self-seeking spirit, and resent it. You have had a terrible and practical illustration of what I say. Are you not a girl of too much mind to make the same blunder again? With your youth you need not spoil your life, or that of others, unless you do it wilfully."

She leaned back in her chair, and bitter tears came into

her eyes.

"Yes," she faltered, "my lesson has been a terrible one; but perhaps I never should have become sane without it. I have been exacting and receiving all my life, and yet to-night I feel that I have nothing. Oh," she exclaimed, with passionate utterance, "I have been such a *fool*. Nothing, nothing to show for all those gay, brilliant years, not even a father's love and little claim upon it."

He came to her side and kissed her again and again.

"You don't know anything about a father's love," he said. "It survives everything and anything, and your love would save me."

Never, even under the eyes of Graydon Muir, had she been so conscious of her heart before. Had he seen her when she departed on the earliest train in the morning he would have witnessed a new expression on her face.

CHAPTER XXXVI

MADGE ALDEN'S RIDE

Methodical Henry Muir found that the events of the last few days had resulted in a reaction and weariness which he could not readily shake off, and he had expressed an intention of sleeping late on Monday and taking the second train. When he and his family gathered at breakfast, the removal to Hotel Kaaterskill was the uppermost theme, and it was agreed that Madge and Graydon should ride thither on horseback, and return by a train, if wearied. Mr. Muir then went to the city, well prepared to establish himself on a safer footing. Graydon and Madge soon after were on their way through the mountain valleys, the latter with difficulty holding her horse down to the pace they desired to maintain.

After riding rapidly for some distance, they reached long, lonely stretches, favorable for conversation, and Graydon was too fond of hearing Madge talk to lose the opportunity. He looked wonderingly at her flushed face, with the freshness of the morning in it; her brilliant eyes, from which flashed a spirit that nothing seemed to daunt; the sudden compression of her lips, as with power and inimitable grace she reined in her chafing steed. Never before had she appeared so vital and beautiful, and he rode at her side with something like exultation that they were so much to each other. He was turning his back on a past fraught with peril, over which hung the shadow of what must have been a lifelong disappointment.

"The girl who would have taken me, as Henry chooses among commercial securities, cannot now make me an adjunct to her self-pleasing career," he thought. "I am free—free to become to Madge what I was in old times. No one now has the right to look askance at our affection and companionship. What an idiot I was to endure Stella's criticism while she was playing it so sharp between Arnault and myself! No wonder crystal Madge said she and Stella were not congenial!

"I call Madge crystal, yet I don't understand her fully, and have not since my return. She has had some deep, sad experience, which she is hiding from all. From what Mrs. Wendall said at the funeral yesterday, Madge must have revealed more of it to that dying girl than to any one else. How my heart thrilled at those strange whispered words! How dearly I would love to help her and bring unalloyed happiness into her life! But whatever it was referred to I cannot touch upon till she of her own accord gives me her confidence. Could she have formed what promises to be a hopeless love in her Western home, and is she now hiding a wound that will not heal, while bravely and cheerfully facing life as it is? Perhaps her purpose to return to Santa Barbara proves that she does not regard her love as utterly hopeless. Well, whatever the truth may be, she hides her secret with consummate skill, and I shall not pry into even her affairs. I only know that as I feel now I should prize her friendship above any other woman's love."

"What are you thinking of so deeply?" she asked, meeting his eyes.

"My thought just then was that I should prize your friendship above any other woman's love, and I had been felicitating myself that Stella Wildmere would never have the right to criticise the fact."

"Oh, Graydon, what a man of moods and tenses you are!" Then she added, laughing, "There has been indeed a kaleidoscopic turn in affairs. Mr. Arnault disappeared yesterday, and Mary learned that the Wildmeres left by the early train this morning."

"Yes, Miss Wildmere followed Arnault promptly. They are near of kin, but not too near to marry. Their nuptials should be solemnized in Wall Street, under flowers arranged into a dollar symbol."

"I feel sorry for Mr. and Mrs. Wildmere, though; especially the former. I think he might have been quite different had the fates been kinder."

"I would rather dismiss them all from my mind as far as possible. Don't think me callous about Stella. If she had decided for me at once and been true I would have been loyal to her in spite of everything; but the revelation of her cold, mercenary soul makes me shudder when I think how narrowly I escaped allying myself to it."

"You have indeed had an escape," Madge replied, gravely. "If she were a young, thoughtless, undeveloped girl her womanhood might have come to her afterward. I hope I am mistaken, but she has made a singular impression on me."

"Please tell me it. You have insight into character that in one so young is surprising."

"I have no special insight. I simply feel people. They create an atmosphere and make some dominant impression with which I always associate them."

"I am eager to know what impression Miss Wildmere has made."

"I fear this would be true of her, even after she becomes a mature woman. A man might be almost perishing at her side from mental trouble of some kind, and, so far from feeling for him and sympathizing, she wouldn't even know it, and he couldn't make her know it. She would look at him quietly with her gray eyes as she would at a problem in the calculus, and with scarcely more desire to understand him, and with perhaps less power to do so. She would turn from him to a new dress, a new admirer, or a new phase of amusement, and forget him, and the fact that he was her husband would not make much difference. Some deep experience of her own may change her, but I don't know. I fear another's experience would be like a tragedy without the walls while she was safe within."

"Oh, Madge, think of a man with a strong, sensitive nature beating his very heart to death against such pumice-stone callousness!"

"I don't like to think of it," she replied. "Come, I ask with you now that we forget her as far as possible. She may not disappoint a man like Arnault. Let them both become shadows in the background of memory. Here's a level place. Now for a gallop."

When at last they pulled up, Graydon said, "Your horse is awfully strong and restless to-day."

"Yes; he has not been used enough of late. He'll be quiet before night, for I am enjoying this so much that I should like to return in the same way."

"I am delighted to hear you say so. My spirits begin to rise the moment I am with you, and you are the only woman I ever knew from whose side I could not go with the feeling, 'Well, some other time would suit me now.'"

Her laugh rang out so suddenly and merrily that her horse sprang into a gallop, but she checked him speedily, and thought, with an exultant thrill, "Graydon now has surely revealed an unmistakable symptom." To him she said:

"You amuse me immensely. You are almost as outspoken as little Harry, and, like him, you mistake the impression of the moment for the immutable."

"Now, that's not fair to me. I've been constant to you. Own up, Madge, haven't I?"

With a glance and smile which she never gave to others, and rarely to him, she said:

"I own up. I don't believe a real brother would have been half so nice.".

"Let the past guarantee the future, then. Shake hands against all future misunderstandings."

She was scarcely ready to shake hands on such a basis, but of course would have complied. In the slight confusion her hand relaxed its grasp on the curb-rein, and at the same moment a locomotive, coming along the side of the opposite mountain, blew a shrill whistle. Instantly her horse had the bit in his teeth, and was off at a furious pace.

At first she did not care, but soon found, with anxiety, that he paid no attention to her efforts to check him, and that his pace was passing into a mad run. The gorge was growing narrower, and the lofty mountains stood, with their rocky feet, nearer and nearer together. She could see through the intervening trees that the road and rail-track were becoming closely parallel, and at last realized that her horse was unmanageable.

When the engineer of the train saw Madge's desperate riding he surmised that her horse was not under control, and put on extra steam in order to take the exciting cause of the animal's terror out of the way. He thought he could easily reach the summit of the clove where the carriage-drive crossed the track before Madge, and then pass swiftly over the down-grade beyond; but he had not calculated on the terrific speed of the horse; and when at last the track and roadway were almost side by side the frantic beast, with his pale rider, was abreast of the train. For a moment the engineer was irresolute, and then, too late, as he feared, "slowed up."

The narrow road, with a precipitous mountain on the left, was so near to the flying train that the passengers in an open car could almost touch Madge, and she was to them like a strange and beautiful apparition, with her white face and large dark eyes filled with an unspeakable dread.

"Oh, stop the train!" she cried, and her voice, with the whole power of her lungs, rang out far above the clatter of the wheels, wakening despairing echoes from the mountains impending on either side.

The speed of the cars was perceptibly checked; the passengers saw the foam-flecked brute, with head stubbornly bent downward and eye of fire, pass beyond them. An instant later, to their horrified gaze and that of Graydon's, who was following as fast as a less swift horse could carry him,

Madge and the locomotive appeared to come together. The young man gave a hoarse, inarticulate cry between a curse and a shout, and whipped his horse forward furiously.

The speed of the train was renewed, and he saw through the open car that Madge must have passed unharmed before the engine, just grazing it. It also appeared that she was gaining the mastery, for her horse was rearing; then cars of ordinary make intervened and hid her from view a moment, and the train clattered noisily on.

When he crossed the track Madge was not where he had last seen her. The road beyond ran at a greater distance from the railway, and was lined with trees and bushes. Through an opening among these he saw that the horse had resumed his old mad pace, that Madge was still mounted, but that she was no longer erect, and sat with her head bowed and her whip-hand clutching the mane. He also saw, with a sinking heart, that the road curved a little further on, and evidently crossed the track again.

A moment later—Oh, horror! An opening in the foliage revealed Madge dashing headlong, apparently, into the train. He grew so faint that he almost fell from his horse, and was scarcely conscious, until, with a strong revulsion of hope, he found himself under the track which, about an eighth of a mile from the previous crossing, passes just above the roadway. Not aware of this fact, and with vision broken by intervening trees, he could not have imagined anything else than a collision, which must have been fatal in its consequences.

With hope his pulse quickened, his strength returned, and he again urged his jaded horse forward, at the same time sending out his voice:

"Madge, Madge, keep up a little longer."

The road had left the car-track, the noise of the train was dying away in the distance. At last, turning a curve, he saw that Madge's horse had come down to a canter, and that she was pulling feebly at the rein.

As he approached he shouted "Whoa!" with such a voice of command that the horse stopped suddenly and she almost fell forward.

"Quick, Graydon, quick!" she gasped.

He sprang to the ground, and a second later she was an unconscious burden in his arms.

He laid her gently on a mossy bank under an oak; then, with a face fairly livid with passion, he drew a small revolver from his hip-pocket, stepped back to the horse that now stood trembling and exhausted in the road, and shot him dead.

He now saw that they had been observed at a neighboring farmhouse, and that people were running toward them. Gathering Madge again in his arms, he bore her toward the dwelling, in which effort he was soon aided by a stout countryman.

The farmer's wife was all solicitude, and to her and her daughter's ministrations Madge was left, while Graydon waited, with intense anxiety, in the porch, explaining what had occurred, with a manner much distraught, in answer to many questions.

"The cursed brute is done for now," he concluded.

Madge's faint proved obstinate, and at last Graydon began to urge the farmer to go for a physician.

The daughter at last appeared with the glad tidings that the young girl was "coming to nicely."

Graydon breathed a fervent "Thank God!" and sank weak and limp into a seat on the porch. The farmer brought him a glass of cool milk from the cellar, and then Graydon sent in word that he would like to see the lady as soon as possible.

When he entered the "spare room" of the farmhouse Madge, with a smile that was like a ray of sunshine, extended her hand from the lounge on which she was reclining, and said:

"You didn't fail me, Graydon. I couldn't have kept up a moment longer. I should have fainted before had I not heard your voice. How good God has been!"

He held her hand in both his own, his mouth twitched nervously, but his emotion was too strong for speech.

"Don't feel so badly, Graydon," she resumed, and her voice was gentleness itself; "I am not hurt, nor are you to blame."

"I am to blame," he said, hoarsely. "I gave you that brute, but he's dead. I shot him instantly. Oh, Madge, if—if—I feel that I would have shot myself."

"Graydon, please be more calm," she faltered, tears coming into her eyes. "There, see, you are making me cry. I can't bear to see you—I can't bear to see a man—so moved. Please now, you look so pale that I am frightened. I'm not strong, but shall get better at once if I see you yourself."

"Forgive me, Madge, but it seems as if I had suffered the

pangs of death ten times over—there, I won't speak about it till we both have recovered from the shock. Dear, brave little girl; how can I thank you enough for keeping up till I could reach you!"

She began to laugh a little too nervously to be natural. Her heart was glad over her escape, and in a gladder tumult at his words and manner. He was no shadow of a man, nor did ice-water flow in his veins. His feeling had been so strong that it had almost broken her self-control.

"Some day," she exulted, "some day God will turn his fraternal affection into the wine of love."

"I'm so nervous," she said, "that I must either laugh or cry. What a plight we are in! How shall we go forward or backward?"

"We shall not do either very soon. Mrs. Hobson is making you a cup of tea, and then you must rest thoroughly, and sleep, if possible."

"What will you do?"

"Oh, I'll soothe my nerves with a cigar, and berate myself on the porch! When you are thoroughly rested I'll have Mr. Hobson drive us on to the nearest station. We are in no plight whatever, if you received no harm."

"I haven't. Promise me one thing."

"Anything—everything."

"Do no berating. I'm sorry you killed the horse; but he did act vilely, and I suppose you had to let off your anger in some way. I was angry myself at first—he was so stupid. But when I found I couldn't hold him at all I thought I must die—Oh, how it all comes back to me! What thoughts I had, and how sweet life became! Oh, oh—" and she began sobbing like a child.

"Madge, please—I can't endure this, indeed I can't."

But her overwrought nerves were not easily controlled, and he knelt beside her, speaking soothingly and pleadingly. "Dear Madge, dear sister Madge. Oh, I wish Mary was here!" and he kissed her again and again.

"Graydon," she gasped, "stop! There—I'm better;" and she did seem to recover almost instantly.

"Law bless you, sir," said Mrs. Hobson, who had entered with the tea, "your sister'll be all right in an hour or so."

Graydon sprang to his feet, and there was a strong dash of color in his face. As for the hitherto pallid Madge, her visage was like a peony, and she was preternaturally quiet.

"Try to sleep, Madge," said Graydon, from the doorway, "and I won't 'worry or take on' a bit;" and he disappeared.

There was no sleep for her, and yet she felt herself wonderfully restored. Was it the potency of Mrs. Hobson's tea? or that which he had placed upon her lips?

CHAPTER XXXVII

"YOU ARE VERY BLIND"

As a general rule Graydon was not conscious of nerves, and had received the fact of their existence largely on faith. But to-day they asserted themselves in a manner which excited his surprise and some rather curious speculation. He found his heart beating in a way difficult to account for on a physiological basis, his pulses fluttering, and his thoughts in a luminous haze, wherein nothing was very distinct except Madge's flushing face, startled eyes, looking a protest through their tears. It was not so much an indignant protest as it was a frightened one, he half imagined. And why was he so confused and disturbed that, instead of sitting quietly down in the porch, as he had intended, he was impelled to walk restlessly to a neighboring grove! For one so intensely fraternal he felt he was continuing to "take on" in a very unnecessary style.

"Confound that woman!" he muttered. "Why did she have to come in just then, and why should I blush like a schoolgirl because she caught me kissing one that I regard as a sister? And why did the word sister sound so unnatural when spoken by Mrs. Hobson? 'Great Scott!' as Henry says, I hope I'm not growing to love Madge. She would overwhelm me with ridicule, infused, perhaps, with a spice of contempt, if I gave her the impression that I had fallen out of love one week and in the next. Hang it! I'm all broken up from this day's experience. I had better get on my feet mentally, and then I shall be able to find out where I stand."

The demon of restlessness soon drove him back to the house again, and he learned that there would be a train in about two hours. They would still have time to dine at the Kaaterskill and return before night. He therefore made arrangements to be driven to the station, also to have the horse he had ridden and the saddles taken back to the Under-Cliff House.

There was a faint after-glow on Madge's cheeks when she joined him at the substantial repast which Mr. and Mrs. Hobson insisted upon their partaking before departure; but in all other respects she appeared and acted as usual. With a fineness of tact she was at home among her plain entertainers, and put them at ease. Mrs. Hobson continued to speak of her as Graydon's sister, and he had darted a humorous glance at the girl; but it met such grave impassiveness of expression that he feared she was angry.

When parting from her hostess Madge spoke words which left a genial expression on the good dame's face for hours thereafter, and at the station Graydon put in Mr. Hobson's hand more than he could have gathered from his stony farm that day, although he had been called from the harvest field.

During the first mile or two in the cars Madge was very quiet, and seemed almost wholly engrossed with the scenery. At last Graydon leaned toward her and asked, "Are you vexed with me, Madge?"

"I find that I must maintain my self-control when with you, Graydon," was the grave reply.

"Forgive me, Madge. I scarcely knew what I was doing. Let your thoughts take my part a little. Remember that within the hour I had believed I had lost you. I haven't had a chance to tell you yet, but when you passed under the train you appeared from where I was to dash into it, and I nearly fainted and fell off my horse. Think what a horrible shock I had. I also was nervous and all broken up—the first time in my life that I remember being so. I couldn't cry as you did, and when off my balance kissing you was just as natural to me as—" Madge's mouth had been twitching, and now, in spite of herself, her laugh broke forth.

"Please forgive me, Madge;" and he held out his hand.

"On condition that you will never do so again, or speak of it again."

"Never?" he repeated, ruefully.

"Never!" she said, with severe emphasis.

"I won't make any such promise," he replied, stubbornly.

"Oh, very well!" and she turned to the window.

"Confound it!" he thought; "I'm not going to tie myself up by any such pledge. I'm not sure of myself, or sure of anything, except that I'm a free man, and that Madge won't be my sister. I shall remain free. She herself once said in effect that I could take a straight course when once I got my bearings, and I shall permit no more promises or trammels till I do get them."

They passed speedily on to the end of their journey, and were the perfection of quiet, well-bred travellers, he disguising a slightly vexatious constraint and sense of unduly severe punishment, and she secretly exulting over the fact that he would not make the promise.

When leaving the Kaaterskill station her eyes first rested on the adjacent lake, and its wide extent suggested the opportunity to pull an oar to some purpose. As the stage surmounted the last approach to the hotel, and the valley of the Hudson, with the river winding through it like a silver band, broke upon her vision, the apparent cloud passed from her brow, and her pleasure was unaffected. A few inquiries and the study of a map of the vicinity made it evident that the region abounded in superb walks and drives, while from the front piazza there was a panorama that would never lose its changing interest and beauty. A suite of rooms was selected, with the understanding that they should be occupied on Wednesday.

Madge soon found herself the object of no little curiosity and interest. The story of her mad ride had reached the house, and she was recognized by some who had been on the train; but Graydon met inquiries in such a way that they were not pushed very far. To a reporter he said, "Is this affair ours or the public's? We have not trespassed on any one's rights."

He reassured Madge by saying, "Don't worry about it; such things are only the talk of a day."

They returned during the afternoon. Graydon's manner was courtesy itself, and but little more; but he was becoming a vigilant student of his companion, and she soon was dimly aware of the fact.

"I will understand her," he had resolved. "I intend to get my bearings, and then shape my course, for I cannot help feeling that the destiny of the little girl who used to sit on my lap, with her head on my shoulder, is in some way interwoven with mine. Even when I believed myself in love with another woman she had more power over me than Stella—more power to kindle thought and awaken my deeper nature. I begin to think that all her talk about being a friend, good fellow, etc., is greater nonsense than my fraternal proposals. No friend, fellow, or sister could make my heart beat as it did to-day. No human being in mortal peril could have awakened such desperate, reckless despair as I felt at one time, and" (with a smile to himself) "I never knew what a kiss was before. I'm not the fool to ignore all these symptoms. I'll fathom the mystery of this sweet, peerless girl, if it takes all summer and all my life."

But the fair enigma at his side grew more inscrutable. Neither by tone nor glance did she indicate that he was more to her than she had said.

"Do you wish to recognize the scenes we passed over this morning?" he asked, gently, as they approached them.

"No, not yet. I don't wish to think about it any more than I can help."

"Your wishes are mine."

"Occasionally, perhaps."

"You shall see."

"I usually do," was her laughing answer.

But she began to appear very weary, and when they reached the Under-Cliff House she went to her room, and did not reappear again that day.

Graydon made even Dr. Sommers's ruddy cheek grow pale

by his brief narrative, adding, "Perhaps her nerves have received a severer shock than she yet understands. I wish you would tell Mrs. Muir the story, making as light of it as you can, and with her aid you can insure that Miss Alden obtains the rest and tonics she needs. You can also meet and quiet the rumors that may be flying about, and you know that Miss Alden has a strong aversion to being talked to or of about personal affairs."

In youth, health, and sleep Madge found the best restoratives, and the morning saw her little the worse for the experiences of the previous day. The hours passed quickly in preparations for departure and in a call on Mr. and Mrs. Wendall, who gave evidence that they were becoming more resigned.

"I am at work again," said the farmer, "and so is Nancy. There's nothing else for us to do but plod toward home, where Tilly is."

Regret was more general and sincere than is usual when the transient associations of a resort are broken. Dr. Sommers's visage could not lengthen literally, and yet it approached as nearly to a funereal aspect as was possible. He brightened up, however, when Madge slipped something into his hand "for the chapel."

They were soon comfortably established in their new quarters, and in the late afternoon Madge was so rested that she took a short walk with Graydon to Sunset Rock, and saw the shadows deepen in the vast, beautiful Kaaterskill Clove. Then they returned by the ledge path. At last they entered the wonderful Palenvilie Road, a triumph of practical engineering, and built by a plain mountaineer, who, from the base of the mountain to the summit, made his surveys and sloped his grades by the aid of his eye only. They had been comparatively silent, and Graydon finally remarked: "It gives me unalloyed pleasure, Madge, to look upon such scenes with you. There is no need of my pointing out anything. I feel that you see more than I do, and I understand better what I do see from the changing expression of your eyes. Don't you think such unspoken appreciation of the same thing is the basis of true companionship?"

"Oh, Graydon, what an original thought!"

He bit his lip, and remarked that the evening was growing cool.

At supper and during the evening his vigilance was not rewarded in the slightest degree. Madge appeared in good spirits, and talked charmingly, even brilliantly at times, but she was exceedingly impersonal, and it was now his policy to follow her slightest lead in everything. He would prove that her wish was his, as far as he knew it.

"Some day," he thought, "I shall find a clew to her mystery."

The next morning Graydon went to the city, and would not return till Friday evening of the following week, for it was now his purpose to resume business. In the evening he and his brother discussed their affairs, which were beginning to improve all along the line. Then their talk converged more upon topics connected with this story, and among them was Mr. Wildmere's suspension.

"His failure don't amount to very much," Henry remarked; "he has always done business in a sort of hand-to-mouth way."

"I am surprised that Arnault permitted him to go down," Graydon said; "it couldn't have taken very much to keep him up."

"It is said that Arnault will have nothing to do with him, and that this fact has hastened his downfall."

"Well, so she played it too sharp on him, also. I was in hopes that she would marry and punish him. I don't wonder at his course, though; for if he has a spark of spirit he would not forgive her treatment after she learned that you had not failed. Oh, how blind I was!"

"Yes, Graydon, you are very blind," said Mr. Muir, inadvertently.

"'Are?' Why do you use the present tense?"

"Did I?" replied Mr. Muir, a little confusedly. "Well, you see, Madge and I understood Miss Wildmere from the first."

"Oh, hang Miss Wildmere! Do you think Madge—"

"Now stop right there, Graydon. I think Madge is the best and most sensible girl I ever knew, and that's all you will ever get out of me."

"Pardon me, Henry. I spoke from impulse, and not a worthy one, either. I tell you point blank, however, that Madge Alden hasn't her equal in the world. I would love her in a moment if I dared. Would to Heaven I could have spent some time with her immediately after my return! In that case there would have been no Wildmere folly. I declare, Henry, when I thought she must be killed the other day I felt that the end of my own life had come. I can't tell you what that girl is to me; but with her knowledge of the past how can I approach her in decency?"

"Well," said Mr. Muir, shrugging his shoulders and rising to retire, "you are out of the worst part of your scrape, and Madge is alive and well. This is not a little to be thankful for. I shall confine my advice to business matters. Still, were I in your shoes, I know what I should do. 'Faint heart,' you know. Good-night."

Graydon did not move, or scarcely answer, but, with every faculty of mind concentrated, he thought, "Henry's explanation of his use of the present tense does not explain, and there is more meaning in what he left unsaid in our recent interview than in what he said. Can it be possible? Let me take this heavenly theory and, as we were taught at college, see how much there is to support it. Was there any change in her manner toward me before we parted years since? Why, she was taken ill that night when she first met Miss Wildmere, and I stayed away from her so long—idiot!"

From that hour he went forward, scanning everything that had occurred between them, until he saw again her flushing face and startled eyes when he kissed her, and his belief grew strong that it was his immense good-fortune to fulfil the prediction that Madge should be happy.

The thought kept him sleepless most of that night, and made the time which must intervene before he could see her again seem long indeed. He did his utmost to get the details of his department well in hand during business hours; but after they were over his mind returned at once to Madge, and never did a scientist hunt for facts and hints in support of a pet theory so eagerly as did Graydon scan the past for confirmation of his hope, that long years of companionship had given him a place in Madge's heart which no one else possessed, and that his blindness or indifference to the truth was the sorrow of her life. This view explained why she would not regard herself as his sister, and could not permit the intimacy natural to the relation.

When he examined the attitude of his own heart toward her he was not surprised that his affection was passing swiftly into a love deeper and far more absorbing than Stella Wildmere had ever inspired.

"The old law of cause and effect," he said, smiling to himself, "and I can imagine no effect in me adequate to the cause. Even when she scarcely cast a shadow she was more companionable than Stella, but it never occurred to me to think of her in any other light than that of little sister Madge. Almost as soon as the thought occurred to me, and I had a right to love her, love became as natural as it was inevitable. Even in the height of my infatuation for Stella, Madge was winning me from her unconsciously to myself."

Such thoughts and convictions imparted a gentle and almost caressing tone to his words when Madge welcomed and accompanied him to his late supper on his return to the mountains.

This significant accent was more marked than ever when she promenaded with him for a brief time on the piazza. Nor did a little brusqueness on her part banish the tone and manner which were slight indeed, but unmistakable to her quick intuition.

"Could Henry have given him a hint?" she queried; and her brow contracted and her eyes flashed indignantly at the thought.

As a result of the suspicion, she left him speedily, and in the morning was glad to hope, from his more natural bearing, that she had been over-sensitive.

The sagacious Graydon, however, was maturing a plan which he hoped would bring her the happiness which it would be his happiness to confer.

"She is so proud and spirited," he thought, "that only when surprised and off her guard will she reveal to me a glimpse of the truth. If I consulted my own pride I wouldn't speak for a long time to come—not till she had ceased to associate me with Stella Wildmere; but if she is loving me as I believe she would love a man, she shall not doubt an hour longer than I can help, that I and my life's devotion are hers. Sweet Madge, you shall make your own terms again!"

CHAPTER XXXVIII

"CERTAINLY I REFUSE YOU"

Having heard that one of the finest views among the mountains was to be had at Indian Head, a vast overhanging precipice facing toward the entrance to the Kaaterskill Clove, Graydon easily induced Madge to explore with him the tangled paths which led thither.

How his eyes exulted over her as she tripped on before him down the steep, winding, rocky paths! As he followed he often wondered where her feet had found their secure support, so rugged was the way. Yet on she glanced before him, swaying, bending to avoid branches, or pushing them aside, her motions instinct with vitality and natural grace.

Once, however, he had a fright. She was taking a deep descent swiftly, when her skirt caught on a stubborn projecting stump of a sapling, and it appeared that she would fall headlong; but by some surprising, self-recovering power, which seemed exerted even in the act of falling, she lay before him in the path, almost as if reclining easily upon her elbow, and was nearly on her feet again before he could reach her side.

"Are you hurt?" he asked, most solicitously, brushing off the dust from her dress.

"Not in the least," she replied, laughing.

"Well," he exclaimed, "I don't believe you or any one else could do that so handsomely again if you tried a thousand times! Don't try, please. I carried you the other day some little distance, and found that you were no longer a little ghost."

"You carried me, Graydon? I thought the people from the farmhouse came."

"Oh, I didn't wait for them! I was half beside myself."

"Evidently," she replied, a little coolly.

Her tone made him falter in his purpose, and when at last they reached Indian Head, she was so resolutely impersonal in her talk, and had so much to say about the history and the legends of the region of which she had read, that he felt that she was in no mood for what he intended to say. As the time passed he grew nervously apprehensive over his project, and at last they started on their return with his plan unfulfilled. They agreed to try a path to their left, which was scarcely distinguishable, and it soon appeared to end at a point that sloped almost perpendicularly to a wild gorge that ran up between the hills.

"That must be what is down on the map as Tamper Clove," said Madge; "and do you know, some think that it was up that valley Irving made poor Rip carry the heavy keg? Oh, I wish we could get down into it and go back that way!"

"Let me explore;" and he began swinging himself down by the aid of saplings and smaller growth. "Some one has passed here recently," he called back, "for trees are freshly blazed and branches broken. Yes," he cried, a moment later; "here is a well-defined path leading up the clove toward the hotel. Do you think you dare attempt it?"

"Certainly," she answered; and before he could reach her she was half-way down the descent.

"Madge!" he cried, in alarm.

"Oh, don't worry," she said; "I was over worse places in the West."

"Well, what can't she do!" he exclaimed, as she stood beside him in the path.

"I can't give up my own way very easily," she replied. "You have found that out."

"That don't trouble me in the least. I don't wish you to give up your own way. It's warm down here, and our walk won't be so breezy as if we had followed the ridge."

"We will take it leisurely and have a rest by and by."

The gorge grew narrower and wilder. They passed an immense tree, under which Indians may have bivouacked, and in some storm long past the lightning had plowed its way from the topmost branch to its gnarled roots.

At last the path crossed a little rill that tinkled with a faint murmur among the stones, making a limpid pool here and there. Immense bowlders, draped with varied-hued mosses and lichens, were scattered about, where in ages past the melting glacier had left them. The trees that densely shaded the place seemed primeval in their age, loftiness, and shaggy girth.

"Oh, what a deliciously cool and lovely spot!" cried Madge, throwing down her alpenstock. "Get me some oak leaves, Graydon, and I will make you a cup and give you a drink."

In a moment she made a fairy chalice with the aid of little twigs, and when she handed it to him, dripping with water, his hand trembled as he took it.

"Why, Graydon," she exclaimed, "what on earth makes you so nervous?"

"I am not used to climbing, and I suppose my hand has a little tremor from fatigue."

"You poor thing! Here is a mossy rock on which you can imitate Rip. You have only to imagine that my leaf goblet is the goblin flagon of Irving's legend."

"Where and what would you be after twenty years?"

"Probably a wrinkled spinster at Santa Barbara."

"You wouldn't go away and leave me?"

"Certainly I would, if I couldn't wake you up."

He looked into her mirthful eyes and lovely face. Oh, how lovely it was, flushed from heat and climbing! "Madge," he said, impetuously, "you have waked me—every faculty of my soul, every longing of my heart. Will you be my wife?"

Her face grew scarlet. She sprang to her feet, and asked, with half serious, half comic dismay, "Will I be your *what!*"

"I asked you to be my wife," he began, confusedly.

"Oh, Graydon, this is worse than asking me to be your sister!" she replied, laughing. "Your alternations fairly make me dizzy."

"Truly, Madge," he stammered, "a man can scarcely pay a woman a greater compliment—"

"Oh, it's a compliment!" she interrupted.

"No," he burst out, with more than his first impetuosity; "I'm in earnest. You, who almost read my thoughts, know that I am in earnest—that—"

By a strong yet simple gesture she checked him.

"You scarcely realize what you are asking, Graydon," she said, gravely. "I have no doubt your present emotion is unforced and sincere, but it requires time to prove earnestness. You were equally sure you were in earnest a short time since, and I had little place, comparatively, in your thoughts."

"But I did not know you then as I do now."

"You thought you did. You had vivid impressions then about me, and more vivid about another woman. You are acting now under another impression, and from impulse. If I ever give myself away it shall not be in response to an impulse."

"Madge, you misjudge me—" he began, hotly.

"I think I know most of the facts, and you know how matter-of-fact I am. You may think I do not know what love is, but I do. It is a priceless thing. It is a woman's life, and all that makes a true woman's life. It is something that one cannot always give at will, or wisely; but if I had the power to give it at all, it should be to a man who had earned the right to ask it, and not to one who, within a few short days, had formed new impressions about me. Love is not the affection of a friend, or even of a sister. There is no necessity for me to marry."

"Then you refuse me?" he said, a little stiffly.

"Certainly I refuse you, Graydon. Has my manner led you to think that I was eager for a chance to accept you?"

"Oh, no, indeed! You have checked my slightest tendencies toward sentiment."

"Thank you for the assurance. I do not care in the least for sentiment."

His airy fabric of hope, of almost certainty, had been shattered so suddenly that he was overwhelmed. There seemed but one conclusion.

"Madge," he said, in a low, hoarse voice, "answer me, yes or no. You loved some one at Santa Barbara who did not return your love? That is your trouble of which Mrs. Wendall spoke—I could not help hearing her words—that is the mystery about you which has been haunting me with increasing perplexity; that was the sorrow I heard in your voice the evening you sang in the chapel, and which has vaguely, yet strongly, moved me since? Tell me, is it not so? Tell me, as a friend, that I may be a truer friend."

She had turned away in a manner that confirmed his thought.

"You are suggesting a humiliating confession, Graydon."

"Yes, humiliating to the man who saw you, knew you, yet

did not love you. Tell me, Madge. It will make my own course clearer."

"Yes, then," she replied.

He sighed deeply, and was silent for a few moments.

"Madge," he at last resumed, "look at me. I wish to tell you something."

She turned slowly toward him, and he saw that her lip was trembling, and that tears were gathering in her eyes.

"You may think me cruel in wringing such a confession from you, but perhaps you will forgive me when you hear all I have to say. You may look upon me now as a creature of impulses and impressions. The memory of my recent infatuation is fresh in your mind, but you yourself said I could be straightforward when once I got my bearings. I have them now, and I take my course. As a friend you have revealed to me much of your woman's nature, and, having known the best, I shall not look for anything less than yours. I shall be devoted to you through life. I will be to you all that I can be—all that you will permit. It is said that time heals all wounds. Perhaps some day—well, if it ever can be, I should be content to take what you could give. You said I was kind and patient with the little ghost. I should be far kinder, gentler—"

She had felt herself going fast, and had almost yielded to the impulse to exclaim, "You, Graydon, are the one who did not return my love; and although your love has been so brief and untested compared with mine, I will trust you;" when voices were heard on the same path by which they had come, and the figures of other ramblers were seen indistinctly through the foliage.

She gave his hand a strong pressure, seized her alpenstock, and hastened swiftly forward. The path soon afterward emerged on the public road. The breeze cooled her hot cheeks, kissed away her tears, and half an hour later they approached the hotel, chatting as quietly as the strictest conventionality would require.

CHAPTER XXXIX

MY TRUE FRIEND

They found that Mr. Muir had arrived, and no family party in the long supper-room appeared more free from disturbing thoughts and memories than the one gathered at the banker's table. In Madge the keen-eyed man could detect nothing that was unusual, and in Graydon only a trace of the dignity and seriousness which would inevitably follow some deep experience or earnest purpose. They all spent the evening and the greater part of the following day together, and Madge was touched more than once by observing that Graydon sought unobtrusively to comply with even her imagined wishes and to enhance the point and interest of her spoken thoughts.

In answer to his direct question she had acknowledged the absolute truth, and yet it had proved more misleading than all the disguises which her maidenly reserve had compelled her to adopt. It seemed now that she would have no further trouble with him—that he had defined his purpose, and would abide by it. She was glad that she had not yielded to his appeal and rewarded him in the first consciousness of his new regard for her. This feeling had seemed too recent, tumultuous, and full of impulse, and did not accord with her earnest, chastened spirit, that had attained the goal of its hope by such patient endeavor. She preferred that the first strong outflow from his heart should find wide, deep channels, and that his love for her should take the same recognized place in his life that her love had occupied so long in her own. She also had a genuine and feminine reluctance that the suitor of Stella Wildmere should be known as her lover so speedily, and something more and deeper than good taste was the cause of her aversion.

Yet she was exceedingly happy. The hope that had sustained her so long, that had been so nearly lost, now seemed certain of fulfilment, and no one but she and God knew how much this truth meant. Only He had been her confidant, and she felt that she had been sustained in her struggle from weakness to strength by a Power that was not human, and guided during the past weeks by a wisdom beyond her own.

"He has proved to me a good Father," was her simple belief. "He led me to do the best I could for myself, and then did the rest. I also am sure He would have sustained me had I failed utterly. That my life would not have been vain and useless was shown when I saved little Nellie Wilder."

Thus it may be seen that she was quite unlike many good people. In her consciousness God was not a being to be worshipped decorously and then counted out from that which made her real life and hope.

The future now stretched away full of rest and glad assurance. Graydon's manner already began to fulfil his promise. He would quietly accept the situation as he understood it, and she saw already the steadying power of an unselfish, unfaltering purpose. He appeared by years an older and a graver man, and when he sat by her during the service in the wide parlor, there was not a trace of his old flippant irreverence. Whatever he now believed, he had attained the higher breeding which respects what is sacred to others.

She had but little compunction over his self-sacrificing mood. It was perfectly clear that by quiet, manly devotion he proposed to help "time heal the wound" made by that "idiot" at Santa Barbara, and she that she could gradually reveal to him so much improvement that equanimity and at last hope would find a place in his mind.

They parted Monday morning with a brief, strong pressure of hands, which Graydon felt conveyed volumes of sympathy and mutual understanding. She had said that he could write to her, and he found he had so much to say that he had to put a strong constraint upon himself.

Mr. Muir had watched them curiously during his stay in the mountains, and felt that something had occurred which he could not fathom. Graydon's manner at parting and since, during business hours, had confirmed this impression. He was almost as grave and reticent as the banker himself, and the latter began to chafe and grow irritable over the problem which he was bent on seeing solved in but one way. He looked askance and discontentedly at Graydon during dinner in the evening. When they were alone he was fidgety and rather curt in his remarks. At last he burst out, "Confound it! What has happened between you and Madge?"

"She has refused me, that's all," was the quiet reply.

Mr. Muir gave a low whistle.

"Oh, I understood you the other evening," resumed Graydon. "The phenomenal penetration on which you so pride yourself is at fault for once."

The banker was so nonplused that he permitted his cigar to

go out, but he soon reached the conclusion, "He has bungled." "Well," he asked at last, "what do you propose to do?"

"To be to her all that she will ever permit, and die a bachelor for her sake if I must."

Mr. Muir lighted his Havana again and puffed in silence for a while, then said, "I like that. Your purpose is clearly defined. In business and everything else there is solid comfort in knowing what you can depend upon."

Madge's replies to Graydon's letters were scarcely more than notes, but they were breezy little affairs, fragrant with the breath of the mountains, and had an excellent tonic effect in the hot city. They usually contained a description of what she had seen or of some locality visited. On one occasion she wrote:

"Late in the afternoon there had been a shower, not gentle and pattering, but one of those frightful, passionate outbursts which are not infrequent in these mountains. The wind appeared to drive black masses of clouds from all directions save one, which, meeting over the height occupied by the hotel, discharged torrents of rain. At last the wind left the writhing trees in peace, and carried the deeply shadowing cloud away beyond the hills. The sun broke forth, and nature began some magic work. Calling the mist fairies to her aid, she gathered from every ravine and clove delicate airy clouds, which formed a large and rapidly increasing mass of vapor. Soon the plain below—the wide Hudson valley—was entirely shut out, as though a great white curtain had dropped from the sky to the mountain's base. Just then the setting sun, which had been temporarily obscured, shone forth in glorious brightness, casting on the beautiful cloud-curtain the dark, clearly defined shadow of the mountain-top, with its crown of buildings, even the towers and turrets showing with startling distinctness. It was like a mammoth, well-cut cameo, or a gigantic magic lantern effect, with the sun as a calcium light.

"The spectacle lasted only a few moments. Then the cloudy curtain parted, and the valley of the Hudson was seen again, spanned by a rainbow."

The days lengthened into weeks, Graydon coming every Friday afternoon, and wondering slightly at the demurely radiant face that greeted him. "Truly," he thought, "in the words of the old hymn she 'puts a cheerful courage on.'"

At times, however, she would be a little pensive. Then his tones would have a greater depth and gentleness, and his sympathy was very sweet, although she felt a little guilty because she was in no need of it. She could stifle her compunction by thinking:

"There was such a long, weary time when I did need it, and was desolate because of its absence, that I must have a little now to offset those gray, lonely days."

She had thought she loved him before, but as she saw him patiently and unselfishly seeking to brighten her life in every possible way, with no better hope than that at some time in the indefinite future she might give him what was left of her heart after the old fire had died out, her former affection seemed as pale and shadowy as she was herself when first she learned that she had a woman's heart.

Late one Friday afternoon he startled her by asking abruptly, "Madge, what has become of that fellow out West?"

"Please don't speak about that again," she faltered.

"Oh, well, certainly not, if you don't wish me to; but I thought if there was any chance—"

"Chance for what, Graydon?"

"Confound him! I don't suppose I could do anything. I want to make you happy, Madge. I feel just like taking the idiot by the ear, bringing him to you, and saying, 'There, you unconscionable fool, look at that girl—' You know what I mean. I'm suggesting the spirit, not the letter of my action. But, Madge, believe me, if I could help you at any cost to myself—"

"Is your regard for me, of which you spoke, so slight that you could go to work deliberately to bring that man to me?"

"There is no regard about it. My *love* for you is so great that I would do anything to make you happy."

"Madge," called the voice of Mrs. Muir, who was following them with her husband, "where are you and Graydon?"

"Here!" cried Madge, springing up. Then she gave her hand to him, and he saw that there were tears in her eyes. "Graydon," she said, "I couldn't ask a stronger test than that. I can't tell you how I appreciate it. I shall never impose any such task upon you."

"Don't hesitate on my account. I admit that it would be harder than one of the labors of Hercules, but you command me now and always. Nothing is so bad as to know that you are unhappy."

"Do I seem very unhappy?"

"No, you brave little woman! but who could guess the truth

if you were? My knowledge is not derived from your usual manner."

"It is a pity if I cannot be patient when you set me so good an example," she said, as Mr. and Mrs. Muir approached.

When they were alone again for a brief time during the ramble, Graydon resumed: "I wish to make sure of your confidence, Madge; I wish you to take me at my word. I don't think you have been quite just to me. I am not a cold-blooded fellow, and, no doubt, am given to impressions and impulses; but I think constancy is one of my traits. I never wavered in my affection for you until I misunderstood you immediately after my return, and then that very misapprehension kept me worried and perplexed much of the time. I was true to Miss Wildmere as long as there was anything to be constant to, and yet for years she was scarcely anything more than a fancy, a preference. Since my return you know just what she was to me. Nothing is more certain than that I never loved her. I did not know what the word meant then. There is a chapter in your history that I don't know much about, but I am sure I could make good my word to do anything within my power to bring you happiness. I have imagined that a little management, guided by tact and absolute fidelity—"

"Don't say anything more about that, Graydon," she said, firmly. "Not if my heart broke a thousand times would I seek a man or permit him to be sought for me in any such way as you suggest."

"That's settled, then."

"That's settled forever."

"Well, in that case," he said, with a short, nervous laugh,

"there may be a chance for me within the next hundred years."

"Are you so willing to take a woman who had once given her heart to another?"

"I don't know anything about '*a* woman.' I would take *you*, Madge, under any circumstances that I can imagine."

"Graydon," said Mrs. Muir, suddenly appearing around a turn in the walk, "what is the matter with you? Why can't you and Madge keep with us more? For some reason we are getting separated all the time. This is a lovely spot. Let us sit down here like a family party and have a little music. I just long to get back home, so that Madge may sing for us as much as we wish. Here she would attract the attention of strangers, and that ends the matter; and so I feel as if I had a rare singing bird, but never a song. In this secluded place no others will hear you, Madge."

"Very well. What do you wish? I feel like singing."

"Make your own choice."

"I'll give you an old song, then, about friendship;" and with notes rivalling those of a hermit-thrush that had been chanting vespers in the dense woods near by, she sang a quaint melody, her voice wakening faint echoes from the adjacent rocks. When she came to the last lines she gave Graydon a shy glance, which seemed to signify, "These words are for you."

"Kinder than Love is my true friend.
He'd die for me if that would end
My sorrow. Yes, would live for me—
Suffer and live unselfishly,

And that for him would harder be
Than at my feet to die for me."

As she ceased she again encountered his steadfast gaze with a glance which said, "Have I not done you justice?"

He was satisfied, and felt that the presence of his relatives had secured a sweeter answer than might otherwise have been given—an answer that contained all he could hope for then.

"Humph!" ejaculated Mr. Muir, very discontentedly.

"What an appreciative remark, Henry!" said Madge, laughing.

"It was; and it expressed my views," said the banker, dryly. "Come, Mary, let us go home to supper."

"Now, I think the song very pretty," said Mary, "only there are no such people nowadays."

As Madge followed with Graydon she continued laughing softly to herself.

"You are not hiding vexation at Henry?" Graydon asked.

"Oh, no, I understand Henry. You think I am always hiding something. You at least should have understood my song."

"Yes, Madge," he said, gravely, "and you also made it clear that you understood me. I am content."

She laughed, imitating the ejaculation.

"Henry's 'humph!' was too rich for anything. It meant

volumes. What sentimental fools he thinks us to be!"

"Henry could no more understand such a song than sing it," was Graydon's somewhat irritable response.

"No matter. Such men are invaluable in the world. My nature is very much in accord with Henry's, and so far as he has had experience, he is very sound."

"With your saving clause in mind, I agree with you perfectly about Henry, but not about yourself. Your nature, Madge, like your voice, has a wide compass."

With this one exception there was no other spoken reference during the remainder of the summer to the attitude toward her which he now maintained in thought and action. The season was drawing to a close, and she had enjoyed the latter part of it beyond her fondest hopes and expectations. She made a few congenial acquaintances at the hotel, and with them never wearied in exploring the paths that converged at the great caravansary, and in visiting the various outlooks from which the same wide landscapes presented ever-changing aspects. Chief among these friends was a middle-aged artist, who was deeply imbued with the genius of the mountains, and who had no little skill in catching and idealizing the lovely effects he saw. He proved her best guide, for he had long haunted the region, and the majority of the paths were due to his taste and explorations. In such congenial tasks he acted as agent for the sagacious and liberal owner of the vast property, who was so wise that in his dealings with nature he employed one that loved and understood her. To Madge the artist showed his favorite nooks and haunts, where the wild beauty of the hills dwelt like a living presence, and the scenery not yet painted which, from certain standpoints, almost composed itself on the canvas. Thus he taught her to see the region somewhat as he did, and to find in the general beauty definite, natural pictures that were like flowers in the wilderness. She greatly enjoyed watching with him the wonderful moonlight effects on the vast shaggy sides and summit of High Peak, that reared its almost untrodden solitudes opposite the hotel. This mountain was the favorite haunt of fantastic clouds. Sometimes in the form of detached mists they would pass up rapidly like white spectres from the vast chasm of the Kaaterskill. Again a heavy mass would settle on the whole length of the mountain, the outlines of which would be lost, and the whole take the semblance of one vast height crowned with the moon's radiance. Nothing fascinated Madge more than to observe how the artist caught the essential elements of beauty in the changing cloud scenery and reproduced the effects on a few inches of canvas, and in her better appreciation of similar scenery thereafter, she saw how true it is that art may be the interpreter of nature.

The fine music and varied entertainments at the house served also to beguile her time. On one occasion the young people were arranging a series of tableaux, and she was asked to personate Jephtha's daughter. When the curtain rose on her lovely face and large, dark eyes, the Hebrew maiden and her pathetic history grew into vivid reality against the dim background of the past.

After all, the time that intervened between Monday and Friday afternoon was spent in waiting, and even the hours toward the last were counted. The expression in Graydon's dark blue eyes was always the same when he greeted her, and recalled the line:

"Kinder than Love is my true friend."

On Saturdays they took long tramps, seeking objective points far beyond the range of ordinary ramblers.

CHAPTER XL

THE END OF THE WOOING

Madge had often turned wistful eyes toward High Peak, and on the last Saturday before their final return to the city she said to Graydon, "Dare we attempt it? Perhaps if we gave the day to the climb, and took it leisurely—"

"There's no 'perhaps' about it. We'll go if you wish. I should like nothing better than to get lost with you."

"There is no danger of getting lost," she replied, hastily. "The hotel must be visible from the whole line of its summit, and I am told that there is a path to the top of the mountain."

"I will be ready in half an hour," he said.

It was a lovely day in early September. The air was soft, yet cool and bracing enough to make climbing agreeable. Graydon had a lunch basket, which he could sling over his shoulder, well filled, and ordered a carriage. "There is no need of our tramping over the intervening miles of dusty roads which must be passed before we begin our climb," he said, "and the distance we ride will make a pleasant drive for Mary and the children."

Madge and Graydon reached the summit without any great difficulty, Mary having returned with the assurance that they would find their own way back to the hotel.

As the hours passed, Graydon began to gather more hope than he had dared to entertain since his shattered theory had so disheartened him. In spite of his fancied knowledge about Madge, it was hard to believe she was very unhappy that morning. There was an elasticity to her step, a ring of genuine gladness in her tones and laugh, which did not suggest that she was consciously carrying a heavy burden.

"She certainly is the bravest and most unselfish girl I ever imagined," he thought, as they left the highest point after enjoying the view. "With an art so inimitable as to be artless, she has tried to give me enjoyment. Instead of regarding herself as one to be entertained, she has been pouring forth words, fancies, snatches of song like sparkling wine, and I am exhilarated instead of being wearied."

When at last they found a spring at which to eat their lunch, he told her so, concluding, "This mountain air does you good, Madge."

"So do you," she replied, with a piquant nod. "Don't be conceited when I tell you that you are good company."

"No; but I can't help being happy."

"Oh, indeed! It doesn't seem to take much to make you happy."

"Not very much from you."

"Pass me a biscuit, Graydon; I want something more substantial than fine speeches after our climb. Isn't all this truly Arcadian—this mossy rug on which we have placed our lunch, the trees whispering about us overhead, and the spring there bubbling over with something concerning which it murmurs so contentedly?"

"I wonder what they think of us! I can imagine one thing."

"You are always imagining. The idea of your being a banker! Well, there is a loud whisper from the trees. What was remarked?"

"That yonder little girl doesn't look so very unhappy."

"No, Graydon," she said, earnestly, "you make Saturdays and Sundays very bright to me. No girl ever had a truer friend than you are becoming."

"Have become, Madge."

"Graydon," she said, eagerly, as if hastening from dangerous ground, "the hotel is there just opposite to us. Don't you think we could scramble down the mountain here, and return by Kaaterskill Clove and the Falls? It would be such fun, and save such a very long distance!"

"We'll try it," he said.

"Come," she resumed, brusquely, "you are spoiling me. You say yes to everything. If you don't think it safe or best you must not humor me."

"We can soon learn whether it's safe and practicable, and there is no danger of losing our way. We have only to return over the mountain in order to strike the path somewhere at right angles."

"Let us hasten, then. I am in the mood to end our sojourn in the Catskills by an hour or two of contact with nature absolutely primitive. The scenes we shall pass through will be so pleasant to think of by a winter fire."

"Winter fire? That's capital! You are not going back to Santa Barbara, Madge?"

"I haven't promised that—I haven't promised anything."

"No; I have done all the promising."

"You did so of your own free will."

"And of my own free will shall keep my promises. No, don't let us leave any remnants of our lunch. Should we get lost you will want something more substantial than fine speeches."

"I shall indeed."

Graydon filled from the spring the bottle which had contained milk; and then packing his little hamper he led the way downward, over and through obstacles which often involved no little difficulty, and sometimes almost danger.

"May I help you all I please?" he asked.

"Yes, when I can't help myself."

Then he began to rejoice over the ruggedness of the way, which made it proper to take her hand so often, and at times even to lift her over a fallen tree.

"What fun it is!" cried Madge.

"The best I ever had," he replied, promptly. But they had not realized the difficulty of their attempt; for when little more than half-way to the foot of the mountain they came to a ledge down which there appeared no place for safe descent. As they were skirting this precipice perilously near the edge, he holding Madge's hand, some loose debris gave way beneath his feet.

Instead of instinctively clinging to Madge's hand, even in the act of falling he threw it up and around a small tree, which she grasped, and regained her footing, while he went down and disappeared.

At first she was so appalled that she could do no more than clutch the tree convulsively and look with blank horror at the spot where she had seen him last. Then came the thought, "His life may now depend upon me."

The distance he had fallen would not be necessarily fatal, and below the ledge there were low scrubby trees that might have broken the impetus of his descent. She called in tones that might have evoked an answer even from the lips of death; then, with a resolution in her pallid face which nothing could daunt, she sought to reach her side.

At first Graydon was utterly unconscious. At last, like a dim light entering a darkened room, thought and memory began to revive. He remembered that he had been at Madge's side, and had fallen; he had grasped at branches of trees as he passed through them, and then all had become dark. He tried to speak, to call his companion, but found be could not. He almost doubted whether he was alive in the flesh. If he were he must have received some terrible injury that had caused a strange paralysis.

His confused thoughts finally centred wholly on Madge. Had

she fallen? The thought of her, perhaps injured, possibly lying unconscious or dead near him, and he helpless, caused a dull, vague dread, like a cold tide, to overwhelm his very soul. He tried to move, to spring up, but only his mind appeared free. Then he thought he recognized her voice calling in the distance. Soon, with alternations of hope and fear, he heard her steps and voice draw nearer. She had evidently found a way down the ledge, and was coming along its base toward him—coming swiftly, almost recklessly.

She was at his side. Her low, terror-stricken cry chilled his heart. Was he dead? and was it his soul only, lingering in the body, that was cognizant of all this?

Her hand was on his pulse, then inside his vest against his heart.

"Oh," she moaned, "can he be dying or dead? I can't find his pulse, nor does his heart seem to beat. He is so pale, so deathly pale, even to his lips."

He knew that she was lifting him into a different and easier position, and wondered at the muscular power she exerted, even under excitement.

"Why, why," she exclaimed in horror, "he is cold, strangely cold! His hands and brow are almost like ice, and wet with the dew of death."

She was not aware of the fact that extreme coldness and a clammy perspiration would be among the results of such a severe shock.

"Graydon," she gasped, "Graydon!" Then after a moment: "O God, if he should never know!"

She chafed his hands and wrists, opened the lunch basket, and found that the bottle containing water was not broken, for he felt drops dashed on his face, and his lips moistened; but the same stony paralysis enchained him. Then she sent out her voice for help, and there was agony, terror, and heart-break in her cry.

Realizing the futility of this on the lonely mountainside, she soon ceased, and again sought, with almost desperate energy, to restore him, crying and moaning meanwhile in a way that smote his heart. At last she threw herself on his breast with the bitter cry:

"Oh, Graydon, Graydon, are you dying? Will you *never* know? Oh, my heart's true love, shall I never have a chance to tell you that it was you I loved—you only! It was for you I went away alone to die, I feared. For you I struggled back to life, and toiled and prayed that I might be your fair ideal; and now you may never know. Graydon, Graydon, I would give you the very blood out of my heart—O God, I can't restore him!" she moaned, in a choking voice, and then he knew from her dead weight upon his breast that she had fainted.

This mental anguish and the effort he put forth to respond to these words caused great beads of sweat to start out upon his face. Suddenly, as if a giant hand was lifted, the effects of the shock resulting from his fall passed away. He opened his eyes, and there was Madge, with her face buried upon his breast, in brief oblivion from fears that threatened to crush at once hope and life.

To his great joy he found that he could move. Feebly, and with great difficulty, he lifted her head and tried to regain his feet. He found this impossible, and soon realized that his leg was broken. He now saw that he must act wisely and carefully, or their plight would be serious indeed; and yet his mind was in such a tumult of immeasurable joy at his discovery that he would not in the least regret the accident, if assured of her safety.

At last, in response to his efforts, she began to revive. The sense of responsibility, the necessity for action on her part, had been so great immediately before she had fainted under the stress of one overwhelming fear, that her mind, even during unconsciousness, may have put forth effort to regain its hold upon sense. She found herself leaning against a prostrate tree, and Graydon sitting near, speaking to her in soothing and encouraging tones.

In response to her bewildered, troubled look of inquiry, he said, cheerfully, and in natural tones, "Don't worry, Madge, or be frightened."

"What has happened, Graydon?"

"I'll tell you what I know, and you must supply the rest. We were proceeding along that ledge above us, and trying to find a safe place to climb down."

A slow deep color began to take the place of her pallor, showing that her own memory was supplying all that had occurred.

"You know I fell, Madge. Thank God, I did not carry you down with me!"

"Any other man would," she said, almost brusquely. "You threw my hand back around a tree."

"Did I?" exclaimed Graydon, very innocently and gladly. "Well, everything became very confused after that. I must have been unconscious. I do remember grasping at the branches as I passed through these low trees above us—"

"You must have caught one of them, Graydon," she said, eagerly, turning toward him again, "for a large limb had broken off and was lying upon you."

"Was it so? Perhaps I owe it a good turn, for it may have so broken my fall as to have saved my life. Well, in some way, you, true, brave little girl, you must have reached me, and, finding that you could not restore me, and imagining I was dead or dying, you fainted yourself from the nervous shock of it all. When I recovered the use of my senses I found evidence that you had been trying to revive me. Now, Madge, we must both be brave and sensible. We must regain the full possession of our wits as soon as possible. Can you be very brave and sensible (to use your favorite word) if I tell you something?"

"Yes, Graydon," she said. "I can do anything, now that I know you are going to live."

"I am very much alive, and shall be thoroughly conscious of the fact for some time to come. You must keep perfectly cool and rational, for what has happened is a very serious affair under the circumstances." Her scarlet face was turned from him again. "Madge," he concluded, in quiet tones, "I've broken my leg."

"Is that all?" she said, with a look of intense relief.

"Isn't that enough? I'm helpless."

"I'm not," and she sprang to her feet "Why, Graydon, it might have been a hundred-fold worse. I thought it was immeasurably worse," she said, suppressing a sob. "You might have been killed. See how far you fell! I feared you might have received some terrible internal injury—"

"I have; but that's a chronic affair, as you know," he interrupted, laughing.

His mirth and allusion did more to restore her than all else, for he appeared the same friend that she thought she had lost.

"Now that it is so evident that you will survive all your injuries," she resumed, with an answering laugh, "I am myself again. You direct me what to do."

"I shall, indeed, have to depend on you almost wholly; and the fact that another must look to you in such a strait will do more to keep you up than all cordials and stimulants. I can do very little myself—"

"Forgive me, Graydon. You know I am not indifferent. Are you in much pain?" and her voice was very gentle.

"Not yet. You must act contrary to your instincts for once, and exert all your ingenuity to attract attention. First, we must have a fire; meanwhile I shall light a cigar, which will help me to think and banish the impression that we are lost babes in the woods. The smoke, you see, will draw eyes to this spot—the smoke of the fire, I mean."

"I'm following you correctly."

"You must have followed me very bravely, heroic little woman that you are! You are indeed unlike other girls, who would never have reached me except by tumbling after—"

"Come, no more reminiscences till you are safe at the hotel, and your leg mended."

"Very well. I direct, but you command. As soon as we have a column of smoke ascending from this point you must try to find an open space near here, and wave something white as a signal of distress."

He had scarcely concluded before she was at work. The prostrate tree against which he had managed to place her at such pain to his broken limb served as a back-log, and soon a column of smoke was ascending. At times she would turn a shy, half-doubting, half-questioning glance at him, but he would smile so naturally and speak so frankly that the suspicion that he had heard her words almost passed from her mind.

"Madge," he said, "in finding an outlook toward the hotel or valley, don't go far away, if possible. It makes me awfully nervous to think of you climbing alone."

She found a projecting rock beneath them within calling distance, and on an extemporized pole she fastened the napkins. At his suggestion she waved them only downward and upward, at the same time sending out her powerful voice from time to time in a cry for help.

He, left alone, sometimes groaned from an unusually severe twinge of pain, and again laughed softly to himself over the situation. He knew that the question of their being sought and found was only one of time, and he would have been willing to have had all his bones broken should this have been needful to secure the knowledge which now thrilled his very soul with gladness. The past grew perfectly clear, and the pearl of a woman who had given herself to him so long ago gained a more priceless value with every moment's thought, "Ah, sweet Madge! I'm the blessed idiot you loved and toiled for at Santa Barbara! I shouldn't have believed that such a thing could happen in this humdrum world."

Nor would it seem that the attention of even a fraction of that great world could be obtained. The shadows of evening began to gather, and Madge, at Graydon's call, returned, wearied and somewhat discouraged.

"Cheer up," he said. "It is only a question of time. We shall soon be missed, and our signals will be more effective when it is dark. See, we shall not starve. I have been getting supper for you. Keeping the remnants of our lunch wasn't a bad idea, was it?"

"Keeping up your courage and mine is a better one. Graydon, I fear you are suffering very much."

"Oh, Madge, armies of men have broken their legs! That's nothing but a little disagreeable prose, while this adventure with you is something to talk and laugh over all our lives. I've cut my boot off and bandaged my leg as well as I could, and am now hungry. That's a good sign. I shall be positively hilarious if you make as good supper as this meagre spread permits. Take a little water, for your throat must be parched. You will have to drink it from the bottle, Pat's fashion, for my rubber cup is broken."

"Indeed, a little water is all I want at present, and I must gather wood for the fire before it is darker."

"Very well," he said, laughing; "supper shall wait for you."

The vicinity appeared as if never before visited, and there was an abundance of dead and decaying wood lying about. When she had secured a large quantity of this she came and sat down by the fire, and said, "I will take a little supper now, and then it will be so dark that we can signal in some other way."

"Madge," said Graydon, earnestly, "it has cut me to the heart to lie helplessly here and see you doing work so unsuitable."

"Nothing could be more suitable under the circumstances. You do think we shall be found soon? Oh, I'm so worried about you!"

"More, then, than I am about myself. I shall have to play invalid for some time. Won't you be my nurse occasionally?"

"Yes, Graydon, all I can."

"Why, then, don't worry about me at all. The prospect makes me fairly happy. Come, now, eat the whole of that sandwich."

She complied, looking thoughtfully into the fire meanwhile. By the light of the flickering blaze he saw the trouble and worry pass from her brow and the expression of her face grow as quiet and contented as that of a child's. At last she said, "Well, this does seem cosey and companionable, in spite of everything. There, forgive me, Graydon; I forgot for the moment that you were in pain."

"Was I? I forgot it, too. Sitting there in the firelight, you suggested the sweetest picture I ever hope to see."

"You can't be *in extremis* when you begin to compliment."

"Don't you wish to know what the picture was?"

"Oh, yes, if it will help you pass the time!"

"I saw you sitting by a hearth, and I thought, 'If that hearth were mine it would be the loveliest picture the world had known.' Now you see what an egotist I am. You look so enchanting in that firelight that I cannot resist—I would try so hard to be worthy of you, Madge. Make your own terms again, as I said once to you before."

"My own terms?" she repeated, turning a sudden and searching glance upon him. "Then tell me, did you hear what I said this afternoon when I first found you?"

He hesitated a moment, and then said, firmly: "Yes, every word; but, Madge, you must not punish me for what I could not help. It would not be right."

"Could you hear me and yet—"

"I could hear you and yet could not move a muscle until you fainted, and then my intense mental excitement and solicitude must have broken the paralysis caused by the shock of my fall. Oh, Madge, look at me! Only a false pride can come between us now. My love is not worthy to be compared with yours, but it is genuine, and it will—it *will* last as long as I do. I shall bless this accident and all the pain I must suffer if they bring you to me."

She sprang to his side, and putting her arm around his neck said, "Graydon, on the evening after your return I told you I couldn't be your sister. You know why now, and you uttered these words, 'I shall have to take you as you are if I ever find out.' I meant to win you if I could, but only by being such a girl as I thought you would love. Now you know the mystery of the little ghost, and you can bring to me that 'idiot' who didn't return my love, as often as you choose."

"Thank Heaven for what I escaped! Thank God for what I have won!" he exclaimed.

"Won? Nonsense! *You* have been won, not I. Oh, Graydon,

wouldn't you have been amazed and horrified if you had been told, years ago, that the little ghost would go deliberately to work to woo a man and take him from another girl? Think how dreadful it sounds! but you shall now know the worst."

"It's music that will fill my life with gladness. How exquisitely fine your nature is, that you could do this with such absolute maidenly reserve! Suppose I had become Stella Wildmere's bondman?"

"I should have gone back to Santa Barbara, and kept my secret."

"Horrible!"

"I said you knew all, but I am mistaken. Now, don't be shocked back into your kind of unconsciousness again. I did another horrid thing. I listened and learned about the plot by which Arnault meant to bring Miss Wildmere to a decision against you;" and she told him the circumstances, and what had passed between herself and Henry.

His arm tightened around her almost convulsively. "Madge," he cried, "you have not only brought me happiness—you have saved me from a bitter, lifelong self-reproach far worse than poverty. How can I ever show sufficient devotion in return for all this?"

"By being sensible, and telling me how to make signals, now that it is as dark as it will be this moonlight night."

"Let me lean on you, as I ever shall figuratively hereafter. We will go down to the outlook you found, build another fire, and wave burning brands."

This was done. Henry Muir, who had grown very solicitous, saw their signals, and promptly organized a rescuing party. A wood-road led well up toward their position, and with the aid of some employes of the house he at last rescued them. Graydon was weak and exhausted from pain by the time he reached the hotel, yet felt that his happiness had been purchased at very slight cost. The next day he was taken to his city home, and Madge filled the days of his convalescence with such varied entertainment that he threatened to break his leg again. She had so trained her voice that she read or sang with almost tireless ease. To furnish home music, to shine in the light of her own hearth, had been the dream of her ambition; and to the man she had won she made that hearth the centre of the gentle force which controlled and blessed his life.

But little further remains to be said concerning the other characters of this story. The severe lesson received by Stella Wildmere had a permanent effect upon her character. It did not result in a very high type of womanhood, for the limitations of her nature scarcely permitted this; but it brought about decided changes for the better. She was endowed with fair abilities and a certain hard, practical sense, which enabled her to see the folly of her former scheme of life. Blind, inconsiderate selfishness, which asked only, "What do I wish the present moment?" had brought humiliation and disaster, and, as her father had suggested, she possessed too much mind to repeat that blunder. She recognized that she could not ignore natural laws and duties and go very far in safety. Therefore, instead of querulousness and repining, or showing useless resentment toward her father for misfortunes which she had done nothing to avert, she stepped bravely and helpfully to his side, and amid all the chaos of the financial storm that was wrecking him he was happier than he had been for years. Her beloved jewelry, and everything that could be legally saved from their dismantled home, was disposed of to the best advantage. Then very modest apartments were taken in a suburb, and both she and her father began again. He obtained a clerkship at a small salary, and she aided her mother in making every dollar go as far as possible.

Arnault had thought, under the impulse of his pride, that he could renounce her forever, but found himself mistaken. She would not depart from such heart as he possessed, nor could he break the spell of her fascination. His interest grew so absorbing that he kept himself informed about the changes she was passing through, and her manner of meeting them. As a result, his practical soul was filled with admiration, and he felt that she of all others would be the wife for a man embarked on the uncertain tides of Wall Street. At last he wrote to her and renewed his offer. The reply was characteristic.

"Your offer comes too late. If, instead of being one of the principal actors in that humiliating little drama of my life, you had stood by me patiently and faithfully, I would have given you at once my deepest gratitude and, eventually, my love. I did not deserve such constancy, but I would have rewarded it to the extent of my ability. You thought I was mercenary. I was, and have been punished; but you forget that you made my mercenary spirit your ally, and kept me from becoming engaged to the man whom you well knew that I preferred. My regard for him is not so deep, however, but that I shall survive and face my altered fortunes bravely. If you had been kind to me during those bitter days—if you had kept my father from failure, instead of deserting him after he had done his best for you—he did do his best for you—I should have valued *you* more than your wealth, and proved it by my life. I have since learned that I am not afraid of poverty, and that I must find truer friends."

Arnault, like so many others, turned from what "might have been" to his pursuit of gold, but it had lost its brightness forever.

An old admirer of Stella's, a plain, sturdy business man, to whom she had scarcely given a thought in her palmy days, eventually renewed his attentions, and won as much love as the girl probably could have given to any one. By his aid she restored her father's broken fortunes and established them on a modest but secure basis, and she proved to her husband a sensible wife, always recognizing that in promoting his best interests and happiness she secured her own.

Dr. Sommers is still the genial physician and the Izaak Walton of the Catskills. Mr. and Mrs. Wendall are "plodding toward home" with a resignation that is almost cheerful.

Henry Muir continues devoted to business, and his wife is devoted to him. He rarely permits a suitable opportunity to pass without remarking that the two sisters are the "most sensible women in the world."

Choose from Thousands of 1stWorldLibrary Classics By

Friedrich Kerst
Friedrich Nietzsche
Fyodor Dostoyevsky
G.A. Henty
G.K. Chesterton
Gabrielle E. Jackson
Garrett P. Serviss
Gaston Leroux
George A. Warren
George Ade
Geroge Bernard Shaw
George Cary Eggleston
George Durston
George Ebers
George Eliot
George Gissing
George MacDonald
George Meredith
George Orwell
George Sylvester Viereck
George Tucker
George W. Cable
George Wharton James
Gertrude Atherton
Gordon Casserly
Grace E. King
Grace Gallatin
Grace Greenwood
Grant Allen
Guillermo A. Sherwell
Gulielma Zollinger
Gustav Flaubert
H. A. Cody
H. B. Irving
H. C. Bailey
H. G. Wells
H. H. Munro
H. Irving Hancock
H. R. Naylor
H. Rider Haggard
H. W. C. Davis
Haldeman Julius
Hall Caine
Hamilton Wright Mabie
Hans Christian Andersen
Harold Avery
Harold McGrath
Harriet Beecher Stowe
Harry Castlemon
Harry Coghill
Harry Houidini
Hayden Carruth
Helent Hunt Jackson
Helen Nicolay
Hendrik Conscience
Hendy David Thoreau
Henri Barbusse
Henrik Ibsen
Henry Adams
Henry Ford
Henry Frost
Henry James
Henry Jones Ford
Henry Seton Merriman
Henry W Longfellow
Herbert A. Giles
Herbert Carter
Herbert N. Casson
Herman Hesse
Hildegard G. Frey
Homer
Honore De Balzac
Horace B. Day
Horace Walpole
Horatio Alger Jr.
Howard Pyle
Howard R. Garis
Hugh Lofting
Hugh Walpole
Humphry Ward
Ian Maclaren
Inez Haynes Gillmore
Irving Bacheller
Isabel Cecilia Williams
Isabel Hornibrook
Israel Abrahams
Ivan Turgenev
J. G.Austin
J. Henri Fabre
J. M. Barrie
J. M. Walsh
J. Macdonald Oxley
J. R. Miller
J. S. Fletcher
J. S. Knowles
J. Storer Clouston
J. W. Duffield
Jack London
Jacob Abbott
James Allen
James Andrews
James Baldwin
James Branch Cabell
James DeMille
James Joyce
James Lane Allen
James Lane Allen
James Oliver Curwood
James Oppenheim
James Otis
James R. Driscoll
Jane Abbott
Jane Austen
Jane L. Stewart
Janet Aldridge
Jens Peter Jacobsen
Jerome K. Jerome
Jessie Graham Flower
John Buchan
John Burroughs
John Cournos
John F. Kennedy
John Gay
John Glasworthy
John Habberton
John Joy Bell
John Kendrick Bangs
John Milton
John Philip Sousa
John Taintor Foote
Jonas Lauritz Idemil Lie
Jonathan Swift
Joseph A. Altsheler
Joseph Carey
Joseph Conrad
Joseph E. Badger Jr
Joseph Hergesheimer
Joseph Jacobs
Jules Vernes
Julian Hawthrone
Julie A Lippmann
Justin Huntly McCarthy
Kakuzo Okakura
Karle Wilson Baker
Kate Chopin
Kenneth Grahame
Kenneth McGaffey
Kate Langley Bosher
Kate Langley Bosher
Katherine Cecil Thurston
Katherine Stokes
L. A. Abbot
L. T. Meade

L. Frank Baum
Latta Griswold
Laura Dent Crane
Laura Lee Hope
Laurence Housman
Lawrence Beasley
Leo Tolstoy
Leonid Andreyev
Lewis Carroll
Lewis Sperry Chafer
Lilian Bell
Lloyd Osbourne
Louis Hughes
Louis Joseph Vance
Louis Tracy
Louisa May Alcott
Lucy Fitch Perkins
Lucy Maud Montgomery
Luther Benson
Lydia Miller Middleton
Lyndon Orr
M. Corvus
M. H. Adams
Margaret E. Sangster
Margret Howth
Margaret Vandercook
Margaret W. Hungerford
Margret Penrose
Maria Edgeworth
Maria Thompson Daviess
Mariano Azuela
Marion Polk Angellotti
Mark Overton
Mark Twain
Mary Austin
Mary Catherine Crowley
Mary Cole
Mary Hastings Bradley
Mary Roberts Rinehart
Mary Rowlandson
M. Wollstonecraft Shelley
Maud Lindsay
Max Beerbohm
Myra Kelly
Nathaniel Hawthrone
Nicolo Machiavelli
O. F. Walton
Oscar Wilde
Owen Johnson
P.G. Wodehouse
Paul and Mabel Thorne
Paul G. Tomlinson
Paul Severing
Percy Brebner
Percy Keese Fitzhugh
Peter B. Kyne
Plato
Quincy Allen
R. Derby Holmes
R. L. Stevenson
R. S. Ball
Rabindranath Tagore
Rahul Alvares
Ralph Bonehill
Ralph Henry Barbour
Ralph Victor
Ralph Waldo Emmerson
Rene Descartes
Ray Cummings
Rex Beach
Rex E. Beach
Richard Harding Davis
Richard Jefferies
Richard Le Gallienne
Robert Barr
Robert Frost
Robert Gordon Anderson
Robert L. Drake
Robert Lansing
Robert Lynd
Robert Michael Ballantyne
Robert W. Chambers
Rosa Nouchette Carey
Rudyard Kipling
Saint Augustine
Samuel B. Allison
Samuel Hopkins Adams
Sarah Bernhardt
Sarah C. Hallowell
Selma Lagerlof
Sherwood Anderson
Sigmund Freud
Standish O'Grady
Stanley Weyman
Stella Benson
Stella M. Francis
Stephen Crane
Stewart Edward White
Stijn Streuvels
Swami Abhedananda
Swami Parmananda
T. S. Ackland
T. S. Arthur
The Princess Der Ling
Thomas A. Janvier
Thomas A Kempis
Thomas Anderton
Thomas Bailey Aldrich
Thomas Bulfinch
Thomas De Quincey
Thomas Dixon
Thomas H. Huxley
Thomas Hardy
Thomas More
Thornton W. Burgess
U. S. Grant
Upton Sinclair
Valentine Williams
Various Authors
Vaughan Kester
Victor Appleton
Victor G. Durham
Victoria Cross
Virginia Woolf
Wadsworth Camp
Walter Camp
Walter Scott
Washington Irving
Wilbur Lawton
Wilkie Collins
Willa Cather
Willard F. Baker
William Dean Howells
William le Queux
W. Makepeace Thackeray
William W. Walter
William Shakespeare
Winston Churchill
Yei Theodora Ozaki
Yogi Ramacharaka
Young E. Allison
Zane Grey

www.ingramcontent.com/pod-product-compliance
Lightning Source LLC
LaVergne TN
LVHW090546110826
845146LV00001B/40

* 9 7 8 1 4 2 1 8 8 8 2 3 1 *